HUNTED

ALSO BY D. E. BECKLER

Missing

Writing as David Beckler

Antonia Conti Thriller series

A Long Shadow

A Stolen Memory

A Nuclear Reaction

Mason & Sterling series

Brotherhood

The Profit Motive

Forged in Flames

The Money Trap

Anthology

The Road More Travelled: Tales of those seeking refuge

PRAISE FOR D. E. BECKLER

'A dark and gritty read set in the homeless community with a real sense of authenticity and a sure touch. The setting is superbly drawn, the characters real and complex . . . A cracking read.'

—Trevor Wood, author of the Jimmy Mullen and DCI Jack Parker series

'Tense and gripping, with a likeable down-at-heel detective. Beckler knows these streets, and it shows.'

—Antony Johnston, award-winning *New York Times* bestselling author

A CITY STREETS MYSTERY

HUNTED

D. E. BECKLER

This is a work of fiction. Names, characters, organizations, places, events, and incidents are either products of the author's imagination or are used fictitiously. Any resemblance to actual persons, living or dead, or actual events is purely coincidental.

Published by Thomas & Mercer, Seattle

www.apub.com

Amazon, the Amazon logo, and Thomas & Mercer are trademarks of Amazon.com, Inc., or its affiliates.

EU Product Safety Contact:
Amazon Media EU S.à r.l.
38, avenue John F. Kennedy, L-1855 Luxembourg
amazonpublishing-gpsr@amazon.com

ISBN-13: 9781662528309
eISBN: 9781662528293

Cover photography and design by Dominic Forbes

Printed in the United States of America

To my lovely Aunty Eunice, who ignited my love of books before she even met me. When, as a young boy, I lived on a farm in Ethiopia, she sent us parcels of books from London, the arrival of which was a highlight I still recall with pleasure.

CHAPTER 1

I woke with a start and sat up. The cacophony that had woken me continued, and I gathered my wits. Shouts and banging came from outside the door of my flat. Memories of the Grenfell fire in London, which I'd watched with my family in Bristol, jerked me into action. I jumped out of bed, grabbed my phone and slipped my feet into trainers. A dog barked. Was that Oscar?

I put my glasses on, stepped outside my room and turned on the light, squinting. Oscar stood in the narrow corridor outside my bedroom.

'Was that you?' I asked him.

He studied me with disdain. ***Did it sound like me?***

Someone banged on my door and the thunderous barking started up again.

Oscar's expression changed to alarm as I reached for the lock. ***What are you doing?***

'It could be a fire.'

I released it and the door flew open, smacking me on the forehead and dislodging my glasses. As I fell back against the wall, a brown blur flashed past me. The stench of weed which permeated the corridor outside almost overwhelmed me. Oscar's bark of alarm came from the kitchen.

A large, angry figure stood in the open doorway and grabbed my arm as I went to Oscar's aid. 'Oi, I want a word.'

A deep growl punctuated Oscar's cries for help.

I threw the hand off. 'Your dog's attacking mine in there.'

'I'll attack you, mate.'

I punched three nines into my phone. Oscar stood on the counter while a large XL Bully type lunged up at him. Without thinking, I grabbed the lead trailing from the spiked collar round its neck and jerked on it. I might as well have tried to rein in a rhino.

The dog had its front paws on the work surface and its enormous jaws gaping. Oscar pushed himself against the back wall between the toaster and kettle.

I thrust the phone into my pocket and used both hands to grip the lead. My efforts didn't seem to even register with the huge, lunging beast as its rear claws scrabbled against the floor. Lacking an elephant gun, I could only go on jerking the lead until a hand grabbed my sleeve and wrenched me back to the kitchen doorway.

'Leave my fucking dog alone!' The intruder – a large, shaven-headed individual with a bushy beard which made him look like he'd put his head on upside down – jabbed a finger into my chest. Muscular limbs stuck out of his shorts and a vest. Tattoos covered most of his exposed skin, including his face.

'Leave your dog alone?' I said. 'Get it out of my house!'

The intruder barked some sort of reply, but I lost it in the wave of dizziness that washed over me. A jabbing pain radiated from my forehead. I dabbed at it and my hand came away red.

A tinny voice said, 'Which service do you require?'

I freed my other arm and retrieved my phone. 'Police. A psycho with a dog is attacking me in my flat—'

'Who you calling a psycho?' The intruder looked even angrier.

The dog let out a growl and Oscar barked in panic.

'Please come quickly,' I yelled into my phone. 'We're at Strangeways View, flat one a.'

The intruder snatched at the phone, knocking it out of my hand. I swung my elbow and smacked him in the face with it.

The man reared back, clutching his nose. 'Oi, bastard!'

His wild-eyed beast wheeled on me, jaws agape. I had just enough time to grab a stool and swing it between us. He sunk his teeth into the crosspiece between two of the legs, destroying it and leaving the legs unbraced. I retreated towards the corner, the remains of the stool in my hand.

'The hell's going on here?' a familiar voice demanded.

We all stopped, even the vicious dog, and looked at Zack Cermak, the building manager. An ex-military type, Cermak didn't believe in small talk or smiling.

'This psycho and his animal broke in and attacked me and my dog!'

'I didn't break in. You let me in.'

Oscar had recovered his confidence. ***He's right, you did. I told you not to.***

Before I could respond to Oscar, the intruder released his nose and pointed a bloody hand at me. 'This guy's dog is eating the food I put out for Tyson.'

Oscar gave an indignant bark. ***I wouldn't touch that muck.***

'He wouldn't touch that muck,' I echoed.

'Oh yeah, so who's eating it, the faeries?'

'Probably you,' I muttered.

He lunged at me and I lifted the remains of the stool between us. Seeing an opening, his dog charged. I brought the stool down and the animal ran into a leg, nose first. It yelped and stopped. When its owner hesitated, I shoved the stool into his chest, pushing him into the kitchen table. A bowl of sugar and the salt and pepper set Zofia had bought me crashed to the floor.

'Hey, stop this, now!' Cermak stepped into the cramped kitchen. 'You.' He pointed at the dog owner. 'Get out and take your dog.'

The thug pushed himself off the table and pointed at me. 'He hit my dog!'

'What's your dog doing in his flat?'

'I told you, he's stealing Tyson's—'

'I don't give a damn. Now get back to your place, while you've still got one.'

The man glared at him, then bent to pick up his dog's lead and headed past the manager for the front door, muttering to himself.

Oscar stepped towards the front edge of the worktop and barked after the retreating dog. ***Go on, you coward. I'd have had you!***

The dog turned back with a growl.

Oscar yelped and leapt back towards the toaster, knocking over a glass, which smashed on the floor.

'Come on, Tyson, let's leave these two losers.' His owner heaved on the lead, giving me a look that should have killed me.

I lowered the stool and followed them to the door, closing it behind them. Once I'd secured the rim lock, Oscar jumped to the floor and strutted. I found my miraculously undamaged glasses behind the door and put them on.

Left alone with me in the flat, the manager wagged a finger in my face. 'First, you shouldn't let your dog on the work surface. It's unhygienic.'

Oscar gave him an incredulous stare. ***Unhygienic? Have you*** **seen** ***the state of the rest of the building?***

I shushed Oscar and replied, 'I don't "let" him up there. That dog attacked him, and he had to get away.'

'Second,' he went on, 'you'll need to repair or replace that stool.' He examined it. 'And get that blood cleaned off it.'

'What? His dog did that, you saw—'

'I don't care. It's your responsibility. And if we have any more trouble from you, you'll be out on your ear.' He pointed at the broken glass. 'And replace that.'

Too stunned to speak, I stared at him with my mouth open. Kasper and Zofia, my employers, had bought all the glasses in here when they found me this place.

Sirens sounded in the distance, coming closer.

'What the hell's happening now?' he asked.

I picked up my phone from the floor. 'I called the police.'

'What the hell you do that for?'

'We were being attacked in our own home!'

'I warned you when you moved in. Don't cause any trouble. The other residents don't like having the pigs around. It unsettles them.'

'What was I supposed to do? Let them kill us?'

Oscar lifted his muzzle. ***I was handling that Tyson, no problem.***

'It looked like it.'

'You what?' The manager gave me a puzzled frown.

I was just lulling him into a false sense of security. If you hadn't interfered . . .

The pain from my cut head and Oscar's false bravado pushed me over the edge. 'You were terrified, you coward.'

'What you call me?' The manager looked ready to punch me.

'I was talking to the dog.'

'Yeah, right.' With a shake of his head, he left, turning at the front door. 'Any more trouble, and you're out.'

The slam echoed.

That went well.

'Shut up and go back to bed.'

Oscar had started talking to me after we'd been on the streets for a few months. Part of me had hoped it would stop once we moved into the flat, but so far, he was more vocal than ever.

After washing the blood off my hand, I checked my forehead in the bathroom mirror. The blood had dried, and I wiped the excess off with damp toilet paper. The wound, which had stopped bleeding, sat on a bump the size of a plum, but it didn't need stitches. I returned to the kitchen and replaced the items on the table. Luckily, they'd survived their fall. Then I swept the broken glass into the dustpan and put it in the recycling. The stool didn't seem too bad, provided I sat on it straight. I wiped the bloody handprint off with a sponge and put the stool back at the table.

Two thirty. I had four hours before I had to get up for work.

A thump on the door set my pulse hammering, and I stared at it.

'Police. Are you okay in there?'

Relief making me tremble, I opened the door, letting in a fresh dose of weed. Two uniformed officers, looking much too young to be out alone, studied me.

'You call us out?' said the smaller but marginally more fully grown of the two.

Cermak hovered behind them.

'A misunderstanding, officers,' I assured them. 'A neighbour's dog got excited and bit my stool there.' I pointed towards the kitchen.

The officer with the speaking role stared at the bump on my forehead. 'You want to press charges?'

'No, as I said, a misunderstanding.'

'Right,' he said, looking relieved. 'In future, don't ring us unless it's necessary.'

'I'll remember that. Thanks, Officer.'

The arrival of the police had created a stir, and several people lingered in the corridor behind them and the manager. One of them muttered, 'Fucking grass,' as I shut the door on the lot of them and leant against it.

Great. Already unpopular with my neighbours because I'd stopped several of them taking advantage of a fellow resident with learning difficulties, now I'd upset the resident psycho and the manager, and everyone considered me a snitch.

CHAPTER 2

Jodie lay in her stinking bedding, unable to sleep, despite her exhaustion. Why the hell had she volunteered for this? A sound made her freeze, and she strained her ears. Then a crash as a door smashed. Shit! Someone was coming, and they weren't sneaking in.

'Toff, wake up.' Jodie shook his shoulder and grabbed her trainers.

Like others on the streets, a well-developed sense of survival meant Toff usually slept lightly, but the relative safety of his billet had made him careless. Still groggy from the effects of whatever he'd taken the night before, he struggled to get out of his sleeping bag even as shouts and screams came from the corridor outside.

Jodie finishing tying her laces and shook him again. 'Come on.'

He at last pushed his bedding off. 'Where are my trainers?'

Faint light leaked in through the windows lining two walls of the large ground-floor classroom they'd chosen to sleep in. She found his shoes and thrust them at him as he struggled to his feet. Before he'd finished putting them on, the door from the corridor crashed open. The shouts grew louder as those who'd been sleeping in the next room fought with intruders. Smoke drifted in, bringing with it a stench that made her eyes sting. She scooped up her backpack.

Torch beams cut through the haze and illuminated the struggling figures in the doorway. The intruders looked like giant bugs the size of men. Was she still under the influence of the weed they'd smoked last night? Then she noticed their gas masks.

Toff, mesmerised, couldn't drag his gaze away from them.

She pulled at his sleeve. 'Come on, let's get out of here.'

Her tug stirred him, and he followed her. Glad she'd explored before going to bed, she headed for the other door, in the far corner. It led to the stairs and a way out, but as she reached it, Toff crashed to the floor behind her with a cry of alarm. She turned to check on him.

A torch beam swinging across the room revealed Toff kneeling beside a prone figure. It was Sawney. As Toff tried to rouse him, the bulky, bug-faced figures came closer. Apart from torches, they carried clubs. Two at the rear held the leads of large dogs, whose snarling filled Jodie with terror.

'TOFF!' she shouted from the far corner. 'LEAVE HIM!'

One intruder lifted what looked like a fire extinguisher and aimed the nozzle at Toff, who ran as a stream of evil-smelling liquid hit the prone body he'd abandoned, splashing up on Toff's retreating back and legs. The stench appalled Jodie and intensified when he joined her. She pushed him through the door and plunged after him, slamming it shut.

To her left was the route out, but she could see the torches of more men coming towards them.

Toff had stumbled to a halt behind her. Without waiting for him, she ran right, towards the stairs, taking them two steps at a time. At the top, she paused, chest heaving and throat rasping. Toff was still on the half landing.

'COME ON!' she urged him.

Boots clattered on the steps below and torch beams cut the air. When Toff had almost reached the top of the stairs, she ran, nearly tripping on a fallen light fitting in the dark. Toff caught up with her, bringing the stench with him.

Ahead, a pale strip indicated a door, and she shoved her shoulder against it. Toff added his weight, and they tumbled through it into a large space marked by moonlight leaking in through big windows. Several figures huddled together in the far corner. Two bookshelves stood by the door they'd just entered through, and desks had been pushed around the walls, leaving a sleeping area clear.

'Let's barricade this door.' Jodie gestured at the bookcases.

Toff helped her slide the nearest one against the door. Galvanised by their actions, the others pushed desks towards them.

'Help me with this one.' She strode towards the other bookshelf.

Someone banged on the door. Toff jumped, then, as the door pushed open, he leapt against it, shoving with all his might. His slight frame, weakened by months on the street, was no match for whoever was pushing.

'THEY'RE IN HERE, LADS!' the man pushing Toff shouted.

The gap widened until an arm came through it, holding one of the fire extinguishers. A rotten stench wafted from it. Toff slid back, his body trembling with the effort. Although paralysed by fear, Jodie forced herself to move and barrelled into the bookshelf, slamming the door against the arm.

'AAARRGGGHHH!' The man dropped his extinguisher and withdrew his hand. 'YOU FUCKERS!'

Fighting back had exhilarated the terrified Jodie. Kicking the dropped cylinder under the pile of chairs, she slammed the door shut and, along with the others, shoved the second bookshelf into place, along with a profusion of desks. Made for small kids, the desks didn't have the bulk to form a solid barrier, but still they stacked them against the door. More shouts and swearing came from outside. Jodie realised the barricade wouldn't hold them up for long.

'Is there another way out?' She examined the people she and Toff had disturbed. None looked big enough to be much help.

Something heavy smashed against the door, shaking their flimsy barrier.

One of the people in the room pointed. 'Window!'

Jodie ran to the nearest window and peered outside. Though they were only one floor up, the drop looked higher than she'd expected – at least five metres, and onto concrete.

The barricade juddered.

There was nothing for it but for her to pick up a chair, smash the window, and set about using the legs to clear the jagged glass.

'LOOK!' Toff shouted.

The door behind them had opened twenty centimetres, and the pile of furniture teetered.

'Everyone out.' She pointed at the opening.

Nobody moved.

Toff ran to the window and turned back to them. 'I'll lower you.'

At his intervention, they formed a queue. The first, a young woman with greasy hair and tattoos, climbed onto the windowsill. He lowered her, grunting with the effort. Jodie went to the window and watched as she dropped the last three metres. When Jodie turned back to the door, she saw a head and a torch poking through the gap. There was no way they'd all get out.

'Next.' Toff helped a middle-aged man with a limp onto the windowsill.

Jodie took off her backpack and reached into the bottom. The cold glass told her she'd found what she wanted. She'd wrapped the bottle in an old towel when she'd collected it from home, and now she tore a strip off it, unscrewed the top and stuffed one end into the clear liquid. She found her lighter in a side pocket and, hands shaking, lit the rag. A blue flame hovered above the fabric, illuminating the bottle.

'What's that?' Toff asked.

'Some vodka I was saving for an emergency.' Jodie grinned. 'I reckon this counts as one.'

She threw the bottle at the doorway as the figure in the opening shoved his torso through it. The bottle smashed on the floor near his feet, the liquid leapt across the tiles, and then – did absolutely nothing. Just as Jodie had accepted she'd failed, a ball of blue flame expanded and enveloped the man's lower body. He screamed and his colleagues dragged him out. The flames licked at their sorry barricade, then spread hungrily across the timber desktops.

Jodie ignored the man's screaming and helped Toff lower two others to the ground. A third, an older man with a shuffling gait, waved them away.

'Leave me. I'd break me legs if I fell that far.'

'Come on, Ziggy,' Toff cried. 'We can't leave you.'

He shook his head and shuffled away into the far corner, coughing. By now, smoke filled the top half of the room. With streaming eyes, Toff gestured to Jodie to go next.

'We can't leave him.'

'What do you suggest,' Toff demanded, 'we throw him out? Come on, you next.'

Jodie shook her head. 'No, you go.'

'Don't fucking argue.'

A crash stopped them. She threw herself to the floor and peered at the far end of the room. A hole had appeared in the wall, near the corner. A battering ram of some kind withdrew, then smashed through the plasterboard, enlarging the opening. Adrenaline flooded her system.

Toff grabbed her shoulder. 'Jodie. Go.'

As she straightened, a fit of coughing seized her. She pushed Toff, and he got the message. He jumped onto the windowsill and lowered himself before dropping out of sight. She controlled her coughing as the battering stopped and boots clattered on the tiled floor. She crouched down, took a breath and pulled herself onto the windowsill. A figure appeared out of the thick smoke. At the next window, a metre away.

He saw her and lunged. She kicked at him, dislodging the man's mask. He screwed his eyes shut and coughed so she kicked him again, but waving his hand blindly, the man blocked her foot. She snatched up a shard of glass at her feet and slashed at his gloved hand.

He recoiled. 'Fuck!'

She didn't have time to lower herself. She peered through streaming eyes and jumped, hoping she landed right.

CHAPTER 3

Kasper Dąbrowski lifted his mug and inhaled, hoping the aroma of coffee would mask the stink of fried food from the shop below his office as he powered up his computer. He opened his emails and scanned the list of new messages. Mostly junk, but one address drew his eye. He clicked on it and read the message. His good mood evaporated.

'What's up?' his sister asked from the next desk.

'Robertson.'

The one word was enough to make Zofia join him at his screen. 'Just delete it.'

'He'll realise I've read it.'

'You didn't send a read receipt?'

'Of course not. But he'll realise I've received it when it doesn't bounce back.'

'That's not to say we've received it. It could be in your spam folder.'

Robertson wasn't someone he wanted anything to do with, but nor was he someone he wanted to piss off. 'What do you think I should do?' As usual, he was passing on the decision to his big sister. If only he'd done it when Robertson first got in touch.

Zofia exhaled in exasperation. 'We can't undo what's happened. Why don't you find out what he wants? Start by telling him how busy we are so we can turn him down.'

He doubted that would work, but no other route presented itself. He used a secure VPN and encrypted app to call the number Robertson had emailed him. The ringtone echoed, and he prayed nobody would answer.

'Yes?' The educated Scottish accent told him he'd dialled the right number.

He checked anyway. 'Mr Robertson?'

Silence.

'It's Kasper Dąbrowski, how are—'

'Good morning, Kasper. I've a job for you—'

'We're very busy at the moment, Mr Robertson.'

'I want you to look into a property in Miles Platting. It's a disused school called Mill View Academy which is on a site we're interested in. Find out who's responsible for it and let me know.'

'That will be the Department for Education, won't it?'

Robertson's chuckle sent a chill down Kasper's spine. 'There will be an individual. I prefer the personal touch.'

Kasper swallowed. 'We're snowed under. I'm not sure we can fit it in. If you like, I can recommend someone who can do it sooner.'

'I don't like dealing with new people, Kasper. I know you and your sister. You won't let me down. Shall we say next Monday?' He paused for a moment.

Kasper's mouth dried.

Robertson filled the silence. 'Verra good. Here's the address.'

He dictated it as Kasper searched for a notepad, stopping when he saw his sister scribbling on hers.

'Speak to you on Monday, Kasper. Ring me on this number.'

'Oh, Mr Robertson?'

'Yes?'

'What about payment?'

'The usual. I'll send it this morning.' Robertson ended the call.

Kasper only kept a crypto wallet for his dealings with Robertson, and every time he accessed it, he felt like a drug dealer or kidnapper.

They sat in silence.

'That went well.' Zofia ripped the top page off her notepad and dropped it on his desk.

'What would you have done?'

She sighed. 'I'd imagine the same as you.' She ripped out the next three pages to make sure she hadn't left an impression.

Mollified, Kasper used the VPN and InPrivate mode to open the map app on his desktop and typed in the address. 'Why's he interested in an old school?'

'Don't you think it's best if we don't find out?'

She was right. 'I imagine he wants to put in an early bid if it's for sale.'

'Yeah, right.' She didn't sound convinced. 'But whatever he wants, he'd better keep us out of it.'

'Amen to that.' Kasper considered how to achieve that. First step: they couldn't leave a footprint from any of the enquiries they made for this project.

'I realise you were trying to put him off, but we are very busy,' Zofia said. 'Shall we get one of Victor's friends on it?'

'We're trying to be discreet.'

'Considering they were present at the scene of a massacre and, unlike us, none of them got questioned by the police, I'd say they're one up on us as far as discretion goes.'

She had a point. 'Okay.' He checked the time. 'Victor's supposed to be in by now. I'll find out why he's late.' He rang him.

'Morning, Kasper. You saved me a call. I'm going to be late—'

'You're late already. We've got a full day planned. I need you here now.'

'Something's come up. Toff's in trouble.'

'Can't you deal with it after work?'

'I owe him.'

Kasper forced himself to take a breath. Victor did indeed owe the young Scouser. He'd helped them find Victor's teen-aged daughter.

'Yeah,' Kasper said. 'Okay.'

'I shouldn't be too long. It's only Miles Platting.'

Kasper checked the address on the piece of paper. 'Where in Miles Platting?'

'An old school—'

Kasper recited the address Robertson had just given them.

'Yeah,' Victor said. 'How did you know?'

'What's the matter with Toff? What's happened?'

'I'm not sure. That's what I'm doing now, going to have a look. I'll do it in my own time, so don't worry about paying me.'

'I'm not, but report back what you find.' He ended the call.

'Did I get that right? Victor's going to the place Robertson's interested in?' Zofia frowned and chewed her lip.

'Yeah.'

'He didn't say what's happened?'

'No, but something has, and it wouldn't surprise me if it's going to cause us problems. Too unlikely it's a coincidence.' A horrible thought he'd been trying to suppress fought to the surface. 'Do you think Robertson's planning to move his operation into Manchester?'

'Why would he?'

'With the Novak boys off the scene, there's a power vacuum in the Manchester underworld.'

'I bloody hope not, but hasn't the dad, Alex, stepped up?'

With what they knew about Robertson, and he about them, the thought of having the man as a neighbour filled Kasper with terror. But even more worrying was the thought of Alex Novak wanting revenge for his sons' deaths.

CHAPTER 4

By the morning, the lump on my forehead had gone down, courtesy of the ice pack I'd applied, and the cut didn't look bad. Zofia might notice it, but Kasper definitely wouldn't. On my way to the office, Toff rang, asking for my help. I ended the call, then opened the map and saw how close we were. I could take the path along the canal. Before I did, my phone buzzed. Kasper – just like him, to complain that I'm a bit late. He'd be even less impressed when I told him I was going to be delayed further.

To my surprise, after his initial bluster, he asked me to report back about the school where I'd agreed to meet Toff. How had he known where I was going? The thought made me uneasy. I consulted the map again and put the phone away.

'Come on, Oscar.' I tugged on his lead.

That's not the way to the office.

'Slight detour. We're going to see Toff.'

I could see Oscar checking his memory to see if Toff gave out treats.

'I can let you off the lead if we go along the canal.'

Now you're talking.

I waited until we got onto the towpath before letting him off. Toff's garbled message had made little sense, but I'd soon sort it out.

Toff. Is he the one who smells like two-week-old roadkill?

'Don't be nasty. He can't help not having washing facilities.'

I wasn't. It was an observation, not a criticism.

Oscar enjoyed sniffing the path, and we made good time. I checked the map. We were almost there. A ramp led up towards a bridge and I clipped Oscar's lead on before we reached the top. Mill View Academy stood on the side of the canal, bounded by it and a busy road. The building didn't look too old and a sign boasting about the school's status as 'Good' from their last inspection hung on the wire fencing.

Why had they closed it down? I looked for Toff, but Oscar detected him first.

Is that your mate? He pointed his nose towards the corner of the building.

I peered through my glasses at a figure lurking behind the wall. He waved, and waving back, I approached. 'Don't mention the smell.'

As if I would. Anyway, he doesn't stink like two-week-old roadkill now. I'd guess three months. And that IS a criticism. Sheesh.

'Shut it.'

As I got closer, though, I got what he meant. The stench caught the back of my throat. 'You okay, Toff?' He looked awful.

'Thanks for coming, Vic. No, I'm not.'

'You want to tell me what happened?'

'Some guys turned up around three. They smashed their way in and—' He gestured towards the school building. 'I'll show you.' He limped towards it.

'What happened to your leg?'

'When they attacked us, I had to jump out of the first-floor window. I twisted me knee when I landed.'

As I could attest, attacks on the homeless in Manchester were not uncommon. A group of hoorays had subjected me to a beating, and men trying to shut me up had killed two rough sleepers, mistaking them for me. I was pretty sure those killers were now dead, murdered, but that didn't mean the homeless community was safe.

Security screens covered the ground-floor openings at the front and side of the building. Toff led us to the back of the school and stopped outside an unscreened fire exit.

'We got in through the front, but they sent some blokes round this morning to block up the doors and windows.' He gave me the name of the contractors and I noted it down.

'Why have they left this unsecured?'

'They ran out of material. I was watching them, and they'd emptied the lorry. They've not done upstairs, either.'

I looked up and down the main street. 'We'd better hurry.'

Oscar stuck his snout into the opening and recoiled. ***Bloody hell! I'm not going in there.***

I'd caught a whiff of what he'd detected. 'You stay here and keep a lookout.' I unclipped him.

A relieved Oscar retreated and sat on the grass five metres away.

Toff led the way in. The stench made me gag. It was a more intense version of the odour clinging to Toff's clothes.

'What is that?'

'That's what I'm going to show you.'

With most of the windows boarded up, little light got into the corridor we found ourselves in. I used the torch on my phone, and he led me to the stairs. It grew brighter as we ascended, and on the first-floor corridor, I switched the light off. Someone had punched a hole in the wall next to a door.

Toff hesitated. 'In there.'

I reached for the door handle.

'No! It's blocked.' He pointed at the opening, and I squeezed through it, brushing plaster dust off my clothes on the other side.

Another stink – a composite of smoke, ash and burnt plastic – had joined the disgusting odour which had accompanied us. A pile of burnt desks, their tops consumed, but the metal frames in a tangled mess, blocked the doorway. Soot stained the walls around the door and the ceiling above. Yet another foul stench came from a pile of bedding in one corner.

I pointed at a broken window. 'Is that how you got out?'

Toff had paused in the opening and didn't answer straight away. A slight tremor betrayed his trepidation.

'Toff?' I walked towards the window.

'Sorry.' Toff entered the room. 'Yes. Six of us got out through there. But Ziggy didn't make it.'

'What happened to him?' I examined the ground outside. A drop of five metres ended on the concrete car park. I wouldn't have fancied it.

'They gave him a good kicking, took his photo, and told him he'd be dead if they caught him again.'

Bastards. 'Okay, what was it you wanted to show me?'

'In there.' He pointed towards the pile of blackened desk skeletons.

A small cylinder the size of a domestic fire extinguisher lay in the twisted metal. Pieces of broken glass were scattered on the floor, and I brushed them aside. I crouched and hooked the cylinder out using my right foot, without bringing the entire structure down on my head. Soot covered the surface, and I held it up.

'What's so interesting about this?'

'The stuff that stinks. It's from there. They spray it on our gear and on anyone they catch. After they've beaten them up. It smells like rotting flesh, and you can't wash it off. It's called Skunk Water.'

'That's quite a report.'

Toff reddened. 'I looked it up after last time.'

'You've come across it before?'

'A few people got sprayed down on Pollard Street East by the canal, and some guys off Oxford Road. I thought if you could find out where it came from . . .'

How come I didn't know about this? I'd only been off the streets a few weeks, yet it seemed like a lifetime. I found a worn top which didn't smell too bad in the pile of bedding and used it to rub at the soot on the cylinder.

'So, you going to do it?' Toff looked at me expectantly.

'What?'

'Find out who's doing this. You're a detective now, ain't you?'

I was, and I owed Toff. 'Of course.'

'Good man.' He punched my shoulder.

The feeling I could help him gave me a boost. If I was going to detect, I should get my brain into gear. 'Did you recognise any of the people?'

'No chance. They wore gas masks. Looked like aliens.'

I doubt the yobs who'd attacked me would have done this. This seemed too organised.

'How many of you slept in the building?'

'About a dozen, mainly young, like me. Quite a few girls. They felt safer here than outside.' Toff snorted. 'Used to feel safer.'

'That's quite a few people who'd know about this place.'

'Yeah, but we didn't blab. We didn't want just any dickhead coming here. Like I said, there were women here. Some guys on the street are animals.'

I didn't need telling. 'Any on drugs?'

Toff grinned. 'Behave. How many people on the streets don't have a bit of something?'

'Yeah, fair point.' During the months I'd slept rough, I'd come close to succumbing. 'Talk me through what happened.' Faint text had appeared under the soot I was rubbing off. I kept at it.

'I came in about eleven,' Toff began. 'Ziggy was on the door—'

'On the door?'

'Yeah, lookout, just in case . . .' He shook his head. 'Anyway, he told me he'd seen a van drive past earlier. Security company.'

I had experience of unsavoury employees of security companies. 'Did he remember the name?'

'Droylsden Shield or something like that.'

Not the same company I was thinking of, but it was easy to change names. 'You know who owns the building?'

'The council? It's a school, innit?'

'Possibly, but it was an academy. Zofia will find out.' I finished cleaning the soot off the canister and used my camera on it. 'Okay, let's get going.'

Toff didn't need telling twice.

The odour followed us out into the corridor.

'Who started the fire?' I asked him. 'Someone trying to keep warm?'

'One of the girls had a bottle of vodka and a rag.'

I could picture it and that explained the broken glass I'd found. 'Lucky nobody got hurt.'

'It splashed one of them as he broke in and burnt his legs.'

'That could be a good lead. He'd need to get treatment.'

As we descended, I put the torch back on.

A door near the bottom of the stairs stood open, and Toff hesitated as we approached it. 'Do you mind if I check in here?'

The thought of being trapped by the returning workmen made me nervous. But Oscar would give us a warning.

'Be quick.'

He switched on his phone light and stepped into a large classroom. The furniture in it looked like an angry bear had smashed it. Piles of bedding and clothes lay in the centre of the room, looking like they'd been turned over by the same bear. Toff headed for the biggest pile while I waited in the doorway. He kicked over the evil-smelling bedding, then bent down and picked up a backpack.

'Shit!'

'What?' I stepped towards him.

'He's dead.'

A leg stuck out from under the pile of bedding. In the gloom, I made out a familiar tattoo on the calf. Before I could examine it, Oscar's shrill barking came from outside. Then sirens sounded, very close.

CHAPTER 5

'Richard III was much maligned by the English because he lost the war against Henry VII. Never lose a war.' Alex Novak had fixed the men standing in front of him with his fierce gaze. 'They called him a hunchback and accused him of murdering his nephews. Both scurrilous lies. All because he lost a war. Never. Lose. A. War.' He slapped his desk, making the leather writing pad on it jump.

His men stared dully back at him across the vast expanse of mahogany. Already subdued by being in the unfamiliar surroundings of the sumptuous private office of his South Manchester mansion, they shifted uneasily. None were very clear what the hell he was talking about, and they waited for someone else to respond, just in case they'd misunderstood.

Since a group of unknown gunmen had killed Novak's sons and their most trusted lieutenants, the remaining forces available to him comprised men well past their best or unproven youngsters. As usual, Dean Hemsworth, one of the latter, put himself forward.

'Good advice, Boss. The winners write history.'

'Exactly, Dean. And we're going to write our own history.'

The others' reactions ranged from relief Dean had got it right to resentment for the same reason.

'How do you want us to write the next page of your story, Boss?'

Novak gave Dean a sharp look. Was he taking the piss? He decided he wasn't. The lad had what it took to succeed, and Novak hadn't spotted too much potential in the others. The older guys were solid and dependable, but none of them had leadership potential and, at their age, they wouldn't develop it.

'Our informants in the cop shop don't seem to have a clue about who was behind the murder of Milan and Marko. I want you lot to find out.'

Barry, one of the older men, cleared his throat. 'But, Boss, if the pigs can't do it, how are we supposed to find out?'

'Barry, you can't have forgotten how we do things already?'

Barry scuffed his feet and stared at the floor between them.

'Carrot and stick. The carrot is ten grand. Let everyone know that's on the table for anyone who can tell me who did it. And the stick?' He studied their faces. 'I don't need to tell you.'

That had been two days ago. Now Novak sat in a small room on the upper floor of one of the pubs he controlled. He could fit this room onto his desk at home, and instead of the aroma of expensive tobacco and wood polish, the stink of stale beer and carpet mites assailed his nostrils. He stifled a yawn.

The two years of semi-retirement when he'd let his boys run his business empire had made him soft. Since their murder, he'd been working fourteen-hour days and hitting the gym at dawn. Every part of him ached. His personal trainer's suggestion he should take testosterone supplements had angered him. He didn't need help in that department.

Novak studied the man seated before him. An impressive physical specimen, well over six foot and built like a heavyweight, but the heart and balls of a mouse. The man had hidden his weaknesses from his employers and, using smarm, treachery and cunning, he'd risen to a reasonable level in the local police. A level that made him very useful to Novak.

The entrance to the room stood next to the toilets, so upon his return to his cronies, Novak's visitor could pretend he'd suffered an attack of the shits if questioned.

'What you got for me?' Novak said.

The man hesitated until Novak produced a brown envelope and emptied its contents onto the round table between them. A band round the bundle of notes declared it enclosed a thousand pounds. The man's eyes lit up, and he slid them into an inside pocket.

'Our people suspect a team from out of town,' he reported.

'You don't say?'

'Probably Birmingham.'

Novak went through the crime groups he knew from that city. 'None of them would dare take me on.'

Mouseheart leant forward, wearing a smug expression. 'One of them did.'

A glare from Novak knocked him back into his seat. 'You any idea which one?'

'Sorry, no.' He patted the pocket containing his payoff.

Novak's mind raced. Hadn't Milan been shagging the wife of a family from up north? The Robertsons, he was pretty sure. Would they have risked starting a war with Novak just because of that? 'Are you sure it's not a Scottish gang?'

'Why do you say that?'

If the police weren't already looking at Scotland, he didn't want them sticking their size twelves in and spooking the locals. 'Just thinking aloud.' He took a deep breath. 'If they were from Brum, they must have had help from up here. You got any names for me?'

'We've not heard anything.'

'What the hell do you do all day? No wonder crime is at an all-time high. You're too stupid to catch anyone.'

The snout almost reacted, but then remembered what Novak had on him. 'There was a private eye involved. She claimed she was being held prisoner by Milan. I assumed you knew about her.'

'Of course I fucking did.' He took another deep breath. He hated swearing, but this maggot made him want to. The truth was, he'd known little about what the boys were doing and while the money flowed and trouble stayed low-key, he hadn't cared. That had been a mistake. 'How involved was she?'

'Well, not involved as such. But she was there when . . .'

When my sons were murdered in cold blood. Mouseheart lacked the stones to say it aloud. 'You've questioned her?'

'I'm not part of the investigation—'

'I was using the collective you, including your colleagues.' This guy really was a dimwit.

'Of course, the investigating officer questioned—'

'Who was it?'

'Does it matter?'

'If it didn't matter, I wouldn't pay you a grand to find out.'

'Grimes, DCI—'

'Yeah, I know him.' He gave a sharp look. 'He's not on my payroll.' He wasn't discussing his business with this snake. 'He's saying she wasn't involved?'

'We questioned her and her brother. Her business partner. But took no further action.'

Hmmm. Maybe he needed to speak to them. 'Names?'

'If they're not involved, why do—'

'You don't seem to understand how this works. I pay you. You talk. Capiche?'

'Their names are in the public domain.'

Novak glared at Mouseheart. 'Their names.'

'Dąbrowski. They've got an office on Cheetham Hill Road.' The smell of fear wafted off him.

'Right. Now piss off.' He waited until the door closed before lifting his glass. The peaty aroma filled his nostrils, and he took a sip. The silky liquid slid down his throat. Time he spoke to these Dąbrowskis. Carrot or stick?

CHAPTER 6

The first police car screeched into the car park as Toff and I burst out of the back door of the school. It disappeared around the front of the building. Hopefully, they hadn't seen us. We couldn't go back the way we'd arrived, and I looked to Toff, whose expression of panic told me he had even less idea about how to get away.

Oscar ran to the school property's back wall and barked. I followed him. The wall, a metre and a half high, had a wire fence along the top. Someone had cut a hole in it and Oscar led me to it.

'Good boy.' I patted him and pulled back the fencing. 'You go first, Toff. Leave that. I'll pass it down to you.' He took the backpack off and I boosted him onto the wall. He lowered himself over, landing with a grunt and rubbing his sore knee. I leant over and dropped the backpack into his waiting arms. 'You next, Oscar.' I lifted him onto the wall. 'Can you catch him, Toff?'

'Yeah, I think so.'

You think so?

'Go on.' I lowered him and released my grip.

Whoa! Not so fast! He let out a yelp as he fell into Toff's upraised arms.

I dragged myself onto the wall and pushed my legs through the gap in the fence. The canal path lay three metres below me. Toff and Oscar waited, looking up at me. I checked both ways, but saw nobody coming. I rolled onto my front, slid my legs over the edge and lowered myself, dropping the last metre.

'This way.' I pointed in the direction we'd come earlier and retrieved Oscar's lead. He let me hook it to his collar, and we set off.

'Slow down, Toff, and don't keep looking back.'

'Sorry.' He slowed, unable to resist checking over his shoulder.

The sound of more emergency vehicles arriving came from the school. The stench from the chemicals we'd encountered in it clung to my nostrils and grew stronger every time the breeze wafted past Toff. My thoughts returned to the body he'd found under the bedding. I'd glimpsed the distinctive tattoo of a thistle on the man's calf.

'Are you sure he was dead?'

'Yeah. His leg was stiff. I touched it.' He shuddered.

Had he left prints? I wasn't sure if you could get them from skin. 'Do you know who he was?' I waited for his reply, my heart racing.

'Yeah, you know him.' He looked into my eyes. 'Sawney.'

'You sure?' I don't know why I asked. I'd had no doubt.

'He was there last night, but we left him when we ran upstairs. He was still asleep.' A note of despondency entered his voice. 'If we'd stopped to wake him, he might be okay—'

Although distressed at discovering Sawney's death, I didn't want Toff to blame himself. 'You sure he was asleep?' I tried to remember the stages of rigor mortis. Didn't it usually wear off after twelve hours?

'Whadja mean?'

'He might have been dead last night, when you thought he was asleep?' Although he'd been clean for a few weeks, his heart might have given out.

'Oh yeah, I suppose so.' It didn't seem to cheer him much.

'I'm pretty sure that's what happened. If they'd killed him, wouldn't they have disposed of the body?'

By the time we reached Butler Street, Toff had calmed down. With a promise to tell him if I found out anything, I left him to get some clean clothes and I continued my interrupted journey to work. Despite my reassurances, I wasn't convinced Sawney's death was innocent. I needed to speak to John.

Within moments of Toff leaving, the stench overwhelming my sense of smell wore off. I took a deep breath through my nostrils, enjoying the stink of exhaust fumes and dogshit.

'That stuff they sprayed on him is disgusting.' Was it toxic? If Sawney had got a lungful, it might have been enough to finish him off.

It will take a week for my poor olfactory nerves to recover.

'I wonder where they got it from?'

No idea, but if you find out, tell me so I can avoid it.

We reached the office, and the effect had almost worn off. Although the usual fried-food odour from the takeaway downstairs seemed far less pungent. Maybe they weren't frying. I waited for Kasper to buzz me in and took the lead off Oscar as he climbed the stairs before me. I pushed the door at the top open and he trotted in.

'What's that stink, Oscar?' Zofia called. 'You been rolling in something?'

Don't blame me. He barked and pointed at me.

'You'll have to take that dog out and clean him up.' Kasper was obviously still pissed off about something.

He couldn't still be annoyed about me being late. 'That's me. I went into the school building. A gang of thugs, probably employed by the owners, broke in and chucked out the rough sleepers who were using it. They'd sprayed some disgusting liquid around. Toff called it Skunk Water. He'd come across it before.'

Kasper got up and opened the windows at the back. 'What did you find out?'

I mentioned the one thing that had stood out: 'There's a dead man there.'

'What?' Zofia's eyes widened. 'Have you phoned the police?'

'Didn't need to. They arrived as we were leaving.'

'Did they see you?' Kasper said.

'I don't think so.'

'Do you know how he died?' Zofia asked. 'Or anything about him?'

'I barely saw him, just a leg, and Toff said he was cold and stiff.' I took a deep breath. 'He's a guy called Sawney. I got to know him quite well on the streets. He was trying to get clean.'

'Oh, I'm sorry, Victor. Do you want some time off?'

Kasper looked horrified, but she stopped him with a glare.

'I'm better off working. I want to find out who broke in. And if they had anything to do with Sawney's death.'

Zofia's eyes widened. 'You think they might have?'

'I don't know what to think.' I remembered our last conversation, less than three weeks ago. 'He . . . He said stuff about people wanting to kill him, but I put his paranoia down to drug use.'

Kasper raised a finger. 'Just because you're paranoid doesn't mean they're not out to get you.'

'That's not funny, Kasper.'

He reddened. 'Did they leave any clues behind?'

'A canister of the stuff they'd sprayed. I'd imagine it's not widely available.'

'Here it is.' Zofia tapped her screen. 'Skunk Water. It's only available from three places in the UK, plus a few mail order outlets that deliver here.'

I opened the image I'd taken on my phone and enlarged the text until I could read it. 'There's a postcode here.' I recited it.

'Okay, got it. Alpha Security Supplies.' She read some more. 'It says they only deal with police forces or government departments.'

'Contractors came to board the building up today. I got their name from Toff, and a security company, Droylsden Shield, was round last night, just before they raided the place.'

Kasper entered the name. 'There's a good chance the thugs worked for the security company.'

'And the owners would employ them. I thought it would be the education authority, but it's an academy, so could belong to anyone.' I remembered when Em's junior school became an academy just after Helen moved up to senior school. 'We need to find out who they are.'

'Already on it.'

'Yeah, how come you already knew about the place?' I thought back to his response to my call.

He exchanged a look with his sister, then turned to me. 'Do you want to sit down?'

I didn't like the sound of this, and sat at my desk.

'We got a call this morning. Mr Robertson—'

'The guy who killed the—'

'No need to say it out loud.' Kasper tugged at his collar.

'You've checked for bugs?' I gestured at the walls. Since the agency's inadvertent entanglement in the murder of members of the Novak gang, including the two sons, Kasper swept the office for bugs every morning.

'Of course.'

I breathed a sigh of relief. 'So, what did he want?'

'He's interested in the school, Mill View Academy. More specifically, the site it's on. What's it like?'

'There's a mill across the canal, as the name suggests. But it's just a school with a playground—'

'Playing fields?' Zofia's fingers stroked her keys.

I tried to visualise what I'd seen. 'One football pitch.'

Kasper shook his head. 'That doesn't sound like enough land to interest Robertson. Especially in that part of town.'

'It isn't. But look what's next to it.' Zofia tapped her screen, and we joined her. A 3D map of the area showed a large, cleared piece of land next to the school. 'It would be interesting to see who owns that. The only access to that plot is that minor road which goes under the railway line.' She pointed at the bottom of the screen. 'If they owned the school, they'd have direct access to the main road.'

My mind raced. 'You think Robertson owns the wasteland?'

'We'll find out.'

'Do you reckon he's planning to move down to Manchester?' Robertson didn't know of my involvement in leading his men to the Novak brothers. But he knew of Zofia and Kasper's part, and had even paid them. While Robertson was in Aberdeen, he and they could pretend it wasn't a problem. If he moved down here to Novak's turf, Robinson would be reminded every day. And how long before he felt he needed to deal with the loose ends they represented?

CHAPTER 7

Victor and Oscar had left, taking the evil stench with them, and Zofia almost welcomed the return of the odour of frying from the takeaway downstairs. She considered her brother, whose air of studied indifference didn't fool her. The contact from Robertson had upset him, as it had her. They should never have got involved with someone so dangerous.

It was too late for regrets. They needed to deal with where they were and avoid getting further embroiled in the man's business. The quicker they found the information he wanted, the sooner they'd be free of him. She returned her attention to the database on the screen. The bell made both jump.

Kasper stood. 'I'll see who it is.'

Although they'd got the offices so they could meet clients, the odours from their neighbour meant they discouraged visitors. They mostly got clients via the website and through advertising on social media.

The bell rang again. Kasper stood at the entry phone, staring at the screen.

'What's up?' she asked him.

The only visitor who had that effect on Kasper was Grimes, a detective chief inspector with the local police. He was the one investigating the killing of the Novaks. Had he uncovered evidence disproving the statements she made after the incident?

'Novak.' Kasper's voice was a croak.

'What?' She joined him and stared at the screen. 'Shit! What does he want?'

Novak leant forward, and the bell rang again.

'I don't know, but he's not giving up.' Kasper's hand trembled. 'We'll have to let him in.'

'I'll do it. You sit down.' She waited until he reached his desk and pressed the talk button. 'Good afternoon, can I help you?'

'Ah, someone is home. Alex Novak. I'd like to consult you about a matter. Can you let me in?'

'Of course.' She took a deep breath and pressed the lock release.

Novak pushed the door open, spoke to someone off-screen, and came in. She glanced round the office. It looked okay, although she suspected the stench Victor had brought with him lingered.

She entered the reception as Novak reached the top of the stairs. Above average height, he had a muscular build and, despite his age, hadn't run to fat, although his tailored three-piece suit could be hiding a multitude of sins. His deep-set, dark-brown eyes studied her with undisguised curiosity.

'Good afternoon, Mr Novak, I'm Zofia Dąbrowski.' She offered a hand.

'I know who you are, Ms Dąbrowski.' Although spoken in a gentle tone, the words sent a chill down Zofia's back.

She untangled her hand from a firm but not fierce grip and gestured at the door behind her. 'Do you want to go through?'

He stepped into the office and scanned the room before fastening his gaze on Kasper. 'And Mr Dąbrowski. Good, that you're both here.'

Kasper stared with a panicked expression and Zofia broke the silence. 'Shall we go into our consulting room?' She gestured at the first door on the right. 'Can I get you a drink?' It would give her time to compose herself.

'Coffee, please.' He showed his perfect teeth.

'I'll get it.' Kasper jumped up and charged towards the kitchen.

Bugger! *So much for marshalling her thoughts.* 'Thank you, Kasper.'

Novak walked into the room they labelled the boardroom, because it contained a dining table and six chairs. 'Dining room' sounded too domestic. He took a seat at the head of the table.

Zofia stood in the doorway. 'I'll get my tablet.' What the hell does he want? She returned, took the seat at the opposite end, and opened a new note. 'How may we help you, Mr Novak?'

'Shall we wait for your brother?'

Kasper took an age. While she grew more uncomfortable by the minute, Novak seemed unperturbed. When her brother at last arrived with a tray, she grabbed the cafetiere and a mug. 'Milk, sugar?'

'Neither.'

She took the cup to him, noticing Kasper had only put two out. He backed towards the door.

'I hope you'll be joining us, Mr Dąbrowski.'

'Errm.' He cleared his throat. 'I've got quite a lot on. I'm sure Zofia can deal with anything you need.'

'Yes, I'm sure she can. But I want you in the meeting.'

He took a seat and Zofia, seeing the tremor in his hands, grabbed the second cup before he could. 'Okay, Mr Novak, do you want to tell us what you need?'

'I believe you were at the location where someone murdered my sons.'

Kasper's tremor increased.

Zofia leant forward, hoping Novak hadn't noticed her brother's agitation. 'Yes, I was. Your sons almost killed me.' A surge of anger overrode the fear that had seized her since Novak arrived. 'Are you here to apologise?'

Novak's fury-filled eyes held her gaze. Then, when she thought he'd explode, he laughed. 'You've got balls, young lady. As Elizabeth I said, "I might have the body of a weak and feeble woman, but I've got more balls than the rest of you put together."' He stared at Kasper, who shifted in his seat.

Zofia frowned. 'Actually, I don't think—'

'No, I'm not here to apologise. I'm here to find out who killed my sons.'

Kasper opened his mouth, but Zofia gestured to him to shut up.

Novak had noticed. 'What were you going to say, Kasper?'

Novak's use of her brother's first name chilled her. 'If it's me you want to speak to, why is my brother here?'

'I want you both to tell me what you saw.'

'Nothing,' she said. 'I saw nothing. I'm sure you've read my statement to the police. And the one my brother made, so you're aware he knows even less than I do.'

He didn't deny seeing their statements. 'You know what statements are like. You tell the police what you think they want to know.' He studied the siblings one after the other. 'And make sure you don't get yourself in trouble.'

Did he see Kasper swallow? He missed little. 'In your world, maybe, Mr Novak. We find it easier to tell the truth.'

'The truth. Yeah, that elusive concept. "Half a truth is often a great lie", as Benjamin Disraeli said.'

'Franklin.' The word fell out of her.

'What?' His eyes flashed.

She swallowed. 'That was Benjamin Franklin.'

'Was it now?' His scowl softened. 'You're obviously a clever young woman. You understand memory sometimes plays tricks on us.'

'What your sons and their men did to me isn't a trick of my memory.'

He had the grace to look away. 'I didn't suggest it was.' His gaze returned to her. 'But you know details come back to you long after the incident.'

'Yes, and so do the police, which is why I have DCI Grimes's number, in case I recall something else.'

'Oh yes, DCI Grimes.'

She waited for him to continue.

'He's a bit of a stickler. If he feels you did something wrong, he'll do you for it. Others might look upon your minor misdemeanours and decide ignoring them would serve the greater good.'

'If I commit any minor misdemeanours, I'll bear that in mind. Now, is that all you wanted?' She pushed her chair back.

'No! That's not all. I want you to find whoever killed my sons.'

'We don't do that sort of work. That's why we have a police force.'

'I'm offering a very generous fee.'

Kasper cleared his throat. 'How much?'

She'd almost forgotten he was there. 'Mr Novak, why the hell do you think I'd want to find their killers? So I could shake their hands and thank them?' She glanced at Kasper to check he'd also got the message.

Novak reddened. 'It's all very well having balls, Ms Dąbrowski, but you also need brains.' He stood. 'Talk to your brother. You can treat the fee as a sort of compensation, if it makes you feel better.'

'Compensation?'

Kasper got up. 'Okay, Mr Novak. We'll consider your offer. I'll show you out.'

Zofia stayed in her seat. Through her anger, she recognised Novak's threat. He obviously didn't believe her confected statement, recognising it as something he'd have come up with. But unlike the police, who had to accept it unless they could prove it false, he didn't.

CHAPTER 8

After speaking to Kasper and Zofia, I arranged to meet Toff and some people who'd been with him last night. The discovery that Robertson, who I'd not met, was taking an interest in property in Manchester alarmed me as much as it did Kasper. His people were killers, and he'd used Kasper and Zofia, implicating them in his crimes. Why the hell was he coming to Manchester?

Oscar dragged me out of my reverie. ***Aren't we seeing Toff?***

'What?' I realised with a start we'd arrived at Angel Meadow Park, where we'd agreed to meet.

I can smell him over there.

We entered the park, and I let Oscar off his lead, climbed the steps, and stood at the top, searching for any sign of my friend.

He's up here. Oscar stood on the path leading to the top end of the park.

I followed him, my breathing straining. Two figures sat on a bench. Toff waved and stood, as did his companion. A bit shorter than him, she had cropped black hair, delicate features and a nose piercing. Although her wary expression made her seem older, she looked to me only about the same age as my Helen. How would I feel if she ended up on the streets?

'Hello, Oscar.' Toff petted him. 'Jodie, this is Victor, the man I told you about.'

Her blue eyes studied me with suspicion. 'Toff says you're a private eye.' She had an educated local accent.

'That's right. He said you saw something last night that might help us find who attacked you.' Close up, the stench from the school clung to both.

'Us? You're not an us, you're a them.' She gestured at my clean clothes. 'Why should I trust you?'

'Come on, Jodie, I told you he is one of us. He's only just got a place off the street.'

'Oh yeah. Where are you staying?'

'Strangeways View.'

'That shit heap? I wouldn't stay there.'

I laughed. Part of me agreed, but having seen where they'd slept last night, I had no desire to swap. Where I was now was a stepping stone to a decent home – not anything like the one I'd left behind in Bristol, but something I could invite my daughters to without shame.

'So, you're happy to talk to me?'

'Don't you lot pay for information?'

I glanced at Toff. 'Our clients pay, and in this case, that's Toff.'

She folded her arms. 'Okay, what do you want to know?'

'What did you notice last night?'

'From when?'

'Talk me through from when you arrived at the school until you left via the window.'

'Okay.' She took a deep breath and closed her eyes. 'When I arrived, around midnight, I saw a dark van parked on the side road opposite. The one where they've got the little Noddy houses with the wooden cladding.'

A 'Noddy house' anyone living on the streets would be grateful to live in. 'A van or a minibus?'

'It might have been a minibus. I think there were people in the back.' She closed her eyes again. 'Yeah, there were.'

'You say it was dark. Were there any names or markings on the sides?'

'I couldn't see any, but there were two darker patches, one at the front door and the other near the back.'

It sounded like they'd covered up identifying marks on the vehicle. 'What size, shape?'

'Square. No, rectangular. About the width of the front door and half as high. Sorry, I'm not much use.'

'You're brilliant. We know the minibus is dark, but not black because the patches were darker. Probably blue. And that they've got two markings identifying them, and their rough sizes.'

'Really.' She brightened.

'And they were just waiting?'

'I didn't get too close, but I got the feeling they were watching me. Girls develop that sense early on, especially if they live on the street.'

'I can imagine.' I gave her a smile. 'Then you went inside?'

'Yeah, Ziggy was just turning in and putting the barricades up.'

'Barricades?'

'Yeah. We stack furniture against the doors to stop people coming in at night. And if they break through, they make enough noise to warn us.'

'Is that what woke you?'

Her face screwed up in thought again. 'No. That's why I thought it strange. The men in the van made me nervous, so I didn't sleep, but I heard nothing until someone screamed in the next room. We were in the room nearest the entrance, so they should have reached us first.'

'Were there any other doors?'

'Yeah, the main entrance, but that's shuttered, and you can't get in—'

'Unless you've got the key,' I finished for her.

Her brow furrowed as she studied me. 'You think the owner sent them? But that's the council. I assumed they were those right-wing vigilantes who've been attacking homeless people in posh areas.'

That was another line of enquiry. 'Do you recall anything else about the people who attacked you?'

'They had radios. I heard the crackling sound they make.'

'Yeah,' Toff cut in, 'the guy who almost caught me had an ear thing. He also had a tattoo on his neck.'

'Do you recall what it was?' So many people had tattoos it was almost useless unless he could identify it.

'Sorry, no.'

I hid my disappointment. 'Do you remember anything else, Jodie?'

'No, sorry.'

'Don't apologise. What you've told me is helpful. Thanks.'

'Okay.' She didn't sound convinced and stood. 'Laters, guys, and you, Oscar.' She gave a small wave and set off towards Victoria Station.

Toff didn't hide his disappointment at her leaving, but finally turned to me. 'What you going to do now, Victor?'

'We're going to find out who might have keys for the school.' Not only would this aid my investigation, but it would also keep Kasper happy.

'Can I come with you?'

'Sure, but you can't come into the office.' Apart from his appearance, the stench clinging to his clothes would put anyone off.

My phone rang. John returning my call. 'Morning, Brother, what's so urgent?' Although I'd psyched myself to give him the news when I rang, I felt unprepared and took a couple of breaths. 'You okay?'

'Yeah. Sorry. Sawney's dead.'

Sensitively done. Oscar shook his head. ***Idiot!***

I mouthed, 'Shut up,' to him.

John replied after a long pause. 'Was it an overdose?'

'I don't know. He told me he'd been clean for a while.'

'Same here, but you know how it goes.' He exhaled. 'Thanks for telling me.'

'Some thugs raided his billet before he died.'

'You think they might have had something to do with his death?'

'I don't know, but I aim to find out.'

'Count me in. I'll get Craig and we'll meet up later.' John ended the call.

The fact I'd be doing something to find out how Sawney died made me feel better. We made our way along Great Ancoats Street, lined with high-end furniture stores. My home lay half a mile away, on the other side of the trendy mill conversions, which were a world away from the scruffy flat in which I lived. We arrived at the Department for Education offices, and I left Oscar in Toff's care. I showed my card and told the receptionist that I was working for a firm of estate agents based in New York.

She studied the business card Zofia had insisted they supply me with. 'I've never dealt with a private detective before.' She examined my jeans, scuffed trainers and creased shirt.

'I bet you have, without knowing it. We blend in.'

'Oh yeah.'

'Which part of Bristol you from?' I laid on the accent, calling it Brizl.

'Henleaze. You?'

'Redland.'

'Ooh, posh.'

'The bit I live in is almost Kingsdown, but you know.' I winked.

She laughed. 'Okay, what did you want?'

'My client has someone interested in setting up a chain of education establishments in the UK. They want to accelerate the process by taking over good-quality disused schools. We're compiling a list and noticed Mill View Academy is empty. Would it be possible to visit and take photos? We can then ensure that's exactly what they're looking for.'

Her hesitation almost convinced me she would turn me down, but she relented, punched keys and studied the screen. 'The person you want is out, so I'll give him a message to contact you?'

'Can I ring him?'

'I'm not giving you his number.'

'Okay, how will I know it's him?'

Suspicion returned to her eyes.

'Okay, I'm sure he'll introduce himself. Cheers. Thanks for passing on my message.' Hiding my disappointment, I returned to the entrance.

'How did it go?' Toff asked.

'The guy's ringing me back.'

'Oh great. And I've remembered something about the guy's tattoo. It was the head of a red snake.'

That stopped me like a punch in the gut. One of the men working for Novak had had a tattoo like that. But I thought he'd died. If he'd survived, what he knew could put me and my employers in prison, or worse.

CHAPTER 9

I returned to the office to discover both Kasper and Zofia deep in a gloomy funk. I'd expected it of Kasper, but his sister was made of sterner stuff. She didn't even greet Oscar, upsetting the poor creature. This probably wasn't the best time to tell them my bad news.

It was up to me to lift the mood by giving them the better news first. 'Guys, I'm going to get you-know-who off our backs.'

Kasper looked at me sharply. 'Who told you about that?'

'You did, earlier on.' Was he suffering from fear-induced amnesia?

'No, not—'

'Let him tell us.' Zofia gestured for Kasper to let me speak.

Something was going on, but I continued. 'I've spoken to someone in the Department for Education and the person in charge of Mill View Academy is going to ring me. We'll be able to let Robertson have his name and contact details.'

'Oh, that.' Kasper's lack of enthusiasm threw me.

'I thought you'd be pleased.'

Zofia broke the thick silence. 'Victor, you'll have to excuse my brother. We've had a visitor—'

'Has Grimes been here?' The policeman scared me, and he terrified Kasper. That would explain his wariness.

'Not Grimes. Worse.'

Who was worse than Grimes? I searched her face for a clue.

Kasper said, 'Alex Novak was here.'

'Shit!'

'Yeah, shit.'

'What the hell does he want?' I thought of his man with the snake tattoo. Had he told Novak about our involvement in his sons' deaths? He couldn't have, otherwise Kasper and Zofia wouldn't be here, not alive anyway.

Zofia explained, 'He wants us to investigate his sons' deaths.'

'You're joking!'

'Yeah, look at my smiling face.' Kasper stood. 'I'm making a coffee. Anyone want one?'

We both declined the offer. I went to my desk and turned on my computer while I absorbed this new information. Kasper came out of the kitchen holding a steaming mug. He spilled a few drops as he placed it on a coaster.

I waited until he regained his seat. 'What have you agreed?' I couldn't believe they'd consented to work for Novak.

Zofia said, 'He told Novak we'd look into it.'

'We had no choice.' Kasper pouted.

'He knows his sons tried to kill you?'

Zofia nodded.

'And he still wants you to help him? Why didn't you refuse?'

'I tried. I suggested my motive to find the killers would be to shake their hands and thank them.'

Much as I admired Zofia's courage, I sometimes worried it would get her into trouble. 'I bet he didn't like that.'

'No, but he still insisted we took the job.'

How do we get out of this? I might as well tell them about the guy with the snake tattoo. The mood couldn't get any worse. 'Toff told me something worrying.'

Kasper muttered an expletive.

'One of the guys clearing out the school had the tattoo of a red snake on his neck.'

Zofia gasped. 'He can't have. He's dead.'

'Evidently not.'

Kasper said, 'I bet your junkie friend imagined seeing the tattoo.'

'Why would he make that detail up? We must assume the man didn't die.'

'So why hasn't he told Novak what happened?'

I couldn't say. He could link us to the killing of Novak's sons. We stayed silent, deep in our thoughts.

Zofia spoke first. 'I mentioned him during one interview with the police. Their reaction suggested he'd been murdered.'

Kasper turned to his keyboard. 'They released the names of the people killed.'

'What's the use of that? We don't have his name.'

I understood what he was getting at. 'But we can find photos of the dead and we know what he looks like.'

We gathered round Kasper's screen while he searched the reports of the incident. One showed images of the men and one woman who'd died that day. I recognised the Novak brothers, but the others looked like extras from a clichéd crime show. Two had shaved heads and broken noses and either might have been the one we were looking for.

Zofia pointed at the screen. 'That looks like him.'

I peered at the image. 'I'm not sure.' The last time I'd seen him, I'd been terrified, and blood had covered half his head. 'I can't see his neck. Are there any other pictures?'

Kasper scrolled down the screen.

Zofia returned to her desk. 'I'll see if they mention the survivors.'

I stayed at Kasper's screen, but none of the images were clearer.

Zofia had no better luck. 'I can speak to the police and ask if the man with the snake tattoo died.'

'And say what? You're worried he might pin a murder on us?'

'Don't be stupid, Kasper. She can explain she thought she'd seen him and was terrified.'

'I've got a card for Sergeant Bowling somewhere.' She checked the time. 'I'll ring her tomorrow.'

I took that as my cue to leave. Traffic filled both sides of Cheetham Hill Road and Oscar sat patiently on the kerb until a woman driving a huge van took pity on us and let us cross. Oscar hated walking along the busy main road, so we took a slightly longer route, past the Jewish Museum, down the side of the shopping centre and onto the green spaces behind it where he could roam off the lead.

The realisation that one of the men who'd threatened Zofia was still alive, and knew my name, filled me with trepidation. I could change it again. Victor Mitchum wasn't my real name. But enough people knew me as Victor that anyone searching for me could get lucky. In fact, if he'd spoken to the police, they'd realise who I was. Were they already looking at me? Overcome by a surge of paranoia, I checked the streets around me and hurried home.

As we crossed the River Irk, my phone rang, and I checked the caller before answering. 'John? You get hold of Craig?'

'Hello, Brother. Where are you?'

I told him.

'We can meet you at Angel Meadow Park in fifteen.'

I changed direction.

Where are we going?

'Slight detour. We're meeting John and Craig.'

Will we be long? I want my dinner.

'Trixie will be there.'

The thought of seeing Craig's Yorkshire terrier overcame Oscar's reluctance, and he almost dragged me to the park. They arrived five minutes after we got there. Trixie, today wearing a yellow ribbon in her hair, greeted Oscar.

'Hail, Brother, and your loyal hound.' John saluted us.

Craig, wearing a scowl that would terrify anyone who didn't know him, made do with a lazy salute. 'Nasty business with Sawney.'

John sat on a nearby bench. 'Do you want to tell us exactly what happened?'

Craig joined him and I stood facing them. 'Sawney was with Toff and a few others, sleeping in a disused school, when a gang of hired thugs broke in, spraying Skunk Water everywhere and beating up anyone they caught.'

John and Craig exchanged a look. 'Sounds like the other places.'

'Yeah, Toff said something about other premises being raided.' I still felt embarrassed I knew nothing of them.

John nodded. 'You think the thugs had something to do with Sawney's death?'

'I'm not sure, John. But I want to investigate them.'

Craig said, 'Why d'you think it wasn't an overdose?'

'Sawney told me he was clean.'

'How many people do you know who've relapsed?'

'Too many, but I'm sure he meant it. He asked me to go with him to that drug and alcohol rehabilitation centre last month.'

John frowned. 'You think they killed him by accident? They meant to rough him up and went too far?'

'I didn't get the chance to examine his body, so can't say.'

Craig said, 'That must be the only other explanation. Why would anyone target him?'

I'd been thinking about that. 'He told me he thought he might be in danger. He claimed to know things about powerful people.

I wasn't sure how much to believe. He's been paranoid since I met him, and you know how people talk.'

'We certainly do, Brother. He said the same to us, but I didn't take it seriously. How do you want to approach this?'

'I'll ask Zofia to use her contacts to discover what the police think. In the meantime, we need to find out who was there at the raid. Discover if any of them knew Sawney. If they targeted him, was it personal or were they acting on behalf of someone else?'

Craig leant forward to stroke Trixie. 'You mean the people who ordered the clearing of the school?'

'Someone must employ the men who were there. We need to find out who that is and who hired them to do the work.'

'We've had no joy with the former and we've been trying to discover who owns the other buildings they've cleared.' Craig listed three addresses where uniformed thugs used similar tactics. 'I've had a look online at the library, but we could do with accessing Kasper's land registry database.'

'I'm sure it won't be a problem. Would tomorrow be okay?'

Craig nodded. 'We'll ring before we call in.'

Oscar and I took our leave and continued on our way home. Now we were well into spring, it was still light when I crossed the canal. The tower block we lived in loomed over the houses ahead, but the joyous lift I'd got on seeing it when I first moved in had gone, replaced by a sense of dread. Oscar felt it too, and his steps slowed.

'Come on, mate. I'll be cooking shepherd's pie tonight.'

He wagged his tail, but the sense of wariness wafting off him deepened as we neared the tower. The stench of weed leaked out of the building as I punched in the code, which opened the main door. Inside, I glanced at the reception desk. Two people lurked behind the security glass, both young trainees who didn't give us trouble. With a sense of relief, I nodded a greeting. A resident I recognised from my time on the streets stood at the counter and scowled at me. I ignored him and used my bipper to open the door to the corridor leading to my flat.

Another stink overpowered that of the weed, which pervaded the entire building. I turned the corner and stopped. Someone had written 'STINKING GRASS' across my door in dogshit.

CHAPTER 10

Banging woke me again, and I dismissed it as a nightmare. It continued, though, and I opened my eyes. Bugger! The sound besieged me and as full consciousness returned, I recognised it: four nights ago, one of my neighbours had staged what felt like a rave in the flat above. I'd used earplugs before going up to complain, but they'd made little difference. Despite my objections at that time, he'd obviously decided to have another.

This time it was louder, and the walls vibrated. My phone showed ten past two and, giving up on sleep, I put my glasses on and went to the kitchen to make a coffee.

Oscar lay under the table with his paws over his ears. ***At least on the street we could move on and avoid this sort of thing.***

I mouthed, 'Okay, I'll speak to them,' and pointed at the ceiling.

Although they'd been aggressive and scary when I'd spoken to them last Saturday, they'd turned the music down. That was before I got the reputation for being a snitch. Suspecting I'd get an even more unfriendly reception, I tightened my laces and pulled on a jacket.

'Do you want to come with me?' I reinforced my words with gestures.

He buried his head further under his paws. On reflection, it was just as well. If Tyson was with his owner, Oscar wouldn't thank me.

I locked the flat and made my way to the next floor. The cacophony quietened on the stairs but hit me like a blow when I entered the corridor above mine. Thick smoke filled the space, and a moment of panic passed when I recognised the stink. A few figures lolled about, leaning on the walls. Most were out of it, but two of them glared at me.

The sound blasted out of the open doorway halfway down the corridor. My head vibrated, provoking an incipient headache. I shouted into the open doorway, to no effect. In the gloom, I made out a few figures. The sensation I was having a heart attack grew as I stepped into the flat and my ribcage vibrated. The stench of weed increased, and smoke attacked the back of my throat.

A hand grabbed my shoulder and a figure I recognised thrust his face centimetres away from mine. I looked around for his dog. His mouth worked and spit landed on my glasses. From his manner and lip movements, I guessed he wasn't welcoming me.

I gestured to my ears. 'I CAN'T HEAR—' My voice sounded loud in the sudden silence. 'Thank you.'

'Well?'

I looked at him, puzzled.

'What the fuck d'you want?'

'This. Silence. Some of us are trying to sleep.'

'Yeah? Some of us are trying to have a good time.'

'Fine. But you should consider other people—'

He prodded me in the chest. 'You think you've got more rights than all of us here?' He gestured to the people standing around. Aggression wafted off them.

I swallowed. 'No. But I'm sure there are others trying to sleep.'

'Oh yeah? And where are they?' He made a show of checking the corridor.

'I don't want to get into the mechanics of why there isn't a queue of people coming to complain. Let's just agree to keep the noise down at this time in the morning and everyone will be happy.'

'And if we don't, you going to report us?'

'Fucking grass!' someone behind me said.

'Yeah, squealer!' A push accompanied this comment.

My pulse raced and I readied myself to run.

'Alright, everyone. What's going on?'

I recognised the voice of one of the staff from the reception with a sense of relief. Before I could speak to him, the dog owner greeted him.

'Alright, Jez. We're just having a quiet chat with our neighbourhood snitch here.'

Jez turned his attention on me. 'Ah, I was looking for you. You need to clean up the . . . crap on your door.'

A few people sniggered.

'I didn't put it there.'

'Oh yeah, who did, then?'

I looked at the dog owner, almost certain he'd done it. 'Someone else with a dog.'

'Well, if you've got evidence . . .'

'Of course I haven't.'

'You'd better clean it up, then.'

'But why should I have to—'

'Do you want me to report that you've been defacing the property?'

I took a deep breath. 'No.' I pushed my way out into the corridor, feeling the hostility accompany me to the stairs, and returned to my flat.

Well done. Oscar wagged his tail in greeting.

I put on the rubber gloves I'd bought when I'd moved in and collected the mop bucket. Before I could fill it, the sound resumed.

If anything, louder. Oscar's disappointed expression accompanied me to the front door. Trying not to gag, I cleaned off the offensive message before washing the mop, bucket and gloves in bleach and returning to bed.

I soon gave up on sleep and found a miserable-looking Oscar under the kitchen table. He'd pulled his sleeping pad and blanket over his head.

I patted his shoulder and mouthed, 'Let's get out of here.'

He didn't need persuading. I put my shoes and coat on and led him to the reception. I ignored Jez behind the counter, and we stepped out into the crisp night air.

The sounds of the party faded the nearer we got to the canal bank. Locals described this area as having been a no-go zone, even in daylight. Now the canal path was a well-lit thoroughfare, linking the delights of the city centre to new housing estates.

Where are we going?

'We're just getting away from the racket. I'm sure they'll finish before too long.'

What if they don't?

I didn't answer.

You could talk to them again.

'You being funny?'

No. They stopped, didn't they?

We walked on.

You could report them.

'Fat lot of good that would do. They already hate me.'

My thoughts strayed to the problems of Kasper and Zofia. Problems that could entangle me. While living on the street, I'd dreamed of a job and somewhere to live. Now I had both and my problems seemed as great. Then I thought of what Toff and the others at the disused school had gone through just one night ago.

And poor Sawney, who hadn't survived. How and why he'd died, I still had no idea, but I would find out.

We'd reached the New Islington Canal Basin. Oscar had run ahead, and he branched off to the left. Happy to meander, I followed him past shuttered restaurants and bars occupying the ground floors of the new tower blocks. Barges with their colourful curtains drawn lined the waterway. The thought of living in one of them appealed. I could find out how to get on the waiting list tomorrow.

Oscar led me through the basin and then followed the Ashton Canal, doubling back towards home. We rarely walked these banks, preferring the greener Rochdale Canal. We left the new-build apartments and reached the section flanked by houses and older industrial buildings.

Halfway home, we passed under a road bridge, and Oscar, who'd been meandering across the path exploring, froze and stared at a series of brick industrial buildings.

'What's up, boy?'

I heard something.

I listened. 'Well, I can't hear anything.'

Amazing. Humans have worse hearing than dogs. Shock horror.

'Okay, smartarse. What was the sound?'

I'm not sure. He trotted back to the road bridge and climbed the steps to the road.

'Oscar, come back.' I followed him across the bridge towards the buildings he'd been studying.

Open metal gates three metres high led to a large, concreted yard and he shot through them. I followed. Away from the streetlights, I struggled to see him, despite his pale grey fur. The darkness deepened nearer the buildings. Was that a van? Then I picked up movement. I almost fell when I tripped over a lump of concrete but righted myself. In doing so, I lost sight of Oscar.

A sixth sense warned me not to shout out, and I made my way to where I'd last seen him. Then flames flared through the windows of the building, highlighting an open doorway. The smell of smoke reached me at the same time. The fire grew, lighting up the yard. I couldn't see Oscar. He must be inside.

I ran to the open doorway and stuck my head in. Thick smoke gathered under the ceiling, and I crouched low. Flames reflected off the smoke, illuminating movement at floor level ten paces away.

'OSCAR!' The fumes hit my throat, making me cough. 'COME HERE!'

Here, I need help.

Bent double, I ran towards him. As I got closer, I saw he stood at the head of an unconscious man. The smoke grew denser, and flames crackled. Fuelled by panic, I grabbed the man's collar and pulled. With a jerk, he slid and, with Oscar gripping a sleeve, we got him to the door.

A figure stood outside the doorway, his face obscured by the smoke.

'Give us a hand, mate.'

He stepped towards me and raised his arm. In a blur of movement, what he held raced at my head. I moved but was too late to avoid it. My head snapped back, then a sharp pain exploded in my skull.

CHAPTER 11

The stink of smoke filled my nostrils, and heat scorched my skin. Hands grabbed me and dragged me across rough ground.

I opened my eyes. It was still dark, but flames flickered in front of me. Oscar barked in alarm. The person stopped dragging me and lowered me to the ground.

'You okay, mate?'

I remembered the man we'd found. 'There's someone else inside.'

'Don't worry, we've got him.'

I sat up and adjusted my glasses, which had almost fallen off. Oscar barked again before pushing himself against me. 'It's okay, boy. I'm fine.'

Sirens sounded in the distance. I coughed and looked around. I'd been dragged twenty metres from the entrance. Two uniformed police officers bent over a prone body a few paces away. In front of me, it looked like the whole of the building was on fire. Flames flickered behind every opening on the lower three floors and my skin tightened against the heat.

I got to my feet, staggering as a searing pain filled my head. I touched my forehead, but the skin wasn't broken. The pain eased, and I stepped towards the police officers. One of them turned to me.

'You okay?'

'Fine. How's he?'

The man they crouched over stirred, and they helped him sit up. The sirens got closer, and with them, the noise of a powerful engine. Then, blue light flickered across the scene. A fire engine raced through the gates and hissed to a stop. Its doors exploded and figures poured out.

I helped the police officers get the man to his feet and got a look at him for the first time. His clothes, and the smell, made it clear he was a rough sleeper. His gaunt features stirred a memory. Did I know him, or just recognise him from my own time on the street? The headache made thinking challenging.

We helped him away from the building, towards the police car, although I doubted my contribution made much difference. A second fire engine arrived, then another. The policeman I'd spoken with opened the back door to the car and the two of them guided the injured man to sit down. I looked back at the building.

Several firefighters in breathing apparatus gathered at the door, and the pump on the first fire engine screamed. The cacophony from the crews and the fire engines competed with the roar of the fire. I bent down and patted Oscar.

'Well done, boy. You saved that man's life.'

It was nothing. He looked pleased, but bashful. He peered at the bump on my head. ***Are you okay?***

'Yeah, I'm fine.' I touched my wound again and winced. It felt the size of a golf ball. It was a good thing the one on the other side, from when the door hit me, had gone down, otherwise I'd have looked like a demon with emerging horns.

A paramedic approached and examined the man in the police car. A colleague arrived with a chair and, after attaching an oxygen mask over the patient's head, wrapped him in a blanket and wheeled him away. The first paramedic returned and stood in front of me.

'Can I check you over?'

'Yeah, okay.'

She asked me a few questions, examined the bump on my head and shone a light in my eyes. 'Do you have a headache?'

'Definitely.'

'You don't know how long you were out?'

'Sorry, no, but it can't have been long, or I'd be dead.'

'The other guy said you and the dog dragged him out.'

'Oscar found him, but those two lads got us out of the building.' I gestured at the police officers.

'Is there someone who can keep an eye on you at home?'

'Just Oscar, why?'

'You might have suffered a concussion, which can affect you up to twenty-four hours after the head injury. If you live alone, we can check if there's a bed available.'

'What about Oscar?'

She studied him. 'What breed is he?'

'A standard Schnauzer.'

He pricked up his ears and wagged his tail.

'Sorry Oscar, we can't put you up. I can ask the coppers if they can get him a night in kennels, just while you're in hospital.'

Oscar's manner changed. ***Kennels! What do you think I am?***

'No,' I told her. 'I'll be fine.'

She peered into my eyes. 'If you're sure. I can give you some paracetamol for your headache and go to Casualty if you feel worse.'

She listed several symptoms, including the inability to sleep. I couldn't help smiling. That's what had got me in this mess. I refused the drugs and thanked her, then checked the time. Almost four. The 'party' back at ours should be over by now and I could get a few hours before going in to work.

I examined the building. The fire had died down, but flames still flickered behind upper-floor windows and a mixture of smoke and steam poured out of the openings. A crew of firefighters came out of the main entrance and removed their face masks. The sweet stench of burnt plastic accompanied them.

'Come on, Oscar.' I set off for the gates we'd come in through.

One of the coppers who'd rescued me stood at the back of the ambulance, noting the homeless man's details. As I walked past, the copper waved me down.

'Excuse me, sir, I need your details.'

I gave them to him, remembering to use my real name, Peter Timothy. Being able to give an address rather than 'no fixed abode' made a nice change, but his reaction when I provided it confirmed he knew the place.

'How long you been there?'

I considered. 'Two months today.'

'I bet you remember to the hour.'

We shared a smile. 'I wanted to say thanks to both of you for getting me out. How did you find us?'

He pointed to Oscar. 'This chap flagged us down. Well, he ran out in front of us, then we saw the flames.'

Oscar adopted his insufferable expression. ***You can thank me later.***

'Naughty boy. I've told you not to play in traffic.' I winked at the copper, thanked him again and set off.

We'd just reached the gates when I heard a voice that populated my nightmares.

'If it isn't Mr Timothy, our favourite down-and-out.' The huge figure of Detective Chief Inspector Grimes loomed over me. 'What you been up to this time?'

'Morning, Mr Grimes. What brings a senior police officer to a job like this?'

A slimmer figure stood just behind him. 'We're investigating a series of—'

'Alright, Sergeant Bowling, we don't have to explain ourselves to the likes of Mr Timothy.'

'Hello, Colette,' I greeted his assistant, who I remembered as a more sympathetic figure.

'Hello, Victor. Who's this?' She bent down to stroke Oscar's ears.

'Oscar. He's been with our family for—'

'Very nice,' Grimes cut in. 'I hope you've got a licence for him. Now, if you two have finished, a uniform tells me you're a witness. What did you see or hear, and why?'

'What do you mean?'

'You're going to tell me you suffer from insomnia and decided to go for a walk in the early hours?' His expression hardened. 'What were you doing here at this time in the morning?'

My mind froze. I found him terrifying and hated myself for it.

'Let's go through some possible scenarios, shall we? You broke in to find somewhere to sleep and accidentally set fire to the place? You decided to—'

'I've got somewhere to sleep.' I told him where.

He grimaced. 'Rather you than me. But in that case, why were you not tucked up in bed?'

'One of my neighbours had a party and we couldn't sleep. The music hurt Oscar's ears.'

'Ahh, diddums,' he directed at Oscar, who growled and showed his teeth. Grimes laughed. 'Tell your dog not to write cheques he can't cash.'

Who the hell still writes cheques? Oscar snarled.

I stepped between the two of them. 'Leave him, Oscar. He's not worth it.'

I'll be the judge of that!

Bowling waited for Grimes to continue, but he seemed intent on a staring contest with Oscar, so she took over. 'Can you tell us what you saw when you got here?'

I paused to recall the events. A sharp pain flashed across my forehead, making me wince. 'Oscar heard something as we crossed the bridge there.' I indicated the canal behind me. 'He ran into the yard and disappeared through that doorway, so I followed him.'

'Into a burning building?'

'I couldn't leave him in there. Then I found Oscar next to the guy in the ambulance.'

'What happened next?'

'I helped Oscar drag the man to the door and then someone appeared outside. When I asked him to help, he hit me.' I touched the egg-sized lump on my forehead.

'Did you get a good look at him?' She couldn't hide the hope in her voice.

'Sorry, it had got pretty smoky. I just saw a shape.'

Grimes had finished his stare-down with Oscar and joined us. 'What did you see before you went in?'

'Nothing. It was dark.' I cast my mind back and relived the moments. 'Now I think about it, there was a vehicle in that corner.' I pointed to a part of the yard that had been in deepest shadow.

'Did you notice what kind?'

Again, I tried to picture what I'd seen. 'Something big and boxy.'

'A van?'

'Or a minibus.' I concentrated on what I'd seen, but all I did was intensify my headache.

Bowling gave me a sympathetic smile. 'You'll remember more when you recover from the bump on your head.'

I doubted it, but nodded, provoking another shard of pain.

A shout came from the entrance of the building and firefighters converged on it.

'Find out what the excitement's about, Sergeant,' Grimes ordered Bowling.

We waited for her in uncomfortable silence as she spoke to the fire officer.

Bowling rushed back, her eyes glistening. 'They've found a body on one of the upper floors.'

CHAPTER 12

'WHERE THE HELL DO YOU THINK YOU'RE GOING?' Grimes's shout stopped me in my tracks.

'I assumed you'd be busy.' I pointed towards the doorway he was heading for.

'Sergeant, keep him here until I get back.'

'Are you arresting me?'

'Don't tempt me.'

Oscar looked for a corner and curled up on the concrete.

Bowling studied me. 'Can I trust you not to do a runner?'

She was a decent officer, and I'd rather have her on my side than face Grimes alone. 'You can, Sergeant. I'll wait here with Oscar.'

She joined Grimes at the entrance. He pointed at me and said something, but she must have reassured him because they ignored us for the next twenty minutes. My thoughts strayed to Sawney. Was this body linked to his death? How could it be? I wasn't sure, but I'd ask Bowling, if I could do it without dragging myself into the investigation into my friend's death.

The fire died down further, and all the firefighters left the building. More vehicles arrived, including a van whose overall-clad occupants spoke to the two detectives before going inside.

Can we go home soon?

'I hope so.'

I could go now. It's only you they want to speak to.

'Please yourself. How are you planning to get into the flat?'

I'll wait outside in the corridor. I'm sure they'll let me in at the main door.

'Go on then. I bet that Bully from upstairs will be pleased to see you.'

Oscar gave me a baleful glare, but sat. ***I'll wait here with you. I wouldn't want you getting lonely, and if Grimes starts anything, you'll need my help.***

'Thanks, I'll bear that in mind.'

Bowling joined us. 'Can you show us how far you went into the building?'

'Sure.' I followed her back to join Grimes at the entrance.

Do you want me to come?

I peered into the opening. Debris covered the floor. 'No,' I called back, 'you'll damage your paws.'

Bowling looked at me with a puzzled frown.

'I was talking to Oscar.'

'Oh, right. Provided he doesn't start talking back.'

Oh, dogs should be seen and not heard, is that it?

I ignored him.

'Right,' Grimes said. 'I want you to show our forensic team how far you went in and where you found the rough sleeper.' He pointed through the opening at metal plates which someone had laid on the floor. 'Step on them and don't contaminate our scene.'

Through the thin haze, I looked at the mess on the floor on each side of the plates. How could I contaminate that? The stench of smoke intensified as I stepped onto the nearest plate. My eyes stung and fumes caught at the back of my throat. One of the overall-wearing figures stood on a plate several paces in.

'Can you show me where you found the injured man?' A fibre mask muffled her voice.

I stepped towards her then looked around, picturing the scene when I'd come in and found Oscar. How many steps had I taken? I'd been bent over, keeping below the smoke.

'It was over there, I think.' I pointed at a section of corridor just beyond her.

'Near this doorway?'

I hadn't noticed a doorway.

It was further than that.

'What are you doing here, Oscar?' He stood on the plate I'd just vacated.

'Who let that dog in?' Grimes demanded to know, and I guessed his sergeant would get the blame.

'Come on, Oscar.' She held out her hand.

'Go on,' I told him, 'before you get me into trouble.'

Okay, but it was further on by the second door. I knew you'd mess it up.

'Enough of your cheek. Now go.'

He let Bowling lead him out.

'Sorry about that,' I said to the crime scene technician. I peered along the corridor. 'It might have been by that doorway.' I pointed to it.

'You sure about that?'

Oscar had been confident. 'Yes.'

'Okay, thank you. You can go out now.'

My eyes were stinging, and I stifled a cough as I stepped outside. I moved away from the door and took a deep breath. Behind me, the technician spoke to Grimes in a low voice. Having unburdened herself of Oscar, Bowling passed me with a smile and a nod and joined them.

I looked for Oscar, who'd returned to the corner where I'd left him.

'I told you to stay here, didn't I?'

Good thing I ignored you. You'd have cocked up the entire investigation.

'Well, I'm a lot higher than you. The smoke was much thicker.'

Always an excuse.

'It's not an excuse.'

'Not interrupting anything, are we?' Grimes and Bowling stood a couple of paces away.

'No.' A local TV reporter had arrived and was doing a piece to camera.

'Good. We'll need you to make a statement. The car's over there.' He jerked a thumb at an ancient Land Cruiser.

'I've given you a statement.'

'You answered a few questions when we were investigating a case of suspected arson. We're now investigating a suspicious death.' His gaze challenged me to disagree.

'Okay, how long will it take?'

'As long as it needs. Sergeant.' He handed Bowling some keys. 'Take Mr Timothy and stick him in the back of my car. I need to speak to the water-squirters.'

'Come on, Oscar.'

'Not the dog.'

'I'm not leaving him.' I held his gaze.

He rolled his eyes. 'If he makes a mess, it's on you.' He prodded a stubby index finger at me before continuing on his way. 'And keep him off the seats!'

I trudged towards the car alongside Bowling. My headache worsened at the prospect of more questions. Oscar trotted along beside me.

Will they feed us?

'Sergeant, can my dog have something to eat and drink?'

'I'm sure we can sort something out.' She unlocked the back door and swung it open.

Oscar stuck his nose in and backed out. ***Have you seen the state of that?***

'Come on, don't be such a soft bugger.' I glanced into the rear, illuminated by a faint overhead light. The stench of stale exhaust mingled with the odour of decay. The floor looked like Grimes used it as his bin. 'Can I put him on the seat, Sergeant?'

'Sorry, you heard the DCI.'

'Look at the state of the floor.' I stepped aside to let her look in.

She grimaced. 'Okay, let him on the seat.'

He jumped in and I clambered in after him. I took my chance. 'Are you investigating the dead man from Mill View Academy?'

She gave me a sharp look. 'How do you know about that?'

I swallowed. 'It was on the news.' I'd not heard anything, but I was sure one of the outlets would have mentioned it. 'Do you know how he died?'

'We're not releasing any details yet.'

'Please, Colette. Sawney was a friend.'

Her expression darkened. 'They've released his name?' She slammed the door. 'Bastards!'

Bugger! Once left in the dark, I sank into the upholstery and, in seconds, fell asleep. I woke with a jerk as the car lurched to one side and a door slammed.

'What part of not on the seat didn't you understand?' Grimes demanded.

I wiped drool off my chin. 'The floor's like a skip—'

'I said he could, Boss.' Bowling climbed into the passenger seat and handed Grimes his keys.

The engine roared to life. Grimes aimed the car at the road, and we made our way through town. The policeman seemed to have no concept of changing speed gradually and we held on for dear life, me gripping Oscar's collar to stop him sliding across the seat. Despite the rough ride, I leant against the door and dozed on the journey, waking in confusion when Grimes opened my door, and I almost fell out.

'Right, inside, sooner we start, the sooner you can get off home.' He looked at Oscar. 'And you can get out. I'm not leaving you in here.'

'It's alright, Boss. I'm going to get him fed. Come on, Oscar, let's go.'

I clipped on his lead, and Bowling took him away.

I surveyed the surroundings, which resembled an upmarket commercial park. Last time I came, I'd been handcuffed in the back of a patrol car, nursing bruises after I'd fallen. A grumbling Grimes led me to the main entrance of the police station, rather than the side entrance they'd previously brought me to. It looked like the headquarters of a multi-million-pound company. Grimes booked me in and took me to an interview room.

Unlike the one they'd brought me to a couple of months earlier when they had questioned me about a mass shooting, this one had carpet and didn't stink of bleach. It even had a paper cup of water on the table. He directed me to a chair and left. My phone showed four thirty. The door opened ten minutes later, and the two detectives came in.

'One of the dog handlers is looking after Oscar.' Bowling placed a pad on the table. 'You understand you're not under arrest—'

'But if you discover I've broken the law, that may change.'

Grimes frowned. 'Why don't you let the sergeant finish?'

I did, and they made me go over the events, repeating everything I'd told them earlier.

Bowling studied the statement she'd typed into a tablet. 'And you never noticed the dead homeless woman?'

The information that the body they'd just found was a woman sent my thoughts into a spin. Were we looking at another killer preying on women? In which case, it couldn't be linked to Sawney.

'Victor?'

'Sorry. I didn't even notice the doorway. I saw Oscar and the man through the smoke and focused on them. Do you know who she was?'

They ignored my question and pressed on. Then came another comment that derailed me. 'My sergeant tells me you're asking about the victim we found at Mill View Academy.'

I gave Bowling an accusing stare, which she returned with interest. 'You told me you'd read about it on the news. But funnily enough, nobody's mentioned the victim's name. We only confirmed it this morning.'

I swallowed.

Grimes slapped the table, making me jump. 'How the hell did you know who he was?'

CHAPTER 13

I looked from Grimes to Bowling, but found no comfort there. What could I say without dropping myself further in it and entangling Toff in the investigation?

'Well?' Grimes studied me as you would a recalcitrant pupil.

I sipped water from the cup in front of me. 'My mates on the street knew about it. From the people he'd been with. And before you ask, I don't know who was with him.'

They let the silence build until Bowling broke it. 'You claim he was a friend, so I'm sure you'll be doing all you can to help our investigation.'

'Do you think he was killed?'

They glared at me.

'Do you think the two deaths are linked?'

Grimes leant towards me, giving me the benefit of his stale breath. 'What we do or don't think is none of your business, but if I find you've been keeping vital information from us, you'll regret it. Is that clear?'

Sweat ran down the back of my neck as Grimes studied me. I fought the urge to gabble and swallowed. After what felt an age, he nodded to Bowling.

She slid her tablet towards me and gave me a stylus. I signed my name in the box and she took it back.

'Okay, Victor,' she said. 'You can go, but don't leave the area.'

I stood, eager to escape, and made for the door.

'Hang on,' she said to my back.

I stopped and turned, waiting for them to tell me they were detaining me.

'I'll take you to Oscar.'

'Oh, right. Thanks.'

Feeling like a soggy lettuce, I followed her to a room at the back of the building where Oscar lay on a rug in a corner, an empty food bowl alongside him.

'Come on, Oscar, let's go.' His lead lay on a desk and I picked it up.

Do you want to come back later, when I've digested my breakfast?

'Come on. I'm not in the mood.' I clipped his lead on him and he got up.

Two women in the office rose from their desks and crowded round him. 'Ahh, you're going now. Make sure you come back and say hello, lovely.'

'Come on, boy. We need to get home.'

You hate seeing me make friends.

'Yeah, whatever.' I led him to the exit, and we stepped out into the car park at the rear.

Bowling accompanied us. 'Take care, Victor.'

I tried once more. 'Can you tell me anything about what happened to Sawney?'

'Don't push your luck, Victor. You'll find out when we announce it. Go home before Grimes changes his mind.'

'Yeah. Thanks.' I trudged round the building, Oscar following.

It was already past six. I needed a few hours' sleep, otherwise I'd be useless. Kasper would complain, but tough. Ahead lay a roundabout with a steel sculpture resembling a leaf, illuminated by spotlights. A van parked up on the road off to the right made me nervous. The buildings round here all had car parks. In the dark, I couldn't tell if it contained anyone, but Oscar felt the same and growled at it.

We turned left, under an elevated tram stop with a roof like a wide-brimmed hat. I put on a spurt, checking over my shoulder. We passed under the railway line and stopped at the main road, waiting for a gap in the traffic, and checked again. A vehicle came towards us.

'Come on, Oscar.' I spotted an opening and ran across the road, accompanied by blaring horns. On the other side, we took a path through a housing estate. Behind us, the lights at the junction changed, and an engine screamed, moving faster than it should. I got my bearings. If we travelled straight, we should hit the Ashton Canal.

We ran past parked cars and into a grassed area. We crossed it and burst out onto a road. In front of us stood a spiked fence almost two metres high. From our left came the roar of an engine. It stopped at the junction. If they saw us, there was nothing to stop them following us onto the grassed area. Opposite, two wheelie bins stood against the fence.

'Come on, boy.' I put my glasses away and ran towards the bins. I picked Oscar up and clambered onto the nearest one.

The lid bowed as I stepped on it. I lifted Oscar above the fence.

Not again, please.

'Come on, don't be difficult.' I leant over and peered at the ground on the other side.

Behind me, the engine growled. They'd seen us. I lowered Oscar, then let him go, hoping he'd get a soft landing. The roar behind me grew louder. I gripped two railings a shoulder width apart. The lid sagged as I prepared to push off. In that instant, the van hit the bin, whipping it from under me.

By some miracle, the impact propelled me upward and over the fence. I landed on my knee. Agony exploded from the joint, but I struggled to my feet. My leg didn't want to obey me and I massaged the muscle around the knee. The van screeched to a halt and two men jumped out. They wore dark clothes and ski masks. One ran towards the fence and gripped two uprights. He stared at me while the other ran towards the bins.

He swore and kicked the remains of the shattered containers. They'd be no use to them. Instead of waiting to see what they'd do next, I hobbled off, Oscar at my heels. Once we reached the canal, I realised my mistake. The footpath was on the other side. The sound of falling water made it difficult to tell if my pursuers had got over the fence. In a panic, I cast about, but a bark from Oscar led me to a footbridge next to the lock. We crossed and once on the path ran – in my case, limped – homeward. My heart thumped in my chest and my breath wheezed. I kept glancing back as we went.

I saw nobody, until two figures appeared behind me on the path, running towards us. They must have found a way over the fence. Infused with panic, I speeded up, ignoring the pain from my knee. Still, their footsteps came closer, but I had no more to give.

CHAPTER 14

Zofia increased the volume on the TV, which hung off the wall in the kitchen she and Kasper shared.

> 'Rudy Glass has set up a charity, Homes for Heroes, which is aimed at providing housing for ex-servicemen living on the streets of this country. We have an interview with Mr Glass at the site of his latest project.'

A man of around fifty, wearing artfully casual clothes, stood in front of a dilapidated office block. A young woman wearing a bright peach skirt suit and strained smile held a mic towards him.

> 'Mr Glass, you've used your own money to buy this disused office block in Edgeley and are planning to turn it into accommodation.'
>
> 'It's a disgrace that we have thousands of service-men who've served this country living on the streets—'
>
> 'Thousands?' The reporter looked shocked.

'Yes, we've had reports of thousands of ex-service personnel having nowhere to call home after risking their lives for our safety.'

'Is this a national initiative?'

'That's the plan. We're running the project in Manchester as a pilot. I'm a local, and it grieves me to see my beloved city full of homeless people.'

'I don't trust that charlatan.' Kasper made his sister jump. He stood in the open doorway to the hall in his pyjamas, his hair uncombed and features still sleep-softened. A sense of despair radiated from him.

Zofia reduced the volume. 'It sounds like a good initiative. Victor's friend Craig could benefit.'

Mentioning Craig, who'd been key to helping her escape the Novak brothers, seemed only to deepen Kasper's air of gloom. 'Yeah, I'll believe it when I see it. Blokes like that Glass poser latch onto a cause to use it to raise their profile, then, once the fuss dies down, they quietly drop it.'

'Do you want a coffee?' She got up without waiting for a reply and poured him a mugful. 'Toast?'

'Yes, coffee, but I'm not ready for toast.' He slumped into the seat alongside hers, his gaze glued to his screen.

She put the mug in front of him and returned to her seat. 'I think we should give Victor all the support we can in investigating his friend's death.'

'Shouldn't we leave it to the police? The guy had probably OD'd.'

'Yeah, that's what the police will say and not investigate properly.' What was up with her brother?

Kasper sipped his drink. 'We can't cover for the police.'

'He was Victor's friend. Just because we're busy, we can't stop Victor from doing all he can. How would you feel if one of your friends died under suspicious circumstances?'

'I just mean . . . Ignore me.' He stood and walked to the toaster. 'Do you want any?'

'No, thanks.' A figure she recognised appeared on screen and she increased the volume. 'Look who it is.'

Detective Chief Inspector Grimes was walking away from the TV reporter, who then faced the camera.

> 'Following the discovery of a dead man in a disused school building yesterday, a woman was discovered in a warehouse on Beswick Street this morning. Firefighters found her body under debris while putting out a fire, which they believe was started deliberately. Two men were rescued at the incident.'

The screen cut to a brick industrial building with flames, smoke and steam pouring out of the windows. A fire engine stood in the foreground and firefighters in breathing apparatus exited the building. The camera panned. In the darkened yard, a few people stood near an ambulance. Further to its right, a dog stood next to a man with his back to the camera.

Zofia pointed. 'Is that Oscar?'

Kasper peered at the screen, but the camera moved away. Zofia stopped the image and rewound it. Kasper edged closer to the TV. 'Could be, but it's too dark and too blurred.'

'It's close to where Victor lives, isn't it?'

He checked the map on his phone. 'About a third of a mile, but have you seen the time stamp? What would he be doing out at that time?'

'Maybe he heard something.'

'Five hundred metres away? Anyway, we can't be certain it's him.'

No, but Zofia had a nagging feeling it was him. She restarted the screen.

> 'One is still in hospital, suffering from the effects of smoke inhalation. The other has been released by the police. Chief Inspector Grimes has asked anyone who was in the area to contact the helpline below.'

Zofia muted it. 'At least he's not the one in hospital.'

'It won't be him. You just saw a dog and assumed it's Oscar. Shall we wait until we speak to Victor later?'

She nodded. She knew Kasper was feeling the stress of not just Novak's visit, but the fact Robertson had got in touch. They'd both hoped to never hear from him again. Why the hell had Kasper agreed to work for him in the first place?

Neither spoke much on their drive in to work and the familiar stench of burnt cooking oil greeted them when they arrived. She waved to the young guys in the fried-chicken shop below their offices before following Kasper upstairs.

An email waited for her from a client. An insurance company they'd worked for before wanted them to check on a claim. She recognised the address. The same street where she thought she'd seen Oscar on the television. It must be the same building. There can't have been two fires on that street.

'Have you seen this?'

He came up behind her and read off her screen. 'I'll ring Victor.' He punched the speed dial.

'We have been unable to connect your call,' said the recorded voice.

He tried again with the same result.

Zofia's neck prickled, and she retrieved her mobile. 'Let me try.'

The same happened.

'Right,' Kasper said. 'I'm going round.'

'I'll come with you.'

'You'd better stay here in case he turns up. It could just be a fault with the phone.'

It made sense, but she didn't want to do nothing. 'I'll keep trying and let you know if I get anywhere.'

Each time she rang, the same message greeted her, increasing her sense of foreboding. She kept checking the time until Kasper surely should have got there.

She rang again.

Nothing.

CHAPTER 15

The urgent knocking at the door to my flat startled me. I hobbled to it and paused. With a sense of trepidation, I opened it, expecting to find the shaven-headed thug and the mad dog who'd woken me yesterday morning. The stench of weed seeped in.

'Kasper? What are you doing here?'

'What are you doing here? You should have been at work an hour ago.' He studied the lump on my head but didn't comment.

'I've just got up. Do you want to come in?'

'What's this?' Kasper indicated the faint outline of 'STINKING GRASS' in the paintwork of my door.

'My charming neighbours—'

'Oi!' A shout from the corridor stopped us. 'What are you doing here?' Cermak, the officious building manager who'd been at the desk when I made it home at almost seven, marched up to Kasper.

'I'm here visiting my . . . friend.'

'No visitors.' He turned to me. 'You know the rules. I've told you this before.'

'I didn't know he was coming.'

He returned his attention to Kasper. 'You. Out.' He gestured back down the corridor.

'Are you serious?'

'If you don't want your friend back on the streets, I suggest you leave.'

'Is this a new policy? We helped him—'

'It's alright, Kasper, there's a café if you go left out of the main door. I'll join you there.' I didn't want to cause trouble for the young social worker who'd let Kasper and Zofia help me move in and clean the filthy flat.

Cermak glared at me, sniffed and followed Kasper down the hall. I hobbled back into my flat and took a quick shower. My knee had stiffened up in the few hours I'd slept. As the hot water loosened my joint, I relived the events of four hours ago.

I'd resigned myself to being caught by the two men from the van and glanced back to see how close they'd got, but then I'd noticed their clothing. Bright running gear with reflective strips. I'd slowed almost to a stop, my breath rasping in my throat, and nodded a greeting as they ran past us.

Once we'd got back to the safety of the apartment, I'd noted down the parts of the van's registration number I remembered while Oscar lapped water noisily.

He'd finished drinking and studied me. ***That was the bloke who hit you at the fire.***

'Who?'

The guy who stared at you through the fence.

'How could you tell? He was wearing a mask.'

I didn't look at his face. I could smell him. He looked heavenward. ***We've been* through *this, yeah?***

We had, when Oscar had used his superior senses to locate the home of a woman we'd been looking for.

I finished showering, got dressed and took Oscar to the café. Warm air infused with coffee fumes and cooking smells enveloped me. Kasper sat at a corner table nursing a coffee and studying his phone, but glanced up as we came in. I ordered breakfast, got myself a coffee and joined him. The staff knew Oscar and greeted him with a bowl of food and water.

Kasper gestured at my knee. 'What happened to you?'

I told him about being chased by the van.

He blanched. 'Why were they chasing you? Did you recognise them?'

'Oscar recognised one, but I only caught the first two letters of the van's registration.' I recited them and he made a note.

'You say Oscar recognised him?'

Oscar stopped eating. ***Yeah, I recognised him. What of it?***

'He was the guy who gave me this.' I fingered the lump on my forehead. It was still red, but hadn't bruised.

'You said you got away.' Kasper looked bemused.

'I did. This happened earlier.'

'You'd crossed swords with these guys already? Is that why they chased you?'

'Yeah. At the fire where we dragged the old bloke out. Someone hit me. They must have thought I could identify them.' A delicious aroma announced my food's arrival. Kasper refused the offer of something to eat but accepted another coffee.

In between mouthfuls of bacon, eggs and sausage, I told him what had happened at the fire.

He stared at Oscar.

Oscar stopped eating again. ***What now?***

Kasper turned back to me, but nodded towards Oscar. 'Zofia thought she saw him on telly, at the fire.'

I can't help being photogenic.

If she'd seen Oscar, who else might have? I'd been tracked down by someone who recognised Oscar before, and I still didn't feel safe.

'Did Grimes question you?' Kasper's expression displayed his horror at this prospect.

'Only twice.'

'And he let you go?'

'Of course. I did nothing wrong.'

'Except turn up where they found a dead body on two consecutive mornings.'

I checked the nearby tables. We were between breakfast and lunchtime, so there weren't many people in the café. A folky soundtrack burbled in the background.

'He doesn't know that. Unless you want to tell him. Blabbermouth.'

Kasper reddened. 'Sorry.'

I completed my breakfast in silence. Kasper's comment had got me thinking, was I right first time? Were the two deaths linked? I'd assumed the second was accidental. There were no indications that the Skunk Water-spraying thugs had been at the second site.

Kasper pushed his chair back. 'Shall I give you a lift to work?'

'Thanks.'

We drained our mugs, and I left a few coins under my plate. Oscar trotted out behind me, and I scanned the street, feeling vulnerable. A dark van sat fifty metres away, two wheels on the pavement. My pulse spiked until I checked the number plate. It wasn't the one I'd run from.

Despite the habitual mess in the back of Kasper's car, Oscar didn't make a fuss. He could sense my mood. We drove in silence.

The familiar fried-food stink greeted me as I followed Kasper into the entrance and climbed the stairs. Zofia was on the phone, but her eyes widened when she noticed my injury. She ended the call and stood.

'Victor, what happened to you?'

Kasper brought her up to date with input from me to correct the details he got wrong.

'Kasper suggested the two deaths might be linked.'

Zofia looked thoughtful. 'We can't discount that. Did you get a feeling for what the police are thinking?'

'I asked Bowling about Sawney, but they hadn't released his name, and she told Grimes. He gave me a hard time before making it clear he wasn't sharing any information with me.'

At the mention of Grimes's name, Kasper winced. 'As long as he doesn't come round here.'

'Errm . . . I may have let it slip to his sergeant that I work here.'

'Let slip? You don't let things "slip" to coppers, especially Grimes.'

'Leave him, Kasper. Colette, was it? She was alright.'

'She's still Grimes's lackey.' Kasper stomped off to the kitchen. 'Anyone want a brew?'

The doorbell rang.

Kasper froze. 'Well done, Victor! That'll be him.'

CHAPTER 16

Neither sibling seemed able to move, so I picked up the intercom. John's monk-like head filled the screen, and I buzzed him in. The hulking figure of Craig followed him through the door, and I replaced the receiver.

'John and Craig, they're helping me with a few things.'

Is Trixie with them? Oscar roused himself from his sleeping pad under the printer.

'I didn't see her.'

The siblings, used to me talking to Oscar, ignored our exchange.

In his relief it wasn't Grimes, Kasper forgot to be annoyed I'd not consulted him. The two visitors had reached the top of the stairs by the time I opened the door into the tiny reception area. An earthy odour accompanied them, and they exchanged greetings with the siblings. Oscar, seeing Trixie wasn't with them, returned to his bed.

'I thought you were going to ring?' I accused Craig.

'Dead battery.' He held up his handset and John did the same.

'I'll charge them up.' Remembering the problems I had getting my phone charged up before I got my own place, I found the right leads and plugged them in.

'Are you looking into your friend's death?' Zofia said.

'You don't mind?' I asked. 'I'll make the time up to you. We just need to use your database . . .'

'Of course we don't mind. We've been asked to investigate the fire in Beswick Street and that could tie in. I'll join you, if you don't mind.'

John and Craig gave me puzzled looks.

'I'll explain.' I pointed to the conference room.

The last time they'd been here was after they'd risked their lives to help us and that bought them a huge amount of credit. Kasper even made the drinks while we retired to the conference room. Once we were round the table with our drinks, I told John and Craig about the incident at Beswick Street.

Craig had the first question. 'You say the man you rescued is homeless? Do you know him?'

'I recognised him, but he's not someone I knew.'

'Can you find out his name?'

I realised I should have got that at the incident.

'And the woman who died, Brother?'

'The police let it slip that she was homeless, but I didn't even see the body.'

John exchanged a look with Craig but didn't speak.

'Never mind,' Zofia said. 'Bowling might not tell us much, but I made a couple of contacts while working on a missing person's case. I'll give them a bell, and I can also ask them how your friend Sawney died.'

Kasper, feeling left out, said, 'Before you arrived, we were discussing whether there's a link between the two deaths.'

I'd been thinking about it. 'An organised group raided the school where Sawney died, but there was no sign of such a raid at Beswick Street.'

'You told me the van that followed you had been there.'

'Yes, but they'd set fire to the building. The people who raided Mill View Academy arrived mob-handed and weren't trying to damage the building, just get rid of the people sleeping there.'

'Are you suggesting the woman's death was an accident?' Kasper asked. 'The two men who chased you were just trying to destroy the building?'

'I don't want to make a guess, but it felt very different.'

John raised a hand. 'There's another possibility. Two other homeless men have been killed in the last six weeks. One had his head bashed in and they found the other beside his dog in the canal—'

Zofia cut in. 'I thought the police ruled that an accident?'

'Very convenient for them.' Craig's scowl told what he thought of that verdict.

I'd considered John's information. 'Do you think there's someone killing homeless people?'

'It's a possibility we can't ignore.'

A silence descended on the room as we digested this.

Kasper cleared his throat. 'We're not equipped to investigate something like that. Best for us to—'

'I'm not ignoring Sawney's death,' I jumped in. 'He was a good mate.'

'Kasper isn't saying that.' Zofia used a conciliatory tone. 'We should focus on Sawney's death. I'll tap my contacts to see if we can find out how he died.'

'Thanks, Zofia. John, Craig and I will investigate similar raids on buildings in the city. See if there's a link. If someone killed Sawney, it will be one or more of the men who raided it.'

John shook his head. 'Or someone else sleeping in the building?'

I hadn't considered that. 'We can speak to Toff and Jodie—'

'Jodie?'

'She's new. We'll speak to everyone who was there. But while you're here, we can check on the ownership of the other buildings involved.'

Kasper said, 'What's the point of that?'

'So we can identify the people who raided the school. Jodie mentioned they'd covered the markings on their van.'

'That doesn't sound like the actions of someone with nothing to hide.'

Zofia put her hands together. 'Right, I'll speak to my contacts, and you can tell us what you need once you've identified the buildings' owners.'

I stood. 'Thanks, we really appreciate it.'

Kasper said, 'Do you want to use my computer, Craig? I'll work in here on my laptop.'

We trooped out into the office. Oscar raised his head and thumped his tail on his bed in greeting.

John and Craig gathered round my desk, and I opened the map of the city. 'This is where the school is.' I marked the site of the building where Toff got attacked, alongside the Rochdale Canal. 'Shout out the others, Craig.'

Without reference to notes, Craig recited three addresses. The first one, on Pollard Street East, backed onto the Ashton Canal, less than half a mile away. Were all the sites near canals? My excitement lasted until I entered the other two. One was on Chester Road, west of the city centre, and the other off Upper Brook Street, on the south.

'Did you find any links between them?' I asked them.

'Not yet, Brother.' John's brow furrowed. 'That's what we're hoping we can find out here.'

I logged Craig into Kasper's machine and opened the database that KZD Investigations – Kasper and Zofia's company – used to find the owners and occupiers of the different premises. I checked the land registry while Craig found out who paid the business rates and John checked who had last occupied them. Zofia had already done that work on the school, and had identified the education authority as the owner, and it didn't take us long to find the details of the other three.

I pushed myself away from the keyboard. 'There's no link between them.'

Craig tapped Kasper's screen. 'Nothing here. Who are the owners?'

I recited the names of the three limited companies.

'The owners are paying the rates. Makes sense if they're empty. I'll check on Companies House.' Craig's sausage-like fingers moved across his keyboard in a blur.

John stood behind Craig but addressed me. 'You think the companies are owned by the same people, Brother?'

'It would make our job easier if they were, but I suspect they'll hide behind proxies.'

'If they've disguised who owns them, we can assume they're controlled by the same people.'

Craig shook his head. 'Sorry, guys. Each company seems to be legit. They've listed their directors, and I've checked the first couple.'

John recited some names of directors, and I checked them. They were all real people with public profiles. Craig checked the rest, and we compared our results. None of the companies shared officers, and we found no obvious links between the personnel at the different companies.

We sat in disappointed silence until Zofia, working at her desk, spoke up. 'Have you looked into who does their security?'

As usual, she'd come up with a good idea. I looked at John and Craig. 'People working for a security company called Droylsden Shield were hanging around the school. Did you see any sign of them near the other buildings? They might have put their details up on the external boundaries.'

'Nobody mentioned them, Brother, but we'll get onto it.'

Zofia said, 'Didn't you get the name of the boarding-up company, Victor?'

'They're contracted by the council. I'll give you the name, John, and can you see if they did the other buildings?'

With promises to keep me appraised, the two friends gathered their belongings and prepared to leave.

'Oh, Craig,' Zofia said. 'Have you found somewhere to live?'

'Errr, not really.'

'I saw a guy called Rudy Glass on the news saying he's providing accommodation for ex-service guys. Hang on.' She carried out a search. 'This is the contact for donations. I'm sure they'll be able to point you in the right direction.'

'Right, ta.' He punched the details into his phone, and they departed, leaving the office feeling empty.

The fear Grimes could still call didn't leave me and after an afternoon in which Kasper and I jumped every time the doorbell rang, I got off early. My nerves already tight, the walk home shredded them further as I treated every van or vehicle I encountered as a threat. I entered the main reception area of the flats with a sense of relief, which increased at the sight of the friendly young social worker behind the counter.

Something about her demeanour suggested discomfort, though. She didn't even give Oscar his customary friendly greeting. I'm sure I'd stopped Kasper blurting out the fact she'd let him into my flat. So, why the cold shoulder?

I collected my post, one hand-delivered letter, and made my way to my flat. One of my eccentric neighbours was having another episode and his shouts carried to the corridor as I unlocked my door. As I stepped inside, my phone rang. Helen. I let Oscar off his lead and closed the door behind me.

'Helen. Lovely to hear from you.'

'Hiya, Dad. When are you coming down to see us?'

Although still at school, Helen worked at the market in the centre of Bristol on Saturdays and I'd intimated I'd go down and see her there. 'What about next weekend?'

'It's Easter. Why don't I come up to you—'

'GOD WILL PUNISH YOU FOR YOUR SINS!'

'What the hell was that, Dad?'

'Just one of the neighbours. The walls are paper thin.' I moved to the furthest point in the flat, my bathroom, and sat on the lid of the toilet.

'I can get the bus,' she went on, 'and you can meet me.'

Panic made my mind freeze. Apart from the horror of this place, I could imagine Cermak's reaction if I had someone to stay. 'I'll speak to your mum about it. Isn't she planning to take you anywhere?'

'She and Garfunkel want to take us to Center Parcs, but it's so lame—'

'Garfunkel?' I knew Carol, my wife, was seeing someone, but Garfunkel?

'Alan, Mum's boyfriend. I told you about him. He's always saying, "you can call me Al", you know, like the song by Paul Simon that you made us listen to. So, Em and I call him Garfunkel.'

The memory made my throat thick. 'Yeah.' I took a deep breath. 'I'll talk to your mum, but it's probably better if you came here during the summer holidays. In the meantime, I'll come down in the next few weeks. You'll enjoy Center Parcs.'

I ended the call and stared into the distance, thinking of how much I missed my family.

Oscar licked my hand. ***You okay?***

'I will be, thanks.' I ruffled his ears. 'Let's see what this letter's about.' I ripped it open and read it. 'SHIT!'

What?

'Here.' I held the letter for him to read.

You know I can't read.

'They're giving me a final warning. One more infraction and we're out on the street.'

That's ludicrous. Why?

'Apparently, it's in my contract that I must have permission if I'm going to spend the night away from my flat. They're claiming because I wasn't here all last night, I'm in breach.'

But you were being questioned by the police.

'Do you think that makes it sound any better?'

Oscar nuzzled his head against my leg and licked my hand. ***We'll be okay.***

I wasn't sure. Now I'd escaped from life on the streets, I wasn't sure I could face it again.

CHAPTER 17

The discovery of Sawney's body in the very room she'd been sleeping in had given Jodie a dilemma. On one side, she had spoken to him a few hours before he died, and that gave her a human-interest angle. On the other, she'd missed the big story of his death following the raid on the school by those thugs.

She also felt guilty she'd left him behind, and although Toff reassured her the man was probably dead before they abandoned him, she couldn't help but reproach herself. If he was right, then the death had nothing to do with the raid, and that didn't help her. A story about thugs harassing the homeless would have much greater weight if they'd killed one, even accidentally.

Could she link the death to the two she was investigating? If so, that would make whoever did it a serial killer. She could see the headline now, 'The Homeless Hunter'. Maybe not. She'd come up with a better title.

She hurried away from the others who were sitting under the trees by the Peterloo Memorial. Once out of sight, she powered up her phone and checked the online news channels.

Shit! Toff hadn't been lying. Not that she'd thought he was. He was too upset to be acting. But with these people, you could never tell if what they said had happened, or they just believed it had happened. They weren't trying to deceive you, but many had psychological problems or had damaged their minds because of the drugs they'd consumed.

She needed to speak to Colin asap, but she couldn't risk the others overhearing her. At the Great Northern Square, she paused, but despite the cold, dull weather, the yells of the kids in the play area would be too intrusive. She crossed Deansgate and made her way to St John's Gardens. Nobody was braving the benches round the stone cross.

She took the one facing the entrance and, after composing herself, punched the number for 'Uncle Colin'.

'Ah, Nellie Bly checks in.'

'Ha, ha.' She wished she'd never mentioned being inspired by the late nineteenth-century American journalist who'd published under that name to expose the mistreatment of inmates of a New York City asylum. The tiresome bastard had flogged it to death ever since.

'I was beginning to think you'd left the country.'

She ignored his rebuke. 'I've got something on the body they found—'

'The one at the fire?'

'What? No, the one at Mill View Academy.'

'The one everybody has been talking about for twenty-four hours? The one you never mentioned in your report?'

'Believe it or not, I don't spend twenty-four seven online. I'm down to fifteen per cent now and it's not like I can charge it up whenever I want.'

'Is that why you didn't send any pictures? You do realise we're a visual medium? People expect images, videos even. How are we supposed to post snippets on social media?'

'I told you, it was pitch-black.' She wouldn't mention that in her panic to escape, she'd not thought once to take pictures of the raid. 'Do you want to hear what I've got to say?'

'Right, okay, what you got?'

'I was with him in the school building when the thugs raided. He stayed downstairs while we got out of an upstairs window.'

'You saying the guys who raided the school killed him?'

Jodie hesitated. She had no evidence to back up that claim. 'I've got witnesses who say he was dead when they raided.'

'Right, so what have you actually got for me? "Homeless man dies of natural causes" isn't a story.'

A woman pushing a pram while leading a French bulldog and talking on her phone came into the park. Jodie waited for her to move out of earshot.

'You still there, Jodie? Have you got the name of the victim? That would at least be something. The police haven't released it.'

'Shouldn't we wait for the police? I'm assuming they're trying to contact his family.'

'That could take them days. Look, if his family gave a shit about him, he wouldn't be on the streets. Do you want to be a reporter or what?'

She took a deep breath before answering. 'His name's Sawney and he came from Ayrshire.'

'Is that it?'

'We don't exchange life stories whenever we meet someone. Most people won't even give you a name until they've seen you a few times.' She remembered Sawney telling her he knew things that could get him killed. She'd dismissed him at the time, but what if he wasn't bullshitting? She should have paid attention and asked questions.

'Jodie, you still there?'

Shit! He must have asked her something. 'Reception's awful.'

'I said, what you been doing? You've been there two weeks. You've got nothing on the dosser killer and nothing on the developers attacking the homeless—'

'I can't just manufacture evidence.' 'Dosser killer': is that what he's thinking of going with?

'Talk to people. You must know a few by now.'

'Of course I do, but I only met him once before I saw him at the school.' She realised she'd raised her voice. The woman had made a circuit of the small park and was coming back out. She gave Jodie an annoyed glare, which Jodie returned with interest.

'You must know someone who knows him.'

'I can't just interrogate people. I'll blow my cover.'

'Not my problem, my girl. You asked for this assignment. Now get back to me with something I can use before I read about it on our rivals' websites.' He ended the call.

'Twat!'

Two old ladies had just entered the park and glared at her with disapproval.

And you can bugger off.

She punched the power button. Although she'd exaggerated how low its charge had been, it was now almost down to fifteen. She'd need to find somewhere to get a boost.

She made her way back to Toff and the others, thinking about how to get the information she needed without bringing attention to herself. Toff and three others sat on the steps below the monument.

'Alright, Jodie, look what we got.' He held up a pizza box. 'Wrong address, so the delivery guy let us have this.'

The thought of pizza made her nauseous. Didn't they realise how bad it was for them? But she didn't want to make them suspicious, and joined them on the steps. Luckily, fewer than half of the slices remained. The aroma of melted cheese and oregano enveloped her as she took one and chewed slowly, trying not to imagine the damage it was doing to her.

Toff finished his last slice and licked his fingers. 'Where did you get to?'

She took another mouthful of pizza to give her time to come up with an answer. She needed to get onto the subject of Sawney, find out what the others knew. An idea came to her and she swallowed.

'I just needed some space. I was upset about what happened to Sawney.'

'Oh, right.' Toff looked away.

'What happened to Sawney?' one of the others asked.

Jodie waited for Toff to speak, but he said nothing, so she said, 'The police found him in the school after they threw us out.'

'That was him? Bloody hell. Poor bastard. He used to say someone would kill him.'

Had he told everyone he knew?

'Did anyone see him at the school after the raid?' she asked.

Nobody answered.

She risked a second question: 'Did anyone see him before the raid?'

One said, 'I think he buggered off around two. Ziggy said he went to see his dealer.'

She was sure Sawney told her he was clean. She'd dismissed it as another lie, like the one about someone wanting to kill him. But what if both were true? 'Are you sure about that?'

'Ask Ziggy yourself if you don't believe me.'

'Okay, thanks.' Keep your shirt on!

Another chimed in. 'I heard he'd been shot.'

These two comments resulted in a flurry of speculation, none of which helped Jodie. They grew bored of the subject, and she decided to leave it. Nobody seemed to know much and more questions from her would just raise suspicions. They split up, and she fell into step beside Toff.

'Does the guy with the dog know about Sawney?'

He studied her with narrowed eyes. 'Victor? What do you mean?'

'Did he know you'd found him?'

'Yeah. He was with me.'

Was Victor working for one of their rival news outlets? She'd given him some information about what she'd seen before the raid, but she'd steered him the wrong way with the information about the black van she'd seen, wanting to keep it fresh for her story. He now thought it was a dark-blue minibus.

'Do you trust him?'

'Yeah. Why?' Toff's expression suggested he trusted Victor more than he did her.

'He seemed a sound guy, but he's a private detective. What if he's working for the people who threw us out? Trying to find out how much we know about them?'

It was clear Toff hadn't considered this, but he shook his head. 'No way, Victor wouldn't work for someone like that.'

'If his boss told him to do it, he wouldn't have much choice.'

He considered this. 'Nah. Zofia wouldn't, either.'

There couldn't be many women running private detective agencies, and Zofia was an unusual-enough name. She'd get Colin to investigate them. She didn't fancy talking to the jerk again today, and texted him before turning in for the night.

◆ ◆ ◆

As usual, she slept badly, a mixture of cold, discomfort and fear keeping her awake. At around five, she got up and put her bedding away, a grubby collection including a sleeping bag, stained duvet, foam mat and pillow she'd gathered to replace the ones she'd abandoned inside the school. After a while, she almost didn't notice the stink.

In the pre-dawn gloom, she made her way to a bakery, which sometimes let you have leftover items from the previous day. As she chewed on a cream cheese-filled bagel, she mulled over Colin's reply to her text.

> I hope it's not just us here doing this 'investigation' while you swan around doing bugger all.

'Prick!'

As dawn approached, signalled by the grey light becoming brighter, she headed towards the Mill View Academy, unsure of what she'd do there, but hoping to take some pictures and discover something of use. The main building stood in darkness, and, with a sense of unease, she worked round the side, crossing the small car park.

She peered round the corner. A faint glow came from the back of the building they'd slept in. Her unease increasing, she crossed the corner of the playground and huddled behind the thick hedge separating it from the school. The light seemed to come from inside. Her heart thudding, she worked round the hedge until she could see the building.

Although someone had boarded up most of the openings, one, a roller-shutter, was untouched. The illumination came from inside the gateway it protected. In the light spilling out from it, she could make out two vehicles. A dark van and an expensive-looking car. Too far away to make out the registrations, but not wanting to move closer, she woke her phone.

While she waited for it to activate, she stared into the opening. It led to a well-lit loading area. She couldn't see anyone, and both vehicles looked empty. The phone beeped, and she held it against her body. Nobody seemed to hear. She pointed it at the vehicles and took three pictures. She opened the first to check it was in focus.

Before she could, a dog barked. A loud, deep sound that a large animal would make.

A dark shape appeared at the far end of the loading bay and lurched towards her. She ran, heading across the playground. Her pulse thundered in her ears. Above it the scrabbling of the beast's claws on concrete. Ahead, a fence. Would she reach it in time?

Her legs thrust her forward and her arms pumped. Only a few paces now. The beast sounded very close, but she dared not look round. Now only two steps. A low growl came from behind her ear as she launched herself, seizing the top of the fence and pulling. A spike punctured her hand, but ignoring the pain, she hauled herself up.

Agony as teeth grabbed her foot and a heavy body slammed into the fence below her, almost dislodging her. She held on and lashed out with her free foot. With a yelp, the dog released its jaws and her foot came free. She pulled herself to the top and dropped over the other side. As she landed in a heap three metres below, she heard voices, shouting.

She scrambled to her feet and looked around her. Behind her, the dog lunged at the fence and barked at her, a frenzied, frustrated sound. She stood on the canal bank, perilously close to the water. From her right came another shout. She turned away to the left, but a figure came at her from that direction. Beside him, another dog.

CHAPTER 18

The day after speaking to his informer, Alex Novak was having a very different type of meeting. He checked the time. He didn't like being kept waiting. Frowning, he lifted his glass of wine. It came out of a bottle that had cost over four hundred pounds. He savoured the rich aroma and was about to sip it when voices approached from the corridor outside. A discreet knock and the waitress stuck her head in.

'Your guests, sir.' She stood aside to let them enter.

Two fat slugs in well-cut suits. One, his guest, but the other, a stranger.

'Sorry we're late, Alex.' Guy's smooth, cultured voice put his teeth on edge, reminding him that although he had his suits made by the same tailor, he didn't belong to the same strata of society. 'This is Roger, my business adviser.'

'I'll set another place?' The waitress waited for his nod and scurried off.

Alex studied Roger, who had the same shiny face and air of smooth confidence as the man he advised.

'Glad to meet you, Alex. I've heard a lot about you.'

He held out a manicured hand, which Novak felt compelled to take. A firm grip, unlike Guy's flabby grasp. Novak returned the pressure and then some. His workout regime had strengthened his grip and given him callouses. To his credit, Roger didn't wince.

The waitress returned, laid another place setting and took their order. Once she'd gone and everyone had a full glass, Novak cracked his knuckles. 'Okay, what does Roger know?'

Guy gestured to his adviser. 'I'll let him tell you.'

'I'm aware you're keen to diversify from your core . . . business interests.' He gave a sly grin. 'And are looking for something less . . . challenging? And want to increase your property portfolio.'

King of the euphemisms, eh? 'Guy will have told you that my core business interests generate excellent returns. And I'm looking for similar.'

'Obviously. But your current activities aren't without . . . downsides.'

Novak's fist tightened round his glass, making it squeak. Was the slug referring to the murders of his sons as 'downsides'?

'What Roger means, Alex,' Guy hurried to say, 'is the property business will run smoothly with our involvement. You're the expert at running your business, and we, and in particular, Roger, are the experts in ours.'

'Okay, so why aren't I dealing directly with you, Roger? Why do I need him?' Novak pointed at Guy, who swallowed.

The waitress arrived, breaking the awkward silence, and placed their starters before them. The aroma of langoustine, lemon and garlic enveloped Novak. He inhaled it and sipped water while he waited for her to leave.

'Guy and I have different roles.' Roger picked up his fork. 'I work with the developers and Guy deals with the . . . political side.'

'So, you're the project manager and he's the bagman? I can hire one of the former and I've got one of the latter. Why do I need either of you?'

Guy, red-faced, leant forward, but Roger stayed him with a gesture. 'What I offer is far more than a project manager. I ensure that every step of the development comes in on time and under budget, guaranteed.'

Guy stepped in. 'And my role is to ensure the planning process works in our favour. For the current project, I'll make sure the council withholds permission until you've purchased the land that makes up the last piece of the jigsaw, depressing its price. Once you've got your ducks in a row, we get the planning permission, and you can either sell the land for a fat profit—'

'In which case, why do I need you, Roger?'

Guy sat back and attacked his starter, avoiding his adviser's glare.

Roger cleared his throat. 'Or you develop it for an even fatter profit. With my help.'

Alex picked up a langoustine and sucked out the sweet flesh. He suppressed a smile. The two slugs looked ready to rip each other apart.

The three ate in silence until Novak finished and dipped his fingers in the bowl of warm, lemon-scented water.

'Okay,' he said, 'I'll work with both of you, but you take your money out of Guy's share.'

'But that's—'

Novak held up his dripping hand and wiped it on the linen napkin. 'Guy brought you in as his adviser—'

'Our adviser.' On seeing Novak's expression, Guy looked like he wished he'd not spoken.

'There's no our. It's me' – Novak jerked a thumb at his chest – 'and you.' He pointed first at Guy, then Roger. 'Now, you either honour our agreement, or I go elsewhere.'

Guy's face reddened and his fists clenched, but Novak knew he'd do nothing. Roger was another proposition.

'What's to stop us from going elsewhere?'

The colour drained from Guy's features.

'You do that, and you'll find out. As Napoleon said, you can't make a soufflé without breaking eggs.'

'Omelette.'

'WHAT?'

This time, it was Roger's turn to wish he'd kept his mouth shut.

Guy broke the silence. 'That will be fine. Roger will get paid out of my share.'

Novak considered telling the smug git his share was now 20 per cent instead of a quarter, but he'd made his point. 'More wine, gentlemen?'

Two hours later, he jerked awake as his car stopped outside his house. He probably shouldn't have ordered the third bottle. He'd pay for it in tomorrow morning's gym session. Already, he was regretting bringing Guy on board. He had few contacts on the council, but how difficult would it be to bribe or intimidate a few councillors? The trouble was, his boys had taken over that side of the business and they'd had the contacts, not him.

A surge of emotion made his eyes shine. Time his men reported back on the search for their killers. His driver opened the door.

'Iggy, get the guys together first thing tomorrow.' He checked the time. 'Get them here by eight.' He'd have to get the personal trainer there by half six, unless he cancelled the session, but that led to a slippery slope.

'Dean's taken one of the lads to Birmingham,' said Iggy.

'That was last night, wasn't it?'

'He said he's got some more people to speak to this evening.'

'But not tomorrow morning?'

'I'll tell him to get back here.'

'You do that.' Fucking hell! Not Iggy as well.

◆ ◆ ◆

A good night's sleep followed by an intensive workout and a cold shower left him feeling almost well. He made his way to his study, which he'd had modelled on the Athenaeum in Liverpool with green-panelled walls and cream ceiling illuminated by a crystal chandelier. What was more, he'd read most of the books lining the walls, although he doubted he'd have time to read any for the foreseeable.

At eight on the dot, a respectful knock announced his men, who trooped in and stood in a rough semicircle before his desk.

'Where's Dean?'

Iggy replied. 'Sorry, Boss, he was stuck in traffic outside Stoke but should be here soon.'

Novak checked his anger. He'd speak to the lad later. 'Okay, which one of you has something to report?'

They shuffled and fidgeted, but none of them looked about to speak.

'You telling me you've done nothing since I last spoke to you?'

'No, Boss,' said Iggy. 'It's just that we've hit a wall. Nobody knows anything—'

'Or nobody's telling you anything. That's not the same.' He took a deep breath and pointed to the man on his left. 'Right, you, what have you done?'

'Nothing, Boss.'

'Nothing?'

'No. What I meant was, we've been asking around, but nobody knows nothing.'

'I'm sure that's not what you meant.'

'Boss?'

'Never mind. Now, I want you to tell me exactly what you've done.'

'Like I said, I asked around, but nobody—'

The slap on his desk echoed, and his Mont Blanc jumped. He stopped it rolling. 'Where did you go? Who did you ask?'

'Right, Boss. I went to the Golden Harp and asked the lads there if they'd heard anything. I then called in to O'Reilly's, but nobody there had heard nothing.'

By the time he'd asked the fourth man what he'd done, Novak was struggling to hold on to his temper. 'How the hell are you supposed to find out anything if you just speak to the same people in different pubs and nightclubs?'

Iggy broke the silence. 'Boss, we're not investigators. Wouldn't you be better off hiring someone?'

'Well, I'd never have thought of that. Thanks for the advice.' He should chase up the Dąbrowskis and check if they'd done anything. If it was up to the girl, she'd have told him where to get off, but her brother would do what he told him.

'At least now, Boss, everyone knows there's money on the table for information.'

'There has been since some scumbags murdered my boys. You telling me nobody knew about that before this week?'

Iggy swallowed. 'No, Boss.'

'Did any of you discover something I didn't already know?' He hoped Dean had done better down in Birmingham.

One of the younger guys stuck up a hand.

'You're not at school now. What you got to say?'

'Well, Boss, one of the guys who worked for the security company Marko ran said they were looking at a homeless guy.'

The mention of his younger son made his throat thicken. 'Explain.'

'Marko thought a homeless guy was spying on them. The lads sorted a couple of them out, but Ox thought they'd got the wrong one.'

'Ox?' He recalled reading something about this business, but hadn't linked it to his boys.

'Yeah, the lad I was talking to.'

'And why does he think they got the wrong one?'

'The dog.'

Novak waited in vain for him to elaborate. 'What about a fucking dog?' He hated swearing, but sometimes . . .

'Ox saw him with a dog and the ones they did, didn't have one.'

Novak attempted to decipher the gobbledygook. Talking to these guys gave him a headache. 'Let's get this clear. Your mate, Ox, thinks a homeless guy with a dog was spying on my sons?'

'That's it.' The lad beamed as if he'd achieved an impressive feat.

'And why should that be of interest?'

The lad looked confused and reddened.

Iggy came to the lad's rescue. 'Boss. He might have been working for whoever killed them, and even if he wasn't, he might have seen something of interest to us.'

Iggy had a point, reminding Novak why he'd promoted him. 'Right, I want you to find this homeless guy. I know most of them seem to have a dog these days, but he shouldn't be too hard to find.'

CHAPTER 19

'Come back, Oscar!'

As usual, he ignored me and raced along the canal path. The deeper bark of a large dog echoed off the mill opposite. Oscar stopped and looked at a figure on the path, standing perilously close to the canal edge. She looked our way and Oscar approached her, tail wagging. Not reassured by this, she let out a cry and backed away. In the gloom, it took me a second to recognise her.

'Jodie?'

She stopped her retreat and stared at me, looking fearful. To her left was the canal and on her right, a high wall with a metal fence above it.

'It's Victor,' I called. 'Toff's friend.'

From behind the fence on our right, the barking continued, accompanied by shouts from the school where I'd gone with Toff. It would take the dog, and the men with it, minutes to get down to the path. Not enough time to get away, but if we crossed on the lock gates, we could get into the café at the back of the mill opposite. It opened early most days.

'Come on, this way.'

After hesitating for a moment, Jodie followed, no doubt spurred on by the barking dog. We crossed the canal and up the steps through the small park beside the mill. Lights from the windows of the café confirmed I'd made the right decision, and with a sense of relief, I shouldered the door open.

About a dozen people sat at the tables scattered around the high-ceilinged room. Enough to deter most thugs from attacking Jodie. Several wore work clothes and looked sturdy enough to come to the rescue of a young woman.

'What do you want?' I gestured towards the counter.

She looked around, eyes wide. 'Cappuccino, please.'

I got myself a coffee and took the drinks to the table she'd commandeered in the far corner. Her attention stayed on the entrance, even as I placed the cup in front of her.

Nothing for me? Oscar demanded.

'It's coming in a minute.' I sat opposite Jodie, who studied me with a puzzled frown. 'What were you doing at the school?' She'd obviously come over the fence near where Toff and I had escaped two days earlier.

'I wasn't . . .' She lowered her gaze. 'Okay, I was looking around.'

'What for?'

'I'd left some of my stuff behind.'

'It wouldn't have been salvageable. They sprayed Skunk Water everywhere.'

'I didn't realise.' She stuck her chin forward in a manner reminiscent of my Helen.

'How old are you?' Hadn't Toff and I mentioned the Skunk Water last time we spoke to her? I was sure he'd said something about it.

'Why?'

'Just curious.'

'I'm twenty-three, although I've been told I seem younger.'

She was ten years older than Helen. Before I could comment, the barista came over with a bowl of food for Oscar. He fell on it, scattering pieces across the floor.

'Anyone would think I didn't feed you.'

They'd be right. Most of the time.

'Could I get something to eat?' Jodie said.

'Sure. What do you want?' I waved her towards the counter.

'Do they have anything healthy?'

She got up and limped towards the servery.

'What have you done to your leg? Have you sprained your ankle?'

'The dog grabbed my foot.' She pointed at her trainer, which had puncture marks on the side.

I noticed a wound on her hand. 'And that?'

She seemed to see it for the first time. 'The fence.'

'You need to get them cleaned.'

'Yeah, okay. Can I eat first?'

She chose an organic superfood granola with seeds and grains. I couldn't remember anyone I'd shared the streets with opting for anything but high-calorie, filling food, especially on chilly mornings. I paid, baulking at the price. Now I had a job, I wasn't hard up, but sending money back to Bristol to support my girls put a dent in my income.

She wolfed the food down and sat back in her chair. 'Do you think they'll have gone now?'

'I'll check.' I stood.

Do you want me to go?

'Great idea.' I let him out and returned to my seat.

Jodie finished her coffee. 'Can I ask you a question?'

I nodded.

'Toff said you were a private detective. Why are you interested in what happened at the school?'

I shrugged. 'Toff's a mate.' Should I tell her he'd found my daughter when she'd disappeared? 'I was doing him a favour.' That wasn't the whole truth, but she didn't need to know our business.

'You saw the dead man? How do you think he died?'

I laughed. That was something I wished I knew. 'We're not like Sam Spade, always seeing dead bodies.' I checked nobody was in earshot. 'Anyway, I glimpsed him in a darkened room before I had to do a runner when the police arrived.'

'So, someone had called the police before you and Toff found him?'

'What did Toff tell you?'

She didn't answer.

'You seem very inquisitive.'

She reddened and picked up her empty cup. 'I'm just interested in what happened. I was there as well, and I knew Sawney.'

'You did?'

'Well, I spoke to him on the street a few times.'

'Was he back on drugs?' I believed he wasn't, but she'd seen him more recently.

She shook her head. 'He told me he was clean, but someone said—' She stopped.

'Someone said what?'

'Just idle gossip. Someone said he'd been shot.'

I was almost certain that wasn't what she was going to say. 'I'm pretty sure he wasn't.'

'You don't think the guys who attacked us could have done it?'

'Can't see how it would've profited them. And if they had done it, they'd have done more to cover up the death. I think they found him dead and left him there.'

'Oh, really.' She sounded disappointed.

Before I could say anything, Oscar returned to our table. ***All clear.***

'How did you get in?'

Same way you did, through the door.

'I meant how did you open . . . Never mind.' Jodie had finished eating, and I gestured at her injured foot. 'Are you up to walking to my place?'

'What?'

'I've got a first-aid kit. You need to get your injuries disinfected and dressed. I can get you to hospital if you'd rather. Probably be a four-hour wait.'

She considered my offer. 'Okay.' She brandished her phone. 'I'll tell my mate where I'm going.'

'Please do. Shall I type in my address?'

She let me and we left, both of us alert for signs of her pursuers. Oscar ignored us and explored the canal path ahead. Jodie insisted she could manage and limped along. Dawn had risen and a procession of runners and early commuters passed us going both ways.

'What were you doing out on the canal path so early?' Jodie said.

'We'd had an unaccustomed quiet night and woke early, so I took Oscar for a walk. I spend far more time sitting around than I did while living on the street. I'm putting on weight.'

As we approached the tower block, I realised I'd have to sneak Jodie into my flat. I told her to wait beside the entrance and popped my head into the reception area. Two residents from an upper floor stood at the counter berating the member of staff behind the glass screens. I warned Jodie to stay behind me, and we slipped through the inner door into the corridor leading to my flat.

When I opened my door, the murmur coming from next door grew louder. 'REPENT OR YE SHALL BE PUNISHED!'

Jodie looked around in alarm. 'Who's that?'

'Just a neighbour. These walls are thinner than the ones onto the corridor. He sometimes gets a bit agitated.'

'God, I'd be round there telling him to do one.'

'I tried that once, and he just got more wound up. He'll quieten down soon.'

I retrieved the first-aid kit and got her to remove her footwear. Her feet didn't smell as bad as I expected them to. I remembered my time on the street. But I still made her wash them in my bathroom. Oscar sat, looking at the closed bathroom door.

'You okay, Oscar?'

Hmmm. She doesn't smell right.

'She just needs a wash.'

That's not what I mean.

'You and your olfactory antennae. Doesn't she remind you of Helen?'

What? That's the trouble with you humans. You make judgements based on vision, ignoring all your other senses.

The bathroom door opened. 'Who are you talking to?'

'Let's have a look at your foot first.' I gestured to Oscar to get out of the way.

She hopped to one of the two dining chairs flanking the small table in the corner, and raised her bare foot for me to examine. It didn't appear too damaged, two puncture wounds and bruising. I applied disinfectant, and she winced. A plaster on each puncture wound, and she was ready to go. I applied the same treatment to her injured hand.

'You can put your shoes back on now.' I straightened. 'Keep an eye on the bites in case they get infected.'

She looked around the cramped lounge filled with tired furniture. 'How long you lived here?'

Having a visitor, even someone used to living on the street, made me self-conscious. 'A couple of months.'

'Your shower's crap. You should get a new one.'

'Yeah, I was thinking of remodelling the kitchen first, then do the bathroom.'

'I'd do the bathroom first.'

I laughed. 'They're precious about me even hoovering the floor.'

She replaced her sock and shoe.

'How long you been on the street?'

She looked uncomfortable. 'Not long, a few weeks.'

'You local?'

'You ask a lot of questions, don't you?'

She was one to talk. 'It's part of being a PI.'

'Who you working for?'

'Even before I became a PI, I knew that's one question you don't ask. It would be like asking a reporter to name their sources.'

She reddened and concentrated on tying her laces. 'I meant, what sort of people are your clients? Jealous husbands? People looking for long-lost friends or lost pets?'

'Yes, but also corporate work, businesses wanting prospective employees vetted.' And gangsters using us to trace their enemies so they can eliminate them.

'Sounds interesting. You got any vacancies?'

'It's not my call.' I remembered how I'd felt when Kasper offered me some work. I thought I'd won the lottery. This young girl was new to the streets. Things can quickly go south when you're homeless, especially for young women. I checked the time. 'I'm just going in to work now. Do you want to come with me? You can meet Zofia and Kasper. Find out if they need anyone.'

'Yeah, that sounds fantastic. Thanks, Victor.'

Oscar gave me a pitying look. Despite knowing I was helping someone, I couldn't shake off a sense of unease.

CHAPTER 20

Zofia looked up when Kasper left the office to answer the door instead of just buzzing Victor in. They should give Victor his own key. Kasper seemed to take a long time. Perhaps it hadn't been Victor at the door. Voices came closer, and the door opened.

She saw why her brother had felt the need to go out to meet their visitors. For an instant she thought Helen, Victor's daughter, had come in with him. But Oscar's distance from her and a longer look confirmed her error. The young woman was a few years older and her hair darker. She also had the gaunt appearance of an addict, but her posture suggested her addiction was exercise rather than something more destructive. A glance at her clothing suggested another reason for her thinness. He must have come across her on the street. Zofia stood to greet her.

Victor gestured at the newcomer. 'Morning, Zofia. This is Jodie. She's looking for a job.'

'I said we might have something.' Kasper gave a sheepish smile. 'We've got a lot on . . .'

Zofia gave her brother a warning look, but couldn't decipher his response. 'Can you give us a minute, Victor, Jodie?'

She gestured towards their boardroom and waited for her brother to close the door.

'We can't just take someone on like that.'

'I only said we might have something. But we do need more help with all the other jobs we've got.'

'If we were looking for someone, we'd want a person with experience. We know nothing about her, let alone what work she's done.'

'Victor had no experience when we took him on.'

She moved closer to her brother and lowered her voice. 'Do we want strangers to discover we're working for Robertson?'

The blood drained from Kasper's face. 'I'll tell her no, then.'

Zofia remembered how much giving Victor a job had changed his life. 'Hang on.' She sat at the table and gestured for him to join her. 'We can get her to do some of the legwork, like we did with Victor—'

'That could be dangerous. Remember what happened to him?'

'Yes, but . . .' She glanced at the door. 'We're not keeping tabs on dangerous criminals.'

'We're just working for them.'

'Do you want to give her a job or not?'

'You said yourself she could compromise our existing clients.'

'Okay. Let's tell her we've got nothing at the moment, but we'll contact her when suitable work comes up.'

Kasper chewed his lips as he considered her suggestion. 'Okay. Will you tell her, or shall I?'

She stood. 'Leave it to me.' She marched out into the office.

Victor and Jodie had their heads together, looking at the screen of a phone. Oscar was on the floor under the printer and Zofia couldn't help thinking he wasn't enamoured with Victor's new friend. Was he jealous, or was it something else?

Victor held the device towards Zofia. 'Look at this.'

She examined the image, which showed two vehicles in the dark. 'What am I looking at?'

'I found Jodie near Mill View Academy after some men having a look round the school chased her.'

'And I took a picture of the cars the guys came in,' Jodie said.

'I was wondering if the van was the one that tried to run me over.' Victor held out his hand to take the phone. Zofia handed it back, and he peered at the image, enlarging it.

His expression told her the result. 'Not the same one?'

'Nope, but let's see who owns it.'

She sat at her desk and logged in. 'Shout it out.'

Victor recited the number plate, and she punched it into the search engine. 'It's a company car.' She noted the unfamiliar name. 'You got the other one?'

Victor read out a new set of letters and numbers.

'That's a council vehicle.'

'That makes sense. They own the building.'

'It must be the person in charge of the building. If we can find out which member of staff drives it, we can give the—' She looked at Jodie. 'Thanks for this, Jodie. Very useful.'

'Great.' She gave a shy smile. 'What do you think he was doing there at that time of the morning?'

That was the question at the forefront of Zofia's mind.

Victor answered. 'He might have been showing some contractors round. The place must need cleaning after they sprayed Skunk Water everywhere.'

Zofia doubted it, but didn't want to discuss it in front of a stranger. 'You could be right.' She looked at Jodie. 'Thanks for these pictures.' She retrieved a tenner from her purse and held it out.

'What's that for?'

'The photo. Or the information in it.'

'Why are you investigating the people at the school?'

Kasper stepped forward. 'We're not.'

'Right, so the information in my photo isn't worth anything to you.' Jodie folded her arms. 'In which case, keep the money.'

Zofia wondered how many homeless people would refuse a tenner. 'Treat it as an advance for when we use you.'

Victor raised his eyebrows. 'You giving her a job?'

'We've got nothing for you now, but we'll get in touch when we do.'

Jodie took the money and retrieved her phone from Victor before punching in Zofia's number and ringing it. She left with a cheery wave.

Zofia hoped she'd not made a mistake.

Victor looked better than he had in a while. An improved wellbeing had marked the first few weeks in his new home, but he'd since appeared to go backwards.

'Are you okay, Victor?'

'Yeah, fine.' He gave a false smile. 'Why shouldn't I be?'

'Everything okay at home?'

'Sure, me and Oscar have our differences, but show me a couple who don't.'

His joke lacked conviction, and she could have sworn from Oscar's demeanour that the dog had said something to him. Don't be stupid. Pets don't talk back. Even though Victor often acted as if Oscar did.

She retrieved her office keys. 'Do you want to get a set cut and I'll talk you through setting the alarm?'

'Are you sure?' He glanced at Kasper.

'Does he need the keys?' Kasper said. 'One of us is always here.'

'Not always. Anyway' – she turned back to Victor – 'if we're busy, you end up hanging around outside, and you're often in and out.'

'I'll get them done now.' He took the keys and set off.

Before he reached the door, the bell rang. He checked the screen, and the blood drained from his face.

Zofia's first thought was Robertson, but she realised Victor didn't know what he looked like. 'Grimes or Novak?'

'The latter.' Victor swallowed. 'What do you want me to do?'

Kasper stood. 'He's a client. Let him in.'

'Not yet. We didn't agree to work for—' She studied Kasper's expression. 'Tell me you haven't.'

'He paid five grand into our account . . .'

'He can have it back.' How could her brother be so stupid?

An angry buzzing interrupted them.

Victor appealed to her. 'I'm not sure what's going on here, but he doesn't know I work for you and I'd rather it stayed that way.'

Zofia saw how distressed he was at the thought. 'We can say you're another client.'

The doorbell buzzed again.

'Well, are we going to let him in?' Kasper's hand hovered over the intercom.

'He mustn't see me here.' Victor sounded near panic.

'Okay, okay.' Zofia racked her brains. 'You can hide in the boardroom until he's gone.'

'What if you need to use it?'

The buzz this time lasted several seconds.

'Tell him we're just finishing with another client, Kasper, and we want to preserve both his and the other client's anonymity. We'll let him in when it's safe. In the meantime, you hide in the toilets, Victor.'

'Really?' Kasper asked.

'Just do it, Kasper.'

Victor mouthed a silent, 'Thank you.'

Kasper spoke to Novak and came back. 'He's not happy.'

'Come on, Oscar, time to go.' Victor retrieved his lead.

Oscar lifted his head but didn't move.

'Yes, I know we've only just arrived. Now we've got to go again.'

Oscar stood and Victor led him out into the reception and then the toilet. Kasper went to meet Novak, and she heard his grovelling apologies. If he expected the same from her, he'd be sorely disappointed.

She stood as the office door opened. 'Sorry about that, Mr Novak. We take the anonymity of our clients seriously.'

'Yeah? Anyone can see who comes into your office?' Novak glared at her.

'Only if they're spying on us. Anyway, most clients don't come here. What can I do for you?'

'I'm not surprised they don't come here. Apart from the stink, you're not very hospitable, are you?'

Kasper said, 'Can I get you a drink?'

'I'm assuming this isn't a social call.' Zofia called up the memory of her experiences with his sons to give her the fortitude to confront the gangster. 'Can you tell us what you want? We're very busy, as we told you on your last visit.'

'Yeah, looking for my sons' killers, I hope.'

'We haven't agreed to take that job on.' She ignored Kasper.

'You should speak to your brother.' Novak glanced at Kasper. 'You've accepted my five grand.'

Zofia glanced at her screen. 'I'm more than happy to return it.'

'I wouldn't do that if I were you. Apart from being bad for business – you wouldn't want it putting about that you renege on agreements – it might suggest you've got something to hide from me.'

Zofia swallowed. 'Okay, let's assume we are working for you. Having you check up on us every day isn't conducive to efficient working.'

'Nor is taking on other clients like the one who's just left.' He jerked a thumb towards the door. 'I want you to focus on my case. I'm paying you enough.'

Kasper stepped forward. 'I can assure you, Mr Novak—'

Zofia cut him off. 'As we explained, we've got responsibilities to existing clients. If you can't accept that, then we're happy to step aside and let you find someone else.'

She held his gaze until he shook his head. 'One of these days, that mouth is going to get you into trouble, Ms Dąbrowski. Don't you know, discrimination is the better part of valour?'

She suppressed a smile at the misquote. 'I'll bear that in mind. Now, was there anything else you wanted?'

'Yeah. I might have a lead on your case for me.' He chuckled. 'A lead. Get it? I want you to search for a man with a dog.'

An uneasy sensation chilled her. 'A man with a dog? There must be thousands in the city.'

'Yeah. More precisely, a tramp with a dog.'

She swallowed. 'Any reason?'

'I've heard one was spying on my sons before someone murdered them.'

Behind Novak, Kasper gagged, but Zofia ignored him. 'Do you know why?'

'I've no idea why anyone would spy on my sons.' He turned to examine Kasper, who looked ready to faint. 'That's why I want to speak to him.'

She needed to go on the attack. 'Maybe he thought they'd kidnapped someone close to him. They seemed to have a habit of doing that.'

Novak controlled a snarl. 'Just find him for me.' He stood and marched to the exit, where he turned. 'I want updates from you every few days. Next one on Friday.' He stomped down the stairs.

Kasper and Zofia looked at each other. Thank God Victor had insisted on hiding from him.

CHAPTER 21

The smell of hot metal and lubricant filled my nostrils as I examined the display of key fobs. I'd considered adding the office keys to those for my home, but decided to keep them separate. The locksmith stopped the key-cutting machine and placed the mortice key in the vice before attacking it with a file. I picked a key fob off the hook.

Oscar bared his teeth. ***Not that one!***

I studied the silver silhouette of a Schnauzer attached to a key-ring. 'What? It looks perfect.'

It's a miniature, not a standard. You can see how stumpy its legs are.

I checked the price. 'I'm getting it.'

Give me strength. Oscar wandered off, shaking his head.

I checked the time. Novak had arrived at the office twenty-five minutes ago. I was keen to crack on, but wanted to wait until I was sure he'd gone. I rang Zofia, who confirmed he'd left.

'And Victor . . .'

'Yeah?'

'It doesn't matter. I'll tell you once you get here.'

It obviously did matter and, uneasy about what she would be telling me, I returned. I arrived back with a bag of filled bagels and another of doughnuts. Oscar gave the fob the side-eye when I pulled my new keys from my pocket and let myself into the office for the first time.

It felt momentous, but his attitude annoyed me. It was just a keyring.

Zofia and Kasper seemed subdued as I returned her keys. I offered them drinks and took the food through to the kitchen.

I took my coffee to my desk. 'Okay, so what's happened?'

'Well, we're definitely working for Novak.' Zofia glanced at her brother. 'He wouldn't take no for an answer.'

I'd learnt to decipher the siblings' silent exchanges. Kasper had agreed to take Novak on without consulting his sister.

'What was it you wanted to say to me?'

She chewed her lip. 'Novak knows a homeless man with a dog was tailing his sons. He wants us to look for him.'

I almost choked on my coffee and looked at Oscar, asleep on his mat under the printer. 'How does he know that?'

Kasper expelled air through his lips. 'Either through the police or one of his guys.'

I studied the siblings. 'What will you do?'

Zofia didn't avoid my gaze. 'We can't "find" you for him.'

'I still don't understand why you took the job.'

'Oh yeah?' A spark of anger animated Kasper. 'He's not the sort of guy you say no to.'

Zofia supported her brother. 'He also suggested we'd have something to hide if we refused. It wouldn't surprise me if he knew we'd been tailing his sons, too. If he's got contacts in the police, he must know. It's in the statements we made to Grimes.'

'But why hasn't he asked you about it?' I couldn't work out his tactics.

'Maybe he wants us to sweat, like we are now.'

I suspected Zofia was right. The alternative was for him to 'question' the siblings. I knew that would end badly for them, and me, if they gave me up.

Zofia took a deep breath. 'No point in worrying about it. Do you think it's worth contacting the company which supplied the Skunk Water to see who they sell it to?'

'Great idea, but would they tell us?'

'I'll have to finesse it.' She winked. 'Leave it to me.'

She had a much better chance of getting information out of them than I would. I got my head down, catching up with the work I was being paid for.

After a while, Kasper swore. 'Shit!'

Zofia frowned. 'What's up?'

'Robertson's sent me another message chasing me up.'

'I thought he'd given us until Monday.'

'He has, but I sent him a report after we got the car number from Jodie, telling him the guy he wanted to speak to is called Russ Chopra.'

'How did you find out his name?'

Kasper looked embarrassed. 'I rang the council, pretending to be from a nursery near the school, and said he'd helped one of our mums when she'd fallen over, and we wanted to thank him.'

'Hmmm . . . What does Robertson want?'

'He wants me to ring him about some other work.'

'So much for getting him out of our hair.'

I had a bad feeling about this. 'You realise Robertson will be furious if he finds out you're working for Novak?'

'No shit, Sherlock!' Kasper rolled his eyes. 'And vice versa. What do you want us to do? Shut up shop and go on the run?'

Taken aback, I mumbled, 'I just meant it's unlucky we've got both of them chasing us up at the same time.'

Zofia gave me a sympathetic smile.

As Kasper rang, I fretted about what Robertson's interest in Manchester meant for us. I guessed I was safe – he didn't even know I existed. But the siblings were in his sights. The fact he needed them now meant they should be okay for the moment, but what would happen once he finished with them?

'Good afternoon, Mr Robertson, it's Kasper.'

I listened but couldn't make out the other half of the conversation. Zofia's frustrated expression suggested she couldn't either. Kasper did a lot of listening and made notes. We waited until he'd finished. His demeanour suggested bad news.

Zofia stood. 'Shall I get you a drink?'

'A large brandy if you've got one.' He tried to smile. 'Failing that, a strong coffee.'

I curbed my impatience and tried to work while I waited for her to return. Kasper's theatrical sighs and gestures made it clear he wasn't happy.

Zofia put a steaming mug in front of him. 'Right, what does he want?'

'It looks like he is moving into Manchester.'

'He said that?'

'Not in so many words, but he wants us to investigate another building. It's on Pollard Street East.'

The name struck a chord. 'What number?'

They both looked at me.

Kasper spoke first. 'Why?'

'One building I'm looking at with John and Craig is on there. Uniformed thugs attacked the people sleeping in it and sprayed Skunk Water on them a couple of weeks ago.' I dictated the address.

Kasper checked and looked up. 'It's the same one.'

Was Robertson linked to these attacks on the homeless? If he was, why would he want to kill Sawney? Not for the first time, I replayed our last meeting, scouring it for anything that might at least point towards an answer.

◆ ◆ ◆

I remembered crossing the concrete path alongside the fountain in Piccadilly Gardens and shivering as an icy wind blew spray into my face. A figure I recognised sat on the seating encircling the pond. I waved and joined him.

'Sawney, how are you doing?' Pale stubble covered his head like fuzz on a peach. Huge ears stuck out at almost ninety degrees, and it looked like he'd lost even more teeth.

'Victor. Great to see you, son. Whit's new?' He tapped the seat alongside him. 'Sit wi' me.'

I sat. 'You growing your hair?' Despite the chill, he wore his habitual baggy shorts and his distinctive thistle tattoo peeked out of the top of his thick socks. I often wondered if he'd rather not wear a kilt.

'Ach, nay. I need to get my heid shaved.'

'You still going to the clinic?' I'd accompanied him to a rehabilitation centre a few weeks earlier. He'd expressed a desire to come off the drugs, which had been a staple of his life for years.

'Aye. I'm determined this time, son.'

'Good.' He looked clear-eyed and better than I'd ever seen him. Maybe he would make it this time.

'Anyway, I need to keep me wits about me.'

I'd heard his claims of being under threat, dismissing them as paranoid delusions. 'Who's after you this time?'

'Ach! I know you don't believe me, but I know stuff.' He tapped the side of his head with a none too clean, stubby finger. 'Stuff people will pay good money for.'

'That sort of information can be dangerous.'

'You're telling me, son.' He made a show of looking around. 'That's why I've got an insurance policy. If anything happens to me, people will get letters.'

I nodded. He'd asked me for my address the last time I saw him. 'It's always good to have insurance.'

'Aye. And I'll be joining you soon.'

'You're moving to Strangeways View?'

He laughed. 'I hope not. No, I'm going to get some money, get my ain place. You see if I don't.'

'Don't forget to invite me to the housewarming.'

He laughed again, and I left him, not realising that would be our last conversation.

'Earth to Victor.' Kasper stood in front of my desk.

'Sorry, I was thinking.'

'You ready to eat?' He held the bag of bagels in one hand.

'I could. And a tea would be nice.'

While I waited, I carried out a search for a number and rang Life Changers, the organisation I'd accompanied Sawney to. At first, they wouldn't tell me anything, and I asked to speak to the therapist who met us when I took him. She remembered me.

'Victor, I know you're a friend of his, but we can't discuss his treatment or even if he was still a client.'

'The reason I need to know is that, I'm sorry to say, he died in the early hours of Monday morning.'

'Oh! I didn't know. I'm so sorry, Victor. What happened?'

'I don't know yet. The police are investigating. I just want to be sure he wasn't using again.'

'As far as I'm aware, he wasn't. I saw him Saturday afternoon. He looked clean and was bubbly, excited about something he said he'd be able to tell me about the next time he saw me.'

'You think he might have relapsed?'

'It's possible. Never say never. But I've seen a lot of addicts, and he had the air of one who would succeed. I'd be shocked if he had relapsed, especially so soon.'

I ended the call and stared at the handset. If he hadn't suffered an overdose, how had he died? And who had he been so scared of?

CHAPTER 22

After leaving the offices of KZD, Jodie returned to the city centre. The bright spring sunshine meant the Cathedral Gardens weren't empty, despite the cold and it being the middle of the working day. She found an unoccupied stretch of wall. The nearest people, an elderly couple with a shopping trolley, sat over thirty metres away. She had a couple of calls to make and didn't want anyone overhearing her. She retrieved her phone and made her first call.

'Hi Mum.'

They exchanged greetings, and her mother said, 'I'm coming into Manchester on Friday to Harvey Nicks and wanted to take you out somewhere. I'll swing by the apartment around five—'

'I'll be working, Mum.' The last thing she wanted was her mother finding out what she was doing. She already disliked the fact Jodie was working as a reporter.

Jodie would have to get herself cleaned up so she could hide her role from her mum. She'd visited the apartment her parents had bought for her in one of the glass towers at the bottom end of Deansgate only once, for a shower, since she'd started her undercover operation. Although tempted to spend the night there, she knew it would make returning to the streets much harder.

'On a Friday evening?'

'Yes, Mum. Most people work past five, even on a Friday. And I'm working on a special project. Long hours.'

'Why do you do it? You don't need to work.'

'I've told you, Mum, I want to make my own way.'

Her mother sighed. 'There's no point in arguing with you. But take care, there's lots of predators out there.'

'Of course.' As if she didn't know. The thought of her mother's reaction if she ever discovered what Jodie was up to gave her an illicit thrill, even stronger than when she'd bunked off from school in Switzerland to go touring with that band.

She ended the call and steeled herself to make the next one. Colin Newsome took so long to answer, she thought, and hoped, it would go through to voicemail.

'If it's not Nellie Bly.'

'Oh, give it a rest,' she muttered under her breath.

'What did you say?'

'Nothing.'

'Right.' He cleared his throat. 'What you got for me?'

'The dead man in the disused school probably died because of a drug overdose.'

'Probably?'

She'd checked with Ziggy, who, although still groggy after his beating from the men who'd caught him upstairs, confirmed Sawney had sneaked out and returned around two, seeming spaced out. 'It definitely wasn't the thugs who'd raided the school.'

'Hmmm . . . That's not much use to us then. What about the dead woman? The one they found on Beswick Street?'

Was she homeless? Jodie hadn't even looked at that case, but couldn't admit it to Colin. 'I called round to investigate, and they set a dog on me. I only just got away.'

'Oh yeah, did it take a bite out of your arse?'

'No, my foot. It's bloody sore.'

'Put it in the accident book. Now, if you have nothing worth publishing by Friday, I'm pulling you out. The reason I let you do this was because you convinced me you had leads on two good stories. You've given me nothing on the killer preying on the homeless. I hope it's not another urban myth like the Manchester Pusher.'

She was starting to suspect he could be right, but wouldn't admit that to him, either. 'I've been focusing on the developers using violent thugs to clear rough sleepers from their buildings. I spoke to a person they beat up and—'

'Yeah, I read the piece, but you don't name the developers behind it. I need names, Jodie. Get me something by Friday or you're out.'

'You can't—' She stopped when she realised she was talking to an empty line. 'Bastard.'

'The social, was it?'

Toff's question made her jump, and she almost dropped the phone. She'd forgotten homeless people could claim benefits. Best to let him think that was who was on the phone.

'I hate dealing with 'em.' She got to her feet and spun. He stood a few paces away with two older men. The shorter one had a fringe of hair round his skull and, had he worn a habit, he'd have fitted most people's idea of a medieval monk. The taller one towered over him and had matted black hair and a beard. A Yorkshire terrier wearing a turquoise ribbon at his feet belied his fierce expression.

'Alright, Jodie. This is Brother John and Craig.' The dog yapped. 'And Trixie, of course.'

'Hello.' She nodded a greeting. How much had they heard? She replayed her conversation. If they'd heard her discussing Sawney's death, she'd have a job explaining it.

'Did you say a dog bit you, Sister?' Brother John said. 'We couldn't help overhearing.'

'Yeah, I went back to the school to see if I could salvage some bedding. They had a guard dog.'

'Do you want Craig to have a look? He's pretty good at first aid.' The other two seemed to defer to John.

She studied the hulking giant and his none too hygienic attire. 'It's okay, Victor dressed it for me.'

Craig's severe expression softened. 'You know Victor?'

'Toff introduced us, and Victor rescued me from the dog this morning.'

'A friend of Victor's is okay, Sister. If you need any help, come and find us, or let Toff know.' They said their goodbyes and wandered off towards Deansgate.

Toff stayed. 'Where you off to?'

She had to get rid of him, but didn't want to make him suspicious. 'I need to deal with that call if I want to get off the streets . . .'

'Yeah, sure. I'll see you later.' Unable to hide his disappointment, he wandered off towards the cathedral.

Jodie fumbled with her bag and waited until he was out of sight. In the absence of anything concrete about who was behind the thugs with the Skunk Water, she decided to check out the incident on Beswick Street. A search brought up a plethora of articles. She read about the fire and the homeless man rescued by two coppers. What was the betting they took the credit for someone else doing it?

She watched a video of the incident and paused it. Bloody hell, was that Victor's dog and Victor with it? She paused it and enlarged the screen. It could be, and he lived nearby. She'd have to ask him about it.

She read a few more articles with a growing sense of excitement. Whoever set the fire killed one homeless person and almost killed another. If she could link it to the ones she was already investigating . . . She'd show Colin it wasn't a bloody myth.

She had to get there and check it out. Not wanting to walk along Great Ancoats Street, she turned off Shudehill, past the Arndale and towards the Ashton Canal.

The walk to Beswick Street took her half an hour. The building she wanted stood just off the canalside. She stepped into the open gateway and studied the building. Soot stained the brickwork above the window openings, most of which had boards nailed across them. A piece of blue and white police tape fluttered on the doorjamb to the main entrance.

After checking she wasn't being observed, she approached. A smoky stink assailed her nostrils as she pushed at the door and it gave, opening a few centimetres. She checked her surroundings again and pushed harder until the gap was big enough for her. She rubbed the soot marks off her palm and the plaster Victor had applied, retrieved her phone and stepped inside. The stench of burnt plastic and wood intensified.

Her torch app illuminated a blackened corridor. Smudged handprints marked the walls at waist height and above. Some footprints cutting into the mush of soggy plaster coating the floor had the sharp edges of a cookie cutter. A few stained ceiling tiles clung to a framework of wires above head height. The rest joined the mush under her feet. The corridor on her right looked more promising.

Ten paces in, the profusion of marks, footprints and scuffs on the walls identified where people had milled around. Probably where they'd placed someone on a stretcher. Jodie took a few photos. A door on her left led to the room in which the fire must have started. A faint smell of hydrocarbon lingered and mingled with the burnt stink, but nothing remained of its contents apart from a mass of ash, charred timbers and twisted metal. As the stories had hinted, someone had started the fire deliberately. Had the killer moved on from using direct violence? She'd have to check if the man the police rescued had been beaten up.

Looking back from the doorway, she noticed drag marks in the corridor. They led from a door at the end with tape announcing 'DANGER UNSTABLE FLOOR' secured across it. She explored the rest of the ground floor and, finding nothing else of interest, returned to the door.

It wasn't locked, and it led to a concrete staircase. Shadows flickered off the walls as she ascended to the first floor. The stairs continued but, afraid to go too far, she decided to check the first floor and skedaddle. She wasn't sure what she was looking for, but she needed to find something to keep Colin happy and just sticking her head in the ground floor wouldn't cut it. Although she'd already found proof that someone had started the fire. Would that be enough? She was here now and might as well see what else she could find.

The door to the first floor stuck, but a hefty shove moved it. The boarded-up windows let in little light, and her torch beam faded before it reached the edges of the space. On her right, opposite an open, undivided space, stood a stud wall with doors off it. The beam of her light fell on piles of burnt machinery and furniture.

A body-sized patch of clear floor to the right of the door grabbed her attention. This must have been where they found the dead woman. She shuddered and took some more photos. Would these be enough to keep Colin happy? She might as well have a look round now she was here.

She stepped around the patch and headed for the first door. Runnels of sooty water left patterns on the vertical surfaces. The door creaked open and residual fumes caught in the back of her throat. A sound came from the stairs. Footsteps and voices. She turned off her light and stood in the doorway, holding her breath.

The steps paused and the door from the stairs opened. The voices grew louder. Two men.

She couldn't risk closing the door and stepped into the darkness. A powerful beam of light swung across the opening.

'Did you leave the door open?'

Her pulse whooshed so forcefully she feared they must hear her.

'Can't remember.'

Her panic eased until the response.

'We'd better put a padlock on it until the floor's sorted.'

'Right, okay. What else do you want doing up here?'

'I'll show—'

The opening bars of 'I Knew You Were Trouble' rang out from her phone. In her panic, it shot out of her hand. As she snatched at it, the floor gave a loud creak. She leapt for the doorway, but her feet fell from under her, and she screamed.

CHAPTER 23

My thoughts whirred as Oscar and I walked along the canal-side. Zofia had sent me out to visit two premises. The one on Beswick Street where we'd rescued the homeless man and the place Robertson was interested in, on Pollard Street East, which I was also investigating in my effort to find out who might have killed Sawney. What might Robertson have to do with the attacks on the homeless or Sawney's death? As we left the canal, I retrieved Oscar's lead.

'Come on.'

You don't need to tie me up.

'We agreed. You wear the lead when we're working.'

There's nobody around. He stopped and sniffed, then ran up the steps to the road.

'Come back, you bloody . . . Typical.'

I ran after him onto Beswick Street, reliving the events of yesterday morning as he made for the building where he'd found the unconscious man. Not again. I followed him into the yard. He stopped at the doorway. Voices came from inside.

Something's happened. You'd better go in. I'm not risking my paws in that sludge.

I stepped past him and followed the voices. Two men stood in the doorway of the last room off the corridor, near where we'd found the man. Focused on something in the room, they didn't notice me. I peered past and above them, where a powerful lamp illuminated the lower half of a young woman hanging through a hole in the ceiling, like a spotlight on a dancer.

'Get me down, you bastards!'

I recognised the voice. 'Jodie?'

'Who the hell are you?' The torch beam swung into my face.

I shielded my eyes. 'Victor Mitchum. I'm here from KZD to speak to Mr Aitken.'

'That's me,' the other man said.

'Can you ask your friend to move his lamp?'

The beam of light returned to Jodie's legs. 'You know her?'

My mind raced. 'Yes, she works with me.' Which was true: Zofia had said she was going to call Jodie to give me a hand.

'OI!' Jodie shouted. 'Do you want to stop arsing about down there and get me out of here?'

'Hang on, I'll get a ladder.' Aitken's assistant left his torch and hurried away.

While we waited for his return, I helped Aitken move two desks, which appeared to have fallen through a two-metre diameter hole in the ceiling. Jodie hung on to a joist at the edge of the hole, her elbows wedged over it. The man returned with a tall stepladder and helped Jodie down, while I and his boss steadied it.

'Bloody hell, what took you?' Jodie brushed at her clothes and glared at the man who'd assisted her.

Before he responded, I stepped in. 'I told you to wait for me, not go blundering around. You could have been hurt.'

She glared at me, then her brain kicked into gear. 'Sorry, I just wanted to familiarise myself with the building.' She looked around. 'Can I borrow your torch? I've lost my phone somewhere in here.'

Aitken's man hesitated.

'And thanks, by the way.'

He swung the beam around the room. 'Is that it?' The light glinted off the corner of a jet-black screen lying on a pile of wet ashes near the centre of the room.

Jodie stepped across to it and picked it out of the mush. She wiped it against her jeans and pressed a button. The screen lit up, making her smile.

'Is there an office we can use, Mr Aitken?' I asked. The stepladder looked clean, which suggested there were parts of the building untouched by fire.

'Sure, there's an office in the workshop.' He led us back out of the building. 'Oi, bugger off, you!' He clapped his hands.

Oscar didn't seem impressed. ***I accept you've probably never seen such a magnificent specimen, but no need to applaud.***

'He's with me.'

'Oh. I thought you'd have a bloodhound.' His assistant joined in with his laughter, and I forced a smile.

He led us across the yard to a single-storey building with large, blue, wooden gates. Jodie dropped behind, messing with her phone. I hung back with her.

'Did you know about this?' Jodie showed me Zofia's message asking her to ring the office.

'She said she'd ring you.'

'Yeah, that's why I fell through the floor. I dropped the phone when it rang.'

Aitken had reached the gate and stood in the opening. We hurried to him, Jodie limping, and he led us through it. Bright pendant lights illuminated a large open space with a covered inspection pit in the middle of the floor. A workbench with tools on the wall behind it took up half the left-hand wall. Opposite stood two small glass-fronted offices. A smell of sawdust and oil filled the air. Oscar's claws click-clacked on the concrete as he trotted ahead and sniffed the edges of the inspection pit.

'Your dog's found where we buried the bodies,' Aitken's assistant said with a smile.

A glare from his boss wiped it off his face.

To fill the embarrassing silence, I pointed to Jodie's foot. 'You hurt yourself?'

'It's just where the dog bit me. I caught it when I fell.'

'You have been in the wars.' Aitken examined her, frowning as he took in her scruffy appearance. Aitken himself was about my height, one seventy-five, and wore a smart suit with a tie and shined brogues.

'She's been working undercover on another job,' I explained.

'Right. You get a lot of that? I've never met a private eye before.'

'It's mostly computers these days.'

'Before we start, you got any ID?'

'Sure. Here.' I fumbled in my pocket for the laminated KZD card with my photo on it.

He examined it and waited for Jodie, who looked at me in panic.

'We don't carry them when undercover,' I said, 'for obvious reasons.'

'Of course.' Seeming reassured we wouldn't attack him, he gestured to his assistant to leave us and led us into the nearest office. Oscar seemed content to explore the workshop.

Aitken sat behind the desk, facing us. 'You said you're investigating for the insurance company.'

'That's right.'

'Don't they have their own investigators?'

I'd studied their brief, along with the list of questions they wanted us to ask. I'd read between the lines and guessed we were cheaper. 'They won't be called out unless we feel it's necessary.'

'Why would you think that?' He licked his lips. 'I mean, under which circumstances . . . ?'

I smiled to reassure him. 'We've got a series of questions they've sent us.' Zofia had printed them out and I retrieved them from my backpack. 'The first relates to the cause. We know someone set the fire—'

'Hang on, I know nothing about that. You're not accusing me?'

'Of course not.'

He's lying.

'Oscar, how did you get in here?'

Through the door. We've been through this.

'I'll get rid of him.' Jodie stood.

You touch me and you'll regret it.

'Leave him, he'll be fine.' She sat while I regathered my thoughts. 'The people who started the fire attacked me and I'm pretty sure it wasn't you or your colleague.'

'Oh, right.' He leant back in his chair, his relief evident. 'Fire away.'

I studied the questions, but something about his demeanour made me agree with Oscar. 'Do you have any idea who might have done it?'

Aitken looked uncomfortable and shifted in his seat. 'Why would I?'

He's lying again.

Yeah, even I spotted that.

I left a silence for him to fill. Jodie leant forward, but I stilled her with a gesture.

Eventually, Aitken clasped his hands on the desk. 'There was someone, in fact. He approached me a few weeks ago, asking if I'd be interested in selling.'

I waited for him to continue until it appeared he wouldn't. 'What happened?'

'I told him I wouldn't.' Aitken loosened his collar. 'He . . . He suggested I reconsider.'

'Suggested?'

'It was more than a suggestion.'

'And what happened?'

'He made it very clear – very! – that I had to change my mind.'

A surge of excitement made me tremble. This was gold. 'And did you?'

'I've got a family. And he even knew which schools my children go to.'

'Who was it?'

Aitken's focus swung between Jodie and me. 'This will go no further?'

I glanced at Jodie, not sure if I could trust her. But if I asked her to leave, Aitken would clam up. 'I assure you it won't.'

'The guy who came round was just a messenger. He gave me his name, but I'm sure it's fake.'

'We can check.'

'Okay.' He shrugged and gave me the name the man used, and I noted it.

'What's he look like?' I cast around the tidy but outdated workshop. 'CCTV?'

'Sorry, nothing like that.' He looked up towards his left. 'About six foot, a couple of inches taller than you, bulky, but wearing a nice suit. Didn't look like a thug, and he had a posh accent.'

'Hair and eye colour? Beard?'

He blew air through his lips. 'Dark, with a bit of grey. Blue eyes, but no facial hair.'

I made notes. 'When did he come round?' Could we get security footage from neighbours?

'I made a note in my diary but . . .' He gestured towards the burnt-out building.

'Okay, no problem.' A posh thug should be easy to find. There couldn't be many around. 'Who was he working for?'

He hesitated, then blurted out, 'Alex Novak.' He seemed exhausted by the revelation.

Jodie had gasped at the sound of the name, but I'd almost expected the answer.

'I can see you've heard of Mr Novak.' He nodded at Jodie. 'At least she has and knows why I didn't mention his name to the police.'

Jodie spoke to him for the first time. 'Are you sure he represented Mr Novak? He might have used his name to scare you?'

Aitken hadn't considered this. 'You think that's possible?'

'Anything's possible,' she said. 'But did he say why they wanted your property?'

'Canalside location. We're a bit out of the city, but the development envelope is spreading outwards, and we've had a few offers. Each bigger than the last.'

Jodie was taking over, so I jumped in with a question. 'And did he offer you a better deal?'

'No. But I care about my family.'

'So, you're selling?'

He fixed me with his gaze. 'Do you have kids?'

I thought of Helen and Em and nodded.

'What would you do?'

'I'd—'

'Tell him to eff off,' Jodie finished for me. 'I bet it's nothing to do with Novak. Call his bluff.'

'The impetuosity of youth.' He gave a derisive laugh. 'Well, young lady, I'm selling up.'

'Will you be claiming on the insurance?' she asked.

'Of course.'

'Isn't that dishonest? If you're selling it. I assume you're not doing it up first.'

'Right, I want you to leave.' He stood.

I joined him. 'Thank you for your time, Mr Aitken.'

He ignored me and glared at Jodie until she got out of the chair and left the office, waiting for me by the inspection pit.

Furious with her, I tried to salvage something as I stuffed the papers in my backpack. 'Did he say what the company was called?' I asked him.

'What?'

'The buyer.'

He'd walked round the desk. 'So you can tell them to knock my insurance claim off the price?'

I didn't back down. 'If they're behind that fire, I want them caught. I almost got killed in there.'

The colour left his face. 'You can't tell the police anything I've told you.'

'I'm not going to.'

He stared into my eyes. 'Grove Associates.'

'Thank you.' I made my exit, Oscar at my heels.

We passed Jodie at speed, leaving her limping after me. Outside the door, I almost bumped into Aitken's man. The ladder lay on the ground beside him. Had he been listening? How much could he hear from outside? I nodded to him and waited for Jodie at the far end of the yard.

Oscar studied me. ***You don't seem happy. Was it because you needed my help?***

'I didn't— No, nothing to do with that.' I glanced back. Jodie dawdled, examining her phone. Aitken's man was still watching me.

I waited for Jodie. 'What the hell were you playing at?'

'What do you mean?'

'You practically accused him of insurance fraud.'

'I thought we were working for the insurance company.'

'We're not trying to deny his claim.'

'What were we here to do?'

'You're here to listen and learn.' I stomped off towards the street. 'And how do you know about Novak?'

'How do you?'

'It's my job. I'm a private detective.'

'Yeah, well, I like to be well informed.' She limped out ahead of me, then stopped on the pavement. 'Where are we going next? Zofia said you were visiting two addresses.'

'We are, but what were you doing hanging through the floor upstairs?' I jerked a thumb over my shoulder.

'This is where Zofia said I was supposed to meet you.'

'How did you know?'

'What do you mean?'

'You said you dropped the phone when she rang you. You must have already been here when she rang.'

Panic entered her eyes. 'Right. Well, I was looking for somewhere to sleep tonight.'

'What, in a burnt-out shell?'

'Yeah. I thought it would be safer because most people would avoid it.' She took a couple of steps away from me. 'Anyway, you haven't said where we're going.'

Was her being there just a coincidence?

Have you seen him? Oscar indicated the far corner of the yard.

A furry bundle cowered in the corner. I walked towards it and made out a scruffy, underfed dog looking sorry for itself. 'What's up, boy?' I approached, hunched over with a hand extended.

He struggled upright and limped a couple of steps away.

'I won't hurt you.' He let me get close. The poor thing looked starved and had a nasty-looking injury to his back leg.

I approached to within one pace, and he shrank back.

'What's wrong with him?' Jodie stood next to me.

'Can you just give me some space?'

She flounced off, and I eventually got close enough to pick the poor animal up. It looked like someone had kicked him, and he appeared cold and hungry. Had he belonged to the guy I dragged out of the burning building? Or the dead woman? I'd heard of a charity which looked after the pets of homeless people. I'd imagined them looking after Oscar if anything happened to me. With the poor dog across my forearm, I searched on my phone. He was so thin his bones dug into my flesh.

'What you going to do with him?' Jodie said.

The dog growled at her.

'I'm taking him to a vet.'

Oscar looked at her and shook his head. ***You sure you want her along with you?***

I wasn't. Had I made a mistake in trying to help Jodie?

CHAPTER 24

Novak had left the detectives' offices in a foul mood. That Zofia was getting on his nerves. He was all for women having spirit, but they needed to know their place. He supposed she was so used to ruling over her brother, she didn't understand how to behave around a real man. As he crossed the road, Iggy jumped out of the car and opened the back door.

'Trouble, Boss?'

'Not really, just a woman who thinks she's better than she is.' He got in the back and waited until they pulled out into the traffic.

After they'd gone a few hundred metres, he retrieved his phone from the locked cabinet behind Iggy's seat. It beeped a few times, picking up the messages blocked while it sat in the metal box.

'Back home, Boss?'

'Yeah.' He read the encrypted messages. Nothing he needed to deal with now. 'Iggy, did you see who came out of the office we just visited?'

'Just after you went in?'

'Yeah. What did he look like?'

'What d'you mean, Boss?' In the mirror, Iggy's brow furrowed. 'You must'a walked past him.'

'They seemed keen to keep us apart. That's why they made me wait.'

'Oh, right.' Iggy glanced in the mirror again. 'Average height. Thin, like a runner. Not too scruffy or smart, short brownish hair, glasses.'

'Just an average guy, then.'

'You could say. Yeah.'

Novak's anger rose. 'So, nothing that helps us identify him?' Was he making too much of this? The guy was probably another customer.

'There was the dog.'

'Dog? Why didn't you say he had a dog?'

'You asked me what he looked like.'

'Yeah, right, okay.' He took a deep breath. 'Describe the dog.'

'It looked like the one me in-laws have, but more pissed off.'

Novak was waiting for more when an outgoing phone call purred over the speakers.

The dialling tone ended. 'Yes, what do you want now?' Iggy's wife demanded.

'Erm . . . I've got the boss in the back, luv, and he wants to know what dog your dad has.'

'Does he?' A note of respect entered her voice. 'It's an Airedale. Is he thinking of—'

'Right, thanks.' He ended the call. 'You hear that, Boss?'

Novak was already typing 'what dog looks like a pissed off Airedale?' into his phone. He found it on page seven of the search.

'Is it a Schnauzer?'

Once they'd parked up outside his house, Iggy looked at the image and confirmed it. 'What you want to do about the bloke with the dog?' He handed the phone back.

'Get some lads looking for him. Show them the picture.'

'Where did you get it from, Boss?'

'It doesn't have to be that picture. Just find one of a Schnauzer and show it to them.' He stormed off before he could swear at Iggy.

'Boss?' Iggy called after him.

He stopped. 'Yeah?'

'Don't forget, Dean's coming later.'

He had forgotten. 'As if I would.'

In his office, he inhaled the aroma of wood polish as he checked when he was expecting Dean. Time was, he didn't need a diary to recall his schedule. It was all in his head. He had three hours. Enough time for a healthy lunch – superfood salad, whatever that was, and raw fish – followed by paperwork.

He logged on to the company accounting site with his usual sense of unease. The idea someone might hack it and take his money haunted him. Even if they couldn't steal it, the thought of anyone else seeing his business gave him colic. He'd always preferred paper, but this was the system his son Milan had set up, so he'd use it for now.

The casino had been closed down for four weeks by that bastard Grimes, despite the efforts of his lawyer, who'd finally got it reopened. That had been just over a month ago. Reopening the sex club remained out of the question. Still, the latest figures should be up. He opened the spreadsheet and fixed his gaze on the bottom line.

He went on staring at it, feeling sick. There must be some mistake. He spent an hour going through all the figures and rang his accountant, who also fronted the casino, and had his name on the licence.

'Jerry, what the hell's going on?'

'You've seen the figures then, Alex?'

'Of course, I've—' He stopped himself swearing and took a deep breath. 'What's going on?'

Jerry hesitated. 'Obviously being closed didn't help.'

Not that excuse again. 'Yeah, but we've been open a month—'

'It takes time to get the business—'

'You said that a month ago. How come the figures are getting worse?'

'We need the girls back, Alex.'

Novak expelled his breath. 'That won't happen in a hurry. The pigs are still on our case.'

'The girls made most of the profit. I can show you the spreadsheets.'

The thought of more spreadsheets made his teeth itch. 'No need. But even without the girls, we should be in profit. Instead, things have got worse.'

'Just this week, Boss.' Jerry sounded flustered. 'It's coming up to Easter. Many people go away.'

Jerry had been with him for a long time, even before the boys were born. Even so, Novak couldn't help thinking the man might be stiffing him. No need to panic yet, but things needed to improve. 'We must do something.'

'What do you suggest?'

'Let me think about it. I'll see you there at nine tomorrow morning.'

'Nine . . . Yeah, sure.'

Jerry never left before three in the morning. A bit of discomfort should help concentrate his mind. He ended the call and shut down the software. Continuing to look at the figures would just give him a headache and piss him off even more.

A call arrived as he prepared his study for the meeting. He checked the number. Not Jerry. But who the hell was it? Few had this number.

'Alex?'

He recognised the voice. Was something wrong? 'Yeah?'

'Someone's been taking your name in vain. A fat bloke in an expensive suit has been throwing his weight around and using your name, trying to make the owner of the factory in Beswick Street sell up.'

He hadn't looked at any buildings there. 'You sure it's Beswick Street?'

'Yes, why?'

'No matter.'

'Someone fired the building, so if your name's linked to it . . .'

'Right, I'll make some enquiries. Thanks for the warning.' He ended the call. Was one of the fat slugs moonlighting? What the hell was he up to? He'd deal with it later. Now he had to get his game face on.

Dean arrived five minutes later and stood in front of his desk while Novak finished studying his leather-bound copy of The Art of War, a present from his eldest son.

'How'd you get on in Birmingham?' His question seemed to catch Dean by surprise.

'Hmm, okay, Boss.'

He looked up and studied his protégé. Was he someone he could promote? 'You going to tell me what you found out?'

'Right, yeah, sorry, Boss. My contact told me he had proof of the McLarens' involvement in the— what happened to Marko and Milan.'

'Milan and Marko.'

'Sorry, Boss?'

'Milan was the eldest.'

'Yeah, right, Milan and Marko.'

'You're saying he didn't show you any proof?'

'Not yet. The snout he had in their team let him down at the last moment.'

'You trust this guy?' It annoyed Novak that Dean was avoiding naming his source, but he could understand why he hadn't.

'Hundred per cent, Boss. He'll definitely have it by the weekend. I can go down—'

'You got a woman down there? You've been three times in the last week.'

'No, Boss.' Dean reddened. 'But why do we need proof? We're sure they did it. It's not like we're going to take them to court.' He laughed.

'We're not certain they did it. Someone you know just claims they did. That's not good enough for me. Understand?'

Dean gazed at the floor. 'Yes, Boss.'

Novak almost felt sorry for him. '"He will win who knows when to fight and when not to fight." Who said that?'

'Was it Sun Tzu?' Dean nodded at the book lying on the desk.

Novak frowned. Did Dean think he'd just read that? 'Very good, Dean. Do you know what it means?'

'Attack your enemy at the right time.'

'Exactly.'

'Didn't he also say, "The worst calamities that befall an army arise from hesitation"?'

Novak gritted his teeth. Did Dean think he feared the McLarens? 'He did, Dean. But he also said, "Victorious warriors win first and then go to war."'

Dean didn't have an answer.

'Right, you can go.'

Dean cleared his throat. 'I've been thinking about the homeless guy with the dog. Why don't we get someone to pretend to be homeless? They're more likely to speak to them than if we go round hassling them.'

'That might not be a bad idea, Dean. You volunteering?'

He swallowed. 'If you want.'

'Okay, start straight away.'

'Right, Boss.' Dean headed for the door.

'"It's better to be feared than loved. You cannot be both." You know who said that?'

Dean paused, hand on the door handle. 'No.'

'Machiavelli.'

Dean closed the door behind him more firmly than needed.

Novak grinned. That would teach him to bandy quotes with his betters. And to suggest he feared the McLarens. When the boys were alive, he'd have waded in, and they'd have dealt with the consequences, but with the crew he had now, he needed to make sure the other families in Birmingham wouldn't get involved. If he had proof the McLarens had killed his sons, he'd get a free pass.

He picked up the book and took it back to the shelf. He couldn't use quotes from Sun Tzu anymore. What a waste of time learning them. He scanned the shelves until he found his copy of The Prince and checked the quote. Bugger, he'd missed out the 'if' after 'loved' in the better-feared-than-loved quote. Still, he preferred his version.

He took the book back to his desk and considered what Dean had said about disguising himself as a down-and-out. Had the guy with the Schnauzer posed as one so he could spy on his boys? He'd known the brother-and-sister private detectives had spied on them, but the pigs told him they'd stopped a week before some scumbags murdered his sons. What if they hadn't really stopped, just switched to using the guy with the dog?

He summoned Iggy. 'The guy with the dog from the detective's office—'

'We've not found him yet.'

'I didn't expect you to have. I want everyone looking for him. Put the word out. Offer a reward. Ten grand should do it.'

'What about the homeless guy with the dog?'

'Dean's looking for him. Get hold of the lads who were talking about him. Show them a picture of that dog and ask them if it's the same one. I'm pretty sure it's the same guy. Keep someone outside the office where you saw him, twenty-four seven. I'm sure he'll be back there.'

'What do they do if they see him?'

'Follow him and find out where he lives.' If those private eyes were involved in his sons' murders, he'd make them pay.

CHAPTER 25

After taking the injured dog to a local vet, the bill being paid for by the charity I'd contacted, Oscar, Jodie and I then visited the building on Pollard Street East, where the uniformed thugs had attacked a group of rough sleepers taking shelter, including Jodie. A five-storey mill set back from the canal and next to a container depot, it looked ripe for redevelopment. Although they'd boarded up the ground-floor windows, an estate agent's sign offering units to let above the main door suggested it wasn't derelict.

As we approached the entrance at the far end, I spoke to Jodie. 'You keep quiet and let me do the talking.'

'Yeah, okay.' She sounded like a sulky teenager.

'I mean it. If I can't trust you, you can stay out here and take care of Oscar.'

I don't need looking after.

'But she does.'

'You talking about me to your dog?'

I ignored her outburst. 'We're meeting someone from the estate agent's. I've told them we're looking for premises for our import-export business. You'll have to be my assistant.'

We reached the main entrance, a pair of scarred and faded blue doors covered in stickers and graffiti. Signs around the doors advertised the businesses of the occupants.

I looked around the frame. 'Can you see a doorbell?'

A young balding man stuck his head round the edge of the building. 'Mr Timothy?'

'That's me.' I'd used my real name, for which I still had a few business cards, just in case he asked.

Jodie gave me a sharp look, and I introduced her as my import manager before she could speak.

He introduced himself with a too-firm handshake and gestured at Oscar. 'He doesn't bite, does he?'

Not unless you really piss me off, and you've made a good start by wearing that offensive aftershave.

'Behave, Oscar.' I addressed the estate agent. 'No, he doesn't.'

He didn't appear convinced. 'We've got several units on the second and third floors. I'll show you.' He produced a bunch of keys and approached the door.

'Ah, but we need something at ground level. We'll be loading and unloading all the time.' The rough sleepers had been in a ground floor unit when they'd faced the attack. 'I was told you had one empty.'

'Errr . . . It's not ready for viewing.'

I gestured at the building. 'We're not expecting the Ritz. If it's cheap and cheerful, we can tidy it up.'

'Security is much better on the upper floors.'

'Okay. I'll contact your office and tell them you had nothing suitable. Come on, Jodie, let's go. We've got other places to see.'

'Okay, okay. I'll show you around. But I warn you, it's not pleasant.'

He returned to the corner of the building and led us down a potholed driveway leading to a spiked fence at the back, his pace signalling annoyance. He stopped at an arched gateway blocked by a pair of enormous doors halfway along the wall.

Oscar pulled up five paces away. ***Sheesh! It's that disgusting stuff Toff stank of.***

'Okay, wait here then.' I unclipped his lead.

Jodie stopped. 'You mean me?'

The estate agent had unlocked a chain securing the gates and waited. 'Are you sure about this?'

With the door unsecured, I could now smell what Oscar had detected. 'Of course.'

He pulled one leaf of the door open, releasing a gust of foul air.

Jodie held a hand to her nose. 'Bloody hell, it's that stuff—'

'You stay here with Oscar, Jodie.'

I'm not taking responsibility for her.

My inspection lasted less than a minute, just until I needed to take another breath. Someone had removed most of the contaminated bedding, but the stench of rotting meat clung to the fabric of the building. Outside, with the door closed, the queasy-looking agent gave a triumphant smirk.

'I warned you.'

'It will be fine.'

'Really?'

'We can use chemical cleaners to get that sorted. Your office said it's only available three to six months. Could we have it longer?'

'I can ask.' The prospect of letting the unit had cheered him up.

'Why is it such a short let?'

He stepped towards me, making me concur with Oscar's assessment of his aftershave. 'Between you and me, I've heard the whole lot is going to be sold and developed. Council have knocked back the owner's planning application twice, but someone's offered to buy it. Nobody will say who, but I reckon they've got someone on the council in their pocket.' He winked.

Things fell into place and, energised by what I'd discovered, I gave him a mobile number, and we watched him drive away. 'We'll call that a day, Jodie. I don't know if Zofia wants you tomorrow. I've got a meeting first thing.'

She walked away, making a call. I waited until she was out of earshot and rang Zofia.

'How are things with Jodie?'

What to say? 'Can we discuss it tomorrow, when I come in?'

'Sounds ominous. I'm assuming from this call that you found out something interesting?'

'Someone has made an offer for Pollard Street East.' I told her what the estate agent had said.

'So, if the buyer suddenly got planning permission, they'd make millions.'

'Exactly, and the fact Robertson was interested in this place and the school suggests he's the one with someone in his pocket.'

Zofia hesitated. 'Unless he's trying to find out who he needs to pay off.'

That made sense. Was he using us to find the names of people he needed to bribe, such as Russ Chopra? Or coerce? 'But why is someone clearing these buildings?'

'That's easy,' she said. 'The council's made a big thing about not allowing buildings to be developed if they're being used by rough sleepers unless the developers provide alternative housing.'

'Right. That makes sense.' My thoughts raced. 'So, whoever is behind the thugs clearing the buildings isn't necessarily the owner. It could be the person buying them to develop them.'

'You mean Robertson?'

I thought back to the mention of Novak at Beswick Street. 'Or someone like him. We'll discuss it tomorrow. I'm meeting John and Craig in the morning.'

I finished the call and returned home.

After an uneventful night, we set off the next morning to see John and Craig. We met them in a small park in Castlefield. They sat on a bench near a statue of three concrete sheep commemorating peace, which I thought ironic. Oscar brightened up on sensing Trixie, who today sported a pink ribbon.

'Morning, Brother, and your faithful hound. What a glorious day.'

Craig just grunted and nodded.

'It's a nice park, but why are we here, John?'

'Did you see the article online claiming Sawney overdosed?'

'What? No.' How had I missed that? Had my friend relapsed and paid with his life?

'The report suggested someone had seen him sneak out to see his dealer, and he came back around two, looking wasted.' John gave me details of the site.

I waited for the story to load. 'But why are we here?'

'Toff told us Ziggy was on door duty. He thinks the reporter must have spoken to him. He's meeting us here.'

I read the article. The tone suggested the author had first-hand experience of what had happened, but the byline, 'Staff writer', told me nothing. Had they been there, or was this an example of the news channel attempting to create an immersive story? They were always using gimmicks to get people to their sites.

I finished reading. 'What do you think?'

John's brow furrowed. 'Like you, I'm pretty sure he was clean, and he seemed determined to stay that way.'

'What if something had occurred to throw him? If something devastating happened, he might have been tempted to relapse.'

'We spent yesterday questioning people who knew Sawney. None had heard of anything like that. We also spoke to most of the people who'd slept at Mill View Academy the night Sawney—'

'Here he is,' Craig announced.

'Ziggy, welcome, Brother.' John stood to greet him.

A man who could have been fifty or sixty, with a thick chest and long arms, approached us. His thinning brown hair fell to his shoulders, and he studied me with pale eyes. Scrapes and bruises discoloured his cheeks and forehead. The redness wasn't entirely due to a beating. A telltale network of broken capillaries, like the skeleton of a desiccated leaf, meandered over his swollen nose.

I stuck out a hand. 'Morning, Ziggy, thanks for coming.'

Before he could take it, Craig stepped in and gave him a huge bear hug, lifting him off his feet before depositing him on the ground. 'Good to see you, Ziggy.'

Oscar and Trixie studied the newcomer, who stood flushed and panting. 'Good to see you as well, Craig.' His expression reflected the bewilderment I felt. I'd never seen Craig so effusive.

I waited until Ziggy seemed recovered. 'I'm trying to find out what happened to Sawney.'

At the mention of my friend, his expression clouded. 'Bad business, what happened to him.'

'We heard you were on the door. What time did you go upstairs?'

'Upstairs?'

'Yeah. Toff said you were on the first floor when the guys in gas masks raided the place. When did you go up there?'

He shrugged. 'I don't remember.'

Craig, who'd been scrutinising him, said, 'It must have been after two. Otherwise, you'd not have seen Sawney coming back from his dealer, "wasted". Isn't that what you told the reporter?'

Ziggy's mouth worked, but no sound came out.

'Nothing to say to us?'

'I don't know what you're getting at, Craig.' His voice rose. 'I never spoke to no reporter.'

'They made it up, then?'

'I came to help some mates, and you treat me like a criminal. You should be ashamed of yourselves.' He stomped off on unsteady legs.

Craig watched him go. 'Lying bastard.' He turned to me and John. 'When you give someone a kicking, most of their injuries are hidden, on the body and limbs. If he'd received a doing on Monday morning, he'd have been in agony when I picked him up.'

'What are you saying?' I looked from Craig to John.

'Those bruises on his face are for show, to throw us off the scent.'

'You think he was working with the guys who raided the place?' I tried to take this information on board.

'He knew they were coming. That's why he hid upstairs. John and I spoke to someone who arrived around one and he wasn't at the door. Nobody was.'

'So why lie about seeing Sawney?'

John replied. 'We're guessing someone paid him to. He seemed to have money since Monday, and he's graduated to branded vodka.'

I considered this information. What did this mean for Sawney's death? Had he been targeted?

CHAPTER 26

'What do we do now, Brother?'

'Good question, John. We need to find the guys who raided Mill View Academy. I want to know who they were working for.'

'That will be the owners, won't it? Craig and I are going to check the other places the men raided, see if there's a link.'

'Not necessarily.' I told them my theory that the people hoping to develop the buildings could be behind the raids. 'But it might be helpful if we check the other places, just to be sure.'

'Okay, we'll carry on and we'll speak to everyone else who was at Mill View that night. Did you have any joy tracing the van that tried to run you down after you rescued that guy?'

'Zofia tried, but with only two letters, it threw up too many. It's probably a fake, anyway. I found a dog which I'm pretty sure belongs to the man. It's at the vet's and I'm going to visit him in hospital and tell him.'

'Good man.' Craig tapped my shoulder, making me stagger.

'How did you get on with Homes for Heroes?'

He grimaced. 'Nothing doing. I found out where their office was and spoke to someone. I got the impression I wasn't welcome. They said maybe in stage two of the project, but couldn't tell me anything about it.'

'Disappointing.'

He shrugged as if he'd expected nothing less.

After agreeing on our next steps, I set off for the office. On Mosley Street near the art gallery, I bumped into Toff, who was with a young man I'd not seen before. Something rang false about him. Although grubby, his clothes looked decent quality, and the muck didn't look natural. Like he'd applied it on purpose.

'Victor,' said Toff, 'this is Dan. He's been on the streets a few days.'

I greeted him, but Oscar wasn't keen.

Dan, however, seemed very interested in Oscar. 'I might get meself a dog,' he proclaimed. 'I need to speak to someone who's been begging with a dog. You must get more money if you have one.'

'Well, Victor will—'

'There's plenty of people on the street with dogs,' I jumped in, giving Toff a warning look. 'Why don't you ask one?' I wasn't ashamed of my time on the streets, but I had a strong sense that I didn't want this Dan to know anything more about me.

'I will do. Thanks, Victor.' Dan gave an ironic salute.

We left them.

He didn't smell right.

'I agree. He reminded me of the thugs we were watching at the casino.'

I'd tell Toff to avoid him next time we spoke. Now, I had to decide what to do with Jodie. She'd almost scuppered my interview with the factory owner. I didn't think it was deliberate, but we didn't need the hassle.

On the other hand, we could help her get off the streets, which was worth a lot to me. Was I allowing her resemblance to Helen sway me? Oscar thought so, but I'd discuss it with Zofia. As I let myself into the office, I realised Jodie might be there. I'd have to play it by ear.

Zofia was on her own, though. She jumped up, offered me a coffee, and disappeared into the kitchen. I sat at my desk and updated the files on the two jobs I'd done yesterday.

'Here you are.' She placed a mug of coffee on my coaster and held the other in both hands. 'Just three sugars now?'

'That's great, thanks. I'm weaning myself off.'

'How did you get on with Jodie?'

I had a responsibility to my employers, but didn't want to jeopardise Jodie's chance to drag herself off the streets. I sipped my coffee. 'She's a bit impetuous, speaks before she thinks.'

'She's not the only one, is she?' Zofia glanced at her brother's desk.

I laughed. 'No, but she should be okay with some supervision.' Is that what I really believed?

'She's young. That's to be expected. You don't mind supervising her sometimes?'

'I'm happy to.' I hoped I'd not regret either my offer or my reticence – Jodie was very much a wildcard – and updated Zofia on what we'd discovered.

'Do you think Novak is the mysterious buyer for the mill?' she asked as she took her mug back to her desk.

'Could be. I imagine it would be a lot of money; it's an enormous site. He's supposedly interested in Beswick Street, which is a stone's throw away. And we know Robertson's interested.'

'They're not the only ones. I did some research on the developers involved in that part of the city. One name stood out. How did Craig get on with Rudy Glass?'

'Not well.' I told her what he'd said. 'Is Glass a developer?'

'Amongst his other interests.'

The door opened and Kasper breezed in.

'Victor. Didn't think you'd be in the office.'

Before I could reply, Zofia said, 'What happened to you?'

'Oh, this?' Kasper held up his left forearm, swathed in a bandage. 'Just a few stitches.'

I waited for him to elaborate, but he obviously wanted us to draw the information out of him. 'What did you do?' I asked.

'I was advising that client who's being plagued by vandals. He was showing me round the site when I stood on a board. It gave way, and I fell forward. Put my arm through a window.'

Zofia covered her mouth. 'Oh, my God!'

'It's okay. Nothing vital damaged, just flesh wounds.' He turned to me and gave a big grin. 'I also found out where your injured security guard went for treatment, Victor.'

'How did you do that?' I'd always found getting information from the NHS impossible.

'I was chatting to the nurse and asked her if they had a burns unit because one of my friends, a security guard, had suffered burnt legs at work. She recognised him and mentioned he's going in this afternoon to get his dressings changed.'

From his bed under the printer, Oscar gave his opinion: ***Do you want a round of applause?***

'Well done, Kasper!'

You're shameless.

'Did you ask her for a name?' Zofia said.

'Couldn't. Not without making her suspicious. I'd already said I knew him.'

'I suppose so, but we might have trouble recognising him.'

Kasper gave another grin. 'That's where Jodie comes in. She'll be able to recognise him. She was there when he got burnt.'

I cast my mind back to Toff and Jodie's description of the events. 'They wore gas masks, didn't they? She won't have seen his face.'

Kasper's exhilaration deflated. 'Well, she might recognise him by his gait. We can ask her.'

Zofia picked up her phone. 'It's worth a shot. I'll ring her.'

'The burns clinic starts at two' – Kasper checked the time – 'so tell her to get here sharpish.'

Zofia finished her call. 'She's on her way. She thinks she can identify him. Are you taking her?'

'I wasn't planning to.' Kasper held up his bandaged arm.

'Can you take her, Victor?' Zofia retrieved her car keys. 'Use my car. It's insured for any employee of the company.'

'Okay.' I wasn't too keen about working with Jodie so soon, but at least we wouldn't be talking to people. 'North Manchester General, was it, Kasper?'

'Wythenshawe. Do you know it?'

'I saw signs for it when you drove me down to Bristol.'

Kasper explained how to get there. Jodie arrived and Zofia briefed her.

I put my jacket on. 'You coming with us, Oscar?'

He lifted his head and opened an eye. ***Is there somewhere to go for a walk?***

'I'm sure there will be, but we won't have time to stop off.'

Forget it then. He lowered his head and went back to sleep.

'Suit yourself.'

Jodie looked from Kasper to Zofia, who both ignored my exchange with Oscar. She shrugged, and I led her out to the car.

'What's with you and the dog?'

'Don't know what you mean.' I checked it was in neutral and started the engine.

'You talk to it all the time.'

'Everyone talks to their dogs.'

'Yeah, but you act like he talks back to you.'

I pulled out onto the main road. 'He does. Can't you hear him?'

She shook her head and muttered something I didn't catch.

Deep in thought, I drove in silence until we reached the edge of Heaton Park.

'I'm sorry about yesterday,' Jodie said out of nowhere.

I hadn't expected an apology. She'd been adamant she'd done nothing wrong. 'You understand why you were out of order?'

'Yeah, you were right. I shouldn't have accused the guy of swindling his insurance.'

'Most people wouldn't have apologised. It shows your maturity and integrity.'

She reddened.

We drove round the M60 until we reached the opposite side of the city. During the journey, I devised a plan of action. I followed the signs and Kasper's directions until we reached the hospital car park. Jodie became more subdued the closer we got to the hospital, and looked despairing as we pulled in. Had she had an unpleasant experience here?

I reversed into a space with a clear view of the main entrance to the burns unit and checked the time. Five past two. We'd have missed his arrival. Now we needed to wait and see him leaving in order to follow him. I paid for two hours and returned to the car.

'What do we do now?' Jodie fidgeted with her seatbelt.

'We wait for him to come out – and then I will speak to him.'

'What you going to say?'

'I'll tell him I'm working for a personal-injury lawyer and heard he'd suffered a work-related injury.'

'What if he tells you to piss off?'

'He might, in which case I'll piss off. But we see how he gets home, and if he's in his own car, we make a note of the number. If he gets a lift, we'll follow.'

'What if they lose you? This car's not that fast.'

'Let me worry about that. You focus on recognising him.'

She didn't respond.

'You do know what he looks like?'

'Yeah, of course,' she said too quickly and glanced away.

Here we go, I thought. Could I ever believe anything she said? 'Only Toff mentioned they wore gas masks.'

'Not all the time.'

I'd been in the room where Jodie had thrown her bottle of flaming vodka and even hours later, it stank. Why would anyone take their masks off in there? 'You sure you saw his face?'

'Of course.' She fidgeted. 'But he might look different in the daylight.'

Convinced she hadn't seen him, I settled down to watch the entrance. Just before three, a large man in tracksuit bottoms came out. His lower legs looked bulky, like they had bandages on.

'Is that him?'

She peered at him. 'I'm not sure.'

I swore in frustration.

'It's not my fault.'

The big man put a phone away in his jacket pocket and limped to the drop-off zone by the corner of the building. I guessed he was waiting for a taxi. I got out and approached. Before I'd gone ten paces, a van-like vehicle appeared and pulled up alongside him. The back door slid open, and he climbed in, wincing as he caught his shin. The sign on the side read Droylsden Shield.

I ran back to the car and started the engine.

'Is it him?' Jodie said.

'He's got burns on his lower legs and a minibus belonging to the people who attacked you picked him up. So, what do you think?'

She pouted.

We reached the car park exit as the van raced past and I pulled out behind it. The driver seemed to think he was on a racing circuit and Zofia's car struggled to keep up. Fortunately, we didn't have far to go. They drove onto a nearby housing estate and the passenger must have said something, because after they'd cleared the first two speed bumps at pace, they slowed.

Cramped-looking pebble-dashed ex-council houses lined the cracked concrete road. Uneven speed bumps and damaged expansion joints added to the discomfort of the ride. They stopped outside a semi-detached house and the side door slid open. I couldn't stop on the narrow lane without looking suspicious and continued round the semi-circular road.

'Check the number and see if he goes in.'

I drove past, keeping my gaze forward, trusting Jodie would do as instructed.

'Seventeen.' She loosened her seatbelt, twisted in her seat, and peered through the headrest. 'Yeah, he's gone in.'

'Great.'

'What we going to do?'

The van, having dropped him off, had now reverted to racing-car speed and filled my rearview mirror.

'We'll find out who he is and call on him.' The driver behind me looked furious, and I feared they'd rumbled me.

Back on the main road, he overtook at the first opportunity, leaving us in a cloud of fumes, but I didn't relax until he'd left us behind and disappeared.

'Are you going to tell them?'

I glanced at her. 'Tell who what?'

'Tell Zofia and Kasper that I didn't recognise him?'

'We've got his address, which is what we wanted.'

'Thanks. I really needed the money for a hostel.' She shook her head bleakly. 'I'm struggling on the street.'

Memories of days when I couldn't face sleeping rough surfaced. I couldn't imagine how much harder it was for a young woman. And I'd had Oscar to keep me company. I still wasn't sure if I was doing the right thing. She'd lied to Zofia, telling her she'd recognise the security guard.

I took her back, and she showed Zofia her phone. 'I took a photo of the car on his drive when we passed. You can read the registration.'

'Great work, Jodie. We'll make a detective of you yet.'

Jodie blushed. 'It was Victor's idea.'

'You won't go far wrong listening to him.'

Kasper mimed being sick and Oscar laughed.

Once Jodie left, Oscar and I set off for home.

'You know, taking the picture of the car was Jodie's idea.'

Why give you the credit?

I'd wondered that. 'Maybe she was thanking me for not dobbing her in. She didn't recognise the security guard, but I spotted him—'

Using your great detective skills.

'You may mock. But I'm becoming a good detective.'

So, you've detected the man following us, have you?

'Where?' I spun round.

Don't do that. Sheesh.

A large SUV sat at the kerb forty paces back, engine running. The driver was alone. A sense of panic seized me, but my mind raced.

'Let's cross the road. We'll cut across the playing fields.' Once we got over there, he couldn't follow, and we'd get away over the railway line.

Oscar followed me without complaint.

I knew the gate onto the playing fields had a barrier across it to stop traffic. I glanced back. The car had followed. I broke into a trot and headed for the gate. To my horror, the barrier lay on one side. Beyond the gate, at the far end of the football pitches, a groundsman loaded a ride-on mower onto a trailer behind his van.

The vehicle following us paused at the gate, and we ran along the edge of the football field. Long before we reached safety, the motor roared. The groundsman stopped to stare at the gate. I checked. The SUV barrelled towards me. I released Oscar's lead, and he ran towards the play area which lay behind a low fence. I followed him. A pile of grass three feet high stood between us and the playground.

Oscar skirted it and soon reached the fence. Behind us, the engine grew louder. The fence lay ten paces away. Oscar barked a warning and ran towards me. I glanced back to see the car bonnet almost on me. Panic gave me strength, but my foot slipped on the grass cuttings, and I fell.

CHAPTER 27

The next morning, Iggy stood in front of Novak's desk wearing a worried look. 'Sorry, Boss, we lost him.'

Novak wasn't sure if anger or resignation dominated in the surge of emotion that roared through him. 'How did that happen?'

'We were fine until he left the main road and went through a park. Then the lad following him got stopped—'

'Don't tell me they followed him through the park in the car.'

'Sorry, Boss. He was worried about leaving the car there. It's a rough area.'

It was definitely anger. 'Why the hell was the lad on his own?'

'I've got the others looking for the homeless man with the dog.'

'Hang on. You had one lad watching the guy with the dog while you had everyone searching for the same bloke?'

'The same bloke? You said the other one was homeless.'

Novak had been thinking about it and was almost sure it was the same man, but to be fair, he hadn't told his men. 'Okay, so tomorrow, have two lads waiting outside, just in case he goes through the park again.'

Iggy stood there, looking like he wanted to say something but unable to bring himself to speak. 'I don't think we'll be able to follow him again.'

'Why?' Yet again, anger gained the upper hand.

'The man realised he was being followed. His dog bit our lad when he crashed the car—'

'He what?'

Iggy explained what had happened. 'He followed them into the playing fields, but some kids had piled grass over a metal bin. He tried to drive through the grass and smashed the car up.'

Novak took a deep breath. 'So, instead of getting the car nicked, he not only wrote it off, but alerted our target?'

Iggy couldn't speak and just nodded.

'Fuck off out of my sight, Iggy.'

Although said in a quiet voice, nobody could mistake the vehemence of his instruction.

Novak stalked to the gym in the basement and after pummelling the heavy bag for half an hour had calmed down enough to deal with this. He had an idea. Still in his suit, he returned to his desk and summoned Iggy.

'Are you certain the dog is a Schnauzer?' Novak wiped his forehead with his jacket sleeve.

'Positive, Boss. The lad got some photos.' Iggy handed his phone over.

Novak studied the images. Several of the man walking with the dog, none showed his face. The last one showed the dog, teeth bared, leaping at the camera. Despite his mood, Novak grinned.

'He got the action shot, then?' He handed the phone back.

Iggy wiped the drops of perspiration off the screen and pocketed it.

'Right,' Novak said. 'I want you to contact the Kennel Club.'

'Is that the new one in Chorlton, Boss?'

'You what?'

'The club. I heard they let punters bring their dogs.'

'Give me strength. The Kennel Club is where owners register their pedigree dogs. Contact them and find out who owns a Schnauzer round here.'

Iggy was back in forty minutes. Novak had showered and changed by then, so was in a better mood.

'Boss, I've been told there's three kinds of Schnauzer.'

'What?' He muttered a curse and punched keys. 'Right, here we are.' He read the descriptions. 'Let's see those photos again?' He studied them and checked the breeders' website. 'Right, it's a standard.'

Iggy left, returning twenty minutes later. 'They wouldn't give me any names, Boss.'

'Of course they wouldn't. What did you ask them?'

'What you said. The names and addresses of people who own a standard Schnauzer.'

'You need to use a bit of finesse, Iggy.'

'Finesse?'

He studied his henchman. Six three and eighteen stone with a battered face and hands like shovels. 'Confucius said, "Never give a sword to a man who can't dance."'

'You what, Boss?'

'Never mind. Finesse isn't your forte, is it? Give me the details and bugger off.'

He emailed using a VPN and throwaway address, explaining he wanted to buy a standard Schnauzer from a breeder in Manchester and asking for contact details. He also made a call and twenty minutes later, had what he wanted. Then he checked the address. Coventry. He had no interest in schlepping all the way down there. Who the hell did he know in Coventry?

Of course. He rang the number. 'Dean, I've got a job for you in Coventry.'

'Sorry, Boss,' Dean whispered, 'I'm on Market Street talking to a homeless guy with a dog.'

'What the—?' Then he remembered. 'Right, finish there, get cleaned up and meet me at the club in Sackville Square in an hour.'

He'd decided to take a more hands-on approach with the club, starting from now. Iggy dropped him off outside the club, where his arrival caused a stir among the front-of-house staff. After ascertaining his manager/accountant, Jerry Sweeny, was in, he let himself into the back and took the stairs up to the first floor, where they had their offices.

A woman he recognised as his son's PA stood and came out from behind her desk in the reception area. 'Mr Novak, we weren't expecting you.'

'Why not? This is my business.'

Her cheeks darkened. 'Of course. I meant we rarely see you . . .'

He racked his brains for her name. 'Karen, is it?'

'Keira. Keira Foley.' She offered a hand. 'I'll let Jerry know you're here.'

'No need, I'll surprise him.' He stepped towards Sweeny's office.

'He's not there.'

'I was told he was in.'

She looked even more embarrassed. 'He's through there.' She indicated Milan's office.

Novak barged through the door.

Sweeny's expression of irritation changed, and he stood. 'Alex, I wasn't expecting you.'

The pictures of Milan with local celebrities had gone from the walls, leaving ghost shadows behind. 'What are you doing in here?'

'Well, the offices were empty. It seemed pointless to waste the—'

'This will be my office. I want Milan's stuff back.' Novak realised Sweeny had a point. They shouldn't leave the boys' offices as shrines. 'You can use Marko's office. Bring his stuff through into here as well.'

'Right, I'll get that done.' Sweeny leant over the desk and closed his laptop.

'Sit down, Jerry. Get it done over the weekend. Right now, I want to discuss our strategy—'

The door opened and Keira Foley stood there. 'Dean to see you, Mr Novak.'

'Right, I'll use Marko's office. And call me Alex.' He followed her outside.

Dean stood by her desk. Instead of his usual sharp suits, he wore grungy jeans, a T-shirt and a hoodie. Even his trainers looked soiled. 'Alright, Boss. I didn't have time to get changed.'

'Through there.' Novak strode to Marko's door and walked in. Unlike Milan's office, this room still carried the tang of his son's aftershave.

Dean followed, bringing a riper odour.

'Sit.' Novak pointed at the visitor's chair and walked round to take his son's throne-like seat. Marko's office still held his trophies, including the signed United and City shirts. He focused on Dean. 'When are you next in Birmingham? You said you could get the proof that the McLarens killed my boys.'

'I've not heard from my contact there, Boss.'

'So why are you going down there?'

'I'm not going—'

'Don't bullshit me. I don't care if you've got a girlfriend down there. Or a boyfriend. Just don't lie to me.'

'Right.' Dean focused on the paperknife with an eagle's claw for a handle lying on the desk. 'Sorry.'

'You can go down this afternoon. There's a guy I want you to meet in Coventry.' Novak pulled out the fat envelope he'd retrieved from his safe and placed it next to the paperknife. 'Give him this and he'll give you a list of everyone in Manchester who owns a standard Schnauzer.'

Dean frowned with incomprehension.

Throw the man a bone. 'That's the dog we're looking for.'

'Oh, right.'

Novak repeated to him the arrangement he'd made with the man from the Kennel Club. 'This undercover work you're doing. Have you found anything?'

'Not yet, but it's still early days.' Dean picked up the envelope. 'Do you want me to carry on with that after I've delivered this?'

Novak considered. There was no guarantee the man he wanted would be on the list he was buying, and Dean had tried to lie to him. 'Yeah, at least for a few days.'

'Right.' This news had hit him with satisfying force, Novak observed, as Dean stood, placing the thousand pounds in the front pocket of his hoodie. Despite it being his suggestion, he was clearly having second thoughts.

'Alternatively,' Novak added, 'if you get your contact to give you the proof, you won't need to find this tramp.'

'Okay.' Dean didn't seem too confident.

'Your contact has got the bloody proof, hasn't he?'

'He said so.'

'Right, chase him up. Put some pressure on him.'

Novak left him there stinking up that office and rejoined Sweeny in the other, where he was just finishing a call. His expression suggested he wasn't liking what he was hearing. 'Yeah, okay, you do that.'

Novak took a seat in front of the desk. 'Trouble?'

'One of the guys on the door tonight. He's booked in sick. Someone was waiting for him last night and used him to practise their baseball swings.'

'Disgruntled punter he'd thrown out? Or someone whose missus he's been shagging?'

Sweeny let out a long breath. 'Normally, I'd agree. But he's the second one today. The other's still in hospital.'

That didn't sound good. 'They involved in something they shouldn't be?'

'I don't think so. They're not particularly tight. They get on okay, but one's a young lad and the other's been around for years. Never had trouble.'

'Give me their names and I'll look into it.' He'd run their names past a few people, just in case they were freelancing and had stepped on someone else's toes.

Sweeny still looked troubled.

'What is it?'

'Two others rang saying they're not coming in.'

'What, tonight?'

Sweeny shook his head. 'Ever. I think someone's warned them off.'

Novak clenched his fists. Whoever was behind this was going to regret crossing him.

CHAPTER 28

I carried my takeaway coffee to one of the concrete benches overlooking the New Islington Marina and made a call. 'Zofia, it's Victor. I'm not coming in today—'

'Are you okay?' The concern in her voice filled me with warmth.

'Yeah, but someone followed me from the office last night. I think they're watching it.'

'Who are they?' Panic infused her voice.

'I saw him working at Novak's club.'

'Novak? Why would his men be watching us?'

I'd been thinking about it through the night. 'They're watching me. There was a car parked outside when Novak came visiting and I hid in the toilet. I'm sure his driver saw me and Oscar when we left.'

I knew it would be my fault.

'Okay. Give me a minute.' She turned away and spoke to Kasper, but I couldn't pick up the conversation. 'I'm going to put you on speaker.'

'Victor?' Kasper's voice echoed. 'What car was your tail in? I'll nip to the newsagent's for milk and see if he's outside.'

'It won't be the same guy. He crashed his car and Oscar bit him.'

They both laughed. Zofia controlled herself first. 'Where?'

'Where did he crash or where did he bite him?'

'Both.'

I told them about fleeing to the playground and the grass-covered bin. 'He got out and Oscar went for him.'

'Brave boy. Well done, Oscar.'

His ears pricked up. ***At least* they *appreciate me.***

'It wasn't very bright. He could have killed you if he'd had a gun.'

I knew he didn't, though.

'He had a gun?' Kasper said.

'No, sorry. I was . . . It doesn't matter. He actually fell out of the car. He'd taken his seatbelt off and smashed his head on the windscreen. Oscar bit him while he was on his knees.'

'Oh.'

Not content with suggesting I'm an idiot, you diminish my bravery again. You can't stand me getting any praise.

'I was worried about you. That's why I called you an idiot.'

Zofia cleared her throat. 'Is Oscar with you?'

'Yes, sorry.' I had to remember not to talk to him when people were listening, even Zofia and Kasper.

'Another thing. Have you registered with a doctor and dentist yet?'

'No.' Zofia had been on at me to do it, but I was okay and didn't need either.

'I told you to do it while you've got an address. Do it now if you can't come in to work.'

'I was going to follow up the security guard we tracked down yesterday.' I told her what I wanted her to do.

'Do you want to borrow my car?' Zofia offered.

'I can't collect it in case they're watching the office.'

'Shall I meet you at the café on Great Bridgewater Street?'

'Give me twenty-five minutes to get there.'

'I'll need two hours to do what you asked me. Why don't you register with a GP now?'

Feeling she'd railroaded me, I agreed and ended the call.

'Come on, Oscar, let's find a doctor who'll take me on.'

Are you ill? He licked my hand.

'Not yet, but I need to find one before I am ill.'

What about the place you took that Airedale?

'You have to pay, and they don't take humans.'

That makes sense. They'd just take up all the attention by making a fuss.

He wasn't wrong.

I'd looked up the nearest GP practice soon after moving in, at Zofia's urging. I led Oscar there, left him outside and approached the receptionist.

'Can I register with a GP?' I produced the dog-eared card with my NHS number on it.

'Address?'

I gave it to her.

Her manner became colder. 'That's temporary accommodation.'

'I am aware of that. I'll give you the new address if I move.'

She returned her attention to her screen. 'None of the doctors do house calls there.'

'I'll bear that in mind.' I didn't blame them; they had a good chance of getting mugged for the contents of their medical bags.

'Name?'

I gave her the details she wanted. 'Do you know of any NHS dentists nearby?'

She laughed, then stopped. 'You're serious?'

'Why wouldn't I be?'

'Check online.'

I'd do it later, after meeting Zofia.

We arrived outside Canada House but didn't see her car. 'Do you want to explore those trees?' I pointed out the stunted specimens around the small car park.

My phone had pinged while I'd been walking, and I checked the messages while Oscar watered a few trunks. Zofia telling me she'd done everything I'd asked, as if I'd doubted her.

Oscar rejoined me as Zofia's car arrived. She had a passenger and my heart sank.

'Hi Victor. Hello, Oscar. I've brought Jodie.'

Do you think we've gone blind or forgotten her already?

'Don't be rude, Oscar.' I nodded at Jodie. 'Morning. Is Zofia showing you the ropes?'

Zofia frowned. 'I thought she could go with you—'

'Why?'

'You can show her the ropes.'

Whoopee!

Zofia studied Oscar. 'What's up with you, Oscar?'

'He's fine, just been worried about the little Airedale we took to the vet.'

No, I haven't. I've not even thought of him.

'Ahhh.' She ruffled his ears. 'You are soppy.'

'You said you'd tracked down his owner?' I'd been working on the assumption he belonged to the man we'd rescued. Why else was the dog hanging about the building we'd found the man in?

'He's at Wythenshawe, in the burns unit.'

'Great, thanks.' She must have spoken to Sergeant Bowling. 'And the security guard?' I wanted to know who he was working for when Jodie burned him.

'The security guard, Daniel Leonov, is going to meet you in a pub near his house at two.' She produced an envelope from her bag. 'I've created a questionnaire on the lines we discussed. It looks more professional and means we miss nothing.'

'Great idea, thanks.' I took it from her. 'I'll visit the hospital first. If you give me the keys, I'll get going.'

'Oh, you not having a coffee?' Zofia pointed at the café. 'My treat.'

I'd have liked nothing better, but with Jodie in tow, it didn't appeal. 'We'd better get on.' I felt bad on seeing her disappointment. 'Some other time?'

'Sure. See you later.' She handed me the car keys.

As we drove away, Jodie said, 'I know you don't like me—'

'It's nothing to do with liking you. I'm going to see the guy you set fire to. How do you think he'll react if he sees you?'

'Oh. I didn't think.'

I parked in the same place at the hospital. 'You stay here. I'm going to visit the guy whose dog we found. I won't be long.'

Don't mind me. I'll just doze on this back seat.

'I'll leave the windows cracked open.'

No doubt they'll take that into consideration when I'm found suffering from heatstroke.

'Jodie, can you take Oscar for a walk? You can take him down there.' I pointed to the south of the hospital. 'There's a bit of greenery.'

'What if he does a . . .' She shuddered and made a face.

'He won't. He's already been this morning.' I addressed Oscar. 'Will you?'

I'm just allowed the one movement a day, am I?

'Yes.' I got out.

'You going to give me the key,' Jodie asked, 'or shall I leave the car unlocked?'

I hadn't considered that. 'Stay in sight of the car.' I slammed the door and made my way to the hospital.

I found the man we'd rescued in the four-bed burns ward. He confirmed that Toby, the Airedale, was his. I questioned him about what had happened, and he told me what he told the police. Two men had followed him and beaten him unconscious. He hadn't seen either, and didn't even know there was anyone upstairs. The woman who died seemed to have been 'collateral damage'. I gave him the details of where I'd taken Toby and returned to the car, deep in thought.

Once I'd discovered the Airedale, I'd checked the details of the homeless men killed in the weeks I'd been off the streets. At least one had a dog. Was it a coincidence, or was someone hunting homeless men with dogs?

The atmosphere in the vehicle reminded me of long car journeys with my family when my daughters had fallen out about something and were refusing to talk to each other.

'You two been playing nice?'

Neither answered, and I punched the address of the pub we were going to into the satnav. The journey took three minutes, during which I again reminded Jodie to stay out of sight.

'Yes, I'm not stupid.'

No, but you are reckless.

I parked in the far corner of the potholed car park. The one other car in the lot sat alongside the pub in a disabled parking space. The newish two-storey building looked in need of a coat of paint. A flagged terrace with warped wooden furniture on it occupied the width of the building. A few faded parasols tried in vain to bring a touch of cheer to the premises.

'I won't be long.'

You leaving me with her again?

'It's a smelly pub. You won't like it.'

You could at least give me the opportunity to experience it.

'Maybe next time.' I ignored Jodie's incredulous gaze and made my way to the pub.

The combined odours of spilt alcohol and burnt cooking oil rolled over me as I pushed the doors open. My eyes took a few moments to become accustomed to the gloom. I saw Leonov almost straight away, but ignored him and bought myself a sparkling water, earning a scowl from the barman. I made a point of checking out the other drinkers. Leonov was the only one on his own.

I made my way over and nodded at his almost full pint. 'Can I get you another?'

'You the ambulance chaser?'

I gave him the name Zofia had chosen for me.

He picked up his glass. 'Lager.' Then gulped half of it down.

The barman's scowl eased as I gave the order. Leonov had finished his first pint by the time I returned. He wore the same tracksuit he'd had on yesterday when I'd watched him leave the burns unit and his body odour embraced him. I took care to avoid his legs and eased myself into the seat opposite.

'Your secretary said you worked for solicitors who can get me compensation.'

We'd concocted a cover story, and I'd memorised the name of a real firm of solicitors in case I had to convince him of my veracity. 'Sort of. I work for myself, but I get commission from solicitors if I refer people to them.'

'And where does the money for the commission come from?'

'The solicitor. You don't have to pay me anything.'

He took another sip. 'Yeah, but the money you get comes out of my compensation.'

'Yes, ultimately.'

'So, what's stopping me from referring myself to the solicitor and keeping the commission?' He produced a leaflet and placed it on the table.

'Nothing. Except you don't know who they are. The ones I work for take a smaller cut and get a better deal for their clients than these cowboys.' I tapped the leaflet.

'Okay. So, what do you want to know?'

'Who you were working for. Details of your employment contract. What protective equipment they'd provided. We have a form.' I retrieved the envelope Zofia gave me and a pen and passed them over.

He peered at the form in the gloom, his lips moving as he read. 'Some of this stuff's confidential.'

'Everything you tell me is confidential.'

He didn't look convinced.

'We need that information. It's the only way we can work.'

He hesitated, then cleared a space on the table before filling it in with childish letters he formed while sticking his tongue out of the corner of his mouth. I waited for him to complete the form, impatient to get away. He took a swig of his beer, studied the form and slid it across to me. He'd filled out all the parts.

'Do you know who your company was working for?'

'They don't tell me that. Anyway, why do you need to know? I'll be suing my employer, won't I?'

'Yes, but if we find out who they were working for, we can get a bigger claim.'

He considered this. 'I can find out if you want.'

He pulled his phone out of his pocket. It rang before he could dial anyone. He frowned and read the name on the screen, then took the call and looked at me. 'Can you give me a minute?'

'Sure.' I stood, sliding the completed form off the table. 'Another?' I pointed at his almost empty glass.

'Yeah, sure.' He pressed the mobile to his ear.

I folded the form and returned it to my pocket as I approached the bar. 'Another lager, please.'

I got the impression Leonov was talking about me and a sudden urge to get out of there seized me. Only the thought he might give us the name of the people behind the attacks on the homeless kept me there. He put his phone down and I took his drink to him.

'Cheers.' He saluted me with the glass. 'That's me mate who's picking me up. He said he can find out what you want and tell you when he picks me up.'

'Oh, right.' I didn't fancy waiting here making small talk. I was also conscious that I'd left Jodie and Oscar outside. 'Will he be long?'

'Nah.' He swallowed a deep draught.

I drained my glass and waited for him to finish. Eventually, his phone pinged. Without checking it, he stood and pulled on a jacket. I set off for the front door.

'This way.' He pointed in the opposite direction. 'He can get the car closer.'

I hesitated, but he was in no condition to offer a threat, was he?

He sensed my reluctance. 'You can help me into the car. Me mate's not too steady on his pins. If you're there, he won't need to get in and out.'

That could explain why he drove like a maniac, to compensate. I followed him as he made his slow way to the back of the pub. We passed the toilets, perfumed with stale urine and bleach, and followed an exit sign through an internal door. Crates of bottles stood in the short corridor beyond, which ended in a fire exit with a push bar. We reached the door, and he stood aside.

'You push it. I don't want to risk . . .' He pointed at his bandaged shins.

The smell of his beery breath enveloped me as I passed him. I pushed the bar, and the door burst open. A shove in my back sent me sprawling into a large metal bin. My head smashed into the side of it with a clang. Lights flashed before my eyes and the stink of rotting refuse filled my nostrils.

A boot connected with my ribs, emptying my lungs. My last thought in a sea of pain was his mate had attacked me. Leonov was wearing trainers. Then, my attacker half carried, half dragged me across concrete and dropped me. Before I could gather my wits, a vehicle door slid open, and he bundled me into it. My head hit a metal tube, sending shards of pain down my spine.

The door slammed shut behind me and someone jumped into the driver's seat. I had to get out. I attempted to lift myself off the floor, but my limbs wouldn't work. The engine roared to life.

CHAPTER 29

Jodie glanced into the back of the car, from where Oscar studied her. She could swear he knew what she was thinking. And Victor was certainly talking and listening to him. Could dogs talk? Of course they couldn't.

'You don't like me, do you?'

His lips lifted in what looked remarkably like a sneer.

'The feeling's mutual.' She returned her attention to the pub and retrieved her phone. She'd caught up with her correspondence outside the hospital, but emails had arrived since. Including one from Colin.

> Time's almost up. What the hell are we paying you for? If you've got nothing for me by five, you're back in the office.

She checked the time. Half two. She pulled up his number and her finger hovered over the call button. She peered into the back seat and hesitated. A pair of intelligent eyes appraised her. Although sure dogs couldn't talk, she half believed this one could at least understand whatever he heard. She left the car and waited until she was ten paces away before making the call.

'She lives. You got my email then?' Colin's smug voice set her teeth on edge.

'You can't pull me out. I'm just about to make a breakthrough.'

'Oh yeah? You found deep throat then?'

Dirty bastard. 'I can get you done for sexual harassment, you know.'

'What?' He paused. 'Deep Throat is the source Woodward and Bernstein found.'

What the hell is he talking about? 'Who?'

'Even you must have heard about Nixon and Watergate.'

She remembered something about it from a lecture at college. 'Of course.'

'Yeah, of course you have. So, what you got for me?'

'I'm speaking to one of the security guards involved in Monday's raid. He's going to tell me who they're working for, what happened during the raid, including what happened to the man who died.'

Colin didn't respond for a long moment and instead of congratulating her, he just said, 'Why?'

'What d'you mean? It's what you asked me to—'

'Why's he talking to you? You haven't offered him money, have you? There's no budget—'

'Don't panic, Colin. I told him I'm working for a solicitor dealing with injury claims.' If it was good enough for Victor . . . 'One of the homeless people set fire to his trousers and—'

Newsome's laughter cut her off. 'Nice one. Make sure you get all the juicy stuff. Email it to me tonight.' He ended the call before she had a chance to respond.

'Up yours, you smug git.' A minibus drove into the car park, passing within ten metres, and the driver gave her a long look. 'And what are you looking at, you pervert?'

Then her insides dropped. She recognised him. The security guard she'd slashed with the broken glass. And he recognised her.

She ran back to the car and stopped. She didn't have the key. If he came for her, she'd be a sitting duck. She glanced back at him. He remained in the minibus. On the phone. Was he ringing for reinforcements?

Or calling Leonov, his friend inside with Victor.

She ran towards the main road, but after a few paces stopped. He must have realised she was with Victor. Which meant he was in danger.

And now the minibus had gone.

She ran back to the pub and pushed her way into the bar. Her eyesight adjusted to the gloom. The few customers had stopped what they were doing and were studying her.

A bulky barman, his stained shirt straining to contain his gut and too-tight belt cutting into it, stood with a hand on a pump.

'Has my dad been in? Average height' – she held a hand above her head – 'thin with brown hair and hazel eyes?'

He glanced towards the toilets, but shook his head. 'Not seen him.'

Bloody liar. She ran towards the men's toilets.

'Oi! That's private.'

She heard the bar hatch slam, but he'd never catch her. Past the toilets stood a door, and she burst through it. A breeze came from an opening at the end of a short corridor. She snatched up two bottles as she passed a crate of spirits. Outside, the minibus idled. Leonov was clambering into the passenger seat.

Where the hell was Victor? 'Oi, stop!'

She threw the bottle in her right hand at Leonov. He ducked, and it flew into the cab and struck the driver, who yelled in pain or surprise. Then it smashed as it struck something more solid.

Leonov had exited the cab and was advancing, hands outstretched towards her. He was twice her size. She swung the other bottle towards him, and he swayed backwards. She ducked under his swinging arms and kicked his bandaged shin.

'FUUUCCK!' He fell to the concrete, writhing.

She ran round him to the front of the minibus, transferring the bottle to her right hand. By the time she reached the driver's door, he'd opened it and climbed out. Instead of confronting her, he had his back to her and was doing something to his seat. Not questioning her good fortune, she smashed the bottle over his head. He slumped to a sitting position on the step of the vehicle with a groan.

The stench of alcohol filled the air. He shook his head and tried to stand. She held the neck of the broken bottle and jabbed it towards his face. His dazed eyes had difficulty focusing on the razor-sharp shards.

'Where's Victor?'

He didn't respond.

'Where is he?' She thrust the bottle at his face, stopping centimetres away.

'He's in the back.' Blood flowed from a wound on the crown of his cropped head and another on his forehead where the first bottle must have hit him.

She looked up, then registered what he'd been doing. He was trying to extinguish a fire. The blue flame licking his seat reached the fumes from the bottle she'd broken over his head. A ball of flame exploded out of the cab. She leapt back, but it engulfed the driver, who screamed and rolled towards her onto the concrete.

She evaded him as Leonov staggered round the front of the minibus, murder in his eyes. He saw his mate and went to his aid. Jodie ran around the back to the other side but the barman had come out and made a grab for her. She still had the broken bottle in her hand, and he moved back from her with surprising speed.

'Call the fire brigade.'

He stared at her, then she pointed at the flame-filled cab.

His mouth formed an O, and he lumbered away.

She ran to the side door and grabbed the handle. It didn't move. She dropped the bottle and used two hands. It stayed shut. In her frustration, she banged on the window. Through the smoke, she saw Victor, panicking as he struggled with the locked door.

CHAPTER 30

Zofia walked along Portland Street towards the bus stop in Piccadilly Gardens, memories she wanted to forget swirling around. Ever since Victor had mentioned seeing the man with a snake tattoo, Zofia's thoughts had been drawn powerfully back to the last time she'd seen someone with the same markings. Nightmares had disturbed her sleep, and the memories of that night kept intruding. Although Victim Support had offered counselling, she'd avoided it. Her fear that the truth would come out had trumped her belief that therapy would have helped her.

She needed to know what had happened to her tormentor and if he was still alive. Dark clouds threatened and a chill wind blew across the gardens, leaving the area almost deserted. She found an empty bench and retrieved her phone. She'd saved the number for Sergeant Bowling and had punched it more than once, but cut it off before it connected.

This time, she let it ring. 'Colette, it's Zofia. Can you speak?'

'Hmmm . . . Give me a moment.' Bowling spoke to someone she was with, and her footsteps sounded on a hard floor. A door slammed shut and her phone swished against clothing. 'Right, I'm alone. What is it?'

'One of the men who attacked me had a red snake tattoo on his neck. Can you tell me if he survived?'

'Why are you asking?'

'I . . . I think I saw him. He might be stalking me.'

'Okay, I can put your mind at rest. He is not stalking you. Not unless he's doing it from beyond the grave.'

Zofia gave an exaggerated sigh of relief. 'So, they did shoot him.'

Bowling cleared her throat. 'I shouldn't tell you this, although it will come out at the inquest. The others were all shot, but he died of a brain injury. Someone smashed him on the back of the head.'

'Oh, my God!' She didn't need to exaggerate this reaction.

'It looked like someone hit him at least twice. Either blow could have been fatal.'

Zofia's throat closed up and her mouth dried. She managed to thank Bowling before ending the call, then sat, shaking. She, or her brother, probably both, had killed a man.

The wind cut through her, and she shivered, pulling her coat tighter. The sky had grown darker, matching her mood. How long had she been sitting there? Two elderly women with shopping trolleys studied her from a nearby path. Sympathy and curiosity in their expressions. She gave them a smile and stood, walking to the bus stop on unsteady legs.

She checked some details on her phone while she waited for the bus and spent the journey reconciling her thoughts. Uppermost in her mind, how to tell Kasper. But why did she need to tell him? Of course she didn't.

She pushed what she'd learnt to the back of her mind and arrived at the office an hour after leaving Victor. Although he'd introduced Jodie to them, he seemed to have turned against her. Zofia hadn't been too keen on her at first, but the more she spoke to the young woman, the more inclined she was to help her.

She got off the bus and approached the office, her steps growing heavier as she got closer. 'Come on, Zofia, forget about it and get on with the rest of your life. You can't change what's happened.'

A woman in a hijab gave her a startled look, and Zofia responded with a smile. She let herself in, hoping her brother was out so she could bury herself in her work. The lack of an alarm and his cheery greeting as she entered the office told her she was out of luck. She removed her coat and hung it up. The fact he already had a drink and she couldn't face one, scuppered her idea of escaping to the kitchen. She hid herself behind her screen.

Kasper wouldn't let her. 'How did it go with Victor?'

'He didn't like that I'd brought Jodie.'

'Hmmm. Do you think he feels threatened because we've taken her on?'

Her brother's analysis surprised her. 'We're only using her part time. He's a valued member of staff with skills she hasn't got.'

'I just meant, we took him off the streets and now he's no longer our only . . . You know.'

'He's not like that. Don't forget, he brought her here. No, it's something else. I think she may have done something silly which pissed him off. He hinted at something.'

'Something which adversely affected KZD?' Kasper drained his mug. 'If she's done something which damages our reputation, Victor should tell us.'

'I'm sure he would. I suspect it's something minor but rash. She seems a bit . . . enthusiastic.'

'I'll have a word with him. Find out what happened.'

She wanted to tell him to leave it, but it would only start an argument, one she couldn't face now. She opened a spreadsheet and lost herself in her work until a shadow fell across her desk.

'What's up?' Kasper's expression radiated sympathy.

'Nothing, why?' A tear splashed on her keyboard, joining others already gathered there, and she brushed at her eyes with the back of her hand.

'Oh, Zofia.' He held out his arms.

'No, please.' She stopped him with her hands, retrieved a box of tissues from her bottom drawer and dried her eyes.

Kasper watched her patiently.

She took a shuddering breath. 'I spoke to Colette earlier.'

'The policewoman?'

'She said nobody survived in the unit on Riverpark Road—'

'Yeah, I told you Victor's junkie mate was hallucinating.'

'Possibly, but the guy upstairs hadn't been shot. He died from his head injuries.'

Kasper's complexion paled. 'I killed him!'

'Or me. She said either blow could have been fatal.'

'Yeah, but he was still alive after you hit him. It must have been me.'

'I looked it up. If my blow caused a bleed on his brain, he could have survived for a few hours before dying.'

'But the medics would have got to him soon after we left.'

Tears welled up in Zofia's eyes. 'But if they couldn't stop the bleeding . . .'

'I'm not letting you blame yourself. At the very least, my blow made things a lot worse. And let's not forget, he was trying to kill you.'

She stood and let him hold her. Her tears overflowed, and she buried her head into her brother's shoulder. When she could speak again, she said, 'I know, but taking someone's life . . .'

They stood together, not speaking for a long moment.

Kasper broke away. 'You want a coffee?'

She forced a smile. 'That's your remedy for everything.'

'Can't hurt, can it?'

He disappeared into the kitchen and Zofia visited the toilet to check her reflection and repair the damage. By the time he returned with two steaming mugs, struggling to hold both with his uninjured hand, she felt almost normal. She sat at her desktop, and he placed one mug in front of her.

Over the next few hours, she focused enough to get through the work she had to do. As she retrieved some printing, she glanced out of the window. Her car pulled into the car park. Victor and Jodie must be back, but the driver was alone. He must have dropped her somewhere. The driver's door opened and instead of Victor, Bowling got out. With her was Oscar, looking forlorn.

Her pulse racing, she ran out, ignoring Kasper's questions, and charged down the stairs. She met Bowling on the pavement.

'Where's Victor?'

'I'm sorry, Zofia. He's been injured.'

CHAPTER 31

Another coughing fit seized me and I drank water from the pint glass a firefighter had brought me.

'Do you want some more oxygen?' She held out the face mask.

'Thanks.' I inhaled the gas.

Behind her, the rest of her crew cleaned and made up their equipment. The burnt-out remains of the minibus steamed. The plastic lid of the metal bin I'd bashed my head on sagged and the paint on its side nearest the vehicle had blistered. A breeze wafted the stench of burnt plastic towards me.

'Well, well, if it's not our favourite private eye, Mr Timothy.'

My heart sank, and I removed the mask. 'Afternoon, Chief Inspector.' I was pleased to see Sergeant Bowling with him and smiled a greeting to her.

'Do you need to see the paramedics?' She gestured towards the ambulance where my two would-be kidnappers were being treated.

'I just inhaled some smoke.' I handed the mask back to the firefighter.

'Don't ignore the concussion.' The firefighter addressed the two detectives. 'He's got two new bumps on his head, and he confirmed he'd lost consciousness. It looks like he's had previous blows to the head.' She pointed to the bruise from the thug who'd hit me outside the factory on fire. 'He should spend the night in hospital.'

I gestured at Oscar. 'They won't take Oscar.'

'I can sort something out,' Bowling offered. 'He's got a few fans back at the station—'

'We're not here to look after dogs,' Grimes huffed. 'We're here to solve crimes.'

You should set more realistic goals, Grimes.

I spluttered a laugh.

'Something funny?' Grimes glared at me.

I touched the bump on the top of my head. 'I expect it's the concussion making me hysterical.'

He gave me a searching look. 'Right. If you're not fit to be questioned, I'll get you admitted to hospital and your mutt can spend the night in the dogcatcher's kennels.'

'Do we still have dogcatchers?' Bowling said.

Oscar looked nervous.

'I'll be fine to answer a few questions.'

Grimes pointed to a table in the far corner of the terrace. 'We'll sit there.' He nodded to his sergeant. 'Record his statement and make sure he repeats the claim that he's fit to have us question him.'

Bowling gestured for me to go ahead and I led the way to the table, sitting on one side while they occupied the seats opposite. The cold slats chilled my backside. Oscar settled on the grass two paces away and lay his head on his paws, although he kept a wary eye on Grimes.

Bowling produced her phone. 'Do you agree to me recording you, Victor?'

'Sure, I've nothing to hide.' I was the victim here.

'I'm going to caution you—'

'Caution me? Why?'

'You may have not noticed' – Grimes gestured at thc ambulance – 'but two men are being treated for burns.'

'One.'

'You what?'

'One of them had already suffered burns. They're being dressed again because he—' I realised I'd drop Jodie in it if I mentioned her. She'd run off after rescuing me and I owed her my life. 'Because someone kicked his injured leg.'

'And I wonder who that was?'

'Not me. I was in the back of their minibus.'

Bowling held out her phone. 'Shall I cover this when we're recording him, Boss?'

'Go ahead, Sergeant.'

Bowling pressed record and went through the introductions, including the caution. I realised I could incriminate myself if I wasn't careful.

'What were you doing here?' Bowling gave the name of the pub.

'I'd arranged to meet Daniel Leonov. He's the guy with the existing burns.'

'For what purpose?'

I had to be careful how much I told her and Grimes. 'I had reason to believe he was involved in the raid on Mill View Academy.'

Grimes butted in. 'Where we found the dead man?'

'How did he die?'

Bowling replied, 'It looked like an overdose, but we—'

'We don't share information with civilians, Sergeant.'

'I don't believe it. The guy was clean and had been going to rehab for weeks.'

Grimes turned his glare on me. 'When we want a character reference, or a eulogy, we'll ask you. Now, how did you discover Leonov's involvement in the raid?'

I refused to believe the idea that Sawney had relapsed. Someone had murdered him and I would prove it. My mind raced, but I had to forget about him for now and focus on answering their questions. Or not answering them, as the case may be: 'I can't remember.'

Grimes's face reddened. 'You understand what "obstructing the police" means?'

My heart was thumping so hard, I feared they could see it. 'I'm not obstructing you. You're just pissed off that I discovered something you didn't.'

'Shall we park how Victor, Mr Timothy, came by the information, Boss?'

Grimes grunted.

'Can you talk me through what you did, starting with your arrival at the pub?'

I recounted the events until Leonov bundled me out of the pub. 'I must have passed out when I hit the dumpster and the next thing I knew, someone had locked me in the back of the minibus and it was on fire.'

'And you've no idea how it caught fire?'

'I told you, I was unconscious.' I reached for the bump on my head.

'How did you get out of the vehicle?'

How to tell of my escape without mentioning Jodie? I closed my eyes and took a deep breath, buying myself time to think, but it wasn't all an act as my head spun. I sipped some more of the water.

Bowling leant forward. 'Are you okay to continue, Victor?'

'Mr Timothy has already said he's okay, haven't you?'

Grimes waited for me to reply, but I took another sip.

'Do you want me to repeat the question?'

'Yes, please.'

Scowling, he did.

'Someone, I didn't see who, threw a brick through the side window and I managed to scramble out.'

Grimes leant forward. 'You don't know who saved your life?'

'Sorry, no.'

'I find that hard to believe.'

'I don't care if you do.'

The redness on Grimes's cheeks moved along the spectrum towards purple. Why was I antagonising him? The man terrified me.

The firefighter returned, saving me from his immediate wrath. 'Have you given your dog some water yet?'

Oh, please. I'm dying of thirst here.

'Don't be so dramatic, Oscar.'

She frowned at me. 'I didn't want to say anything while I was treating you, but you shouldn't leave dogs alone in locked cars.'

'I didn't. He was with—'

Even enraged, Grimes didn't miss my slip. 'He was with whom?'

'I didn't lock him in, I meant to say, and anyway, I didn't think I'd be long. Who expects to be kidnapped from a pub in Wythenshawe?'

The firefighter disappeared into the pub.

'Sergeant, make a note that Mr Timothy abandoned his dog in a sealed car.'

Bowling frowned at her DCI. 'As he said, Boss, he couldn't have anticipated being kidnapped.'

Grimes let it slide. 'Why did these men seize you?'

'You'll have to ask them.'

'Don't worry, I will. You haven't explained why Mr Leonov agreed to meet you.'

How much was I safe to say? Was impersonating an ambulance-chaser a crime? 'I told him I could help him get compensation for his injuries.'

'How were you going to do that?'

'Put him in touch with a criminal injuries lawyer.'

'Which one?'

I swallowed. 'I hadn't decided yet.'

Grimes gave a sceptical sneer. 'I'm sure you hadn't. Was that why he attacked you, because he realised you were bullshitting him?'

My cheeks grew warm, but I bit my tongue. The firefighter placed a Tupperware container half full of water in front of Oscar, who fell on it like he'd crossed a desert. I nodded a thanks to the firefighter.

'It seems excessive for Leonov to have kidnapped him, Boss.'

Grimes glared at her, then took a deep breath. 'Let's park that until we speak to the two men.' He nodded towards the ambulance, then fastened his gaze on me. 'In the meantime, don't take any trips for the foreseeable. Let's wrap this up, Sergeant.'

Bowling ended the recording, and they both left me and strode towards the ambulance.

'Come on, Oscar.' I stood.

The ground swayed, and I held on to the table.

You okay?

'I will be. Let me get my breath.' Intense pain radiated from the wound in my head.

Maybe you should go to hospital.

'Don't fuss. I'll be fine.' I slumped back into the seat.

What will you do about Jodie?

'What do you mean?'

She attacked those two men.

'Only to save me.' Although why had Leonov attacked me to begin with? 'Did Jodie get out of the car while you were waiting?'

I couldn't possibly comment.

'The other guy must have seen her when she set fire to Leonov and recognised her. Stupid girl. I'd better ring her.' I reached for my phone.

Are you going to warn her the police want her?

'What? Why would they want her?'

Didn't the nice policewoman say someone had murdered your friend Sawney?

'She said he'd overdosed.'

She said, it looks like an overdose and Grimes stopped her saying what they think. I knew you weren't listening.

'I've been hit over the head.' I placed a hand on my bump. He was right. 'Anyway, why would they want to speak to Jodie?'

Didn't she say she was in the same room with him?

'Well remembered, but if she was asleep, anyone could have come in—'

But Jodie said she didn't sleep. So, unless she's lying, she either knows who killed Sawney, or she did it herself.

Again, I'd forgotten this point, but wasn't going to tell Oscar I had. He was already preening from me saying well remembered. 'What possible reason would Jodie have had to kill him? I'm sure she's not involved.'

But was I? I pulled my phone out.

'Still here?' Grimes loomed over me. Behind him, Bowling led Leonov towards the table. 'Sling your hook, I need my office.'

I stood, swaying as a wave of dizziness washed over me. 'Help yourself, Chief Inspector.'

I stuffed the phone back in my pocket and set off for Zofia's car, Oscar trotting by my side. At the car, I opened the back door to let him in. An intense sensation of nausea seized me as I straightened, and I emptied the contents of my stomach onto the back wheel.

Oscar gave a yelp of alarm. The ground swayed, then rushed to meet me with frightening speed.

CHAPTER 32

My night in hospital, in a small ward with three others, should have been restful, but apart from the headache keeping me company, I worried about Oscar. Bowling had assured me she'd take care of him, but she wasn't in charge. Grimes was.

Around midday, a doctor came to see me. She unhooked the clipboard at the foot of the bed and studied it. 'Mr Timothy, you failed to eat your breakfast.'

The lukewarm porridge and prunes had made me heave. 'I wasn't hungry.'

She placed the clipboard on a bracket below my feet, came up to my head, and produced a pen torch from her pocket. 'Can you look up to your right?'

I did, my eyeballs objecting.

'Now to your left.' She peered into my face. 'You've broken capillaries in both eyes because of the blows to your head, but they'll repair themselves. Your pupils are reacting as I'd expect.' Her attention moved to the bump on my head, and she prodded it with a purple-gloved hand. 'Is that sore?'

'A bit.'

'Headache?'

'Not too bad.'

She added to the notes on the clipboard. 'Have you lost consciousness since you arrived?'

Had I? I didn't even remember sleeping. 'I don't think so?'

'But you lost consciousness when you hit your head.'

I thought back. 'Not fully. I couldn't move my arms, but I could see them and I didn't pass out until I bent over at the car and then I fell, hitting my forehead.' I touched the graze.

She frowned. 'Have you had any other blows to the head in the last few days?'

I'd passed out at the fire at Beswick Street when someone hit me and that was four days ago, but if I said anything, they'd keep me in. 'Not for a while.'

'Okay.' She checked the time. 'We'll check you again in eight hours. That will be twenty-four since you arrived—'

'I was here for almost three hours before you admitted me.'

'Eight hours, Mr Timothy.' She made another note on the clipboard and returned it before striding away.

Lunch arrived, and I forced myself to eat most of the flavourless shepherd's pie but couldn't manage the rice pudding. At two, Zofia arrived with Kasper.

'You been in the wars?' she said as she passed me a box of chocolates.

'I'm fine. I just felt dizzy when I bent over.'

'Colette said you collapsed.'

I placed the chocolates on the cabinet by my bed. 'Not collapse, exactly. I felt woozy and lost my balance, but I'm fine now. I'll be back at work Monday.'

Kasper pulled a chair across from the wall by the entrance and placed it alongside the one by my bed. 'Not if you're still here.'

'What do you mean?'

Zofia sat in the one nearest me and I caught a hint of her perfume. 'The nurse said they might keep you in another night.'

'No way. What about Oscar?'

'Don't worry about him. He's fine with us.'

At least he wasn't in the dog pound. 'Have you heard from Jodie?'

Zofia exchanged a look with her brother. 'She rang me yesterday evening and told me what happened.'

'Did she mention what she did to make Leonov attack me?'

'Did she do anything? She said she saw the minibus drive round the back and investigated. She saw them bundle you into it and stopped them. Although she was pretty cagey about how she'd done it.'

I looked around the small ward. The man in the nearest bed had gone for a walk, one of the two opposite had headphones on, and the other was snoring. 'She hit the driver over the head and set fire to the minibus. I just got out after she smashed the window. I didn't see her, but I'm pretty sure the driver did and warned Leonov.'

'She told you that?'

'We didn't speak. She helped me out of the window and scarpered.'

'So, how can you know what happened?'

I'd largely surmised it. 'I heard her hit the driver. As for the rest, ask her when you next speak to her.' I remembered what Bowling had almost let slip: 'Also, the police think someone murdered Sawney, and made it look like an overdose.' I'd surmised that as well, but was confident I was right. 'They'll want to speak to anyone who was there. Jodie and Toff were sleeping in the same room with him.'

I didn't say that Jodie had claimed she hadn't slept. I intended to press her on that point when I next saw her, but the fact was she'd saved my life, despite endangering it in the first place. There was no telling what those men would have done to me once they got me away.

I could see Zofia thinking, but couldn't guess the contents of those thoughts. 'I'm seeing her later,' she said at last, careful not to meet her brother's gaze.

'You'd better warn her, the police will want to talk to her. I said nothing, but I expect someone at the pub saw her.'

Zofia nodded. 'Colette told me when she dropped Oscar and the car off. The landlord saw her. He said she threatened him with a broken bottle.'

'That doesn't surprise me.'

'Did you get anything from Leonov?'

'Sorry, Zofia. I got him to fill in the questionnaire, but I can't find it. I must have lost it when I was in the minibus, and I can't remember what he said.'

'Don't worry, we'll get the information somehow.'

At around half two, Kasper checked the time. United were playing at three and they'd want to follow it, so I let them go. I retrieved my phone and rang Toff, but it hit voicemail straight away. After three attempts, I rang John.

'Have you seen Toff, John?'

'Bad news, Brother. The police lifted him last night, something to do with Sawney's death. Where are you?'

I told him and refused his offer of a visit, assuring him I'd be home soon. The doctor's visit at eight made me a liar, and they kept me in for another night. By Sunday afternoon, my headache had almost gone, and I was wandering round the ward driving the staff crazy. Zofia came to collect me at four. I was conscious that the clothes I'd put on just before she arrived still stank of smoke from Friday as we descended in the lift.

Oscar jumped out of the car and greeted me. ***You stink of smoke.***

'Thanks for pointing it out. I hadn't noticed.'

Why am I not surprised? Now let's get home. I'm starving.

As we pulled out of the car park, Zofia said, 'I spoke to Jodie. She's adamant she knows nothing about Sawney's death.'

I'd been pondering what to tell Zofia and decided she needed to know about Jodie. 'The police are questioning Toff. They still haven't released him. I checked around lunchtime. He was in the same room, but out of it. Jodie, by her own admission, didn't sleep all night. If someone came in and killed Sawney, she must have at least heard them.'

Zofia stayed silent for a long moment. 'You believe she's capable of killing someone?'

I considered what I knew of her. 'She firebombed Leonov and did the same to the driver of the minibus—'

'But that was to save you. She didn't realise he was smoking when she threw the bottle at him.'

'Yeah, I suppose so. And Leonov was so she and Toff could escape from the school. I think it's more youthful exuberance rather than malicious. I suspect she didn't consider the consequences.' Was I making excuses for her because she'd rescued me? 'Why would she possibly have wanted to kill Sawney?'

This provoked another silence from Zofia.

'Do you think she's capable of it?' I asked her. 'You've spoken to her as much as I have.'

'You brought her to us, Victor, but your attitude towards her seemed to change since you took her to Beswick Street.'

'I didn't take her there. I found her hanging through the factory ceiling.'

'What?'

'She fell through the burnt-out floor.'

'What was she doing there?' Zofia glanced at me.

'Looking for somewhere to sleep, she claimed.'

'You didn't believe her?'

'It seems a bit of a stretch. And then, she accused the owner of insurance fraud. He clammed up and almost chucked us out.'

'That's not good. It sounds like she's a bit of a hothead.'

I couldn't disagree, but I didn't want her thrown out. 'I can manage her. We need to choose what jobs to use her on.'

'Hmmm. I was hoping to use her as well as you. If you're always babysitting her, what's the point of having her on the books?'

I couldn't argue with her. Zofia had to do what was best for the business. And now Jodie had questions to answer about Sawney's death, she'd become a liability.

We arrived at my flat and Zofia parked up outside. 'You sure you'll be okay to come to work tomorrow?'

'I obviously can't come to the office with Novak's men watching it, but I can do legwork.'

I got out and Oscar joined me, watching her car disappear round the corner. I looked up at the tower block looming above us.

'Come on boy, let's go home.'

Can't we live somewhere else?

'We will someday. Now, this is all we've got.' I walked towards the entrance and punched in the entry code.

He followed me and we headed for the internal door leading to our corridor. My bipper didn't work, so I made my weary way to the reception counter. The young woman who seemed to get lumbered with the Sunday shifts looked up.

She reddened. 'Hello, Victor.'

'Hi. My tag doesn't work.'

'No. It's been disabled.'

They'd done this before when three went missing and given us new ones. 'You got a new one for me?'

'Sorry.' She slid an envelope across the counter.

I tore it open.

> . . . Despite previous warnings, you have again spent the night away from your designated accommodation. You leave us no alternative but to terminate your tenancy. You have three days to vacate your accommodation.

I looked up at the young woman. 'But I was in hospital.'

'I'm sorry, it's not my decision. But you can appeal.' She pointed to the bottom of the letter.

I read the section. 'But you won't respond to the appeal for up to a month. What do I do in the meantime?'

'I'm sorry, Victor.'

She wasn't to blame, and I stepped back.

'You need to return your tag, and I can buzz you through.' She pointed at the door.

What's happening? Oscar looked alarmed.

'Your wish to move out is coming true, but a bit sooner than I expected.'

Where the hell were we going to go now?

CHAPTER 33

Zofia drove from Victor's place, her thoughts in turmoil. Jodie seemed more of a liability than she'd feared. The information that not only was she quite happy to set fire to people, but she had questions to answer about the death of Victor's friend. Did they need someone like that working for them?

She'd discuss it with Kasper once she got home.

As she got on the Mancunian Way, her phone sounded over the speakers. She hesitated before answering.

'Jodie?'

'Can we meet please, Zofia?'

She didn't want to discuss anything with Jodie until she'd spoken to Kasper. 'I'm just on my way home. I took Victor to his place from the hospital—'

'Hospital? Was he burnt?'

'Concussion. So, can we meet tomorrow morning at the office?'

'I can't come to the office. I just need a bit of advice, Zofia. Please.'

'Okay, where?'

'How about Hulme Park, at the Jackson Crescent entrance?'

'Five minutes.' Zofia ended the call.

By the time she'd found somewhere to park, she'd taken nearer ten minutes. Jodie sat on a bench sixty metres inside the park. Laughter and jeering were interspersed with the rhythmic thrum of skateboard wheels on the metal halfpipe in the skate-park fifty metres away. The aroma of mown grass made Zofia's nose itch.

Jodie saw her and stood. 'Thanks for coming, Zofia. How's Victor?'

'Okay, thanks to you. But maybe it's your fault Leonov attacked him in the first place.'

Jodie coloured. 'Yeah, sorry. I wasn't expecting the other guy to turn up when I got out of the car.'

Victor had guessed right. She'd been identified by the second man. 'What couldn't wait until tomorrow?'

'Please sit.' Jodie gestured at the bench and took a deep breath as Zofia complied. 'I got a call from Toff telling me the police were looking for him and me.'

'About Sawney?'

'You knew?'

'Victor's not as clueless as you seem to think.'

'No. I don't think he's clueless—'

'You told him you hadn't slept the night Sawney died. So how did someone else come in and kill him if you were wide awake next to him?'

Jodie glanced towards the skatepark as a loud cheer and applause broke out. 'I wasn't there all night.'

Zofia waited for her to continue. 'Where were you?'

She exhaled. 'I went home for a shower.'

'Home?'

'Yep. I'm sorry, Zofia. I'm not homeless.'

Zofia took this in, considering the possibilities. 'Do you want to explain yourself?'

'I'm . . . I'm working undercover.'

'Undercover? Who for?' The fear the police had sent her to spy on them sent a surge of panic through Zofia.

'I'm a journalist. I'm investigating attacks on the homeless community.'

Relief and then anger seized Zofia. 'You've been stringing us along and letting me pay you.'

'Sorry.' She reached into her bag and pulled out a bundle of notes. 'This is all of it. I didn't intend—'

'Keep it.' She waved it away. 'Why didn't you come clean when I offered you a job?'

'I . . . It was Victor. I knew he'd been homeless and was still close to people like Toff, and I couldn't risk him letting it out who I was.'

Zofia understood her concerns, but her anger still burned, and she stood. 'Right, thanks for telling me.'

'Please, don't go yet.'

'We've exhausted our conversation.'

'I need your advice. Please.'

Zofia reminded herself that, despite deceiving them, she was still a young woman with serious problems to solve. She sat back down. 'Go on then.'

'Thanks.' Jodie touched Zofia's forearm. 'The police are looking for me, and I don't know what to do.'

'Simple. Tell them what you told me. If you weren't there, you're in the clear. Can you prove you'd gone home?'

'Yeah. The alarm's monitored and there's CCTV in the lobby.'

'There you are, then.'

'I returned to the school, though, so I could have still killed him. But that's not what I'm really worried about. I set fire to the security guard—'

'But you didn't mean to.'

'Of course not. But does that matter? I still injured the man. Then I did the same to his mate. I didn't mean to hurt him, either. You must believe me. I didn't realise he was smoking when I threw the bottle into the cab. I just wanted to stop them taking Victor.'

Provoked though she'd clearly been, Zofia could see how it might look like a pattern of dangerous behaviour. 'I'm friendly with some officers. I could ask—'

'NO!' She clasped Zofia's arm. 'Please, don't drop me in it.'

'I'm just going to find out what they're thinking. You said they're looking for you. What are you going to do?'

'They're looking for a young homeless woman. They'd never look for me if I go back to my day job.'

'You're probably right.'

'And Zofia. I'd like to help you with the cases I've been working on. That's the least I can do.'

How would Victor feel about that? And Kasper? 'I'll speak to my brother.' She removed Jodie's hand and stood again. 'I'll be in touch.'

Behind her, the skaters let out another cheer.

Relieved to find her car undamaged, she continued her journey.

Back home, she let herself in to be greeted by the aroma of chilli and garlic.

'How was Victor?' Kasper stood in the kitchen doorway wearing an apron and holding a wooden spoon.

'Victor's not too bad. I told him he doesn't have to rush back.'

'We could do with him. Good thing we've got Jodie.'

She sighed. 'That's another thing. Do you want to sit down?' She gestured towards the kitchen table.

'This doesn't sound good.'

She followed Kasper, and the cooking aromas intensified. 'Jodie isn't who we think she is. In fact, I doubt Jodie's her real name.' She sat opposite him and brought him up to date.

'The bloody deceitful so-and-so!' His condemnation hinted at admiration. 'And she offered to help us out?'

'You're not serious about taking her up on it?'

'Why not? We'll be shorthanded if Victor's off sick, and I'd imagine she won't want paying.'

Zofia shook her head. 'I'll get cleaned up.' She gestured at the pot bubbling away on the hob. 'How long?'

'Just the rice to go on. Ten minutes.'

She made her way upstairs and got changed into her PJs, looking forward to an evening in front of the telly. She returned to the kitchen to find Kasper staring at his phone.

'Everything okay?'

He shook his head. 'Read this.'

She took the screen off him as he dealt with the food and read the article he'd been studying.

> . . . was a senior member of the council's estates and property department with special responsibility for educational buildings. A police spokesman described it as a particularly nasty murder. The killers broke into Mr Chopra's home and tortured him before stabbing him in the neck and leaving him tied to a kitchen chair.

At the moment, they don't have a motive, but don't believe his murder is linked to his job.

Zofia slumped into the nearest chair. 'Robertson?'

'A coincidence if it wasn't.'

Zofia felt sick. Not again!

CHAPTER 34

Dean looked pleased with himself as he sat opposite Alex Novak, across what had been Milan's desk. Novak had to resist the urge to swipe the smug grin off his face.

'You sure this guy is the one who was spying on my sons?'

'One hundred per cent, Boss.'

'And where do I find him?'

'He's not on the streets no more. He's living in a flat in Strangeways View.'

Novak laughed. 'That's a real name? Where the hell is it, Cheetham Hill?'

'New Islington.'

'Ancoats, you mean.' Novak had no time for the trendy designation of that part of the city. Nobody called it that when he was growing up.

'Whatever.'

Novak answered this with a sharp look. 'I'm not one of your mates down the pub.'

Dean sat up straight. 'Course not, Boss.'

'You know which flat?'

'Not yet, but I'm working on it.'

'Can you do that this week?'

'I expect so, Boss.'

'"Expectation is the root of all headaches." Who said that?'

Dean looked panicked. 'Was it Machiavelli?'

'Shakespeare.' He got disproportionate pleasure from Dean's frustration. 'And your trip to Birmingham? Did you find out who's behind it all?'

'Sorry, Boss, my contact let me down.'

'Again?' Novak was starting to suspect this contact didn't exist. 'You're letting this guy take the piss out of you. And if he's taking the piss out of you, what do you think he's doing to me?'

'He's got real problems, Boss. Someone stabbed one of his men last week and shot another.'

Novak recalled a report he'd seen. 'I read it was two Black lads got attacked.'

'That's right.'

'He's Black?'

'Anything wrong with that?'

'Just surprised. They don't normally work with us.'

'New generation, Boss.'

'Yeah.' Novak felt old. 'Right, focus on the guy with the dog. We can use him to give us the McLarens.'

Dean closed the door behind him and Novak returned to the spreadsheet he'd been studying. The weekend's figures looked no better than the previous ones. Sweeny wouldn't be in until midday, but that would give him time to outline his new plans for the place. Half an hour later, a call broke his concentration.

'What's up, Guy?' He still needed to explain why he was using Novak's name to pressurise people to sell up.

'Can I come and see you straight away?'

Novak waited with a sense of unease. The note of panic in Guy's voice, plus his insistence he couldn't talk over the phone, convinced him something serious had happened. He couldn't even go through the charade of making him wait when he arrived. Guy hustled in on a cloud of expensive aftershave.

Despite his impatience to find out what Guy was panicking about, Novak knew he must address his disrespect and struck before he made himself comfortable. 'What were you doing on Beswick Street?'

'What?'

'You went there threatening someone.'

Guy gave the smile of a condemned man. 'You know what they say about omelettes, Alex—'

'What were you doing using my name to scare people?'

Guy flushed and pushed himself towards the back of his chair. 'We're partners, so I thought—'

'No!' Novak held up an index finger. 'I made it very clear that we're not partners.'

'But we're working together.'

'Again, that's not true. You work for me. Now, what's this place on Beswick Street?'

'It's . . .' Guy's gaze roamed. 'It's nothing. Just a small project I'm working on.'

'Who for?'

'I can't tell you that.'

'Put it this way, Guy. You've been using my name, my reputation, to progress a project for another client.'

'I just mentioned I knew you.'

'Did you mention anyone else you knew?'

Guy studied his feet. 'No.'

'Not your client?'

His cheeks wobbled as he shook his head.

'Of course, you wouldn't want to sully their name. But you're happy to throw mine in the gutter.'

'No. I wasn't. I just thought your name would have more impact.'

'Let me be the judge of that.'

Guy looked puzzled. 'What do you mean?'

'Tell me on whose behalf you invoked my name.'

'He's just a Hong Kong businessman.' He dared to look at Novak.

'His name.'

Guy blurted out a name, which meant nothing to Novak.

'What's the project?'

'It's tiny. One you wouldn't be interested in.'

'Try me.'

'It's just forty units on the canal.' He'd mumbled the number, but Novak heard it.

'And what's the profit?'

Guy held his thumb and forefinger a centimetre apart. 'One. One and a bit.'

'I'll assume it's one and a half.'

Guy didn't deny it. 'I'm really sorry I used your name, Alex.'

'I don't blame you, Guy. "All welfare is based on deception," as Sun Tzu said. You were just deceiving to win.'

'Exactly.' A smile hovered on his lips.

'The problem is, you've hurt my reputation doing it.'

The smile vanished. 'That wasn't my intention.'

'As they say, "intention creates our reality", and the reality here is the damage to my name.'

Guy closed his eyes, and the lid on his left one fluttered. 'How can I undo the damage?'

'There's only one way. The man you spoke to believes the project is mine. The damage to my name will occur if someone else benefits. Therefore, I want—'

'No!'

Novak's temper rose. 'I've not told you yet.'

'You want to take over the project.'

'Very good, Guy. I knew there was a reason I employed you. You're now managing that project for me.'

'I can't do that. What about my client?'

'Tell him the owner refused, and the project has stalled. He'll understand.'

'But I assured him I'd—'

'Use my name to get it over the line?'

'No. I said I'd iron out the problems.'

'You can do them for me. You'll still get your fee—'

'But my reputation . . .'

'If I were you, I'd be more concerned about my more tangible parts.'

Guy swallowed. Sweat was now beading his brow.

'Good. As Sun Tzu said, "If the enemy leaves a door open, you must rush in." Have the papers on my desk by Friday.'

'Okay.' He looked sick.

'Cheer up, we're entering a new partnership. We'll celebrate with another feast. Bring Roger, your adviser.' Novak winked. 'Now, what did you want to see me about?'

Guy's expression suggested he'd forgotten why he'd come, then remembered and wished he hadn't. 'I'm afraid I've got bad news.'

'That's a shame. It takes the edge off the good news you've just given me. Now, spit it out.'

'Did you read about Chopra? The man murdered in his kitchen?'

'It's just round the corner from where my mum lives. It's shaken her right up. Crime has its tentacles everywhere now, even the pleasant suburbs.' The thought of criminals near his old mother filled him with a righteous fury. 'What about him?'

'You recall I said we'd make sure we got everyone onside to smooth our journey? Make sure there were no obstacles to you making millions developing the site near the school?'

Novak could see where this was going, but wanted Guy to spit it out. He stayed silent, giving him an icy glare he suspected would make the man even more uncomfortable.

Guy loosened his colourful tie. 'He was one of our key people.'

'What are you telling me, Guy?'

'Without him, we may struggle.'

Novak glanced at the computer screen now showing images of his sons, but before, it had displayed his spreadsheets, where he could see the exact depth of the shit they were in. 'You love your euphemisms, Guy. "Key person." "May struggle." What I want you to do is explain the problem in plain English.'

'Do you have any water?' Guy looked round the room. 'Please.'

Novak, worried he'd have a heart attack, stood and retrieved a bottle of water from the fridge behind his desk. The unexpected windfall of the extra forty apartments had put him in a good mood, but Guy's abject behaviour related to this dead man alarmed him. Raising his voice wouldn't be productive at this stage. He cracked the bottle's top and handed it to Guy, who gulped half, spilling some on his tie.

Despite the aftershave he wore, body odour wafted off him. 'Without our fixer, we may struggle to get the school—'

'Whoa! That site is key to the project.'

'Yes. Obviously.' Irritation made Guy squint – and speak recklessly.

Novak let it go. 'What do you need to do and how much will it cost me?'

'That's the problem. We approached him after being rebuffed by his two deputies. Now he's gone, one of them will most likely take over.'

'Find out which one's getting the job and up your offer.'

'I got the impression neither will be swayed.'

'Everyone has their price.'

'But there's only so much money in the project.'

'You may recall our earlier conversation, where you used my name as a stick. You may now use the same stick with my permission.'

'I've heard, via my sources, that his murder may be linked to the project?'

Novak sat back but tried to hide his surprise. 'What are you saying?'

'I'm saying you've got competition, and they are prepared to torture and kill.'

'Find out from your sources who it is.' He'd speak to his own police mole.

'If they've got evidence, they're not going to tell us.'

'We're not going to prosecute them.' He paraphrased Dean. 'Just find out who it is, and I'll warn them off.'

'How far are you prepared to go?'

Novak knew how far he'd go. All the way. He'd sunk everything he and his dead sons had worked for into this project, and it would now be their memorial. There was no way he'd give it up. He'd taken on all comers before, but he wasn't sure he still had the resources.

CHAPTER 35

Despite my promise to work on Monday, I couldn't face it. Not only had an incipient headache kept me awake, so had the worry of being made homeless again. Part of me gave in to despair and then a surge of optimism would strike. It gave me the opportunity to find somewhere better. But I didn't have a huge deposit. Zofia and Kasper gave me a reasonable wage, and I had a frugal lifestyle, but I'd been generous with the money I sent to care for my daughters.

I called Zofia as my coffee brewed. 'I'm not coming in today.'

'Of course, Victor, I'll put you on the sick. We'll pay you full wages. You got injured on duty, so take as long as you need.'

'I'm really sorry, Zofia. I know you're pulled out, but could you use Jodie?'

'Jodie?' Zofia laughed.

'Something wrong?'

'Nothing for you to worry about. We'll see you when you're fighting fit.'

I did worry. What had happened to Jodie? Of course, the police must have caught up with her. I rang Toff's number, and he picked up.

'Toff, I presume the police have released you.'

'Yeah.' He sounded half asleep. 'Last night.'

'Are they holding Jodie?'

'Don't think so. She's disappeared.'

That wasn't a surprise. 'Could she have killed Sawney?'

'You what?'

'She told us she couldn't sleep that night. So how did someone sneak in and kill Sawney without disturbing her?'

'Sawney was murdered?'

I could have handled that better. I'd forgotten he didn't know. 'Yeah. Someone made it look like an overdose. They'd either injected him before he arrived—'

'Nah, he was fine when he came in. We had a chat. He spouted the usual paranoid stuff, but he looked and sounded clean.'

'Or they injected him while he was asleep.' Another thought occurred to me. 'Unless he sneaked out.'

'I don't think so. He was asleep before I was, snoring something chronic.'

'So, you think Jodie could have killed him?'

Toff didn't reply for a long moment. 'I . . . She wouldn't have. Why would she do it?'

I didn't know, but she had questions to answer. 'You're probably right, Toff. Take care.'

I poured myself a coffee and sat at the tiny kitchen table. Oscar studied me from his bed in the corner.

What will we do now?

I had no idea. 'We'll find somewhere else. Somewhere better.'

Good. I hate it here.

So did I, but would I be longing to be here if we ended up on the street? At least it was warm and dry. 'Let's have breakfast.'

Oscar stood. ***Great. Are we going to the place by the canal?***

I needed to save every penny. 'Shall we have it here? Our last breakfast in this place.'

If you insist. He lowered himself.

We had a quick breakfast, and I took him for a walk. The young woman at reception wouldn't meet my gaze as I walked past her. As we wandered along the canal path, I mulled over my predicament. At least I'd accumulated some of the stuff I'd need to set up home, thanks to Kasper and Zofia's generosity.

The towpath ended, and I realised we'd reached Canal Street and were almost at Sackville Square, our old haunt. I attached Oscar's lead, and we crossed Minshull Street. The eateries and bars alongside the canal were taking advantage of the early spring sunshine and had laid their tables out. A few brave souls sat drinking coffee and having a late breakfast.

I hurried past until we reached Sackville Street. 'Shall we look at the old square, for old times' sake?'

Why not? You had such a marvellous time there, with your urine shower and almost getting killed.

'Thanks for the reminder. Come on, it won't take long.' I tugged on his lead, and he followed.

A minute later, we arrived, and I stood in the corner and surveyed the scene. A stocky young woman with short hair and a nose ring occupied the best place in the square, my old pitch.

Never go back, don't they say?

'They do, and it's good advice. Let's have a look at St Peter's Square.'

I thought we were going to get somewhere better, not return to the streets.

'As you pointed out, at least we won't have to endure the loud music our neighbours play.'

Great. Why did we wait to get evicted if that's what's driving your move?

'I'm just trying to put a positive spin on it.'

Don't bother.

'I won't.' A sound made me glance up. The pink door at the side of the casino opened, and I tensed. But the thugs who'd terrorised me from behind it were no longer around. Instead, a bulky man in an expensive suit rushed out, mopping his brow.

My mind returned to my visit to the Beswick Street factory. A man fitting his description had made threats using Novak's name, and now he, or someone like him, was rushing out of Novak's club. It couldn't be a coincidence. If I found out who he was, we'd have a better idea of what Novak was up to and if he was behind the attacks on the homeless.

'Come on, we're following him.' I led Oscar after the man.

He paused at Portland Street as a pair of buses shot past but scuttled in front of a taxi, making like he was running but moving at walking pace. We followed, and he entered Nicholas Street. The enticing aromas from the Chinese restaurants distracted both me and Oscar, although our quarry, deep in thought, didn't seem to notice.

We almost lost him on Mosley Street when he ran in front of a double tram, and another arrived on the opposite track. When they'd gone, he'd disappeared.

'Bugger.'

He's gone into that building.

'Where?'

I'll show you. Oscar led me to a restaurant-bar on the next corner. ***In there.***

I checked through the window but couldn't see anyone. 'Can I trust you to stay here if I go inside?'

Where am I going to go? Can you see any trees?

'There are plenty of lampposts.'

Leave me by this one. It's got an interesting medley of odours.

I tucked his lead into his collar and stuck my head in the restaurant. The aromas of coffee and toast wafted in my direction.

'Sorry, mate, we're not open.' A young man wearing a smart black apron over a white shirt and navy trousers stood at a table with a tray of cutlery on it.

'I'm looking for someone. A big guy in an expensive suit wearing a snazzy tie.'

'Guy?'

Maybe he wasn't English. 'A bloke, a person. A man.'

He smiled. 'Guy is the bloke, person, man's name.'

My cheeks grew warm. 'Right. Sorry.'

'Back there.' He pointed towards the entrance. 'There's a door to the offices upstairs just outside.'

'Do you know what they do up there?'

He shrugged. 'It says property development on the plate by the door, but it could be anything. He has some dodgy-looking clients he sometimes brings here.'

'Novak?'

The smile evaporated. 'Not that dodgy.'

'Thanks.' I backed out and found the door, which looked like a wooden panel. A small metal plate by a bell push read 'GE Holdings Property Development'. I snapped a photo, checked it was in focus, and sent it to Zofia with a message to check them out. It could be a front company run by Novak. The guy had looked like he'd received a bollocking from someone inside Novak's club.

I collected Oscar, and we made our way to St Peter's Square. A council pickup with a cage on the back stood at one end of the row of tents pitched alongside the town hall extension. Six bulky police officers accompanied the orange-clad council workers engaged in seizing up the tents and shoving them into the back of the vehicle.

A few tent owners remonstrated with the officials, but most were out collecting money, and would return to find their hard-assembled belongings gone. Oscar growled at a council worker who attacked the nearest tent.

'Show some respect,' I called to him. 'That's someone's belongings.'

'It's a load of rubbish,' he replied without even glancing my way. 'They shouldn't be allowed to make such a mess.' Now he focused on us. 'If your ugly mutt wants to join the rest of the rubbish, send him over here.' He stamped on the tent and scooped up the resulting debris. 'Arrrggh! Fuck!' He fell to his knees.

Two police ran towards us, hands on their batons. 'What you done to him?'

I held up my hands, palms forward. 'I haven't touched him. It's all his own work.'

They studied the man, who held up a gloved hand. A spike stuck through the palm and blood dripped onto the limestone paving slabs.

He shouldn't be allowed to make such a mess.

'Come on, Oscar, let's leave these vandals to their work.'

We set off homeward and my phone rang. 'Zofia?'

'You okay, Victor? I got your message, but I thought you weren't working today.'

'I brought Oscar for a walk into town and saw something interesting.'

'I checked the company whose nameplate you sent me,' Zofia said. 'They're "fixers" for property developers. They sort out planning permissions and acquisitions.'

'I followed a man called Guy there. He came out of Novak's office, and he fits the description the owner of the factory at Beswick Street gave me, of the man using Novak's name to threaten him.'

'That's interesting.' She summoned Kasper. 'I'll put you on speaker and you can tell us what you know.'

I recapped what had happened at Beswick Street and what I'd seen, and the information the waiter gave me.

'You say he looked stressed?' Kasper said.

'Yes, like someone had torn a strip off him.'

'Hmmm. Someone murdered the man responsible for the school you investigated.'

'What?'

'There could be a link.'

I checked nobody was nearby. 'The man whose details you gave to Robertson?'

'The same.'

I mulled this over. Had we done it again, found Robertson a target? People who'd kill for a few grand aren't going to think twice when millions are involved. 'Do you think he was in Novak's pocket and told Robertson to sling his hook?'

'Probably the other way,' Zofia said. 'Robertson got to him, and Novak killed him to get him out of the way.'

'Have you spoken to Robertson?'

'He rang Kasper first thing. He's furious at Kasper, almost accused us of misleading him.'

'Did Kasper manage to placate him?'

'I think so.' She gave an unconvincing smile. 'I hope so.'

So did I. 'What are you going to say to Novak?'

'What do you mean?'

'He's a client, and you suspect he's involved in a murder.'

She took a deep breath. 'I don't know. Kasper and I were just talking about it. We can't pretend it hasn't happened, but if we say anything to Novak, he might figure out we think he's involved. Or that we're working for Robertson.'

'Yes. And even if he doesn't figure it out, if Robertson comes down here and they square off, it might come out.'

'Right. We need to decide how to deal with it.'

I ended the call, thinking my imminent homelessness might not be my biggest problem.

CHAPTER 36

While we were in town, I could discover what accommodation was available. A property website listed hundreds of places to let, but checking each one to find out if it was suitable would be impossible. I found three letting agents within a few hundred metres. All seemed to have plenty of property on their books.

I got to the first one and walked into a bright open-plan space full of desks with a member of staff at each, their gazes fixed on screens. A powerful air-freshener scented the air. After a minute, one agent noticed us and made her way over.

'Can I help you?' She offered an unconvincing smile.

'I'm looking for somewhere to live.'

'Buy or rent?'

'Rent.'

She retired the smile. 'Do you want to follow me?'

We returned to her desk, and I sat in an uncomfortable chair, Oscar at my feet.

'Is that your dog?'

No, he just followed me in and thrust the lead into my hand. 'It is.'

'You're going to struggle.' She turned the screen towards me. A grid of properties filled the screen. She punched keys, and the grid became nine thumbnails. 'I've just put in the "pets allowed" filter.'

She made another change and nine became three. 'These accept dogs.' She glanced at Oscar. 'Cats are easier. I've got a cat.'

Yes, having a pet more intelligent than you would be challenging.

'Don't be rude Oscar.'

Just an observation.

'I talk to my cat as well.'

And I'm betting it doesn't understand a word you say.

I focused on the screen. 'How much are those three?'

She clicked on the first, a two-bedroomed terraced house in Salford which, despite photos taken with a distorting lens to make the rooms appear bigger, resembled a children's playhouse. 'Twelve fifty a month. Deposit of fifteen hundred.'

I shook my head. That was almost three times what I'd saved. 'What about the others?'

Although cheaper, and even smaller, neither was remotely affordable.

'You'd need to look further afield.' She pointed at a map of the city taking up the side wall on her right. 'East to areas like Openshaw or north to Moston or Crumpsall.'

I studied the map. North looked more promising for the office. She took my details and gave me the address of their branch on the north side of the city.

By the time we'd called on the other two letting agents, I was getting used to the feeling of disappointment. The headache which had hovered in the background had burrowed its way into prominence. I fought the urge to go back to the flat and return to bed. We had two more days to find somewhere to live.

You could always get rid of me.

'We've been through this before.'

But this time, it's me or life on the streets. I'm sure I could find—

'I'm not getting rid of you and that's final.'

He looked surprised and then nuzzled against my leg. ***I knew you loved me.***

'It's more I've got used to you.' I ruffled his ears. 'Anyway, even the places that don't accept dogs looked out of my range and Helen would never forgive me.'

He glared at me and growled. ***I can see through you.***

I stepped away. 'Let's get something to eat first and get the bus up to Crumpsall.'

Now you're talking.

We were near the bottom end of Deansgate, where I used to get a hot meal and shower when I lived on the streets. The thought I might need that place again depressed me. As we walked past, a shout stopped me.

'Victor, how are you doing? And you, Oscar.' Digger stood by the open side-door of a micro van. Inside, boxes of tinned food and trays of bread on their sell-by date.

I gestured at the van. 'You setting up for tonight?'

Digger bent down and made a fuss of Oscar. 'We're starting earlier these days so we can fit everyone in.'

The van had given me an idea. 'We're moving on Wednesday. Can I borrow that?'

'I can do better than that. I'll help you. Where are you moving to? I'm free from about three.'

'I'm not sure yet. We've had enough of that place.'

'Yeah, I can't blame you. It's pretty grim.' He straightened. 'If you need me to store your stuff for a while, I've got a lockup with space.'

'Cheers, Digger. We'll see you Wednesday afternoon.'

He declined my offer of help in unloading, and we left, soon turning the corner round the Central Library into St Peter's Square.

The workmen had finished their 'tidying' of the tents and the only evidence of what had been there were a few bewildered-looking people who'd returned to find their homes gone.

We continued to Piccadilly, where we took a tram to our destination. As we left the city, the evidence of construction, cranes and half-completed tower blocks soon disappeared, and the buildings looked tired and in need of attention. I suspected any housing I could afford would fall into that category.

The letting agency had few properties, especially once they knew about Oscar. They were, however, cheaper, and they even had some I could afford. The agent offered to take me to see some and, after a discussion, took Oscar as well.

First, we saw the ground floor of a cramped terraced house with a small back yard. The young agent pushed the door open with a decidedly undeserved flourish. Junk mail stopped it halfway, and I pushed past. The damp air filled my lungs, making me feel I was at the bottom of a swimming pool. Black mould dotted the wallpaper and plaster bulged, held in place by the woodchip. Oscar wouldn't even come in, and it took me a minute to decide.

'How long's it been empty?'

He glanced at his tablet. 'A while.'

'I'm not surprised.'

'The owner's prepared to contribute towards the cost of refurbishing it.'

'Yeah, I'm sure he is. Where's the next one?'

Two hours later, we'd seen five more places, each as depressing as the last. I stood outside the final one with Oscar as the agent struggled to lock the door.

I don't know why he bothers. Nobody's going to break in and if they do, there's nothing to steal. They'll likely leave a donation.

'You're probably right. Let's get back. It will be dark soon.'

The agent scribbled something on his screen and joined us. 'That's it, Victor. All the ones you can afford.'

Oscar bared his teeth. ***Mr Mitchum to you.***

The young man stepped back. 'Right, I'll leave you to it, then.'

'Hang on, aren't you going to take us back to the office?'

'I'm not taking that vicious animal anywhere.' He beat it to his car and roared off, the blowing exhaust letting everyone in the street know it was there.

Sorry. Oscar bowed his head.

'Not your fault. He deserved it.' I checked the map on my phone. 'There should be a tram stop that way.'

It took us another two hours to get to the tram stop and then back home at the other end. Exhausted and hungry, I greeted our arrival back at the tower block with relief. Oscar, however, stood on the pavement, staring at the rear of a car parked round the corner.

'Come on, let's get in and have some food.'

Oscar refused and pulled me towards the car.

'Bloody hell, what now?'

Keep it down!

'Don't tell me to keep it down.' But I did.

We reached the corner of the building and peered round the wall. A resident I recognised from the rave upstairs was talking to someone in the car.

The driver passed him an envelope and said, 'You sure about that?'

'Positive.'

With a start, I recognised the car as one of those that had often pulled up outside the pink door on Sackville Square. What was one of Novak's henchmen doing at a halfway house for the homeless?

Oscar grew agitated and turned to look behind us.

'What you doing, snitch?' The voice of thc Bully's owner made me jump.

It also made the driver of the car turn towards us. I jerked back behind the corner, but not before I recognised him as the nosey 'homeless man' who'd been pumping Toff for information.

The Bully growled and Oscar whimpered.

CHAPTER 37

Jodie had left Victor on the ground beside the blazing minibus and run out of the car park before making her way back to her apartment off Deansgate.

She'd spent Friday night pampering herself. On Saturday, she travelled to Liverpool and enjoyed a big night out with three of her friends, clubbing until four and staying in a five-star hotel in the old council offices. She got home on Sunday afternoon and powered up her phone. Colin had left seven messages, each threatening greater retribution, before he stopped calling on Saturday afternoon.

She should contact Victor, find out how he was and, more importantly, if he'd found out who Leonov was working for. She doubted Victor had got much information out of him before his mate spotted her. Unable to face him, she rang Zofia, who agreed to meet her. She rushed down to the underground garage and took the Maserati. She drove to their rendezvous, parking it out of sight of the meeting place. It wasn't the best area to leave such a car, but in her experience, anyone thinking of stealing it would assume it belonged to a dealer and leave it alone.

Her meeting with Zofia went better than she'd feared, although the fact that Victor had guessed how things had transpired in the car park made her think the dog had told him. But no, dogs couldn't talk. Victor was more astute than she'd taken him for. She wouldn't underestimate him again.

She returned to the street where she'd left her car and found five lads on bikes examining it. Without hesitating, she strode towards it. They watched her approach.

Their leader pushed his pedals and met her twenty paces before she reached it. 'That yours?' He towered over her.

'What do you think?'

He swung round and shadowed her, riding alongside her as she kept on towards the car. 'I reckon you've stolen it.' A mixture of body odour mingled with the stench of weed wafted off him.

'You might be right.'

Another lad blocked her way with his bike, but moved before she got to him. She reached the car and stepped towards the driver's door. Two of the other bikes blocked her car in.

She opened her door. 'You might want to get out of my way. I don't want to scratch the paintwork running you over.'

They glared at her, but a nod from their leader moved them out of her way. She settled into her seat and pressed the ignition. The engine roared into life, and she drove off, giving the wannabe gangsters a finger wave. Despite her confidence they'd not do anything, her pulse raced, and she took deep breaths to slow it.

The knowledge someone had killed Sawney gave Jodie plenty to ponder. Although not an expert, she'd have sworn he'd taken nothing before arriving at the school. He'd been there at least two hours before turning in. If someone had given him enough to kill him, she'd have noticed.

He was always eager to talk, and his two subjects were how long he'd been clean and that he knew stuff that could get him killed. It looked like he'd been right about the latter, but what did he know and who might have wanted to kill him?

She was pretty sure it hadn't been Toff, but any of the others might have come into that room while she was home showering and, stoned as he was, Toff would have been none the wiser. If she'd resisted the temptation to sneak off, she'd have prevented the killing.

Or become another victim. She needed to find out why Sawney died. Was he another victim of the killer stalking homeless men in Manchester, or had the people clearing the school targeted him? Or was it a third possibility, someone who didn't want whatever Sawney knew coming out? She should have paid more attention and questioned him, although he was always careful to be vague.

The more she considered it, the more she dismissed the first two options. The other men were attacked in out-of-the-way places and the people clearing the school hadn't killed Ziggy, so why kill Sawney? And if it was the third possibility – Sawney's paranoia proving not to have been paranoia at all – that only helped her if she solved the case.

Whichever it was, she needed to find out more. Although she couldn't risk going out on the streets to investigate, she still had contacts. She made some calls and by Monday morning, she knew enough to contact Colin.

'Give me one reason I shouldn't sack you?'

Tosser! 'Morning, Colin. And what would be your justification for such an action?'

'Let me see. Being useless. But oh no, I'd have to sack most of the office if that were the case. How about not being at work when you should be—'

'I am at work.'

'I told you, if you had nothing by Friday evening, you were off the story. That means you should be here, at your desk.'

'Don't you read your emails?'

'Yeah, of course.' The sound of keystrokes replaced his voice, then the annoying mumble he made when concentrating replaced them. 'Where did you get this information from?'

'My sources.'

He gave a nasty laugh. 'I don't know who you think you are, luv, but I won't publish anything without knowing the veracity of the information.'

'I'm not your "luv".' Wanker. But she told him her source for the story.

Someone had held Sawney down and injected him with a lethal dose of pure heroin. Tests showed he'd not touched any for several weeks. The police were investigating the motive.

Now she'd confirmed her source, he read it again. 'Okay. That's not a bad story. Keep on your source and let me have updates.' For once, his praise didn't sound grudging. 'Have the police got any suspects?'

Apart from me? 'They've questioned one of the homeless people, but let him go.' Toff's encounter with the police had left him shaken, but it was clear they believed he'd had nothing to do with Sawney's death.

'Nothing to do with the guys who threw you out of the school, then?'

'Not to my knowledge.'

'You still haven't found out who was behind the raid?'

'I'm working on that.'

'Okay, you've got until tomorrow to find out who's behind the evictions.'

'No problem. What about the murdered—' But he'd hung up. 'Wanker!' She shut her phone off.

What she hadn't told Colin was that her source had confirmed the name of the security firm who'd raided the school. Time to find out who they worked for. She made a call.

'My company's having problems with undesirables using our empty premises for sleeping quarters. Is that something you can deal with?'

'Of course, madam. We've done the same for other clients.'

'That's reassuring to know. Can you tell me who?' Surely it couldn't be this easy.

'I'm afraid not. We pride ourselves on giving our clients confidentiality. This is not a service some clients like to advertise having used.'

'It sounds to me like you're making claims you can't substantiate. I need someone with a track record—'

'We've extensive experience, I assure you. We can send someone out to survey the premises and they'll be able to tell you who we've worked for, in confidence, of course.'

'Of course.' Was there somewhere she could get the keys for? But not at this short notice. 'I'm close to you, so I'll pop in and we can discuss it.'

The two men she'd burnt and who could recognise her were probably still in hospital. And if not, they'd be off sick. She'd wear her most intimidating power-suit. She made an appointment for the afternoon and arranged to get her hair dyed blonde.

By the time she'd finished, nobody who'd known her on the streets would have recognised the glamorous young woman who climbed out of the bright blue Maserati MC20. Several faces came to the window of the offices of The Shield Group as she parked in one of the visitor's spaces. A sign by the door listed the companies in the group, including Droylsden Shield, the company Leonov worked for. The confidence she got from her Tom Ford power-suit dispelled any apprehension she felt at coming here.

As she'd expected, even without seeing her car, the smarmy sales guy she'd spoken to on the phone recognised that her outfit and handbag would have cost him six months' salary. Once she'd signed the contract in the name of a firm whose details she'd harvested from Companies House, he couldn't wait to tell her the name of their client.

As he led her to the reception, a commotion ahead roused a slight sense of unease, dampening her euphoria.

A man's angry voice: 'Why should I have to come in when I'm on the sick?'

A lower voice tried to placate him, and the salesman gave Jodie a nervous smile. As they turned the corner and entered the reception area, she saw him. Leonov, the man who she'd set fire to in the school. He stopped his diatribe as he saw her and stared.

Jodie's insides dropped.

CHAPTER 38

Zofia had been at the kitchen table having her porridge when her brother wandered into the room and his phone rang. He stared at it for several seconds.

'Aren't you going to answer it?'

His complexion had paled. 'It's Robertson.'

Zofia put down her mug. 'What does he want?'

Kasper shook his head and took the call. He put it on speaker.

'Kasper?'

'Yes, and my sister's here.'

'Good. Have either of you heard anything about Chopra's murder?'

At the mention of the man in charge of the disused school they were investigating, Kasper's mouth fell open.

Zofia answered for them. 'Only that someone killed him.' She hesitated before adding, 'Do you know anything about it?'

'What do you mean, Ms Dąbrowski?'

Oh hell! She wisely kept quiet.

'You think I had something to do with it?'

'I just meant why would you think we'd have heard anything?'

'Because you're private detectives in the city and you'd just investigated him.'

'As you say, we're private detectives and don't investigate crimes. All we did was confirm that he managed the school property you were interested in.'

'So you did, Ms Dąbrowski. And his removal has created a big problem for me.'

Her first response was relief that their work hadn't led to the man's death. But then she considered who else might be interested in him. Was another client, Novak, responsible for his death? She realised Robertson was speaking.

'. . . find out who's replaced him and get back to me.' He ended the call.

Kasper looked relieved. 'At least he's not coming down yet.'

'What?'

He cocked his head at her.

'My mind wandered. Sorry.'

'He's generally worth focusing on, I'd think.'

'Tell me what he said.'

'He said he might have to come down if we don't give him the information he needs. If he does, he could decide we're loose ends from when he . . . You know.'

When he had his men kill Alex Novak's sons. 'Yes. I know. And we just need to find out who's Chopra's replacement?'

'That's all. By close of play, today.' Kasper poured himself a coffee and slumped into a chair.

'Don't get comfortable, we're going into work in five.'

'I've not had breakfast.'

'Get something on the way.'

'I need something now. I've had to deal with an angry Robertson.'

She stood and took her bowl to the dishwasher. 'I'll see you there then.'

'Hang on.' He gulped his coffee, spilling some on the table, and rushed to catch up with her.

She sensed his resentment on their journey to the office, but Zofia kept her thoughts to herself. Now wasn't the time to tell her brother he should have stood up to Robertson. They had enough on today without this. Her hope that Victor would come into work died when he called. She almost told him, but didn't want to guilt trip him into coming in. It wasn't something he needed to know, and Robertson wasn't even aware that Victor worked for them.

She felt bad she hadn't told Victor the truth about Jodie, deciding to give him that news face to face. He'd be furious that Jodie had fooled him, but she doubted not telling him would put him at risk. He already had misgivings about Jodie and even if he came across her, he'd not say anything to her that could hurt them.

Despite the temptation to use Jodie, she resisted. Both the council and the education department rebuffed her calls, so she got in touch with a contact she'd made at the council admin offices. She'd met him while working on a previous investigation. He replied to her text offering to meet her for lunch, with the name of an out-of-the-way pub.

A text from Victor arrived, and after looking up information for him on the company whose name he'd sent her, she rang him, putting him on speaker for Kasper's benefit. Victor's revelation of Novak's connection to that property development 'fixer' gave them plenty to think about.

While she wound up the call, Kasper punched keys on his computer.

'There's a Guy Ellison on the board of GE Holdings Property Development,' he said. 'He looks like the rattled man Victor described coming out of Novak's office.'

Zofia joined him at his screen and agreed. 'So, this man has contacts with Novak?'

'And it seems he's stressed by Chopra's death.'

'That's an assumption without evidence. It could be something unrelated.'

'But I bet it isn't.'

She checked the time. 'I'd better go. We'll talk later.' She put on her coat and had just reached the door when the entry phone buzzed. She studied the screen. 'What the hell does he want?' Then she remembered they'd promised him an update on their hunt for his sons' killers.

'Who?' Kasper looked up in alarm.

'Novak.'

'Did you send the report?'

Zofia's cheeks grew warm. 'I forgot. Sorry.'

They'd concocted an imaginary dossier based on rumour and innuendo. It didn't come to any conclusions, but they hoped it would be enough to keep him off their backs.

She picked up the handset. 'Come in, Mr Novak.' She took her coat off and returned to her desk. 'Remember, say nothing about Ellison and let me deal with him.'

Kasper gave a relieved nod. 'With pleasure.'

Looking stressed, Novak refused her offer of refreshments, and they took him to the boardroom. He went into attack mode before he'd taken a seat.

'Why didn't I get my update on your hunt for my sons' killers?'

'My fault,' Zofia said. 'The report's almost ready, but I'm waiting to hear from a source in Bucharest.'

'Who the hell's in Bucharest?'

She'd got the idea from the fact that two of the women his sons had killed came from there. 'Your sons had business dealings with some unsavoury characters there.'

'Who?' Novak took a seat.

A police contact she'd made when she'd attempted to contact the family of one of the women had given them the names of the key people-traffickers in Bucharest. 'It's all in the report, which I'll let you have shortly.'

He sat, fingers steepled and deep in thought. He broke the silence before they did. 'Not Birmingham, then?'

She exchanged a look with her brother. They'd laid a false trail to Birmingham following his sons' killings. 'We believe whoever did it flew into East Midlands.'

Novak took this on board. 'You got the names of whoever did it?'

'We haven't got evidence which would stand up in court, but if there were any, the police would have it. We can give you the names of people who were probably behind it.'

This seemed to satisfy him, and still appearing preoccupied, he left them. Zofia saw him to the door and returned to the office. Kasper waited at the top of the stairs.

'Are we going to give him the names the police in Bucharest gave us?'

'That's what we agreed.' She grabbed her coat. She was late.

'But what if he goes over there and starts taking them out?'

She shrugged. 'Those guys are scum. At least one of them trafficked Jehona and her friends and was indirectly responsible for her murder. His loss would hardly qualify as such. With any luck, one of them will kill Novak and he'll be out of our hair.'

She'd pulled on her coat and started for the door when she noted Kasper looking at her with his mouth open. She stopped. 'What?'

'Nothing.'

'Good. I'll get going.' If she hurried, she'd get to her contact before he returned to the office.

She arrived at the pub as he left by the back door. She slewed into a space in the car park and almost ran to intercept him.

'You owe me a lunch.' He gave a sardonic grin.

'Sorry, something came up. I'll make it up to you.'

'I might hold you to that. What was it you wanted?'

'One of my clients wants to know who's taking over from Russ Chopra.'

'Oh yeah. He seems a popular guy.'

A stab of alarm pricked her. 'What do you mean?'

'You're the second person to ask that today.'

'Who's the other?' The fact he was so happy to pass on information gave her pause.

He grinned. 'You know I can't say. I mean, would you want me to tell people you were interested in him or her?'

'No. And I'm sure Mr Ellison will be grateful for your discretion.'

His mouth opened into an O. 'Who told you?'

'You know I can't say.'

His expression darkened, and he scanned the car park. 'I'm not confirming it was him, but whoever I spoke to was very keen to know who'd be stepping in for Chopra.'

'How much?' Would Robertson pay? She was sure he would.

'They were offering five hundred.'

'I haven't got that on me.'

'Don't worry, I'm sure you're good for it. You can give me the money when you buy me that meal you owe me, but let's make it a dinner, somewhere nice.' Evidently recovered from the shock, he winked and gave her a name.

Feeling unclean, Zofia returned to her car and drove back to the office. At least this should placate Robertson. Back at the office, she gave Kasper the name she'd discovered, and how much the information cost, including the five hundred in cash.

He messaged Robertson, finished and placed his phone on the desk. 'That should keep him off our backs.'

'My contact said that Ellison—'

'Who?'

'Keep up. Ellison. The flustered-looking man Victor saw hurrying out of Novak's place. The real-estate process—'

'The process fixer. Right. What about him?'

'Ellison was asking my contact the same thing I was.'

'So Novak's interested in the same thing.'

'Assuming Ellison is working for him.' She could see a big collision between Novak and Robertson and hoped they'd not end up crushed between them.

'It's worrying that your man gave up Ellison's name.'

'He didn't. I gave it to him. He wouldn't tell me.'

'Oh, right, in that—'

His phone interrupted him.

'Yep,' he answered it. 'Is everything—?'

He stopped speaking, and the blood drained from his features.

Before Zofia could work out what was happening, he ended the call.

'Robertson's coming down, to, and I quote, "sort things out".'

Did that include dealing with her and her brother?

CHAPTER 39

Oscar shot away from the Bully, snatching the lead from my hand. He ran round the corner of the tower block, the beast in hot pursuit. The car we'd been spying on just around that corner roared into life and fishtailed away, leaving a cry of alarm and then one of pain in its wake.

I ran after the dogs.

Behind me, the Bully's owner shouted, 'TYSON COME BACK!'

Rounding the corner, it took me a moment to discern what I was seeing. Instead of attacking Oscar, Tyson had fastened his teeth on the arm of the man I'd seen taking an envelope from the driver. The car disappeared round the next corner and Oscar stood on the lid of a dumpster a few paces past the melee.

The man being attacked screamed as Tyson's owner charged past me and tried to get the dog off him.

I circled past the struggling figures and approached the dumpster. 'Are you okay, Oscar?'

I'm fine. That clumsy oaf would never catch me.

'Do you want to come down?'

I'll stay here for the moment. I've got a better view.

Tyson's owner prised his dog's teeth away from his victim. More people arrived, including Cermak.

'What the hell's going on?'

The injured man held his forearm and grimaced. 'This monster attacked me.' He pointed at Tyson.

Panic crossed Tyson's owner's face. 'He was dealing drugs.'

'No, I fucking wasn't.' Blood dripped from between his fingers.

'Yes, he was. You saw him.' Tyson's owner pointed at me.

Part of me wanted Tyson's owner to suffer, but I considered the consequences. They'd put Tyson down and I didn't want that. 'He was up to something. A dodgy guy in a car gave him some money.' I pointed at the pocket where he'd deposited the envelope.

'What? That wasn't for drugs.'

Cermak had looked confused to this point. He'd already evicted me, and he seemed to have a soft spot for Tyson's owner. This latest twist offered him a way out.

'What was it for?'

'You what?'

Cermak stepped towards him. 'If the dodgy guy wasn't paying you for drugs, what was it for?'

The injured man looked at me, then at the concrete between us. 'None of your business.'

'You're on housing benefit. You're supposed to declare any income.'

He opened his mouth, then closed it as he formulated a reply. 'It was a loan.'

Cermak crossed his arms. 'One you were taking out, or was he repaying you?'

Tyson growled and, and although his owner held him in a firm grip, his victim edged away. 'He was paying me.'

Tyson's owner sneered. 'Where the fuck you get money to lend? You're always skint.'

'He was borrowing me the money.'

'Make your mind up.'

'It's yer dog. It's meking me nervous.'

Cermak unfolded his arms and turned on Tyson's owner. 'Take that animal away. I'll deal with you later.'

He pulled on the dog's collar. 'Yeah, but—'

'Later, I said.'

Cermak waited until his owner removed Tyson. 'Right, you,' he pointed at the injured man. 'Get your arm sorted and you can look for somewhere else to live.'

'Hang on, I've not done nothing.' He looked to me for support.

'You were dealing drugs. He saw you.' Cermak waved in my direction.

'No, I didn't. I saw him take an envelope from the man in the car.'

Cermak glared at me, then spun on his heel and stomped off. Oscar leapt off the dumpster and came to my side.

'Do you want me to call you an ambulance?' I nodded at his arm, which had stopped dripping blood.

'You can fuck off, yer grass.'

I glared at him. 'Yeah, you're the one taking money for information and I'm the grass?'

He swallowed and looked away.

'Come on, Oscar.'

Oscar growled at the man as he passed him and followed me. ***What a rude man.***

'Some people have no manners, Oscar.'

You can say that again. I'm glad we're leaving.

Apart from my concern that we'd be back on the streets again, I worried about what I'd seen. The dodgy guy wasn't a dealer or a loan shark. I felt certain he was Novak's man, paying for information on my whereabouts, which meant I wasn't safe here. I should never have agreed to watch the man's sons. If I'd known they'd be killed while I was following them, I certainly never would have.

And now their father suspected I'd played a part in their deaths. How had his men tracked me to my home? I'd been careful since they chased me into the park.

I rang Digger, but he couldn't come over until tomorrow. Disappointed and worried, I arranged for him to collect me mid-morning and told Cermak that I'd found somewhere and would be moving out a day early.

His confused and disappointed look gave me the last enjoyable moment I had in that place. I couldn't sleep, fearing an attack. Unsure where it would come from, I put a barrier against the front door and blocked the inside of the windows as best I could. After lying on the bed in my clothes for hours, I got up, had my last shower there, and packed my meagre belongings to be ready for tomorrow.

At first light, I dozed off, to be woken by banging on my door. I slid off the bed in a panic, slipped my shoes on, placed my glasses on my nose and checked the time. Ten, the time Digger had agreed to collect me.

'Digger?'

'Come on, Victor, let me in.'

I dragged the flimsy chest of drawers aside and opened the door. 'Morning, Digger.'

Oscar ran to Digger and greeted him.

'Morning, Oscar, excited to be going to your new home?'

Oscar studied me with a puzzled expression. ***What's he talking about?***

Digger saved me having to explain by pointing at the chest by the front door. 'Keen to go, are you?'

'That's staying. I wasn't sure if anyone would come for me in the night.' I closed the door, led him into the living room, and told him what I'd seen.

'The people at the diner were talking about a young homeless guy asking questions. I didn't realise it was you he was looking for. Anything I can do?'

'Just help me get out of here.' Digger had already been a big help, and I didn't want him any more involved.

He looked around and pointed at the sofa propped up in front of the window. 'How much of this you taking?'

'Only the TV and stand, plus the throw and cushions.' I pointed to a garbage bag in the corner. 'The rest came with the flat.'

We'd put everything I owned together in a pile in the living room when the key turned in my lock.

Cermak opened the door. 'You're still here?'

'Well spotted. I'll give you the keys once I'm ready to leave.'

Oscar grew agitated, and I noticed an Airedale behind Cermak.

'Your replacement's here.' He stepped aside to reveal Toby's owner. Seeing him with Toby, I was glad I'd gone to the trouble of visiting him in hospital to tell him we'd found his dog.

'Hello, Toby.' Digger bent down to greet the dog.

Oscar stepped towards it. ***Nobody invited you in.***

'Oscar, be nice.'

He's taking our home.

'No, he isn't, and I'd much rather he had it than some stranger.' The fact the man we'd pulled from the flames was taking the flat seemed cruel, but he hadn't forced me out.

'If you've quite finished.' Cermak looked at the pile of belongings. 'You're not taking anything which was here when you moved in?'

I produced my phone and opened an image file. 'Here's the flat the day I moved in.' I showed him the pictures. 'And here are the items I brought with me.'

'Hmmm. Okay, you'd better get moving.' He stomped off towards reception.

Toby's owner spoke for the first time. 'I'm really sorry about this. Can I help?' He pointed at the stack of my belongings.

I looked at his bandaged hands. 'We'll be fine. You check the place out. Oscar, behave or you can come with us.'

I'll keep an eye on this lot. He nodded at our belongings.

Digger and I took bags of clothes and bedding to his small van and returned. Oscar and Toby looked like they'd made peace.

His owner stood in the doorway to the kitchen. 'There's nothing to cook with.'

'There wasn't when I moved in.' I studied my remaining goods, most of which Zofia and Kasper had given me. 'Where's your stuff?'

'Ain't got none. I lost it all in the fire.'

I split my belongings, deciding I didn't need four plates and cups, and left him enough to make a start, while Digger carried the rest to his van. Embarrassed by Toby's owner's effusive thanks, I picked up the last box and left. At reception I returned the keys to a scowling Cermak, glad it would be the last time I saw him.

'Hang on.' He held up an index finger.

'What now?'

'You've got post. A letter.' He placed an envelope on the counter and slid it to me.

Was this a reprieve? Even he wouldn't be cruel enough to do that. But no. The envelope bore a crooked stamp, and my address, written in blue biro, contained an incorrect postcode. 'Thanks.' I picked it up and stuffed it in the box.

Oscar and I returned to the van, where Digger waited.

'Okay, Victor, where to?'

I shoved the box in the back. Even in such a tiny van, my pile of belongings looked pitiful, and with Oscar beside me, I got in the front. 'You said you had a storage unit?'

Digger studied me across Oscar's head. 'I assumed you had somewhere to stay.'

'Yeah, I have, but I won't need all my stuff.'

Digger didn't seem convinced, but took us along Hyde Road to a lockup behind a row of terraced houses in Belle Vue. It smelled of spices, and shelves laden with tins of food, bags of rice and beans lined two walls.

Once we'd emptied the van, I noticed the brackets welded to the sides.

'What are these?'

'It's me mum. She converted it into a camper van, but I took all the bits out when she passed.'

'Have you still got all the units?'

'Sure, do you want to borrow the van until you're sorted?'

An hour later, we'd found all the units, including a narrow bed with a foam mattress. Digger produced a toolkit, and we reattached them to the vehicle. By late afternoon, we had a cramped but serviceable living space containing my bedding and clothes.

'What do you think, Oscar?' Digger asked.

It's alright for him, but where am I sleeping?

I could see his point. There wasn't much floor space. 'You can go on the front seat.'

He frowned. ***I suppose it will do. For now.***

'Right, let's get your water tank topped up, Victor. You can do it at my house when you drop me off.' Digger threw me the keys to the van.

An hour later, with dusk falling, I fed Oscar and sat, exhausted. I'd need to find somewhere to park up for the night.

Are you going to open that letter?

'What?'

The one you got as we left the flats.

Now, where was it? 'I'll read it tomorrow.'

You've forgotten where you put it, haven't you?

'No, I'm just tired.'

It's in here. He scratched at a drawer in the bulkhead.

There it lay, on the top. I ignored his smug expression and opened it. I tried to decipher the tiny script in the dim light.

Well?

'Let me read it.'

> If you're reading this, it means I'm deid.

A bit melodramatic, but not out of character. And true. Should I handle this with gloves? But it would only have Sawney's prints. I read on.

> I've given it to a newsagent friend to post if I don't see him fer three days.

He'd been dead for over a week, but the second-class stamp and misremembered postcode would explain the delay.

> I know you think I'm off me heid. I see you roling your eyes when I mention what I know, but you're far from the worst. Before I lost my job, I worked at Oldham council in the planning department. RC, one of the lads there, was keen on fast cars and expensive clubs.
>
> We became mates, and he took me clubbing with him. We met the owner who slipped RC an envelope. He denied everything when I challenged him, but it was obvious what he was doing. My marriage was a mess, and I needed money, so I forced him to cut me in.

He took big risks, taking bribes from all sides. Some nasty people involved, but he seemed to have a charmed life. I however, didn't. I got caught, lost me job, home and you've seen where I've ended. RC, though, went from strength to strength. I knew he had a network of people greasing the wheels.

I followed his career, and the people who paid him. They got their money's worth, and he climbed the greasy pole.

Wen I first got on the streets, he'd help me out, fifty here, hundred there. I knew stuff about him but didn't have evidence. It would have made his life uncomfortable if I'd said something, but I left under a very big cloud. I'd have been the bitter drunk being vindictive. A few hundred was worth it to avoid the hassle.

Then a few months ago, I saw him with one of his clients I suppose you call them. They met in a park. Each arrived separate with a coffee and sat on the same bench pretending they didn't know each other. I saw them again a week later. The following week, I hid a voice-activated recorder under the bench. It cost me two nights in the hostel but was worth it.

I took photos, not great, but with the recording they're enough. RC lives in a very nice house now. He wasn't pleased to see me, especially when I played the recording. He snatched it off me and gave me a few slaps, but it was a copy.

I'd have been hapy with fifty grand, but that cost him double. He's supposed to be paying me

> the money using crypto. I don't know how that works, but me newsagent mate does.
>
> The recording and photos are safe. I'm sending the details separate. My mate will send them the day after he sends this.

I let the contents sink in, then rang John.

CHAPTER 40

Jodie couldn't believe it when Leonov stared at her but didn't appear to recognise her. He'd had a clear view of her when she'd kicked his shin behind the pub, but she'd been in her street clothes without make-up or dyed hair. Her heels added to her height, and, despite her trepidation, she wore a smile rather than the grimace she'd displayed during her attack. All this, plus her confident demeanour and the other staff's deference, must have been enough to fool him.

She'd driven off at speed, whooping in exhilaration, and returned home. The information she'd gathered gave her plenty to think about. She wrote a story which would keep Colin off her back, but she had others to share the information with before he could publish it.

The next morning, while Victor was moving out of his dingy flat, she made her way to the KZD offices on Cheetham Hill Road. Unsure of the reception she'd get, she experienced trepidation as she waited for Kasper or Zofia to answer the door. She wasn't sure which she preferred. Kasper was easier to manipulate, but that might have changed now he knew she'd deceived them about being a journalist.

Zofia answered and buzzed her in. Kasper looked up when she walked into the office and did a double take. She wasn't glammed up like she'd been for her visit to the security company, but she still looked far sleeker than she had in her street-living get-up.

She scanned the office. 'Victor not in?'

Zofia answered. 'He's having a few days off.'

'He's okay, isn't he?'

'No thanks to you.' Kasper's tone removed any uncertainty she might have had about his attitude towards her.

Her immediate impulse was to snap back, but she controlled herself. 'Yes, I'm sorry. I didn't mean to get him attacked.'

'If you say so. Why are you here now? I imagine it's not just to find out how Victor is.'

'I've got some information which might help you.' She told them who was paying for the properties to be cleared.

Kasper turned to his sister. 'What did I say? I never believed his "Homes for Heroes" bullshit.'

'Okay, you were right. Rudy Glass is a manipulative liar.' She turned back to Jodie. 'Are you going to expose his hypocrisy?'

'I suppose so, but that's up to Colin, my editor.'

'You can't let him get away with it?' Zofia looked horrified.

Jodie shrugged. 'Like I say, it's not my call. One thing I've found doing this job is many of the men in public life are scumbags. If we expose him, he'll be embarrassed for a few days, then he'll go back to doing what he's always done and everyone will forget it.'

Kasper folded his arms. 'Okay, thanks for telling us. I'll let Victor know next time I speak to him.'

'Right.'

'It's not one of our jobs. It was something Victor was doing pro bono. Is that all you wanted? We're pretty busy.'

'Don't be rude, Kasper,' Zofia said. 'Thanks, Jodie. I'll email the information to Victor. I'm sure he'll be very grateful.'

'If you're busy, I can help. I'm good at finding out information.' She looked from brother to sister. 'Or writing summaries . . .'

'Well, we've got—'

'We're busy, but not that busy,' Kasper butted in.

Jodie had had a lifetime of being excluded, so didn't need an interpreter. 'Okay, I'll leave you to it then.'

Zofia accompanied her to the front door. 'You'll have to forgive Kasper. He's still furious you lied to us.'

'No worries. I'll see you around.'

Jodie returned to the Yaris she'd parked on a side street. It went better with her reporter persona. She hadn't wanted her colleagues to know her family had money. By the time she reached it, her fury at the way Kasper had treated her had abated to simmering anger. It wasn't him who'd got his head bashed in, so why was he so annoyed?

She'd go into the office and speak to Colin in person. There was no way she could stay undercover. Victor was sure to have let everyone know what she was. Anyway, she didn't need to do it anymore. She'd uncovered who was behind the attacks on rough sleepers. Someone else could investigate who was killing the homeless men. As for Sawney's death, she'd see how the police got on with solving it. She'd make sure it stayed in the headlines. She owed him that much.

Instead of taking the motorway, she tootled down the A56, arriving in Broadheath almost an hour later. On a whim, she drove on and rang her mum, meeting her for an early lunch in Hale. The worry she might bump into Colin passed in an instant. He hated Hale, and even if he saw her, she could claim she was meeting an informant.

Her mother again told her to leave her job, and that she didn't need it, but that, as always, only made Jodie more determined to make a go of it.

The scruffy office block in the heart of an industrial park wasn't somewhere she imagined herself working, but as Colin said, if she wanted to work in a swanky office building, she should get a job with one of the nationals.

She parked in the grotty corner by the bins, a penalty of arriving late. The stench from the nearest open dumpster made her gag as she locked the car and made her way into reception. A familiar chemical-floral smell and tired faux-leather sofas in the waiting area drained any enthusiasm she'd arrived with.

The receptionist, who had never hidden her dislike of Jodie, slid over the visitor's book. 'Can you sign in, please, miss?'

'Ha, ha. Is he in?' Jodie gestured up towards Colin's office.

The receptionist picked up her phone. 'I'll tell him you're here.'

'I'll tell him myself.' Jodie ignored her protests and took the stairs to the next floor.

Colin looked up from his desk when she knocked on his open door. 'Your email arrived.' He gestured at the screen of his laptop. 'I'll get the legal team to look at it and if it stands up—'

'Of course it will stand up. You've got to run it.' Despite what she'd said to Zofia, she wanted to expose Glass and his ilk. At least people would be forewarned.

'I'll make that decision.'

'I risked my life to get that story.'

Colin scoffed. 'Slept on the streets for a few nights? Give me a break.'

'Anytime you want to give it a go, Colin.'

His grin faded. 'Right. There's a council meeting needs covering—'

'That's not my beat. I'm features and human interest.'

'You're what I tell you to be. You've got an hour. Don't miss the start.' He returned his attention to his screen.

Fuck you, arsehole. Her tyres squealed as she left the car park, but she'd calmed down before she reached the main road. The council meeting proved as boring as she'd feared until they turned to a discussion on planning applications. The mention of an address made her sit up and pay attention.

'. . . an offer for the site which we're minded to accept. The premises are no longer required for educational purposes and the offer is significantly above the current market rate.'

Who the hell were they proposing to sell the school to? She listened to the rest of the meeting with increased attention but, as she'd suspected they would, they hid the name of the prospective buyer by citing the information as commercially sensitive. There must be a source in the council, but this wasn't her usual beat. Colin might know, but she didn't feel like asking him for any favours and she could imagine his scathing putdown. Sod him. She knew exactly who might know.

The meeting finished, and she rang a number as familiar as her own, but he didn't pick up, so she left a message and returned to the office. She finished the report on the meeting and sent it to Colin, who summoned her to his office.

'Can you link the sale of the school to the people behind the thugs who cleared the dos— er, homeless people out of it?'

'Go on, Colin, call them dossers if you want. Nobody to hear you here but me.'

He gave her a sour look. 'Well, can you?'

'Who's your source in the town hall?'

'I haven't got a source. That's your job.'

Her face grew hot. 'That's not my usual beat, so why would I need a source there?'

'Leave it to me.' He sighed and punched keys. 'Bloody amateurs.'

'What did you call me?' Jodie had had enough.

He ignored her and picked up his phone.

Her father's advice came to the fore. 'Take a deep breath and count to ten.' She also recalled the rest of his recommendation, 'Then kick them in the balls.' She smiled, leaving a puzzled Colin on his call.

When the time came, she'd enjoy telling Colin to stuff his job, but she'd do it on her own terms, not as a reaction to him being an arse. She didn't get a response to her message until late afternoon.

'Sorry to call back so late.'

'No problem. You been busy?'

'You could say. The shit's hitting the fan in the next day or so.'

'Anything I can help with?'

'I thought you didn't want to get involved.'

She didn't, but could she really avoid it? 'Be careful.'

'Always. What was it you wanted?'

She told him what she'd learnt at the council meeting.

'Shit! You know who the prospective buyer is?'

So much for him knowing. 'Not yet. Colin, my editor, hasn't found out yet.'

'Let me know when he does.'

'Will do. It's not going to cause you problems, is it?' Was he interested in buying the school?

'No way. It's just a minor detail I need to sort out.'

Despite his bravado, she could tell he was worried. Would whatever he was involved in spill over into her carefully constructed life?

CHAPTER 41

After spending the night at Piccadilly Trading Estate, I got cleaned up using the tiny kitchen sink. I'd hardly slept, a combination of the headache, which lingered, waking every time I heard a noise outside, and trepidation about what I had to do first thing. I'd have to find a proper site tonight.

We had a breakfast of egg and bacon butties from a nearby caff, and I made my way to Strangeways View, nerves tight as I anticipated an ambush round every corner. The only saving grace was that I'd never seen Novak's men out and about before midday. I parked the camper round the corner. Oscar refused to come with me, and I left him in the back with a window open.

I checked the surrounding vehicles before making the short walk to the entrance. Despite the cold, I arrived sweating. I pushed the doors open to be greeted with the familiar stink of weed and unwashed humanity. My heart sank on seeing Cermak behind the counter. He watched me enter the reception with cold eyes. I wouldn't allow him to intimidate me.

'Is there any post for me?'

'No.'

'You going to check?'

'I don't need to. Nobody's got post yet. It hasn't arrived.'

'Right, can you contact me if anything arrives? I'm expecting an important letter.'

He reached under the counter and produced a form. 'Fill in a redirection form and we'll send it on.'

'That will take days. I need this urgently. If I give you my number, can you ring me if something arrives?'

'We haven't time. Fill this in or you can come every day to check. Suit yourself.' He folded his arms.

The thought of coming here every day filled me with dread. I pulled the form towards me. 'You got a pen?'

With bad grace, he recovered a chewed biro from a mug under the counter and threw it to me. I managed to get it working and wrote John's address on the form. Not expecting a result, I scribbled my number across the bottom with a request to ring me if anything arrived. Cermak wouldn't bother, but one of the others might.

I drove to the rendezvous where I was meeting John and Craig. The engine sounded like a sewing machine puttering at just below thirty. The unmistakable figures of Craig, tall with long hair and beard, and John, short, stocky with a large bald head fringed with a ring of grey hair, waited on the pavement. I pulled up in a parking bay past them.

John bent down to my window. 'You going on holiday, Brother?'

'It's Digger's. I'm borrowing it for a few days.'

'Problems with your accommodation?'

I didn't want to burden my friends with my problems. 'Shall we look at this letter?'

'Just the one? I thought you said he sent two?'

'The other hadn't arrived. I've asked them to redirect it to your hostel, like we agreed. You sure it will be safe?'

'No problem.' John jerked a thumb at the back. 'Shall we retire to read the one you received?'

Oscar complained when we turfed him out and he sat on the front passenger seat, chuntering. The suspension groaned when they got in and they sat side by side on the bed, filling the back of the vehicle. I perched on a seat beside the back door. They laid Sawney's letter on Craig's huge thigh and read it in silence.

'Poor Sawney.' Craig passed me the letter. 'Nobody believed him, did they?'

'You going to give it to the police, Brother?'

'I don't know, John. It's just conjecture, isn't it? As he said, he's got no evidence.'

John waved a hand at the letter. 'You want to wait for the second one?'

'If it arrives. He got the postcode wrong, and it was only luck I got the first one.'

Craig frowned. 'I wish he'd put more information in the letter.'

'Let's hope the other arrives.' I looked from Craig to John. 'You said you had some news for me?'

'We've spoken to everyone who slept in Mill View Academy last Sunday night. I'm certain none of them would have hurt Sawney.'

That news made me feel better. 'From the letter, it looks as if this RC paid someone to kill him.'

'One of the men who raided the place?'

'It makes sense. And I met one of them.'

'Do you know where he lives?'

I studied Craig. 'What are you suggesting?'

'You know what I'm suggesting.'

The thought of beating the truth out of him made me feel sick, even if Craig and his mates did it. 'I'll ask Zofia to do a background check. He might not be involved. From what Toff and Jodie said, they arrived mob-handed. It could be any of them.'

'Jodie?' John frowned. 'The young girl Toff's sweet on?'

His tone worried me. 'What about her?'

'Be careful around her. I think she was the one who spoke to Ziggy.'

'You think she's selling information to the press?'

'Or buying it.'

'You heard something? Is she a reporter?' Oscar had said she didn't smell right.

He winked, suggesting I'd guessed right. Bloody hell!

I drove them into town, the engine straining with the extra weight, dropped them in Piccadilly and drove on to the office, pondering this latest revelation. I'd have to tell Kasper and Zofia about Jodie. Zofia had confirmed that they'd not seen Novak's men at the offices since the one had chased me into the park. They must have concluded I'd spotted them and would stay away. Anyway, they wouldn't recognise the camper van, so it was worth a risk.

Was John talking about Jodie?

'Yes.'

I warned you she was trouble.

'How the hell had I let her fool me?'

Because you wanted to be fooled.

He was right, and I drove on in silence. Despite my belief Novak's men wouldn't be watching the office, I still checked as I arrived. Zofia's car was in the car park, but her brother's wasn't. They sometimes shared, so it didn't mean he wasn't in. I wanted them both there when I told them. I let myself in, Oscar rushing up the stairs ahead of me. He waited at the door from the reception into the office, impatient to greet Zofia. I opened the door.

'Kasper?' Zofia called, but then Oscar shot past me and presented himself. She rubbed his tummy. 'Good boy, I've missed you.'

You hear that?

I rolled my eyes and smiled at her.

'Victor, how are you feeling?'

My headache had faded to almost nothing, provided I didn't jerk my head, and I felt guilty I'd not been in to work, or at least rung to keep her updated. 'Not too bad. I've moved out of the flat.'

'What's happened? Have you somewhere to stay?'

'Long story, and yes, I've got somewhere, thanks. Where's Kasper?'

'He shouldn't be long. Do you want a drink?' She stood.

'I'll get it.' I made two coffees and took them back out to the office. I saw now that she looked like she'd been crying. I didn't know what to do, so placed the mug on her desk. 'Everything okay?'

'Just work stuff. Nothing you need to worry about.' She looked away, but her eyes glistened.

'You don't have to tell me. I'm just a member of staff.'

She stared at her screen. 'You'll always be more than that, Victor. You saved my life.' She sipped her drink. 'I spoke to Sergeant Bowling. Told her I'd seen the guy with the snake tattoo.'

I swallowed. 'What did she say?'

'She said I couldn't have.' Her voice broke. 'We'd killed him . . .' She broke down.

Without thinking, I strode to her chair and held her head against my chest. She let me. What could I say? How do you get over killing someone? True, he'd been trying to kill us, but taking a life was an unimaginable step.

The main door opened, and I released Zofia, almost jumping away. She stood and headed to the kitchen, closing the door behind her before Kasper breezed in. I moved away from her desk and headed to mine.

'. . . Some bloody idiot's parked a camper van in my space. Oh, Victor, I wasn't expecting to see you today.'

'Those are my wheels for the moment.'

'You holidaying on the Cheetham Hill Rivera?' He laughed at his joke. 'Coffee?' He headed towards the kitchen.

I needed to give Zofia a minute. 'How's your arm?' I asked, to distract him, and took my seat.

He waved it in the air. 'They took the bandages off and left the stitches exposed to the air for a few days. They itch like hell, but they'll be coming out soon.'

Zofia emerged from the kitchen with a steaming mug.

'You're a mind reader.' He took it off her and sat at his desk.

She looked remarkably composed. As I gathered my resolve to tell them about Jodie, she cleared her throat.

'I've got some upsetting news, Victor.'

Had she not told Kasper about— But no, she was addressing me. What else had happened?

'Jodie isn't who she claims. She's a reporter posing as homeless.'

Relief made me grin. 'Is that all?'

'You knew?' Kasper said. 'When were you planning to tell us?'

'I've just found out. Although they don't name her in the article, I think she wrote the piece about Sawney taking drugs.'

The siblings exchanged a look. This was clearly news to them.

'When did you find out?' I asked them.

Zofia looked troubled. 'She told me Sunday—'

'Three days ago?'

'Sorry. I wanted to tell you to your face.'

As I'd brought Jodie in, I had no room to complain. 'I presume you've sacked her.'

'She gave us some useful intel. The name of the person paying for the school and other buildings to be cleared. It's the anti-homelessness campaigner, Rudy Glass.'

'Bloody hypocrite. No wonder Craig got nowhere with Homes for Heroes.' I considered his offer to get information out of Leonov.

'Can you see what you can find on Daniel Leonov, the guy I met at the pub?'

Zofia punched the name into a search engine. 'I'll check what's available.'

I switched on my desktop and tried to focus on the work I should have been doing while I was off. My headache was threatening to return, making focusing difficult.

Zofia called out that she'd got something. 'Leonov has a record for violence. Look at this – GBH, ABH, arson. Ironic really, that Jodie set him on fire.'

Kasper looked up from his desk. 'What the hell is a security company doing employing someone with that background?'

'Hmmm.' Zofia studied her screen with a distracted air. 'Bloody hell!'

'What?' I got up and stood behind her so I could see the screen.

An article on a crime blog recounted a group of men who the police had accused of running a protection racket and taking money for handing out punishment beatings. The trial collapsed after witnesses withdrew their statements. The comments below suggested the men were well known for violence and one even hinted they'd killed someone. One respondent had published a photo. Four heavyset men with grim expressions stood on the steps of what might be a court building.

I pointed at the screen. 'That's Leonov, and that's his mate who drove the van.'

Had we found the men who'd killed Sawney?

CHAPTER 42

I'd not had time to find somewhere better to park up for the night, so returned to the same spot on Piccadilly Trading Estate. Exhaustion ensured I slept well until the call woke me. I reached for the phone, but hit the kitchen cupboard and knocked the handset.

'Bugger.' It clattered to the floor, buzzing angrily until I located it. 'Yeah, what?'

'Victor, sorry it's so late. A letter arrived for you this afternoon, but I've only just found the form you filled in.'

Despite being sleep-fuddled, I recognised the voice of the young social worker who worked at Strangeways View. I checked my screen. Twelve thirty-five.

'Right, thanks. I'll collect it in the morning.'

But I lay awake, unable to get back to sleep. In addition to my eagerness to discover who RC was, and what Sawney had on him, I experienced a sense of dread about going back there. Two hours later, I messaged John, who called me straight back. He agreed to come with me. We'd go now.

When I pulled up outside his hostel, he wasn't alone. Craig carried a holdall and opened the passenger door.

'Right, Oscar, shift over.'

Not only am I forced to get up in the middle of the night, I'm made to vacate my seat.

'Come on, Oscar, I'll make it up to you tomorrow.'

What, you're going to get us an actual house to live in?

'That's below the belt, mate.'

A contrite Oscar joined John in the back and Craig dropped the holdall at his feet before climbing in. Having John and Craig with me gave me a confidence I'd not had when I drove there the previous morning.

I pulled away from the pavement, the engine straining. 'Are you staying at the hostel as well, Craig?'

'Not officially, and I had to sneak Trixie in, but someone attacked another homeless man with a dog around ten last night.' Craig's sleep-breath filled the space between us. 'I thought it wise to get off the streets for a few days.'

Had whoever attacked Toby's owner done so because he had a dog? Was it Novak's men looking for me? A surge of guilt washed over me. Despite having reinforcements with me, my grip on the steering wheel tightened as I got closer to Strangeways View. I turned a corner and the tower block containing our former home loomed.

Oscar barked. ***I can smell smoke from a fire.***

'Smoke, where?' I peered into the darkness.

'There's something there.' John pointed at a grey smudge drifting from the side of the building. I stopped and pulled over. Had a resident set fire to his flat? I was amazed it hadn't happened before. Then, from the rear of the building, the sounds of combat. The feared attack from Novak's men must have materialised.

I wanted to drive off, but they'd come because of me. And if they went to my old flat, they'd have attacked Toby's owner.

'Let's go, it's Novak's men.'

We all piled out, and after telling Oscar to stay, I started for the back of the building.

'WAIT!' John's shout stopped me.

Craig reached into his holdall and pulled out a short but solid club. 'I thought this might be useful.'

I hefted it, feeling ready for battle. More yells and growls came from the rear of the building. We clattered round the corner, anger dispelling the fear which threatened to paralyse me.

The scene that greeted us resembled something from Dante's Inferno. Against a background of flames, two men struggled while a third battled with a monstrous adversary. It took me a moment to recognise what I was seeing. The flames came from an open dumpster. The monstrous beast was Tyson, the Bully who'd terrorised Oscar, and he had another human victim.

Unsure who was being attacked, we peered at the three men involved. One I recognised as Tyson's owner. The other two must be Novak's men. I pointed them out to Craig and John.

'It's those two.'

We charged, yelling. Everyone froze, including the dog. The two masked attackers ran. Before we could chase them, an engine roared, and lights blinded me. A dark, powerful vehicle exploded out of the darkness and stopped alongside the fleeing muggers. They leapt in and it raced away before they'd closed the doors.

'Come on, you bastards.' Tyson's owner had picked up an extendible cosh and faced us, his dog alongside him.

'Hang on, it's me, Victor.' The flames stretched my skin over my face and the stink of burning rubbish filled my nostrils.

'Yeah, come on, then.' He hefted the weapon and Tyson growled. 'You and your mates.'

'We're after them, Brother.' John pointed in the direction where the vehicle had disappeared.

'You what?' He lowered the cosh.

'They're working with the guy your dog chased on Monday.'

Tyson growled, and I pointed at him. 'Can you keep a hold of his collar?'

His owner patted his head. 'Come on, Tyson, easy.'

We stepped away from the burning bin. 'Can you tell me what happened?'

He shook his head and grimaced. Blood flowed from a cut above his eyebrow and his face bore the marks of a beating. 'Two men came to the door, shouting about a fire outside.' He gestured at the dumpster. 'One hit me with this.' He hefted the extendable cosh. 'They dragged me out and slammed the door on Tyson.'

'How did he get out?'

'I shouted to him, and he came through the window.' He pointed at the shattered pane behind me. Pieces of glass covered the ground outside.

I looked around to get my bearings. 'That's my old room.'

'Yeah, well, I offered to swap with the old guy.' He looked embarrassed. 'It's a better room than mine.'

I couldn't help feeling satisfaction that his selfishness had got him a hiding. Sirens sounded in the distance.

'We'd better go,' Craig said.

From the building came a voice I'd hoped never to hear again. Cermak's. 'I should have guessed it would be you.'

He stood at the back corner, surrounded by several of the residents, come to gawp.

'I didn't do anything.'

'You would say that. What about them two?' Cermak pointed at Craig and John.

'He's right, they didn't do nothing,' Tyson's owner spoke up. 'It was two guys in a car. They scarpered.' He hefted the cosh, as if he'd caused them to flee.

I wanted to run, but if I didn't get my envelope, there was no guessing what would happen to it.

'Have you got my letter?' I asked Cermak.

'What the hell you talking about?'

'I'm here for my post.' Sirens sounded in the distance.

'Come back in office hours. I've got this to deal with.' He gestured at the burning dumpster.

John signalled we needed to go. I ran to the open back door and pushed past the rubberneckers. The young social worker's eyes widened when I ran into the reception.

'You got my letter.'

'Oh! Yes, here.' She handed me an envelope, which I snatched off her.

'Thanks.' I glanced at it on my way back to the van and recognised Sawney's writing.

The sirens were now much closer, and I started the engine before puttering off. Blue lights flickered off the tarmac as we reached the road. A fire engine, slowing. I pulled out in front of it, my pulse thudding as I flattened the accelerator.

The lights disappeared and I let our speed drop to below the limit. I glanced across at the envelope, which was much smaller than I'd expected.

'I think it's a memory stick, Craig. Do you want to open it?'

He did. 'It's a key.'

'A key?'

He held up a silver key with a black grip.

'Is that all there is in there?'

He held up the envelope. 'Yep.'

What the hell did that open?

CHAPTER 43

I took John and Craig to their hostel and drove back to Piccadilly Trading Estate. A huge lorry with Latvian plates sat in the spot I'd left in the early hours, and I slotted in behind it, hoping he didn't decide to reverse without checking behind his trailer.

A roar like a jet engine woke me in a panic until I recognised what it was. I pulled the curtain aside and peered out of the side window. The lorry lumbered out of sight, leaving behind a black cloud. Still exhausted, I let the fabric drop and lay back on the bed. I must have nodded off because I woke again to the sound of a fist beating a tattoo on the roof.

'C'mon, you lazy sods.' The van rocked as my visitor shoved it.

'What the hell you playing at?' I slipped my trainers on and opened the back door. My anger turned to alarm.

Two burly coppers examined me. 'You can't sleep here.' The nearest one pointed to a sign. 'No overnight parking.'

I stepped out onto the tarmac, pushing my sluggish brain to think of something.

We only arrived at seven, Oscar offered from the front seat. ***When the big lorry left.***

'We only arrived at seven. I saw a lorry pull out and thought it would be a good place to rest rather than driving tired.'

He sniffed. 'You stink of smoke.'

'I had a fire at my flat, which is why . . .' I pointed at the camper, amazed at my facility for lying.

His expression softened. 'Right, I'll let you off this time, but find a proper site if you're sleeping in that thing.'

I thanked him as he walked off and watched them leave in their car.

You're a good liar. And you do stink of smoke.

'You gave me the line.' I sniffed, and he was right. I'd washed and changed when I'd parked up in the early hours, but hadn't washed my hair.

I returned to the cramped quarters and folded the bed away. The stink of smoke emanated from my pillowcase. Time to visit the launderette. The tiny sink was too small to get my head under the tap, but I didn't need to worry as it spat out a cup of water and gurgled before dying.

'Bugger!' I checked the water tank. Empty. I'd have to find somewhere to top it up.

It was almost nine, and I'd agreed to meet John and Craig at the office around ten, so I needed to get going. I'd have to wash at the office.

Any water? My bowl's empty.

You'll have to wait.

And I need a walk.

I took him round the car park, ignoring his complaints about the lack of interesting odours. My thoughts strayed to the key Sawney had sent us. It looked like a locker key, but how to find it? Oscar asked for water again and I remembered a drive-through burger place not too far away. I ordered two breakfast baps and filled his water bowl.

Again, I approached the office warily, but saw nobody who looked like one of Novak's men. I suspected they were busy licking their wounds after last night. At the office, Kasper ostentatiously checked the time but, receiving a glare from his sister, said nothing.

I held up my towel and wash bag. 'I'm still smoky from last night. I'll get cleaned up.'

Both looked puzzled, but I'd explain soon enough. After a quick wash, I found a steaming coffee at my desk and Oscar being fussed over by Zofia. I sipped my coffee and told them what had happened.

'You sure they were Novak's men?' Kasper said.

'I recognised the car. It was the same one that was there on Monday night. The driver gave money to a resident, and I suspected he'd paid him for information about me. That's why I moved out and I was right, because they targeted my old flat.'

Zofia looked worried. 'Are you sure you're safe to be here? I know we've not seen his men, but he might be paying someone else to watch our offices.'

Kasper said, 'What were you doing there at two a.m.?'

'I got a call around midnight telling me the second envelope Sawney had sent me had arrived. I couldn't sleep and nor could John or Craig, so we went to collect it.'

'Second envelope. What do you mean?'

I'd not mentioned the first, distracted by the revelations about Jodie and the discovery one or both the siblings had killed someone I'd thought still alive. 'I was going to tell you about the first one once I got the second one. It doesn't give much information.' I retrieved it from my pocket and passed it to Zofia, who read it, her brother looking over her shoulder.

Zofia finished reading and studied me. 'It explains why someone might have killed your friend.'

'Of course, but I was hoping the second letter would name names.'

'He does name names. RC.' She tapped the letter.

'That's not much use.'

'What about the guy Robertson wanted us to look at? RC. Russ Chopra?'

The name struck a chord. 'The one found killed and tortured in his kitchen?' Why hadn't I put his name together with the initials in the letter?

Zofia punched keys, and I joined her. 'Here we are.' She angled the screen so I could read it.

> Police have released further details on the death of Russ Chopra, who was found tortured and murdered in his kitchen. It's suspected Chopra was involved in selling confidential information linked to several major developments in the city, but it's unclear who is behind his death.

'Bloody hell. Do you think whoever was bribing Chopra had him killed?'

'Why would they torture him, apart from nastiness?' She grimaced. 'It's more likely someone was trying to find out who was bribing him. Do you think the same people killed Sawney?'

'I've been assuming RC, Chopra, killed Sawney to shut him up.'

'Can I see what you got in the second envelope?'

'It just had a key in it.' I pulled it from my pocket.

Zofia held out her hand.

I slid out the key and gave it to her.

She examined it. 'Nothing else, no label or address?'

'That's all there was.' I gave her the envelope and returned to my desk.

Kasper took the key off her desk and examined it. 'Locker, I'd say.'

'It's just got a number on it,' I said. 'We might have to search hundreds of sites in the city.'

‘There aren’t many with keys these days,’ Kasper said.

I sighed. ‘Now we just have to contact anyone with lockers to find out if theirs have keys.’

‘Maybe not.’ Zofia, who’d held the envelope up to the light, ripped it open and spread it on her desk.

Kasper and I converged on it. On the inside, in the familiar blue biro, was a street name, Lever Street. I recognised it as one I often traversed in the Northern Quarter.

‘Can we find out what businesses are on that street?’ I racked my brain trying to picture the places I’d passed.

Zofia opened a map. ‘It’s almost four hundred metres long. Is there anything you know about your friend which might narrow it down?’

I stared at the screen.

Zofia opened a new browser tab. ‘I’ll see if any might have lockers.’

The doorbell rang, and I answered it. John and Craig arrived, Trixie with them. Oscar roused himself from his sleeping pad and the clamour of greetings filled the space. I asked the question Zofia had put to me.

Both John and Craig studied the map. Craig tapped the screen with a blackened fingernail. ‘Stevenson Square. Sawney’s got the same surname, Stevenson.’

‘Great, Craig.’ Zofia used the mouse to get a view of the street.

We watched as she traversed the four corners of the junction of Stevenson Square and Lever Street. None of the occupiers looked like they rented out lockers.

John spoke up. ‘I did some work in a kitchen. They supplied their staff with lockers.’

Zofia opened another screen. ‘Excellent idea, John. I’ll list all the places on the corners, and we can check them.’

Craig held up a hand. ‘There’s a Stevenson Place further down.’

Zofia returned to the map. 'Okay, we'll check every premise on Lever Street between those two roads.'

With a sense of excitement that we were getting somewhere, we piled into Kasper's and Zofia's cars and drove to Lever Street. As we only had one key, I held on to it and the others spoke to the occupiers to find out if any had lockers with keys. We'd tried every premise on the stretch between the two Stevensons, but were getting nowhere.

Had we mistaken Sawney's steer? Why the hell couldn't he have left straightforward instructions? I came out of a small takeaway where they had staff lockers, but only twelve, and each was empty or contained a staff member's clothing. Outside on the pavement, a despondent-looking Zofia spoke to John, who shook his head.

In desperation, I asked the manager, 'Anywhere else round here where they might have lockers?'

'You could try the martial arts studio upstairs.' He told me where to find the entrance.

Sawney had mentioned that he'd once done martial arts. I rushed out, down the alleyway at the side of the building and found the weathered door. To my surprise, the ancient intercom worked, and a disembodied voice invited me to the first floor. A stocky man of indeterminate age with delicate features met me at the top of the stairs and introduced himself as the senior instructor. I explained what I wanted, and he led me through a door and along a narrow corridor which smelt of steam and soap. He moved like water over an oiled wooden floor.

The lockers stood along the wall in a side room, and he pointed to the far end where I'd find number forty-seven. Even from the doorway, I could see something was wrong. I didn't need the key. Someone had prised the door open. Not expecting to find anything, I opened it and looked at the bare metal.

CHAPTER 44

I slammed the damaged door in frustration. 'Who has access to these?' I asked the instructor.

'Just members. Everyone has to be buzzed in.'

'Do you have a list of members?' I pointed at the door. 'It looks like one might be a thief.'

He frowned. 'I'll get Sally. She looks after the premises. She'll be able to tell you when someone broke into it.'

He left to return with a slim woman with short red hair. She frowned when I repeated my accusation that they had a thief.

'I broke into that. We're short of space, especially on a Monday, and that's been locked for months. I asked around and nobody claimed it, so I broke in. I'm going to put a new lock on it.'

'No need.' I gave her Sawney's key. 'What did you do with the stuff in there?'

'It's in my office.'

With a sense of relief, I followed her up a narrow staircase to the next floor. We passed a large room infused with the stink of sweat, its floor covered in mats. Her 'office' consisted of a small, windowless room lined with cleaning products. A workbench served as her desk, and she recovered a carrier bag from the top drawer of a filing cabinet.

'This is all there was. Some papers and photos.'

'Thanks.' I reached for them, but the instructor, who'd followed us, placed a hand on my wrist.

'That's Sawney's stuff.'

I tried to free my hand but, despite the gentle grip, I couldn't escape it. 'He's dead.' I explained what had happened and showed him the first letter in which Sawney outlined the corruption he'd witnessed, without naming names.

He finished reading it and returned it. 'Okay. You going to find out who did it?'

'I hope so.' I took the bag and checked the contents. A memory stick and a thin sheaf of papers.

Zofia and the others were waiting at the corner. 'You found them?'

I hefted the bag, which felt insubstantial for something for which a man had died. 'Let's get back and see what he found out.'

I sat in Zofia's car, the bag between my feet and an impatience to read its contents making my stomach fizz. Back in the office, we gathered round my desk. I slid the contents out and spread them over the table. Several sheets of paper had low-resolution images printed on them.

Zofia picked up one showing two men on a bench. 'That's Russ Chopra.' She pointed at a figure on the right end of the bench.

'Is that Robertson?' I indicated the one on the opposite end.

'That's Rudy Glass.'

'The Homes for Heroes guy?'

'Hypocritical bastard.' Craig's tone made me worry about Glass's safety if they ever met.

We split up the papers, not that there were many, and Zofia took the memory stick to her desk while John helped Kasper with the refreshments. Craig and I read the sheets of paper covered in the familiar blue ink. Sawney had listed the people he and Chopra had sold information to, although some read like pseudonyms. Chopra mustn't have trusted him with the most sensitive names.

I didn't recognise any, so I started my desktop and entered them into a search engine. Most seemed to be property developers, but some were wealthy individuals, and I assumed they'd wanted help to get plans for their homes passed. A few didn't seem to have a digital footprint, confirming my suspicion that they didn't exist, and some had died. Sawney mentioned he'd written this from memory. Years of drug abuse might have played havoc with his recollection of events.

The aroma of strong coffee preceded John's return from the kitchen, and he placed steaming mugs on the desk. 'Kasper's gone out to get some turkey rashers, I think he said.'

'Great.' I recalled the last time I'd had them. 'They're not bad. People round here don't eat pork, so bacon's out.'

'How are you getting on?' John picked up a sheet I'd finished reading.

'He's listed people he and Chopra used to take money off. It's a bit haphazard, and he's not included detailed dates or amounts.'

'Would the police be able to trace that from his banking records?'

'Some of these go back years. He'd been on the streets, off and on, for six years.'

Craig placed a sheet in front of us. 'Look at this.'

The name Milan Novak jumped off at me and I read the details. The older of the dead Novak brothers had paid Chopra to get the licence for a nightclub in Oldham. Had the father still been using the corrupt official?

'Is he mentioned again? This was eleven years ago.' I typed in the name of the club and found an old article detailing the battle between residents and the owners to get the place opened. It appeared to have shut five years ago, a victim of Covid.

Craig shook his head. 'Not that I've found yet, but there's two more sheets.'

I'd almost read mine and there were no smoking guns I could see. Between us, we read the last sheets and sat, an air of deflation hanging over us like a black cloud.

Zofia had put headphones on and was typing. Maybe she'd have something. She removed her headphones, and the printer clattered to life, alarming Oscar and Trixie, who slept beneath it.

I stood to collect the papers. 'You get anything?'

Zofia smiled. 'We've got Glass. He was paying Chopra to manipulate property prices by withholding planning permissions.'

'Does he name names?' I scanned the sheets I'd collected.

'I recognised Glass's voice from the radio, and he mentions the school where you found your friend's body. Not by name, but it's obvious where he means and we know from Jodie that he paid the people who cleared it.'

Kasper arrived, accompanied by the delicious smell of cooked meat and fresh bread. We fell on the turkey-filled baps, making sure Oscar and Trixie got one each first. I washed down the last mouthful and wiped my fingers on a napkin.

'So, we can show Chopra took bribes from Glass, and Sawney knew about it. That gives Chopra a motive to kill him, but nothing linking him to the men who raided the school.'

Kasper, who'd read while he chewed, tapped a sheet on the desk in front of him. 'But we have a link between them and Glass.'

Had the high-profile developer paid someone to kill my friend?

'We've got this.' She indicated her screen, her smile suggesting she'd found something good.

We gathered around her desk. She clicked through a series of photos. The first few were the ones Sawney had printed off, then they changed. Chopra sat in a car talking to two men. The photos, obviously taken from a distance, weren't great and you couldn't identify the men. Then they walked away from the car, towards the camera, as it drove away. I recognised them. Leonov and his mate who'd tried to kidnap me.

CHAPTER 45

After a discussion on what they should do with the evidence they'd discovered, Kasper suggested a vote. Zofia had argued they should give it to the police. Although Craig and John hadn't been specific, she didn't want to get involved in anything that smacked of vigilantism. Her brother supported her, and she waited for Victor to break the deadlock.

He avoided her gaze but, to her surprise, said, 'I'm with Zofia. Let the police deal with it.'

'Thank you, Victor.' She picked up her phone. 'I'll speak to Colette.'

She took it into the boardroom and closed the door. Bowling answered straight away.

'Zofia, how can I help you?'

'I wanted to discuss the murder of Sawney Stevenson—'

'We haven't released his surname.'

Zofia swallowed. 'Victor was a friend.'

'Hmmm. Okay, but it wasn't murder.'

'But you said—'

'I misspoke. We're satisfied he accidentally overdosed.'

'But you thought it was murder?'

Bowling didn't answer.

Zofia took a deep breath. 'What made you think it might have been murder?'

'This goes no further.' Bowling lowered her voice. 'We found bruising suggesting someone had held him down, but we've since discovered he'd been in a scuffle earlier, which could account for the bruises.'

'Could?'

'The guy was an habitual user.'

'Does that mean his death doesn't matter?'

'Of course not. You know me better than that.' Bowling didn't hide her irritation. 'But you have to recognise his body would have been weakened by years of abuse and living on the street. We go with what we can prove, and the most likely scenario is the one I outlined.'

Zofia took a deep breath. She must calm down if she wasn't to alienate the detective. 'What if I could show you a link between Russ Chopra, Sawney and Daniel Leonov, who we know was at the school the night Sawney died?'

Bowling didn't reply for a long moment. 'What sort of link?'

Zofia told her.

'Send it to me and we'll have a look.'

Zofia noted her email address and sent the contents of the memory stick. They shared the files from the memory stick on each machine in the office, studied the photos, and read the notes again while they waited.

Zofia's phone rang, and she snatched it up.

'Thanks for this, Zofia. It strengthens our case against Glass, but the pictures of Chopra and Leonov aren't clear enough to prove anything.'

'At least bring him in and question him.'

'That won't be happening.'

'Why not?'

'The decision was taken at a high level. I'm sorry, Zofia.' She ended the call.

They sat in silence for what seemed like minutes until Craig cleared his throat. 'Look at the picture of Leonov at the side of Chopra's car.'

Zofia did so. 'What am I looking for?'

'Chopra hands him something. If you look at the last picture, you can see a phone in Leonov's hand.'

She checked. Although the right size for a phone, she couldn't see enough detail. 'Do you think that's a burner?'

Victor said, 'We need to get hold of that phone. That must be how Chopra gave him instructions about killing Sawney.'

A discussion ensued and eventually, after a back and forth, they all agreed.

'How do we get hold of it?' Kasper, the most reluctant of the five, asked.

Victor said, 'We have to get into Leonov's house and search it.'

'What if he comes back?'

'We need to entice him out of the house to give us time to search it. I've got his phone number. Why don't I tell him we have evidence linking him to the murder of Russ Chopra—'

'Have we?' Kasper looked puzzled.

'We know he met him, but I've no idea if he's involved with his murder. What happened to Chopra sounds personal, and Sawney's killing was clinical, so I suspect not. But he won't want to be tied to that investigation.'

Zofia voiced her misgivings. 'Whoever breaks in will need plenty of time to search the house. If you ask him to travel too far, he might not bite.'

John said, 'If we have a compelling enough narrative, he'll bite. Why don't we say Chopra left detailed notes, with photos, about hiring him to kill Sawney?'

They agreed on a strategy. Zofia wasn't too happy, but she could see how keen Victor and the others were to get justice for their friend. She volunteered to break in and search the house.

'No way. I'll do it,' Kasper offered.

John leant forward. 'Toff will do it. We just need one of you to drive him there and keep a lookout.'

Despite her relief, Zofia felt obligated to help. These men had risked their lives to help her. 'I'll go in with him. We'll take half as long.'

Despite Kasper's objections, she insisted, and they settled on a plan. They talked through it three times, refining it and making sure everyone knew their roles. Victor took his phone into the boardroom to call Leonov and came out seven minutes later. They looked at him expectantly.

'He's agreed to meet us at Vale Park at half ten.'

On hearing the location Victor had chosen, Zofia gasped. He'd discovered an almost dead Jehona there and later feared he'd lost his daughter in the same building when it burnt down. Why would he ever want to revisit the site?

Victor seemed unperturbed, however. Just raised his eyebrows at her reaction and addressed the group as a whole: 'I'll give him the exact address at the last minute.'

John and Craig were grinning in apparent relief. They must have feared Leonov would refuse to meet them, whereas she had hoped for the same outcome. Zofia gave her brother an encouraging smile, although inside she wanted to curl up and hide. Victor left with the others to recce Leonov's place before going to Vale Park to prepare for his arrival.

The office seemed deserted without the other three or the dogs. It got worse when Kasper rang Toff, then left to buy the items they needed. Although she tried to focus on work – they had plenty to catch up on – her mind kept wandering to what lay ahead and what had happened at Vale Park. Why had Victor chosen that location?

Kasper returned with the shopping and lunch. She checked his purchases while eating her chicken wrap and salad. Neither felt like talking. At around four, an email arrived from Victor. Photos and a video of Leonov's house from all sides. They studied them, checked an online map and Google Earth. Once they were happy with what they needed to do, she rang Victor.

'Did you have any problems?'

'A neighbour clocked the camper van but as it won't be going anywhere near there, I'm not worried. Craig broke the lock on the back gate. There's a pallet leaning against the back wall of the flat-roofed extension. Use that as a ladder to get on the roof. The bathroom window lock doesn't work.'

She didn't ask how he knew. 'Is there an alarm?'

'We saw contacts on the doors and windows, but not on the one to the bathroom. I doubt they'll have motion sensors as well, but if they do, scarper.'

They wished each other luck and ended the call.

'We still going ahead?' Kasper's hopeful note broke her heart.

'We'll be fine.'

They left for home around six. Neither felt like eating much but forced themselves to have something. At half eight, they rang Toff and arranged for Kasper to collect him to bring him back to change. Zofia had a shower, tied her hair up and changed into the black painter's overalls and trainers Kasper had bought.

Toff seemed as nervous as she felt, and she realised how young he was. The odour of weed clung to his clothes and Zofia worried it might give them away when Leonov returned home. But once he had his overalls on, you could hardly smell it. With the hood up, it should be even better. The cheap black trainers fitted him well enough. They talked him through their plan until he could repeat it without deviation.

Victor expected Leonov to be gone by ten, so they had an hour. Kasper drove and Zofia's heart rate increased as they got closer. Her hands trembled as she passed Toff disposable gloves from a bag between the front seats. She studied the house as they drove past. Kasper reversed into the small residents' car park. He could see the front of Leonov's house from his seat.

They sat in the car in silence for a long moment, nobody willing to move. She realised they must go now, or they'd lose their nerve.

'Come on, T. Let's go.'

'Okay, Zee.' The tremor in Toff's voice belied his bravado.

She led the way down the alley leading to the back of Leonov's house. She counted the back gates but recognised the mark on the brickwork by the gate Victor's video had lingered on. Holding her breath, she pushed the door, which opened after sticking for a heart-stopping second. Once they were both inside, she pushed it shut and stood for a moment, gathering her breath.

She pulled her hood over her pale hair and Toff copied her. The pallet was where Victor said it would be, and they scrambled up to the flat roof. She'd brought a screwdriver to ease the window open and stood with her head in the opening, listening.

A jet went overhead, and she clambered through the window, placing her foot on the edge of a toilet seat. She closed the lid and slid an air freshener spray to the side of the windowsill before gesturing at Toff to follow. She peered outside, but nothing moved. Now she was inside, she doubted Leonov would notice the stink from Toff's clothing. She'd need another shower when she got out of here.

'Okay, T. I'll go downstairs and you check the rooms up here. If you find something like an office, focus on that. Remember, draw the curtains before putting on your torch.'

'Yeah, okay.' He wasn't joking now they were inside.

She started in the kitchen, signified by the stench from a bin three days past needing emptying. The room didn't have curtains, so she had to search one sector at a time. A torch beam jumping about was far more noticeable than a still light. Glad she wore gloves, she didn't take long to search the filthy room.

She tried the freezer, but it contained nothing but ice and three frozen pizzas. In the living room she found two leather sofas and a huge TV. Everything must be upstairs. She checked the time. They'd been there twelve minutes.

She found Toff in the front bedroom, checking a wardrobe. 'Have you done any others?'

'Sorry, Zof—'

She placed a rubber-coated finger against her lips. 'Zee, remember. I'll go next door.'

Unlike the one Toff was searching, this bedroom didn't stink of weed and unwashed clothing. Someone had made the bed and tidied. A guest room? With a sense of unease, she checked the drawers and wardrobe. These were mostly empty, containing a few folded garments and some ironed shirts arrayed at one end of the wardrobe.

Her pulse spiked when she found an old phone in the bedside cabinet, but it looked too old-fashioned to be the one in the photos. She came out as Toff finished in the main bedroom.

She pointed at the door they'd arrived through. 'You do the bathroom, and I'll do the back bedroom.'

The tiny room contained a desk, a filing cabinet and two low cupboards. Why the hell hadn't Toff focused on this room? She checked the time. Twenty-seven minutes. They should be fine. Vertical blinds hung in front of the window, and she closed them.

She found the phone straight away in the desk drawer. It seemed too easy. Maybe it wasn't the right one. A 1234 code opened it – too easy, again – and she checked the call logs. He'd rung three numbers, but only one person had rung him. He hadn't saved that person's name.

She checked the time again. They'd been there half an hour.

She needed to make sure this was the right phone. If it was, the incoming call must have been from Chopra's phone. Either his killers or the police would have it now, unless they hadn't been able to find it. She suspected the killers had it. That must have been why they tortured him, to get the phone back and remove any link to them.

There was only one way to check. She pressed dial and listened. She couldn't hear a phone ringing in the house, so Leonov hadn't taken it, unless he had it on him.

'Hello?' a wary voice asked.

Her breath caught. Police or killers? She'd pretend she didn't know Chopra was dead. 'Russ?'

'Yeah, Russ here. Who are you?'

It must be the killers. She'd put the wind up them. 'Sergeant Bowling, Major Incident Team.'

A voice she now recognised as Grimes's bellowed, 'Hear that, Colette? You've got a doppelganger. Ha! Now listen, you, I don't know who—'

She ended the call.

A wild-eyed Toff appeared in the doorway and in her pocket, her phone vibrated. Downstairs, the front door slammed.

CHAPTER 46

After carrying out the reconnaissance of Leonov's house and telling Zofia what we'd discovered, we'd clambered back into the camper. We dropped Trixie with a friend of Craig's and drove to where we were planning to lure Leonov. It lay on an industrial estate less than two miles north of our office. It was one of the few parts of Manchester I knew away from the city centre. Kasper had once sent me there to check a surveillance camera he'd planted.

My nervousness grew as we came closer to the site where I'd discovered a badly injured woman and almost got myself killed. Oscar felt it too, and as we turned into the road leading to the industrial estate, he whimpered in the back of the camper.

'It's alright, Oscar, you can stay in the van.'

Why are we here?

'We need somewhere secluded and away from Leonov's house.' I'd calculated it would take him forty minutes to get here, even without traffic.

Neither Craig in the front seat nor John in the back thought it odd that I was having a conversation with Oscar.

Is this the only choice? You don't seem to care if you upset me.

I didn't know what to say to that. I hadn't even considered it might upset him to come here. The building in question, now a shell being rebuilt, lay on our left as I entered the site. Dusk was falling and many of the units were shutting for the night. I knew that soon they'd all be vacated. The workmen had finished for the day and abandoned the building we wanted to see.

I drove up towards it, my insides tense. A crane towered over it and plastic-sheeted scaffolding sheathed the fire-blackened walls. I remembered my terror when the roof collapsed, and I shuddered. We drove round the back. If anyone challenged us, I'd say we were looking for somewhere to doss down.

We completed our reconnaissance without incident and returned to the KZD offices. It felt strange being there without Kasper or Zofia, and I silenced the alarm. We got drinks and sat around my desk, a diagram of the site on my computer screen.

I cleared my throat. 'Craig, you're probably the best person to outline a plan.'

He exchanged a look with John, then turned back to me. 'We've been wondering what would happen if Zofia doesn't find any evidence linking Leonov to Sawney.'

'We just have to hope she does.'

'And even if she links him to Sawney, we might not get the guy who paid him.'

'I'm assuming it was Chopra.'

John joined in. 'What if it wasn't? It might have been one of the men paying Chopra off. They might have been worried that if Sawney exposed Chopra, he might implicate them.'

'And then they killed Chopra?' That had a logic to it.

'How did Leonov react when you said you could link him to Chopra's death?'

I thought back to the call. 'There was a stunned silence. Then he said, "You can't have." I assumed it was because he wasn't involved.'

'If I wasn't involved, I'd have told you to sling your hook.'

'Well, he's agreed to pay me ten grand if I give him the evidence.'

'There you are, Brother, that proves he must be involved. But that might not be enough to convict him. Or whoever is behind it.'

I could see where this was going. 'What do you suggest?'

'We persuade him to tell us all he knows.'

'Torture him, you mean?'

Craig said, 'You don't need to get involved. John and I will deal with him. We were closer to Sawney.'

My immediate reaction was annoyance at the implication that I cared less about the loss of our friend, but I realised they were giving me a chance to get out of a task none of us welcomed. 'I won't shirk my responsibility.'

'Let's see what happens.' Craig outlined his plan.

'I know I told Leonov to come alone,' I said, 'but we must assume he might bring someone with him. We'll need a lookout.'

Craig and John exchanged another look. 'Shall we get something to eat at Digger's diner?'

We locked the office and drove to Deansgate, where Digger ran a centre at which homeless people could get food and a wash. The rich aroma of cardamon and cumin told us it was curry tonight, courtesy of the local Sikh community. Digger greeted us effusively, and we ate well, even Oscar. Word must have got out about the food because they had a full house.

I paid for all of us, although we were eligible for the free food. Digger told me about a caravan park set in a pub car park in Oldham, about eight miles away. I left John and Craig and drove to the site, arriving in darkness. The owner reserved me a pitch, and I drove back into town to collect the others.

John and Craig stood on the street corner where we'd agreed to meet. As before, Craig carried a holdall, but John carried a backpack. He jumped into the back with Oscar, and Craig squeezed himself into the front seat. The holdall clanked as he stuffed it under the seat.

'Digger's meeting us there, after he's locked up on Deansgate.'

I had been worried that the camper, already straining with three men in it, would struggle if we had another. 'Okay. One thing has been bothering me. Leonov will recognise me, and if we . . .' I couldn't say 'torture him'.

'Don't you worry about us being recognised.' Craig tapped the holdall and studied my clothes. 'You don't mind binning those?'

I realised they'd changed and now wore very shabby, dark clothes. I'd not taken much notice of what I wore since Cermak had chucked me out of my flat and these clothes weren't my best. 'Don't worry about these.'

The drive north out of the city took us away from what little traffic there was and apart from the odd taxi or van, we saw few other cars. By the time we reached the industrial estate, even these had disappeared. We drove down the lane leading behind the unit and I killed the lights, covering the last few dozen metres at walking pace.

I turned the vehicle around, ready for a getaway, although not a rapid one, and parked up. Craig distributed ski masks, gloves and the clubs he'd brought the night we visited my old flat at Strangeways View. I cracked the window open to give Oscar air and got out.

That's not enough.

'What do you mean?'

I need more air than that.

With a sigh, I lowered the window further. We waited for Digger, me getting colder and more nervous. Within a few minutes, a car arrived, crawling at slow speed without lights. We watched as it approached and even though I recognised it as Digger's, I released a breath in relief when he got out.

Craig handed him items from the holdall, and I rolled the ski mask over my head, put on the gloves and picked up the club. Once everyone was ready, we left the car and made our way to the rear fence of the unit. Craig still had the holdall and retrieved bolt cutters, which he used to cut a hole in the fence. Even in the darkness, there was enough light to see what we were doing.

We approached the temporary gates at the back of the building. Craig used the cutters to chop the chain securing them, and we stepped into the back of the unit. He produced a powerful lamp and swept the room. The rebuild was just that, and the layout was as I recalled from our last fleeting visit.

I rang Leonov, giving him detailed instructions for our meet while Craig checked the rest of the building. Although Leonov had only just found out where we were, it was best to be sure we were alone. Sweat ran down my neck by the time I finished the call. I was luring a man to a beating, or worse. Craig returned and gave me a questioning look. I nodded, and he squeezed my shoulder, handing me the lamp. We split up, taking up our agreed positions. I stood facing the opening where I'd told Leonov to enter. I checked the time, 10.02. We had almost half an hour to wait.

Time dragged, but eventually I heard a vehicle. A text from Digger told me Leonov was on his own. Despite this, nerves still twisted my insides. The vehicle stopped outside the gates and a door slammed. A shadowy figure walked into the doorway. The shuffling figure, his lower legs swaddled in bandages, was no more. In his place a confident thug who specialised in protection rackets and murder. I had to remember how dangerous he was. Even injured and bandaged, he'd taken me down.

I switched on the lamp and shone it in his face. 'Stop there!' I used the same exaggerated, educated accent I'd used when arranging the meeting, emulating a friend from university, and hoped Leonov wouldn't recognise me from the pub.

He held up an arm, shielding his eyes. 'I've got half the money here.' He hefted a package in his hand. 'Five grand.'

'That's not what we agreed.' I wasn't bothered about the money, but I had to push back or he'd get suspicious.

'You think I'd risk coming here with all of it? I'll lead you to the rest once I've seen what you've got. Now where's the photos?'

I'd brought copies of the photos and notes we'd printed from Sawney's memory stick in a large envelope, and I slid them across the concrete floor. As he bent to pick them up, Craig moved out of the shadows and lifted his club.

'DROP IT!'

I swung my lamp towards the voice. Another figure stood next to their car. In his hand, a large automatic.

CHAPTER 47

Zofia held her finger to her lips and gestured towards the bathroom. Toff looked ready to freak out as the person who'd slammed the door moved around downstairs. After hesitating for a moment, Toff crept to the back of the house. Zofia, heart thudding, followed him. If they locked the door, it might delay Leonov long enough. Had something gone wrong with Victor's plan?

A crash came from inside the bathroom as she reached the door. Toff bent over to pick something off the floor. She prodded him and he stood, almost jumping out of his skin. She propelled him towards the window. He held the air freshener in his hand.

'Who's up there?' Leonov called.

They froze.

'I'm coming up and you'll be sorry.'

She pushed the door shut as steps pounded upstairs. The flimsy lock on the door wouldn't keep a determined cat out. She slipped the bolt and looked for something to barricade the door. Toff was almost out of the window. A fist banged on the door. Then a loud crash came from downstairs.

'WHAT THE FUCK!'

Feet thudded on the stairs, and she rushed to the window to follow Toff. He'd reached the end of the flat roof and clambered over the side. Then, with a cry, he disappeared. She ran to where he'd vanished and peered over the side. He lay flat on his back, the pallet they'd used as a ladder lying across his legs.

She moved away and lowered herself over the side before dropping to the ground. Her ankle turned as she landed in a heap. Shit! She scrambled to her feet and hobbled a step. It didn't feel too bad. Toff was on his knees.

'You okay?'

Shouts came from the front of the house.

With her help, Toff stood.

'Let's go.' She shoved him towards the gate and followed, her ankle on fire.

The car was where they'd left it, only, no Kasper. Where the hell was he? She opened the driver's door. The keys were still in the ignition. Toff jumped into the back, making the car rock. Should she wait for Kasper? She got in the driver's seat and started the engine. She'd drive around looking for her brother.

'There!' Toff pointed across her to their right.

Two figures ran towards them. She locked the doors and put the car into first. The front runner passed under the nearest lamppost. Kasper. He reached the car and skittered around to the passenger side as she unlocked the doors. His pursuer, a big hulk, ploughed into the car, which shuddered. Kasper got in and slammed his door. The hulk grabbed her door handle and pulled it open.

She tried to stop him, but he hardly noticed and made a grab for her shoulder. She let out the clutch and stamped on the accelerator. The front wheels spun until they gripped the slick tarmac with a squeal. Her attacker held the top of her door and ran alongside for a few steps before releasing the door with a roar of rage. The stink of burning rubber assaulted her nostrils. In her mirror, she saw him sprawled in the road and shaking a fist. Despite her terror, she smiled.

Next to her, Kasper panted, his face red. She checked her mirror again and slowed for the main road. 'What happened?'

'The guy walked past me towards the house carrying cans from the corner shop. He wasn't Leonov, but he had a good look at me. I thought he'd walk past, but he stopped at the house. I messaged you a warning, but he had a key.'

'Leonov's got a lodger.' She turned left, towards the motorway, her ankle complaining every time she used the clutch. The neat bedroom should have been a giveaway. 'What was that crash?' She still had her hood on and pulled it back.

Kasper looked sheepish. 'I knew you didn't have time to get out, so I threw a bin through the front window.'

So much for a stealthy operation and not disturbing anything while they searched. She couldn't believe she'd worried Leonov would detect Toff's weed odour.

Toff laughed. 'They'll never know we've been.'

Kasper joined him, then said, 'Did you find anything?'

'Put some gloves on.'

He picked two disposable gloves out of the bag between the seats.

She retrieved the phone from her inside pocket and passed it to him. 'Code is one, two, three, four.'

'Idiot.' He punched in the numbers. 'It's the right one?'

'Only one number rang it. I rang it back and asked for Russ. Shit! Turn it off!'

'Why?'

'The police had the phone. Grimes answered. He'll be tracing it.'

Kasper shut it down. Toff asked to be dropped off in Chorlton, where he was staying in a squat, and they returned home. Zofia half expected to find a squad of police cars outside but told herself they'd have gone to where Kasper switched the phone off. She pulled up outside their house, still wary, and got out of the car, wincing as she put weight on her ankle.

'You okay?'

'I turned my ankle. It will be okay with a bandage.'

He helped her to the kitchen and placed the phone on the table. 'Sit.' He pointed at a chair, then retrieved the first-aid kit from under the sink and strapped up her ankle.

Zofia stared at the phone. 'We're going to need a Faraday cage before we can switch it back on.'

Kasper ran upstairs, returning with a wire mesh box the size of a large shoebox, which he placed on the table. 'I forgot I had that.' He put the phone inside it. 'You remember laughing at me for buying it?'

He'd bought a slew of items when he started the company. She recalled thinking, 'All the gear, no idea,' with a sense of shame. Kasper reactivated the phone inside the cage and keyed in the code. He opened the messaging app.

'There's nothing here.'

'Is that the only messaging app?'

He scrolled through the screens. 'Here's two more, both encrypted.' He opened the first with the same result, then opened the other. 'They've used this one.'

He moved round so Zofia could see the screen. He'd opened a chat with four participants and scrolled down until the last message, letting out a frustrated groan.

'Unless they're using code, it sounds like a group of lads arranging to go for drinks.'

Zofia shared his frustration. 'When was the first message?'

He scrolled back to the start. 'Monday of this week.'

'After Russ Chopra was killed?'

'The news reported his death on Sunday.' Kasper returned to the call log. 'You sure it was Grimes who answered it?'

'Positive. I said I was Sergeant Bowling, and he shouted, "Colette". She must have been in the room with him.'

'It must be the phone they found with Chopra's body. Now we know Leonov and Chopra are definitely linked. They must have discussed everything in calls rather than using messages. Hang on.' He punched buttons. 'The number you rang is on the phone memory, not the SIM card?'

'So, he hung on to the phone, but changed the SIM card.' She should have kept looking. It had seemed too easy. 'If they've still got the old one, they'll get rid of it now we've been there looking for it.'

'I imagine it's in pieces down some drain.'

She agreed. 'At least we can prove they were in contact.'

'But remember what Bowling said when we sent her the photos of them meeting? They need more.'

'Yeah.' A sense of failure weighed on her.

Kasper punched buttons.

'What are you doing?'

'I'm checking who was in the chat group.' He opened the list of participants. 'Four nicknames.'

Zofia recalled the photo they'd found online. 'There were four of them in that picture on the steps of the court.'

'If we assume one was the guy we got away from, that leaves three of them.'

Zofia checked the time. 'We should have heard from Victor by now.'

CHAPTER 48

Despite living in a mansion Victor couldn't dream of owning, Alex Novak was enduring a dreadful week. It had started well enough, with him forcing Guy to hand him the details of a nice development, but that was the highlight of a week that had gone south. And if he was honest, that development would only stave off his other problems, unless he could turn the club round.

His troubles began on Tuesday. First came the news he'd dreaded, that the council was selling the school to someone else. He'd torn a strip off Guy, who he was paying to ensure that didn't happen. He'd made excuses, but promised to discover the name of the buyer. Novak had an idea who it was, but couldn't risk approaching the wrong man. What he proposed was risky enough if he had the right person. The wait for Guy's call put him on edge.

Meanwhile, his problems at the club had grown more pressing and after one too many calls from Jerry on Tuesday, he got Iggy to drive him in. Two lads he didn't recognise were on the door. Big and muscular, they looked the part, from a distance. Close up, he saw uncertainty in their eyes. They'd bottle it if it kicked off.

He swept upstairs to Jerry's office. 'Who's that on the door?'

'Hi Alex, I wasn't expecting you in.'

Novak waited for a reply.

'They're two new lads from a rugby club in—'

'What experience do they have?' Bloody rugby club! They'll be good at drinking, singing and getting muddy.

'One's worked on the door in a club in Alderley Edge—'

'Alderley Edge? What's he had to deal with? Breaking up fights between people who've turned up in the same designer outfit?'

'It's not ideal, Alex, but we've had two more lads cry off. We're desperate.'

Novak gave a sigh. 'Okay, but why have you put them on the door?'

'We'll get the more experienced guys out there later when it gets busier.'

'See that you do. Have you got the latest accounts?'

Jerry's expression warned him what to expect. He sat in Milan's – his, he reminded himself – office and stared at the spreadsheet. No matter how he examined the figures, they didn't appear any better. Jerry was probably right. They needed to reopen the sex club, but that brought many risks, not least Grimes. And if, as the Dąbrowski woman had said, the people in Bucharest were behind the murder of his sons, they'd need an alternative source for the girls.

In the past, during hard times, he'd talked things through with the boys. Brainstormed ideas and came up with solutions. He didn't have that luxury now. Thoughts of the good times took him somewhere darker. The bastards who killed the boys were still out there, laughing at him. The men in Bucharest were out of his reach for now, but they must have had local help, and he'd make them pay.

A gloomy cloud descended and with it, an urge to smash something. A heavy onyx ashtray sat on the corner of the desk. He picked it up, intending to smash it to pieces.

'Boss, you okay?'

'What you doing here, Dean?'

'I work here.'

'Why are you in my office?'

'I knocked, Boss. You sure you're okay?'

Novak wasn't sure if he was. He'd been so preoccupied, he'd heard nothing. 'Now you're here, what do you want?'

'Just to let you know, we've got the guy's address. The one with the dog. We're going to pick him up tonight.'

That was welcome news. 'Where are you going to take him?'

'I thought the railway arches? The one with the room at the back. Nobody can hear you there.'

'Good choice, Dean. Don't damage him unless it's unavoidable. I wanna do it.'

Dean grinned. 'No problem, Boss.'

Novak racked his mind for an appropriate quote and found a perfect one. 'As Scorsese said, "Revenge is sweet and not fattening."'

Dean frowned. 'Erm . . . Wasn't that Hitchcock, Boss?'

Novak blinked at him. 'Fucking Hitchcock might have said it, but Scorsese was first.' He gripped the ashtray so hard it vibrated.

Dean ducked his head and left. Novak replaced the ashtray. He'd struggled to come up with ideas to boost the business and was feeling despondent when an alarm bleeped. He clicked on the security camera icon and a grid of screens filled the monitor. An angry red border flashed around one.

He clicked on it and studied the scene. Three hard-looking lads in leather coats confronted the two lumps Jerry had stuck on the door. So much for replacing them. Even through the screen, he sensed them shitting themselves. He was sick of this. He pulled the top drawer open and studied the weapons Milan had left there for such an occasion. He made his selection.

A flick of his wrist and the extendible cosh snapped open. He fitted the brass knuckles into his left hand and strode out of the office, not hurrying, but moving fast. By the time he reached the bottom of the stairs, one of the rugby lads was down and the other ready to turn tail. Voices carried through the doors from the casino. Reinforcements, he hoped.

'Okay, lads.' He negotiated the last few steps, the extendible cosh concealed by his leg.

'You're Novak, aren't you?' The biggest of the intruders had a Birmingham accent.

'And you are?'

'I'm the guy who's going to be running this place.'

'I don't need a manager.'

Novak had reached the ground floor. The visitor towered over him. Unlike his sons, Novak didn't look threatening.

'I'll tell you what you need—'

The man screamed as Novak swung the extendible cosh low and hard, smashing into his knee. As he fell, a straight left crunched into his cheek, the brass knuckles amplifying the damage. His two companions, shocked by the speed at which their leader had succumbed, didn't react until too late. Novak whipped the cosh across the nearest guy's face, taking him down. The reinforcements from the casino, aided by the second rugby player, who'd rediscovered his courage, dealt with the third one.

Novak felt more alive than he had in years. Adrenaline surged through his system, and he buzzed with energy. He stepped up to the first one he'd hit. Blood flowed from a cut on his cheek, and he sat on the floor, staring at his knee, and groaning in pain.

'If I see any of you again, I'll fucking kill you. Is that clear?'

The thug looked as if he wanted to kill Novak, but nodded.

Novak stepped back and gestured at the three fallen intruders. 'Get rid of this lot.' They should hang on to them, but he didn't have the resources to guard them until he had time to question them.

Blood had splattered on both his left sleeve and the front of his suit. He dropped his bloodied weapons and turned to the fallen rugby player, who was struggling to his feet. 'Clean these up and bring them up to my office. I'll pay you and your mate off for tonight. You're not cut out for this life.'

He didn't argue, and Novak returned to his office. The adrenaline did more than energise his body, it boosted his brain, and by the time the soon-to-be ex-doorman had returned his weapons, he'd come up with some good ideas. He wandered down to the casino floor, glad-handing the regulars and basking in the regard of his staff, who'd all heard about the battle at the door.

◆ ◆ ◆

He was still buzzing when he got home, and he went to his study and poured himself a generous glass of malt. Dean should have lifted the guy with the dog by now. He considered the information the Dąbrowski woman had given him. He could imagine the killers being from Eastern Europe. But Dean assured him it was someone from Birmingham. Which one, if either, of them could he trust? The leader of the intruders sounded like he came from Birmingham. But would his sons' killers wait months before trying to muscle in?

At least they now knew not to mess with him and once they got the guy with the dog, he'd tell them what they needed to know. His phone rang at half three. Dean.

'You got him?'

Dean cleared his throat. 'Sorry, Boss, we ran into problems.'

'I pay you to deal with problems.'

'I know, Boss, but . . . can I come in and explain? I'm outside.'

'What?' Muttering to himself, Novak checked the security cameras at the main gate. Dean's black pickup stood outside. 'The fuck you playing at? Coming here after you've done a job.'

'I didn't use this car.'

Novak took a deep breath. 'Right, get it off the road, now.' He checked Dean was alone and punched the controls to open the gate.

He closed them and used the camera above the front door to watch Dean get out. He strode to the door and opened it as Dean reached for the bell.

'Close the door behind you.' Novak returned to his study, settled behind his desk, and waited for Dean to take a seat. He sipped his drink and studied his visitor. 'What happened?'

'We started a fire outside his—'

'What the fuck for?' He really must stop swearing.

'As a distraction and to make it realistic. We told him there was a fire, so if he saw flames . . .'

And attract attention. Idiot. 'Go on.'

Dean looked at the glass in Novak's hand. 'We grabbed the guy, took him outside, and then all hell broke loose.'

He took another sip and waited. 'You're going to have to be more expansive. "There's no power without knowledge," who said that?'

'Was it Machiavelli, Boss?'

Novak smiled. 'It was Fuckall.'

Dean looked puzzled. 'D'you make it up, then, Boss?'

'No, he was the French philosopher who had a pendulum. Fuckall's pendulum. Even you must have heard of it. Never mind, just tell me what happened.'

Dean looked perplexed but carried on. 'The guy whistled, and this gigantic dog came through the window. It almost ripped Alfie's arm off.'

'Hang on. What did this dog look like?' Novak clicked on the mouse and opened the web page on Schnauzers. 'Here.'

Dean came round to study the screen. 'Nah. Not one of them. It looked like the one Marko was thinking of getting.'

He remembered his sons discussing the relative merits of fighting dogs. 'XL Bully?' He punched the name into the search engine.

Dean stared at the images. 'Yah, that's it.'

'What did the guy look like?'

'Young, like he worked out. Shaved head, tattoos—'

Novak swallowed the curse, which came unbidden. 'You got the wrong guy. So, whoever he was, he got away from three of you? Maybe I should give him a job.'

'We were dealing with him, then three guys carrying baseball bats turned up and we scarpered.'

Novak considered this. 'You think they were the guys your target was working for?'

Dean's reaction said he hadn't considered this. Novak told him to get some rest and locked up after he left. Dean wasn't up to the job he'd considered him for. He'd have to find someone else, but in the meantime, Alex decided to take a more prominent role.

The lack of trouble at the club the next day and the return of one of his men from his sickbed improved his mood further. Although with Alfie off nursing his bites, that still left them short. Despite the low numbers in the club on the Thursday, he left at 3 a.m., feeling more positive. Iggy had parked on the opposite side of the road, not something he usually did.

With a sense of unease, Novak crossed the road. He couldn't see Iggy in the driver's seat. 'Iggy?'

No answer.

His unease became concern. He edged round the back of the car. A dark shape lay on the pavement by the driver's door. He'd left Jerry and a few of the staff in the bar having a nightcap, but before he could get them, four figures came out of the shadows. This time, he didn't carry a club, but they certainly did. He used anger to push his fear away. If this was how he was to go out, he'd take as many with him as he could.

CHAPTER 49

Craig lowered his club but didn't drop it. Leonov reached into the back of his jacket and produced another handgun, which he pointed at me.

'You too.'

My logical brain told me I had no chance against a pistol, but my optimistic brain said I didn't want to leave myself defenceless. Logic won, and I let the club fall before he asked again.

The other man stepped into the opening and jerked the muzzle of the pistol at Craig. 'I won't ask again.' He looked at me. 'And get that bloody light off me.'

Behind him, the boot of their vehicle was open. He must have hidden in there. Before I could move the light, a loud voice bellowed from my right.

'ARMED POLICE. DROP THE GUN!'

I jumped. Thank God! Digger or John must have called for help.

The two gunmen froze.

'DO IT NOW!' This one came from the left.

A low grey shape appeared in the opening, moving at speed. In the same instant, I recognised Oscar and realised it wasn't the police. They'd have used laser sights. I killed my lamp, plunging us into darkness.

The club I'd dropped lay at my feet. I scooped it up and leapt at where Leonov had been. I swung it blindly, but with all my strength. The impact snatched it out of my hand, but Leonov crumpled and fell into me.

Oscar snarled, then a shot rang out, followed by a thud, and a body thumped to the ground. I pushed at Leonov's body to get him off my legs, certain the man had shot Oscar, or Craig. Then light beams cut through the air and voices came closer. I recognised both. Then Craig spoke.

'Well done, Oscar.'

John helped me to my feet, and I realised I'd done something to my ankle. He picked up the torch Leonov had knocked out of my hand when he fell and handed it to me. Leonov lay in a heap on the floor, blood leaking from a wound on his head. I swung the lamp outwards.

The other man lay insensible, and Digger had removed the man's pistol, placing it out of his reach. Craig knelt near him, patting Oscar. My relief made me forget my injury, and I took a step, almost collapsing until John caught me under my arm.

I hissed in pain as the weight went on my ankle. 'What happened?'

'Oscar attacked this guy, giving me a chance.' Craig prodded the fallen man with a toe.

I felt an unjustified pride. 'Well done, boy, you're a hero.'

Only a bit.

Craig added his praise.

Okay, I was pretty heroic, I won't deny it.

'What are we going to do?'

Craig produced a bundle of zip-ties. 'What we came here to do. Ask them questions.'

Digger found a short length of scaffold tubing I could use to support me and they zip-tied the two men's wrists behind them.

Oscar pricked his ears and barked. ***Someone's coming.***

Then we heard it. Sirens. Panic infused me. 'You three get out. Take Oscar.' I retrieved my keys. 'John, take the van. I'll see you back at your place.'

'What about them?' Craig pointed at our prisoners.

'I'll tell the police what they did, and hope Zofia's found something.'

'Come with us.'

'Not on this ankle.' A siren sounded, much too close. 'Now go! And take these.' I gave him my torch, ski mask, gloves and club.

Oscar refused to go. ***I'll stay and take care of him.***

'You're a good dog.'

I waved them off and sat to take the weight off my ankle, Oscar alongside me. In the darkness, we listened as the sounds of their escape faded and the police came closer. Someone must have reported the shot, because the police took an age to approach. In an orgy of bright lights and shouting, armed officers forced me onto my stomach and handcuffed me.

'Oscar's harmless. Please don't hurt him.'

They let him lay beside me. Once the excitement ended, powerful lights illuminated the scene, and they let me sit up. A dozen armed and armoured officers surrounded Oscar, me and my two prisoners. Two held the recovered pistols.

More figures came into the unfinished warehouse and a familiar voice regaled me. 'If it isn't our favourite private eye.' Grimes studied Oscar. 'And my favourite mongrel.'

Oscar bared his teeth.

Grimes did the same, then pointed at the two men we'd captured. 'Who are your friends?'

Neither had moved, and the police had cut the ties round their wrists and put them into the recovery position.

'Can you get the cuffs off, please?'

Grimes nodded and the nearest officer released me. I massaged my wrists and explained who they were as Bowling joined us. Paramedics arrived to tend to the injured.

'Any chance of having a look at my ankle?'

The medics bandaged it, so I could hobble. Grimes got me taken to the station and dumped in an interview room. After half an hour, a cup of weak milky tea arrived. Exhausted by my ordeal, I lay my head on the table and dozed.

'How touching, he likes this place so much, he's decided to make himself at home.'

I lifted my head, dazed and convinced I was in a nightmare. The aroma of good coffee filled my nostrils, and I saw the two takeaway cups on the table.

'Is one of those for me?'

'Have this one.' Bowling pushed it across the table, earning a look of disapproval from Grimes.

I sipped it as they set up the recording equipment and shuddered as the caffeine entered my system. The recording started at 3.07, and I refused representation.

I told them what we suspected, but they kept asking for evidence. We had none. The fact they didn't mention the others suggested they'd got away. They kept asking me who I'd been with, but I claimed I'd been alone and hadn't seen who'd attacked the two men. None of us believed that, but I stuck to my story.

The two men we captured couldn't identify any of us. Leonov hadn't appeared to recognise me before I bashed him over his head. I asked if they'd said anything.

Grimes gave a nasty laugh. 'Neither has regained consciousness, and it looks like one might never do so. You could be looking at murder, or at least manslaughter.'

CHAPTER 50

'Payback time,' the large, limping man said in his Brummie accent, as he and his three companions advanced on Novak.

Novak reached into the back of his belt where he'd secreted his son's automatic. The weapons he'd used last time had worked because his enemies had underestimated him. He'd guessed they'd not make the same mistake twice.

'It is,' Novak agreed, pointing the automatic at the big man. 'As Machiavelli said, "Before all else, be armed."' The man nearest him hefted his club. 'Not advisable. There's one in the chamber.'

The man stopped moving.

Novak pointed the pistol at the big man. 'Tell your mates to drop their weapons.'

Nobody moved.

Novak depressed the barrel until it pointed at the man's injured knee. 'I bet that hurts. Imagine how it will feel with a bullet through it.'

The man's belligerence deflated. 'Alright, drop your weapons.'

Four lumps of wood and metal clanged onto the pavement.

'Now kick them that way.' He pointed to the roadway, away from where he stood.

Iggy groaned.

Without taking his gaze off the four men, he said, 'You okay, Iggy?'

Two of the men moved their hands, as if to reach for something hidden. He kept the pistol on the leader. 'You.' He pointed to the nearest one. 'Get that gun out of your belt. Use one finger and thumb.' He demonstrated. 'And drop it on the ground.'

The man hesitated and Novak straightened his right arm, aiming for the big man's crotch.

'Just do it.' The big man sounded panicked.

The man reached behind his back with his left arm. Is he a southpaw or is this a ruse? Novak took a chance.

'Use the other hand.'

The man was either a great actor, or he'd guessed right. The gun came out, finger and thumb holding the grip.

'Hold it by the barrel.'

The man looked puzzled.

'Use your other hand.'

Iggy groaned again.

'Iggy?'

His reply came with a low groan. 'Yes, Boss.'

Novak focused on the one removing his gun, but kept the others in view. 'Put it on the ground and step back.'

He did so.

Behind him, Iggy huffed and puffed as he struggled to his feet.

'Now you.' Novak pointed to the other man, who'd acted as if he might have a gun. 'This time, use your left.'

By the time he'd lowered his weapon and stepped back, Iggy was on his feet.

'Iggy, come round the back of the car and pick that first pistol up.' Novak pointed at the one nearest the road.

Iggy did so. Blood stained the side of his head. He looked in pain, but steady as he retrieved the first automatic. His expression suggested he wouldn't need much provocation to use it. He stepped to one side, so they covered all four with ease.

Novak addressed the big man. 'You and your mates. Fuck off back to Birmingham before you get hurt.'

The big man glared, his naked hatred on full display. Novak let him delay his inevitable departure to save face. The man turned his back and hobbled towards a large, black SUV parked half hidden around the corner. The others followed him, strutting to make believe this wasn't another humiliating defeat for them.

Novak followed for a few steps and scooped up the other discarded automatic. The men reached their car and doors slammed. The engine roared and Novak tensed, waiting to see which way they went. They pulled out and turned away from him. He relaxed as the driver took his frustrations out on the machine.

'He'll get a ticket driving like that.' Iggy stood alongside Novak.

'How are you?'

'Been better.' He patted his head above the bloodstain and winced.

'You might need stitches. Get the Doc to look at it.'

The Doc was a retired A&E surgeon who looked after Novak's people.

He handed Iggy the second retrieved pistol. 'Stick them in the box.'

Iggy opened the boot and placed both weapons in a locked compartment under the carpet. The door to the club opened and the last stragglers came out, Dean to the fore.

'What's up, Boss?' He gestured at the Glock in Novak's hand.

'Bit of trouble. Can you take Iggy to the Doc?'

He saw Iggy and gasped. 'Bloody hell. Who did that?'

'A big bloke from Birmingham.' Novak described him. 'Anyone you know?'

'Doesn't sound like any of the McLarens.'

'Hmmm. Then who the fuck were they?'

Dean shrugged. 'I'll get going with Iggy.'

Novak took the keys off Iggy and watched him follow Dean. If these weren't the McLarens, he had more problems than he thought. He considered again Dean's failures. The lad seemed to have no end of excuses for his inability to get any info from his contacts in Birmingham, and he'd now cocked up the hunt for the guy with the dog.

He'd have gone to ground after the cock-ups, first with the lad following him crashing the car in the park and now Dean's abortive raid on his flat when he attacked the wrong man. Much as it hurt, he should put the hunt for his boys' killers on the back burner and focus on sorting out the threat to his business.

Novak drove home, still buzzing from the confrontation with the Brummies. It had been invigorating, but he'd had two lucky escapes, especially today, and he couldn't guarantee another, even if he remained vigilant. He needed to deal with these threats once and for all. Back at the house, he drove into the garage and opened the boot. He retrieved the two automatics and placed them in a safe hidden under the floor. Iggy would dispose of them. He let himself in through the side door and stood listening. Apart from the low hum from all his gadgets and the climate control system, he heard nothing.

Now his last child had moved out, he should think of getting another woman to move in. He knew plenty, but none he could imagine living with. He'd think about it when he'd sorted out his other problems. If his plans for the business panned out, he wouldn't be here much. Maybe get a pad in town, like his girl. Not too near hers, of course.

Despite his earlier resolve to pause the hunt for his sons' killers, he couldn't let it go. He took a generous glass of malt to his desk, put the Glock in the top drawer, and revisited the information they'd gathered so far. As he re-checked it, his eyelids grew heavy.

◆ ◆ ◆

He woke with a start. There was someone else in the house. He recovered the Glock and stood, still groggy with sleep. The door burst open. He raised the automatic.

'That's not much of a welcome.'

'Shit! Sorry.' He lowered it. 'What you doing here?'

'That's not much better.'

He could tell she'd had a drink.

'Sorry, love, give your dad a hug.' He put the gun down.

She walked round the desk with a big smile and embraced him. 'I was in Wilmslow with some friends and had a couple of glasses, so got an Uber. Then I decided to see my old dad. I thought you'd be in bed.'

'Just got back from the club.' He remembered something he meant to tell her. 'I found out who's buying that school you've been investigating. Rudy Glass, the guy who's been all over the news championing the homeless.'

'That figures. He was paying the security company to clear the buildings of them.'

'You going to expose him?'

'Pfftt.' She sat on the desk. 'He's a mate of the managing director. Colin's had the word to leave him alone.'

'He probably had that guy who worked for the council whacked, Russ Chopra.'

His daughter's eyes widened. 'You got evidence?'

He didn't, but was sure he could get some, especially if it would scupper Glass's attempt to buy the school. 'What's the point if your boss won't publish it?'

'A story like that, I could take to one of the big boys.'

'I've heard rumours. I'll ask around.' He wasn't sure he liked his daughter working as a reporter and mixing with lowlifes, but he admired her determination to plough her own furrow.

She yawned. 'Right, Dad, I'm off to bed.' She bumped against his monitor as she turned to go and glanced at the screen. 'Why are you looking at pictures of dogs? You getting a pet?'

'No way.'

She looked closer. 'That looks like Oscar.'

'Oscar?'

'Yeah. He belongs to a bloke who works for a private detective I met.'

He was suddenly very awake. 'Do you know where this guy lives?'

'Strangeways View.'

'He's moved.'

'How do you know?'

He tapped the side of his nose. 'I just do.'

'I've got his number. Why?'

He told her.

Her expression hardened. 'Right. I'll ring him in the morning, arrange a meet.'

CHAPTER 51

I stuck to the story that I'd not seen who attacked the two men. Without the weapons used, they couldn't easily pin it on me. Bowling told me they would be questioning the men about the two pistols they'd recovered. I just had to hope Zofia had found something. They finally let me go at six thirty and Bowling fetched Oscar, who sulked because the women who'd spoilt him on his last visit weren't on duty.

They returned my phone, and I powered it up. It beeped as it registered all the missed calls. Zofia and Kasper. Was it too early to ring her back? Apart from wanting to know what they'd discovered, I was desperate to find out she was okay. I checked the calls as we left the station. She'd rung me until midnight, then tried again at six.

She answered straight away. 'Victor, thank God. Are you okay?'

Her tone made me warm inside. 'Not too bad.' I told her what had happened.

'Wait there, we'll collect you.'

'How did you get on?' Had they found the evidence to put Leonov away? 'No problems?'

'I'll show you when we pick you up.'

'It's okay. John's got the camper, so I'll get him to pick me up. Shall we meet at your office?' I ended the call, unsure how they'd got on. She'd avoided telling me what had happened, but they must have something to show me.

John had been waiting for my call and he and Craig arrived in twenty minutes. I pulled the bed out and lay on it to rest my ankle. I woke when Craig shook me.

'We're here.' He handed me a walking stick he'd got from somewhere.

I made it up the stairs without too much trouble. The smell as we walked into the office told me they'd brought breakfast. A smile lit up Zofia's face, and she limped to me to give me a hug.

'Snap.' I pointed at her ankle and then melted into her arms. 'What have you done?' I asked when she released me.

'Shall we go through there?' She pointed to the boardroom.

Plates of breakfast sandwiches and hot drinks had been arranged on the table, and we sat round it, falling on the food, while Zofia and Kasper told us what had happened.

'So, no evidence on the phone?' John sounded as disappointed as I.

'Not quite.' Zofia exchanged a smile with Kasper.

He took over. 'I wasn't convinced Grimes couldn't trace the phone, so I took the battery out and found another SIM card stored inside the phone.'

I waited for him to continue, but he focused on a sheaf of papers. 'And?'

'It's the one Leonov used to communicate with Chopra. There was one thread on an encrypted app.' He grinned and passed round the papers. 'Here, see for yourselves. We took screen shots of what we found and printed them off.'

The first message was dated the Monday Sawney died. I read it with a sense of sadness and excitement.

Job done. Pay us rest.

Done, in ur wallet.

We sed 10k

Chek rate. Its what agreed.

The next message arrived on Friday morning.

Just cashed it. Not enuff

Should have cashed it Monday.

I want my mony

I paid you. I've got no more.

Its not over

Not my fault you're an idiot

Uve got til five

Grow up

Five or else

The next message arrived at five.

Wares my mony

No reply. And Leonov sent the message three times in the next hour with the same response until he sent a final message.

Ure dead you cheating paki.

Zofia studied me as I put the last sheet down, her eyes shining. 'We've got him, haven't we?'

'Maybe not a guaranteed slam-dunk, but it's enough to take to Bowling.' I stared at the message. 'They killed Chopra the following Saturday, didn't they?'

'Or Sunday morning.'

I thought back to last week. 'Leonov would have still been wreathed in bandages then, and so was his mate who Jodie set fire to at the pub.'

'Don't forget, there were four of them,' Kasper said. 'The guy who chased me looked fit and there's another—'

'The one I hit?' Craig said.

I looked back at the messages. 'I don't understand about the payments?'

'Crypto. I bet the rate dropped between Monday and Friday.'

Kasper looked impressed. 'Right in one, Craig. I checked the rates, and most plummeted on the Wednesday.'

I'd been considering how we could get this to Bowling without incriminating ourselves. 'How do we explain where wc got this?'

Zofia said, 'We used gloves when handling the phone, so only Leonov's prints should be on it. I put it in a padded envelope with a note giving Leonov's address and put Grimes's name on it. Kasper gave it to a young lad in a hoodie to drop it off at our local station. Paid him ten to take it and ten afterwards, and we watched him do it.'

The knowledge we'd found Sawney's killers, and had given the police enough to begin a prosecution, should have made me happy, but exhaustion weighed me down. My phone buzzed as a message arrived.

Jodie.

Hi Victor, sorry I lied to you. Can I make it up to you with dinner tonight?

I had no wish to see her again.

Sorry, I'm busy.

It buzzed with a reply.

I've got some dirt on Rudy Glass and Novak. My boss won't publish it, but you might be able to use it.

I stared at it.

'What's up?' Zofia said.

I slid the phone to her.

'Dirt on Novak would be helpful. In case he's still got us in his sights.'

I realised I was being selfish.

Why not? Where?

She named a quiet but well-regarded bistro just outside town.

Zofia nodded approvingly. 'Nice. What have you got to wear?'

I hadn't thought about it. 'I'll nip to the launderette later.'

'You're going to look the part. I don't want you feeling uncomfortable because of how you're dressed. Kasper will have something.'

We split up and after dropping John and Craig off, I drove to the campsite I now lived at and, despite my ankle complaining, got a good six hours. As I drove to Kasper and Zofia's house, I worried that Novak's people were still hunting me. Maybe the 'dirt' Jodie could give me would get him off my back.

I arrived at seven, and Kasper and Zofia were more excited about me going out than I was. Kasper led me upstairs, where he'd laid out three outfits he assured me his sister had vetted.

I chose a get-up of chinos with a button-down check shirt and a jacket. Kasper wasn't at the cutting edge of fashion, but neither was I. I put it on and went downstairs.

Zofia stood and examined me. 'Very nice.' She reached out a hand and straightened my collar, her hand brushing against the side of the jacket as she withdrew it. The intimate gesture surprised me, and I froze.

Kasper broke the silence. 'What time's the meal?'

'Eight.'

'What are you doing with Oscar?' Zofia said.

'He'll be alright in the camper for a few hours.'

'He could stay here for the night.'

I looked at Kasper, and he didn't object.

'Would you like that, Oscar?' She ruffled his ears. 'We can take you to Longford Park and see if that spaniel you seemed to like is there.'

You could adopt me, you know.

'Behave yourself.' I addressed Zofia: 'That would be very kind.'

As planned, I drove to a quiet street near the restaurant and parked up. I didn't want to look weak by using a stick, so I'd wound extra bandages round my ankle and swallowed powerful painkillers. I walked, my ankle easing with each step, looking forward to discovering what dirt Jodie had on Novak. The restaurant lay in its own grounds, set back behind a high hedge on a quiet road. A sign pointed to the car park and a neat gravel path led from it to the restaurant. I couldn't see any lights and a sense of unease burrowed in my insides. A low gate blocked the path, on it a sign.

‘Closed until May Day’.

I heard steps behind me. The hair on my neck lifted, and I spun round. Jodie stood a few paces away; with her, a man I recognised.

‘Hi Victor, do you know my dad, Alex Novak?’

My heart raced and I looked for escape, but at least three of his men stood between me and the road.

CHAPTER 52

'Have you seen this?' Kasper offered his phone to Zofia.

It was open on a social media app showing two women in a fancy restaurant. They were obviously having a good time.

'What am I looking at?'

'The young one in half profile, on the right.'

She enlarged the image. 'Is that Jodie?'

'Read the caption.'

She did.

> Sonia Griffin and Judy Novak enjoying a boozy lunch in Hale. Despite her stepsons' recent murder, Griffin, second wife of notorious businessman Alex Novak, is having a fabulous time. Judy, youngest of Alex's children, is more reserved. Rumours suggested neither was overfond of the two men, who had a reputation for mistreating women.

'Shit! She's his daughter.'

Kasper took his phone off her and punched in Victor's number. It went straight to voicemail.

'He's turned it off.'

Zofia, her insides twisted, opened an app on her phone.

'What are you doing?' Kasper looked over her shoulder.

'I slipped a tracker into his – your – jacket pocket.'

'What for?'

'Uhhh. Something like this.'

'What are you doing with a tracker, anyway?'

'It's one you ordered a few weeks ago. You're always buying that junk.'

'A good thing. Where's Victor now?'

'Not at the restaurant.' She held her phone to Kasper. The map on the app showed a dot moving along a road.

Kasper checked the time. 'He should be there now. Maybe he's late.'

She examined the map. 'He's going away from it. Anyway, that's not his van.'

'What do you mean?'

Her cheeks burned. 'He parked it two streets away and walked.'

'You been checking up on him?'

'I'm worried. I had a bad feeling, and I was right.' She opened her phone and found the number for Bowling.

'Yeah, Zofia, what's up?' She sounded exhausted.

'Victor's in trouble.' She told her what they'd discovered.

'Why's Novak after Victor?' Bowling was wide awake now.

Zofia hesitated. She didn't want the police linking them to the murder of Novak's sons. 'Victor said you attended an incident in the flats he lived in. That was Novak's men after Victor. I'm not sure why.'

'That's what he said. Where is he now?'

'I'll check.' She put Bowling on speaker and returned to the app. 'He's still moving. It looks like they're going south on Princess Parkway.'

'Towards Novak's home? Okay, I'll alert people. Keep this line open. I'll use my work phone.'

Zofia watched the moving dot and heard Bowling alerting her colleagues. Kasper had left the room and returned in his outdoor clothes, carrying her jacket. He mouthed, 'I'll make a flask.'

The dot doubled back on itself. 'Colette?'

'Yeah?'

'They seem to be returning to town.'

'Right. I've got a team going to Novak's house and another heading down the Parkway. I'll warn them.'

In the background, Bowling issued instructions, and Zofia put her shoes and jacket on. Kasper finished making a flask of coffee and, taking Oscar, they locked up and got into Kasper's car.

'Where are they now?' he said.

'Still on the Parkway, near Alex Park.'

He started the engine. 'I'll go along Kings Road.'

Bowling's voice came over the speaker. 'Are you in the car, Zofia?'

She wanted to lie, but realised there was no point. 'We just want to be nearby, see if we can help.'

'You should stay at home.'

'That's not going to happen.'

Bowling gave an exasperated sigh. 'Keep out of the way and let our guys deal with it.'

Zofia watched the dot as it travelled through Moss Side, then it crossed under the Mancunian Way before turning right. 'Colette, they're on the Manky Way going east.'

'Okay, we've stood down the squad on the way to Novak's house. The other one is coming back along the A34. I've got a team standing by at headquarters and I'll tell them they're coming back this way.'

Zofia checked where they were. 'Take the next left onto Chorlton Road, Kasper.'

The lights at the junction stayed green until they reached them, but a sense of haplessness and the certainty they'd be too late made her heart race. They came off the Mancunian Way onto Fairfield Street. They were less than a mile from the restaurant where Victor was supposed to meet Jodie. What the hell were they playing at?

The dot stopped moving, and she spoke to Bowling. 'They've stopped on North Western Street.' She checked the screen. 'Blast! The signal's disappeared.'

'Hang on.' Bowling spoke to someone in the office and came back on. 'There are railway arches there with units under them. If they've gone into one, that explains why you've lost the signal. We just need to find out which one he's gone into.'

Zofia stared at the screen. Where had the dot been before it disappeared?

'What's happening?' Kasper's voice betrayed his tension. They were doing almost twice the speed limit.

In the back, Oscar whined. Even he could tell something was up.

Zofia studied her screen, looking for a clue. 'Is there a river there? I think they're opposite that.'

Bowling spoke to someone, and a man came on the line. 'That's the Medlock. It goes underground there. It could be one of three units. Can you narrow it down?'

Zofia enlarged the map but couldn't be certain exactly where she'd lost the signal. Choosing the wrong one could lead to Victor's death. 'I'm sorry, I'm not sure.'

'No problem. I'll get an unmarked unit down there to observe.'

'When will you go in and rescue Victor?'

'We'll need to find out who occupies the units and get plans.'

'How long will that take?'

'I'll hand you over to Sergeant Bowling.' He disappeared.

'Colette, what's happening?'

'Don't worry, our guys are on it. They'll get him out. You've done a brilliant job getting us here. Now leave it to us.' She ended the call.

Zofia felt excluded and wanted to ring back, but realised they'd not share operational decisions with her. She checked the map. They were almost there, but she didn't want to drive past the unit and spook his captors.

'Next left, Kasper.'

He braked hard and took the left. Ahead, against the darkened sky, the railway line stood out and below it the arches of the bridge, which had been bricked in to provide industrial spaces. Victor was in one of those. To her left, water glinted in the streetlights. This must be where the river resurfaced. She directed him right before they reached the river, and he took the lane.

Their headlights shone on the brick walls that filled in the arches. She couldn't see any openings. These must be the backs of the units. Not wanting to get too close, she signalled for Kasper to stop. He killed the engine and extinguished the lights. Zofia kept the tracker app on and peered into the darkness, hoping Bowling's people would get to Victor before it was too late.

CHAPTER 53

Novak's men had bundled me into the boot of an SUV and driven off. The stink of oil and rubber filled my nostrils. After what felt like a long drive, we stopped, and the engine died. I waited for the boot to open, torn between relief to get out of the box and fear of what would come next.

Bright light made me blink and hands grabbed me, pulling me out. I landed on a concrete floor in a large space with a curved roof. The stench of exhaust fumes mixed with that of damp and decay. Another vehicle stood beside the one I'd arrived in. Novak, Jodie and one of his men, an older man with a bruised face, watched me while two more men held my arms.

'Welcome to our' – Novak's cultured voice surprised me as he struggled to find a word – 'intelligence-gathering facility, Mr Mitchum.'

Jodie looked contrite. 'I'm sorry for the deception, Victor.'

'Bullshit!' Despite my predicament, my anger at Jodie drove me to react. 'You're not even a reporter. You lied to us about that.'

The grip on my right arm tightened, making me wince.

'Oh, she is. And don't call my daughter a liar.'

'What do you call someone who lies about who they are?'

Novak smiled. 'As Machiavelli said, "It's double pleasure to deceive the deceiver." You're not above dissembling yourself, are you, Victor?'

'I don't know what you mean?' I wasn't sure what to make of this man.

'You claim to be a private detective, yet you're a homeless tramp.'

'What?' Irritation overcame my wariness. 'Homelessness isn't a permanent characteristic. Anyone can be made homeless.' I tried to free my arms without success. 'Anyway, you can be homeless and have a job.'

Novak raised an eyebrow. 'All we want from you is the name of your employer.'

How much did he know? At Zofia's bidding, we'd come up with a tale to satisfy the police, that we'd been monitoring the casino/sex club at the behest of the family of Jehona, one of the women who worked there and disappeared. 'I work for KZD Investigations, as you well know. You had one of your men follow me.' I nodded at the thug who gripped my right arm.

'Even while you were living on the streets?'

I hesitated, sensing a threat to Zofia and Kasper. 'Why are you obsessed with the time I was homeless?'

'A homeless man with a dog.' He pointed at me. 'You. Watched and followed my sons before someone murdered them. You either know who killed them, because you were working for them, or you saw them do it.'

'I'd never work for a killer. No offence. But how do you think I followed your boys? In my limo, or do you think I called an Uber?'

'Don't get smart with me.' Novak's eyes narrowed, and I saw the killer beneath the veneer of civilisation. 'Take him over there.' He pointed behind me.

His men spun me round and shoved me towards a doorway in the back wall. The brickwork and the curved ceiling above it showed marks of water damage. Beyond lay darkness, giving the open doorway a sinister air, as if it led somewhere hellish.

The bruised man stepped ahead, entered the doorway and flicked a switch. Strip lights flickered, filling the space beyond with harsh, white light. My two captors led me through the door. The damp smell intensified but was accompanied by the sharp tang of bleach. The room, about eight metres by six, had a lower ceiling, and a bench ran along the right side.

On the back wall, metal brackets stuck out with faded brown stains on the surrounding bricks. The men led me towards these. On the bench nearest these brackets lay a selection of tools. They held me there for long seconds, letting me look at the implements.

'They're all new.' Novak spoke softly. 'So you haven't got to worry about cross-contamination.'

I swallowed. The door slammed, sealing us all together in the space.

'Nice and solid, that door. Like the rest of this place.' Novak waved a hand around the room. 'Great place for a party. You can make an unholy racket, but the neighbours would never hear.'

I directed a pleading glance at Jodie, but she avoided my gaze, looking like she wanted to be anywhere else. 'Why have you brought me here? I've got nothing to do with Milan and Marko's deaths.'

'Don't fucking mention their names.' Novak's aggression was almost like a blow and if his men weren't holding me, I'd have staggered. He regained control. 'I need you to tell me why you were watching my sons. Who was paying you?'

Even in my terror, I realised I needed to be convincing. I put on an act of a man wrestling with his conscience and losing. 'I wouldn't normally disclose the name of a client, but this was a family from Bucharest—'

'Names?'

'They didn't tell me. They just said they were looking for their daughter.'

'Her name?'

She was somewhere nobody could harm her, so I didn't mind telling him. 'Jehona.'

Novak looked at the bruised man. 'Jehona Sorokin, I think, Boss. She's the one someone took to the hospital in a bin.'

The memory of that awful journey made me shudder. Before Novak could respond, the door opened. A young man stepped into the doorway. I recognised him with a start. He was the one who'd been asking about me, the one pretending to be homeless and who'd paid for information on my whereabouts.

'Dean, glad you could join us. Where the hell have you been?'

'Sorry, Alex. I had other business to deal with.' He stepped fully into the room and produced an automatic. Still speaking to Novak, he said, 'You've met my friends.'

Four more men, all holding firearms, trooped in behind him. One, a huge man with a bruised cheek and pronounced limp, carried a sawn-off, pump-action shotgun.

'I'm going to enjoy this,' he said in a Brummie accent.

A series of emotions, starting with anger and ending with resignation, crossed Novak's features.

The guy with the shotgun nodded at me. 'Who the fuck are you?'

My mouth had dried, and I could only croak, 'Victor.'

'Well, Victor, it's your lucky day. Let him go.'

The two men released me and I stumbled, unable to believe I'd survive.

'Thanks.' I gestured at the exit. 'Alright if I go? I'm nothing to do with this lot.'

'Sorry, Victor.' The man bearing the shotgun smirked. 'If it was my decision, I'd let you go, but Dean here doesn't want any witnesses.'

CHAPTER 54

A loud bang from the main entrance made me jump and grabbed everyone's attention.

'ARMED POLICE, DROP YOUR WEAPONS!'

My initial reaction, that it was my friends initiating another performance, passed in an instant. How the hell would they know I was here? It must be the real police, then, but how did they know? I had to assume it was a separate operation, nothing to do with me. In which case, the police would treat me like they would Novak, or this Brummie newcomer's people. As a threat.

I stepped back but hit the bench. The big man swung his shotgun towards Novak, his expression that of a child denied a promised treat. I was convinced he'd shoot, but my mind wouldn't let me believe it. Everyone else froze except for Novak, who charged at the big man. Jodie tried to stop her father. I reached back and picked up a hammer. I'd been on an axe-throwing course at my last job. Team-building bullshit, but I'd been pretty good at it. I aimed at the big man's head and hurled the hammer.

Time slowed and several things happened at once. The big man had his shotgun levelled at the charging Novak. He glanced towards the hammer I'd thrown and ducked, but it hit him and bounced off the top of his head. Another explosion blew the door open. The shotgun blast boomed at nearly the same instant, making my ears ring.

A scream of pain confirmed he'd hit someone. Another shot rang out and Novak's man with the bruised face fell. I threw myself to the floor. Shouts and instructions came from the doorway and pale smoke spread across the room. The chemical tang hit my throat, making me cough and my eyes water. I lay on the floor, covering my head.

'DROP THE GUN!'

Then, two shots rang out. Less percussive than the shotgun. Metal struck concrete and then a heavy body slammed to the floor. In the confusion, I lay there. Boots on concrete came closer.

'Hands behind your backs.'

I obeyed, but nobody touched me. Then my two guards grunted as policemen secured their wrists. Elsewhere, shouted instructions clashed, and someone asked for an ambulance. The boots came closer and stopped beside me.

'Victor?'

I wasn't sure I'd heard right. 'Yes?'

'Get up. Keep your hands where I can see them.' A figure wearing dark fatigues, body armour and a gas mask stood over me, machine pistol cradled in his hands.

I struggled to my feet, swallowing more of the smoke and coughing.

He frisked me and spoke into his radio. 'We've got him.'

As the smoke cleared, I saw the others. My guards and three of the newcomers lay face-down on the floor, wrists secured behind their backs. The big man, now stripped of his shotgun, lay on his side, blood streaming from a wound in his head, another on his torso. Novak's man with the bruised face lay on his back, a hole in his forehead.

Novak himself lay on the floor, covered in blood. Jodie cradled his head. Blood soaked her top, but I couldn't tell if it was hers. Dark-clad officers moved about in the space, picking up the prisoners and taking them out as the smoke cleared. Something about the scene felt wrong, then I realised.

'Dean's missing.'

CHAPTER 55

The explosion made Zofia jump. Oscar barked, and Kasper spilled coffee from the flask he'd just opened.

Zofia opened her door, terrified at what could be happening on the other side of the brick wall alongside them. 'Do you think that's the police?' The icy night air chilled her.

'I don't—' A muffled bang, sounding like it came from a deep well, interrupted him. 'Was that a shot?'

Zofia had had enough of waiting. 'I'm going to have a look.' She got out, wincing as she put weight on her ankle, and Oscar jumped over the seat and followed her out of the door.

'Oscar!' She grabbed his collar, just avoiding tripping over a pile of builders' rubble beside the road. 'Get inside.' She opened the rear door.

Oscar whined and attempted to escape.

'Oscar, don't be difficult.' His lead lay on the back seat, and she clipped it on his collar. 'Okay, you can stay out, but I'm not letting you loose. You'll get in the way.'

'So will you, if you go round to the front,' Kasper said from behind the wheel. 'And if people are shooting . . .'

He was right. She stayed at the back of the car, and retrieved her phone, intending to call Bowling, but realised she probably knew as little as they did.

A figure broke away from the nearest railway arch and ran towards them, crouching and holding something in his hand. By the time she recognised it, he was almost upon them.

He pointed the pistol at Kasper. 'Out, I'm taking the car.'

Kasper froze and Oscar barked.

The gunman aimed at Zofia. 'Keep hold of that dog.' He returned his attention to Kasper, then ran round the front of the car. 'You can drive me.' He pulled the passenger door open.

Zofia had to stop him, but fear paralysed her. If he took the car, they could replace it, but he mustn't take her brother.

The gunman swore and reeled back, hands to his face. 'You bastard.' He still held onto the gun and waved it in Kasper's direction.

Oscar leapt forward, snatching the lead out of Zofia's hand and making her drop her phone. He fastened his teeth on the gunman's wrist. The man swore again and tried to shake Oscar off while wiping at the scalding coffee with his other hand. Kasper's door opened.

Zofia, sick of being scared, picked up a brick from the pile of builders' rubble. Her first strike caught the gunman a glancing blow high on his head. Its momentum almost snatched the brick out of her hand. She held on and adjusted her grip. The gunman had cleared his eyes and threw a fist at Oscar's shoulder. The dog grunted but didn't release him.

This time she swung the brick above one shoulder and brought it down with all her strength, catching the back of his head. He fell, Oscar helping to drag him down, and landed on his knees. Zofia stood above him, brick held in two hands, and brought it down on his head.

The automatic fell with a clatter and he slumped forward, Oscar still clamped to his wrist. Filled with rage, she stepped forward to finish him.

'Zofia, stop, you'll kill him!' Kasper placed an arm around her.

'So what?'

'You don't mean that.'

She studied the fallen man by the light from the car. Blood oozed from the wounds she'd inflicted, and the fight left her. She dropped the brick, and Oscar released the man's wrist.

Kasper picked the pistol up using a handkerchief to grip it. 'Well done, Oscar, good boy.'

Oscar limped away from the man.

'What's up boy, are you hurt?' Zofia crouched down to him.

Oscar licked her hand as she checked him. The memory of the man punching him made her want to retrieve the brick and give him another belt, but he looked out of it. She found her phone under the rear wheel, seemingly undamaged, and rang Bowling.

'Zofia, it's pretty hectic here. I'll ring you back—'

'We've got one of them.'

'What do you mean?'

Zofia let her breathing slow. 'A gunman escaped out of the back and tried to hijack our car.'

'Where are you?'

She could see part of the road sign. 'Chapel something.'

'Chapelfield Road? What's happened to his gun?'

'Kasper's got it. The guy's unconscious.'

This earned a muffled bark of laughter from Bowling. 'Hold on. I'll bring some guys over.'

Less than a minute later, a torch beam appeared out of the darkness, followed by the policewoman. Although a bulletproof vest bulked her out, it didn't appear to be impeding her. In her wake, two officers, like her, wearing vests, but also carrying automatics. Bowling examined the gunman, and one of her colleagues took the man's weapon from Kasper.

Bowling straightened and spoke into her radio. 'Ambulance required on Chapelfield Road. One gunman with severe head injuries.' She ended the message and approached Zofia. 'You okay?'

'Yeah.' She realised she was shaking. 'He hit Oscar.'

'He shot him?'

'No! No, Oscar grabbed the man's gun arm, and the man punched him.'

Bowling shone her torch at the prone gunman. 'That explains why you did such a number on him.' She turned her attention to Oscar. 'Well done, boy. You've been very brave.'

Bowling touched her earpiece and straightened before walking away. Was she getting news about Victor? Zofia watched her, trying to guess what she was hearing by reading her expression. She stopped talking and came back.

'Shall we find Victor?' Bowling said. 'I'm sure he'll be glad to see you.'

Tears welled up and, unable to speak, Zofia nodded.

CHAPTER 56

While I worried about Dean's escape, paramedics came into the space and worked on Novak. Jodie stayed by his side, even though she looked injured. Once reassured I wasn't a gunman, the armed officers had taken me outside and handed me to Grimes.

'Mr Timothy, and you're unharmed.' I couldn't tell if he was disappointed or not.

I looked around for Bowling. 'How did you find me?'

He explained about Zofia slipping the tracker in my pocket and calling them.

I wasn't sure how to respond. Pleased she cared, but what did it mean that she was tracking me without my knowledge?

'Where's Colette?'

'Sergeant Bowling has gone to collect the escaped gunman.'

'You've caught Dean?'

'You seem to be familiar with several of Novak's people.' His suspicion had returned.

'He was another one, like Jodie, pretending to be homeless.'

'Was he now? You and I will have a chat about that. And other things. Don't go away.' He wandered off down the side of the railway arch.

I tried not to dwell on the nature of that chat and studied the structure Novak's men had brought me to. Stark white light spilled out of the opening. Wisps of the pale smoke that had attacked my throat and eyes drifted out. Now the adrenaline had worn off, it appeared my painkillers also had, and I dry-swallowed two more.

Movement came from inside and the light dimmed. A paramedic led a stretcher out, Jodie alongside it, head and arm covered in bandages. A clear face mask covered Novak's mouth and a bag of pale fluid swayed on a bracket above him. I was still having trouble processing the information. I'd brought Novak's daughter into KZD and almost got myself killed as a result.

Oscar's bark pulled me out of my thoughts. But he was back safely in Zofia and Kasper's place. I must have imagined it. Then I heard it again, from the road that went under the railway line. I hobbled towards the sound, then I saw him.

'Oscar! What are you doing here?'

He limped towards me, ahead of several figures.

'What's happened, Oscar?' I bent to hold him.

'Victor, you're okay.' The relief in Zofia's voice almost made me forget Oscar's injury. The hug that followed did.

She stepped back and studied me, eyes glistening. I stared back.

Kasper's 'Great to see you, Victor' broke the spell.

'What are you two doing here?' Then I realised she must have followed the tracker. 'Never mind. What happened to Oscar?'

'The gunman who got out of the back punched him. Oscar bit his arm to stop him shooting us.'

'You did? Brave boy.'

Oh, it was nothing.

'It's not like you to be modest.'

I don't know what you mean. Just because I saved Zofia and Kasper from a crazed gunman, I don't expect praise.

'Okay, I won't disappoint you then.' I returned my attention to Zofia. 'Why were you so close?'

Bowling said, 'That's what I asked them.'

Kasper attacked: 'Why didn't the armed response team cover the back entrance?'

I wondered the same.

Bowling looked embarrassed. 'I'm sure there will be a reason.'

'Reason for what?' Grimes returned.

'Alright, Boss. They were just asking how the gunman got away.'

'According to the Tactical Aid Unit commander, there isn't a rear exit from that unit.'

'That's bullshit!' Kasper seemed to have surprised himself. 'I meant, where did the gunman come from?'

'They think he might have been arriving, saw them and made a run—'

'Sorry, that is bullshit. I saw him in there.' I pointed to the unit. 'He shot the guy with the battered face.' My brain had only put that together in that instant.

'Where's the man's pistol, Sergeant?'

'The two guys I took with me have secured it.'

'Right, make sure they carry out a ballistics test and check the prisoner for gunshot residue.' Bowling left to carry out his orders. 'And you three, four, including you' – he pointed at Oscar – 'wait there out the way until we're ready for you.'

We stood aside as commanded. We needed to make sure we had our stories straight – not about this evening's events, but what had led to them, and why Novak and his daughter would want to kidnap me. The ordeal I'd just endured didn't encourage clarity of thought, but we needed to come up with something. I started by telling Zofia and Kasper what had happened.

Zofia reacted first. 'Do you know who the gunmen were?'

'Only the one you overpowered. Dean.' I told them how I'd met him and when I'd seen him at my old flat.

'But you think he was working with the big guy with the shotgun?'

'I'd have sworn he was working for Novak.' I thought back to the chaos of his arrival. 'Yeah, I'm sure he was because Novak chastised him for being late.'

'But he arrived with the others?'

'Yes, and he didn't look like they were coercing him or using him as a shield. The fact they left him armed suggests he was also working with them.'

Zofia bit her lip and looked at her brother. 'Could the big man with the shotgun have been Robertson?'

'Robertson?' The image I'd built up of him was that of a Scottish robber baron, if not in a tweed jacket and a kilt, at least in a well-cut suit. And if he was to wield a shotgun, it would be to shoot grouse on his moors. 'Does he have a Brummie accent?'

Kasper shook his head. 'Absolutely not.'

'Not him then. Why did you think it might be?'

'He's threatening to come down. He might already be here. They could be men working for him.'

I considered this. 'The big guy hated Novak enough to shoot him, even after the police arrived. He'd be alive if he hadn't fired the shotgun.'

'Something personal?'

I didn't know. Exhaustion suddenly hit me.

The big idiot's back.

I spun round. Grimes was making his way over.

Zofia said, 'Let's remember what we've said about Novak's sons and stick to the story, okay?'

Grimes stepped towards me. 'You, come with me.'

CHAPTER 57

The interrogation I feared from Grimes never materialised and he let me go after less than an hour of moderate questioning.

As I left, he deflated my sense of relief with his, 'Don't forget to come back here at eleven on Monday. I don't want to have to come and get you.'

I took a cab back to my camper, arriving at three in the morning, and slept through until lunchtime. Keen to see Oscar, I rang Zofia and arranged to meet them at Dunham Massey Park to the south of the city. The drive reminded me of trips I took to Ashton Court in Bristol with Carol and the girls. Thinking of my daughters and how little I was seeing of them dampened my mood.

Was Carol's new man taking them there? The memory of Helen calling him Garfunkel improved my mood. By the time I got into the car park and found a space, I felt much better, and was even managing to ignore the looming second interview with Grimes.

I heard Oscar before I saw them and expected him to come running, but he arrived at a more sedate pace, attached to Kasper by his lead.

'Let him off, Kasper.'

Yes, set me free. I'm a wild animal, not a pampered pet.

'Sorry, Victor.' Kasper pointed to a sign. 'Dogs Must be Kept on a Lead'. 'The grounds are full of deer.'

I won't chase them, honest.

'Sorry, Oscar, rules are rules.'

Says the man kicked out of his flat for breaking the rules and who's being questioned by the police. Again.

'I'll take his lead if you want, Kasper.' He'd never got on well with Oscar.

'That's fine. I'm happy to hold him.'

'What's brought about this change of heart?'

Kasper shrugged. 'We were just getting to know each other.'

What he means is, I saved his life by biting that gunman.

I laughed.

I should bite people more often. It seems to make me popular.

'You need to bite the right people.'

A couple with two small children gave me a dirty look and hurried away. Worried I might direct Oscar to bite them? Kasper took Oscar ahead, and I fell into step alongside Zofia. Although the car park was full, we soon lost the crowds as we walked into the country park. The scent of blossom filled the spring air. Despite not being let free, Oscar enjoyed the afternoon as much as we did. After a relaxing time in the sunshine, we returned to the car park.

Zofia stood with her hand on the car door. 'Grimes has asked Kasper and I to go in Monday. I'm at nine and he's at ten.'

'He must want to talk to you two before he has a go at me.'

The knowledge put a dampener on the evening. I drove to the caravan site and fell into bed. The Sunday was a bright spring day, so Oscar and I took a picnic and drove to some of our favourite beauty spots. I'd loved to have gone walking, but my ankle wasn't up to more than a series of short strolls from the car. Despite this, I enjoyed drinking in the beauty of the Pennines. The exhilaration of the day wore off on the drive back to the campsite and, by the time we returned, a dark sense of dread had replaced it. I lay awake, wondering if that would be the last time I saw those views for a while. Following a troubled sleep, I set off for my meeting with Grimes on the Monday morning. I arrived early and found Zofia having a coffee.

'How was it?'

Her smile lifted my spirits even more. 'Fine. He was almost affable.'

'I'm not having that.'

'You're right.' She laughed. 'It was more neutral, but compared to his usual manner . . .'

I made sure nobody could hear us. 'What did he ask you?'

'Why did Novak have a problem with you? Have we done any work for clients from Birmingham? He made it clear he meant gangsters.'

'No questions about the shooting of Novak's sons or you-know-who?' I pointed upwards to indicate Scotland.

'Nothing.'

I was looking around for somewhere I could get a coffee when Kasper returned and Grimes called me. 'We might as well get it over with, Mr Timothy.'

I whispered, 'Affable, eh?' to Zofia and joined him, relieved to find Bowling in the interview room.

Once she'd completed the preliminaries, he took over. 'We found a hammer with your prints on it. The head matched with an injury to a person we found dead—'

'Your colleagues shot the man twice.' They couldn't be trying to pin that on me. 'I didn't kill anyone.'

Bowling replied. 'On the contrary, Victor. You probably saved Mr Novak's life.'

'How is he?'

'He'll be paralysed from the waist down.'

'Shit! What about Jodie?'

'Judy, you mean. She's suffered some minor pellet wounds, nothing serious.'

Grimes leant forward. 'What I was going to ask you before you interrupted me is why didn't you mention throwing the hammer at him yesterday?'

'I was exhausted and traumatised. I'd seen two men shot dead. You clearly understand how that can affect memory, hence this interview.'

'Don't push it.' He held my gaze. 'You claim to have seen both shootings. Did you see who killed Mr Higgins?'

I assumed Higgins was Novak's man with the bruised face, the one the police didn't shoot. 'Dean, the guy who threatened Kasper after he'd somehow slipped away from the scene.'

'That ties up with the evidence we've collected.'

'How did your guys let him escape? He could have killed Kasper and Zofia.'

Grimes reddened. 'The plans we were working to didn't show a concealed passage leading out the back. A recent addition.'

'So, Dean worked for Novak?'

Grimes and Bowling glanced at each other. Neither replied.

'How else would he know about the passage?'

Grimes glanced at a note on the table before him. 'Can we go back to your abduction? You claimed Novak and his daughter were behind it. Did either of them touch you?'

'No, they had staff to do that. It doesn't absolve them of responsibility.'

'Judy Novak claims they were forced under duress, at gunpoint, to act as bait.'

I laughed. 'Who was behind the kidnap, then? And why target me?'

'That's what we were hoping you'd tell us. Yesterday, you said Novak was targeting you, but couldn't say why. Now, if it's someone else, you may be able to enlighten us.'

I had to be careful not to drop myself in it. 'Sorry, it must be a case of mistaken identity. Did you ask the people involved?' The thought of Novak and his daughter escaping punishment rankled, but I didn't want to incriminate myself.

'Funnily enough, they blamed the dead guy. Did you know Higgins?'

I didn't and forty minutes later, they let me go. Bowling led me out of the interview room. I made sure we were out of Grimes's earshot.

'Have you charged the guys who killed Sawney?'

'They're both still in hospital. But you'll be pleased that we've upgraded his death to murder. Fortunately, someone sent us evidence which led us to look into another murder, a guy called Russ Chopra. You wouldn't know about that?'

'No idea.' I held her gaze.

'We then found evidence at Leonov's house linking both, plus two more men, to the two murders, including your friend's. We'll be charging them.'

'Do you know why they killed Sawney?'

'Your friend was blackmailing Chopra, so he paid the four men to kill him.'

'But why did they kill Chopra?'

'A dispute over money. We found a memory stick covered in Mr Chopra's blood at Leonov's house. It contained seven thousand pounds in crypto.'

That wasn't a lot to kill a man for. But at least we'd exposed Sawney's killers. I thanked Bowling, and returned to my camper, wondering if that would be the last I would see of Grimes until the trial.

CHAPTER 58

The May Day crowds had gone, and Oscar and I climbed up to Hartshead Pike on our own. A twinge and stiffness when I got out of bed first thing was the only hangover of my injury from our fight with Leonov. I'd negotiated a good rate for a spot on the caravan site and Oscar was enjoying living on the edge of the countryside. The drive to work wasn't too bad, and I even considered putting my name down for a house around there.

We'd spent the Bank Holiday at Kasper and Zofia's place enjoying a barbecue, with John, Craig and Toff among the guests. Looking at John discussing German literature with a lecturer from South Trafford College, you wouldn't have guessed he'd been living on the street for two years. Even Craig, with Trixie bedecked in her gold ribbon, blended in.

We'd heard nothing more from Grimes or Bowling and the press had had little to say about the events of a week ago. We'd find out about the trial of Sawney's killers in due course. I parked the camper in the office car park and walked round.

I let Oscar and myself into the office and the siblings were both in. They made a fuss over Oscar as I woke my desktop. Kasper seemed particularly happy.

'You won the lottery?'

'Almost.' He grinned. 'Robertson's decided not to come down. He's told me he wants me to stop any work we were doing for him and send a final bill.'

'That's great. You think he'll keep away from Manchester?'

'It looks like it.'

'So, less chance of you two being a "loose end" he feels obliged to tidy up?'

Zofia looked up from petting Oscar. 'Kasper reckons that with Novak in a wheelchair, the chances of him being a threat to Robertson is around zero.'

I didn't agree. 'I wouldn't discount Judy.'

'That's what I told him.'

'No way,' Kasper said. 'Gangstering is a man's job. You only get women heading up crime groups in fiction.'

'If I had to choose between going up against you or your sister as head of a crime group, I'd choose you every time.'

'Ha, ha.'

I made a start on catching up with my workload when Zofia called us over to her desk. She had a news page open on her screen.

> Police have linked a local businessman, Guy Ellison, to the death of homeless man Sawney Stevenson. Mr Ellison, a 'fixer' for wealthy property developers, provided the funds for Russ Chopra, who was himself murdered, to hire a team of hit-men to kill Mr Stevenson. His motive is still being investigated.

Kasper reacted first. 'Bloody hell, so Chopra was only a go-between.'

'He must have told Ellison when Sawney threatened to expose him. He needed Chopra for the deal he was "fixing" so told him to get rid of Sawney.' I returned to my seat, wondering who was behind Ellison. It must come out during the trial.

At ten, the doorbell rang, and Kasper picked up the intercom. 'Uh, oh!'

'Grimes?'

'Novak.'

I was still trying to process this when the door opened and Judy, who I still thought of as Jodie, strode in. She wore a designer suit, heels and a serious attitude. I had no trouble imagining her heading a crime group. I stood.

'Hello, Victor.'

I noticed the slight wound encircled in a bruise on her jawline, almost concealed by make-up. Another mark on the back of the hand she offered showed where a second shotgun pellet had struck her.

I took her hand. 'Hi Judy, how's your dad?'

'Still alive, thanks to you. He won't walk again, but he's not dead, and for that I'm grateful.'

I wasn't sure how I felt being thanked for saving a man happy to torture me, and I stared back.

As usual, Zofia came to my rescue. 'Tea, coffee?'

'No, thanks. Lots to do. Dad said you did some work for him. He'd like to pay you.' She produced a thick envelope from her handbag.

'He's already paid us.'

'That was a retainer. This is for the work you did.'

'We don't want a retainer. We're not doing any more work for your family.' Zofia's eyes looked icy.

'Whatever. Dad said keep it, for your inconvenience.'

'We've not made up an invoice yet.'

She offered it to Zofia. 'Let me know if it's short.'

I gained control of my voice. 'What will you do with your father's . . . business?'

'I'll keep the casino going and focus on property. No more' – she searched for a word – 'questionable projects.'

'Probably a good idea.'

'Hmmm. Dad asked if you'd like to meet him somewhere. He wants to thank you in person.'

She noticed my reluctance.

'You choose the venue.' She handed me a card. 'Let me know when you're ready. And bring your friends.' She indicated Kasper and Zofia before taking her leave.

She left, a residue of exotic perfume and a pile of cash the only testaments to her visit.

Zofia brandished the wad of cash. 'These are fifties. There's ten grand here. Our bill will be about a tenth of that.'

'Take out our bill and split it three ways.'

'Victor should get the bulk, it's obviously a thank you.'

'Kasper's right, three ways.' My share was enough for a deposit on a place, with enough left to pay for me to drive down to Bristol and take the girls away in the camper. It would be tight, but I could borrow a tent.

'Okay,' Zofia said, 'but we're going out somewhere posh, and I'm paying.'

'I'll look forward to it.'

I studied the card.

M & M Investments LLC

Judy Novak

Kasper reached for it. 'M and M Investments?'

'Milan and Marko.' Maybe she hadn't left the old family business. I suspect we'd not seen the last of Judy Novak or her dad.

ACKNOWLEDGEMENTS

A novel, although written in solitude, requires a team to produce. This is where I can thank those who've helped me on my journey to get this novel published.

I've again taken a few liberties with the geography of Manchester, in particular Sackville Square, which doesn't exist, yet.

The support of my family and friends continues undimmed, and I want them to know I never take it for granted.

I read early versions of all my novels to my writing group, South Manchester Writers' Workshop. Despite the fact I've never finished reading one out before it's sent to my agent, they never complain and continue to give me constructive advice on my writing.

My agent, Clare Coombes, from The Liverpool Literary Agency, continues to guide me and be a powerful advocate for my work, even my more challenging stories.

The team at Thomas & Mercer, without whom this book wouldn't have been published. Although Maisie Lawrence has overseen the day-to-day progress of the novel, the entire team has contributed.

David Downing, of Maxwellian Editorial Services, Inc., who made editing this novel as pleasurable as the last four. His continued wisdom and insightful feedback give me great confidence that my novel will be in the best possible shape.

Ian Critchley, who copyedited the manuscript, picking up my verbal tics and innumerable embarrassing errors, while suggesting further improvements.

Jill Sawyer, who did the proofread and eliminated those errors that always slip through and threaten to undermine all the work that has gone before.

Dominic Forbes, whose excellent cover makes the book stand out.

Thank you also to Nicole Wagner, Dan Griffin and their respective teams for all their help.

If your heart was in your mouth as Victor and Oscar raced to find their friend's killers, then you'll absolutely love *A Long Shadow*, starring journalist Antonia Conti. In this dystopian vision of London, public safety is in private hands – and nobody is beyond the reach of the 'law'.

Available now, or read on for an exclusive extract.

CHAPTER 1

Antonia winced as the shorter woman ploughed through her blonde opponent's jab and landed three blows to unprotected ribs before catching her with an uppercut. The blonde fell to one knee, blood streaming from her mouth. The amateur recording of Antonia's next opponent wobbled, but even through the TV screen Antonia could sense the shorter woman's fury. She imagined the same fists ripping into her ribcage as Milo paused the footage.

Milo waved the remote at the screen. 'See her lining up the uppercut? She dropped her left.'

'A right hook and she's history,' Darius said. 'And she so telegraphed it.'

'You'll take her easy, Antonia,' Milo assured her. 'She's only one-seventy, so you've got height and reach on her.' Light glinted off his shaved skull, a huge brown cannonball. 'We got three weeks to sharpen you up.' He grinned and winked at her.

Her mouth dry, Antonia didn't reply. It was easy for them; most of the Dekker brothers' opponents gave up when they saw either of the monsters across the ring and spent the fight keeping out of their way.

Milo killed the screen and Darius said, 'Want a lift home?'

'I'll walk.' She rose out of the shabby armchair in the small TV room at the side of the gym, picked up her backpack and headed for the door. 'Thanks, guys.'

The empty gym smelt of sweat and liniment. Darius had lowered the lights and the heavy bags cast long shadows across the wooden floor. Her trainers made no sound as she reflected on what she'd watched. Despite the brothers' reassurances, Antonia wasn't sure she'd prevail against her unbeaten opponent. Although she'd sparred hundreds of rounds, she'd never fought someone fuelled by so much anger. The memory of a coachload from the gym going to support one of the other fighters in his first bout still mortified her. Despite showing promise in training, he'd frozen at the first bell and had never since visited the gym. The fear she'd do the same haunted her.

Outside, she hesitated. Normally high on the endorphins after a workout, tonight a sense of dread weighed on her. Only the brothers' battered silver Land Cruiser remained in the gloomy car park and she paused beside it. She could say she'd changed her mind.

Don't be a wuss, Antonia. She shouldered her backpack and set off for home.

The familiar route seemed different tonight, the darkened industrial buildings lining it appearing sinister. She shivered and hurried between the pools of light surrounding the scattered lamp posts. Icy air infiltrated layers of clothing and she promised herself a mug of hot chocolate when she got home. Cheered by the prospect, she walked faster.

Instead of fading, the sense of unease grew stronger. *The fight isn't for three weeks. Forget it and pull yourself together.*

Angry voices called out ahead and she faltered. The sounds came from an opening on her left. She glanced up at the nearest camera, for the first time welcoming its intrusive surveillance. As she approached, she saw that the opening led down a narrow potholed lane. In the shadows, thirty metres away, two jeering men bent over a bundle on the ground. One of them kicked it. An old man cried out in pain.

Antonia stepped towards them, shouting, 'Leave him alone!'

The men spun round, seeming unsurprised to see her, and she hesitated. Ignoring the old man, they advanced towards her. Chests thrust out and arms bent, they looked huge, and hostility flooded out of them. *Oh hell, you've done it now.*

Ten metres from her, the men halted. In their mid-twenties, both stood over one-eighty and although not athletes, looked like they could take care of themselves.

The one at the front leered. 'Leave him alone, or else . . . ?'

A gust of wind carried the odour of beer and curry from them. If she ran now, she'd get away, but she couldn't abandon an old man. Although the same height as the one who spoke, she was half his bulk. A sudden movement from the other one made her heart jump until she realised he was pointing behind her.

'Cameras, Arkady,' he said, frowning.

The man called Arkady glared at the camera and then at her as he raised his palms in a gesture of appeasement. 'Come on,' he said and edged past her towards the main road. His small, mean eyes appraised her, making her skin tingle. His principal emotion as he passed Antonia confused her. She expected anger, but she sensed satisfaction, as if he'd achieved something. His companion followed, a scar from his mouth to his ear giving him a macabre grin.

When they reached the corner, Arkady stopped and turned back to her. Her stomach tensed. 'See you around,' he said, blowing her a kiss, and Scar-face laughed.

They left, and she exhaled. Their victim, an unkempt old man, crouched in the gutter retrieving his belongings and she went to help him.

'You okay?' she said, rescuing a grimy, fluorescent-pink sleeping bag from a puddle of filthy water.

A claw-like hand snatched it from her grasp. 'Get your thieving Black hands off!' She recoiled as the old man straightened, his toothless mouth twisted into a sneer. 'Unless you want to give me a gobble,' he said, cackling and spraying spittle.

Cheeks burning, Antonia turned away from him, then stopped. Arkady had reappeared, and now stood between her and the main road along with half a dozen others, the hostility emanating from them like a physical barrier. Her insides fluttered and she checked behind her, along the lane. She didn't even know where it led. The old man, seeming unhurt by the kicking, scurried away and vanished into the darkness.

She remembered what Scar-face had said about the camera. If she stayed within range of surveillance cameras, she should be safe. She set off down the lane away from them. *Don't run, and don't look back. They're just trying to scare you.* The men's heavy steps echoed off the buildings.

Determined to stay calm, she checked the nearest camera. It hung broken, the letters ASL sprayed on the wall under it. Anti-Surveillance League. Although sympathetic to their cause, she cursed them. *Keep calm, there's another one ahead.* She got closer and saw the black paint across the lens. Time slowed. Her pulse raced and the men's steps grew louder. She ran.

She'd pushed herself in the gym and her legs felt leaden. Angry shouts followed her. Heavy footwear thudded on to the road. Images of what they'd do to her filled her with terror. *Save your energy, concentrate on running.* The freezing air scoured her throat. She groped for the mental exercises Milo made her rehearse to block out her fear. The straps of her backpack slapped her shoulders with each stride on the uneven roadway. The sounds of her pursuers grew fainter and she risked a glance behind her. Two men trailed in her wake but she didn't see the others. In a few minutes these last two would give up.

She saw the pothole too late and her foot caught the edge. Her ankle gave way and she stumbled, flailing her arms. Her other foot smashed into the kerb and pain ripped through her knee. She staggered two steps, almost going down. Her pursuers let out yells of triumph. Antonia gritted her teeth and ran.

The knee stiffened with every step but she forced her legs to move, hoping it would ease. The men sounded closer. She must think. If she stayed in the lane, they'd catch her, but if she left it, they'd wait for the others. On her right lay an alleyway. She swerved into it, ignoring the pain as she changed direction, concentrating on keeping her footing.

A shout told her they'd seen her. A distant reply followed a few seconds later, then silence. The path split and she took the left branch. The alley opened out and in front of her lay a stretch of inky water, slick in the faint light. City Road Basin; she'd doubled back on herself. She hesitated, unsure which way to go.

A shout in the distance sounded forlorn. They'd lost her. She relaxed and listened. A yell in reply, much nearer, jolted her into action. She ran left, along a lane bounded by a wall and the water. Each step on the uneven ground jarred her knee. Voices echoed over the water, closer than she expected. They were gaining on her.

A few yards in front, a darker shadow in the wall led to an opening. She plunged through it before skidding to a halt. She found herself in an enclosed courtyard lined with large steel bins. Paralysed for a moment, she turned back, but the men were almost on her. She hobbled to the furthest container and threw herself into it. The stench of rotting garbage made her heave, but she eased the lid shut. Had they seen her? Her pulse pounded in her ears as she listened. When she didn't hear anything for several minutes, she began to hope they'd passed her.

Then a roar of anger and a voice said, 'Where the fuck's she gone?'

She gulped, gagging again at the stink of putrefaction.

'You sure she came down here?' another voice panted.

'Where else would she go?'

'She's probably carried on along the path,' the uncertain one said. 'Come on, Pavlo, we'll soon catch her.'

'What if she *did* come down here?'

'What if she *didn't*?'

She held her breath, willing them to go. A bin lid clanged, sending shockwaves through the soles of her trainers. Plastic rustled and bottles clinked. *Blast!*

'You going to fucking help, or what?' Pavlo said.

'Waste of time,' the other man mumbled, but another lid clanged.

Antonia swallowed. Should she wait until they discovered her or jump out now, surprise them? Would her knee let her?

'Come on, Pavlo, I'm going back.'

'Don't you want the money?'

What does he mean?

'The others might have caught her.'

'Those fat fuckers. No way.' Pavlo's voice came closer.

She could almost taste his anger and she prepared herself, tensing her muscles and inhaling. Bad knee or not, she would do serious damage to whoever found her. Another bin opened, the lid striking the side of hers. She bit back a cry.

'Come on, search under those bags,' Pavlo ordered.

'Shit, it's all over my hands. What the fuck's this stinking crap—'

'Don't be a pussy.'

'Fuck off!' A lid banged shut.

'Where the fuck you going?' Pavlo demanded.

'We don't even know she came down here.'

'Hang on . . .' Something smashed into her bin, making it reverberate. The sound faded and Pavlo muttered a frustrated, 'Shit!'

Their voices grew faint but not daring to hope they'd left, Antonia waited. Her thighs trembled with the effort of keeping her out of the vile-smelling sludge at the bottom of the bin and a chill leached into her weary body. After what seemed an age, she lifted a corner of the lid and drank down the freezing air.

Silence greeted her, so she straightened, easing the cover back against the wall. She flexed her legs, massaging them and grimacing as her circulation returned. Once sure they worked, she grabbed the side of the bin and clambered out. Something made her hesitate; a sensation of danger still close. A dog barked in the distance and a lorry laboured up an incline, its engine complaining. The everyday sounds calmed her and she set about retracing her steps.

Pavlo's words raced round her mind as she tried to make sense of them. *Don't you want the money?* They must have thought she was an illegal. She remembered the outcry when the new company running homeland security suggested offering a bounty for each illegal immigrant handed in. She hadn't realised they'd gone ahead. The stretch of water lay in front of her and she stepped into the open.

A noise like a large animal scratching at the floor made her turn. A bulky figure was almost atop her, charging her with a cry of, 'Got you, bitch!'

Pavlo.

He drove his lowered shoulder into her, hitting her mid-thigh and jarring her teeth. Caught off balance, she flew backward, screaming until icy water engulfed her.

The shock of entering the freezing water paralysed Antonia. Pavlo seized her legs, dragging her under. Foul liquid entered her mouth and nose and she fought not to retch. The numbness faded and she kicked out, twisting her hips. The grip on her thighs loosened, so she kicked again and he released her legs. She struck for the surface but a fist thudded into her shoulder, spinning her. Hands closed around her neck, squeezing. She tore at the fingers digging into her flesh, but couldn't dislodge them. She lashed out, aiming for his head. But the water dragged at her arms, slowing her punches and robbing them of power.

Energy drained from her with each blow she attempted. Her lungs caught fire but she clamped her mouth shut, resisting a desperate need to breathe. A roaring filled her ears and bright lights flashed in front of her. Then anger seized her. How dare this man end her life? After everything she'd survived. She pushed her exhausted body into a final effort. Thrashing feet struck a solid surface and she pushed against it. Her trainers slipped before gripping on a rough patch and she propelled herself through the water. As she emerged from the icy liquid, she gulped for air.

Still blinking to clear her vision, she lashed out. When her hand hit solid flesh and caused him to grunt, she struck again. Encouraged by a cry of pain, she pulled her fist back. Before she could throw the punch, he seized her in a powerful bear hug, pinning her arms to her sides. She fought to free them as he crushed her against his body. The grip intensified, squeezing air out of her lungs. Panic made her mind go blank. Then a small voice told her to stop struggling and let her body go limp.

Pavlo pushed her under the water. As it closed over her, she made herself stay calm. Her feet found the bottom and scrabbled for purchase on its slimy surface, but she kept her upper body limp. After long seconds his hold relaxed. She drove with her thighs, shooting out of the water and smashing her forehead into his face. Bone crunched, and he cried out.

Before he could react, she hit him in the throat. With a strangled cough, he fell back. She made for the bank, scrambled out and lay on the side, panting, muscles screaming for rest. *Come on, don't stop now.* With an effort she pushed herself to get up and crawled away from what had almost been her grave.

A hand seized her ankle and Antonia's heart somersaulted. With the last of her strength, she jerked her leg, attempting to free it, but the grip tightened. Then he pulled her towards the water and an involuntary whimper escaped her lips.

ABOUT THE AUTHOR

Photo © 2021 Steve Pattyson Photography

D. E. Beckler writes fast-paced action thrillers populated with well-rounded characters. Born in Addis Ababa in 1960, Beckler spent his first eight years living on an agricultural college in rural Ethiopia where his love of reading developed. After dropping out of university he became a firefighter and served nineteen years before leaving to start his own business.

Beckler began writing in 2010 and uses his work experiences to add realism to his fiction. Beckler lives in Manchester, his adopted home since 1984. In his spare time, he tries to keep fit – an increasingly difficult undertaking – listens to music, socialises and feeds his voracious book habit.

Follow the Author on Amazon

If you enjoyed this book, follow D. E. Beckler on Amazon to be notified when the author releases a new book!
To do this, please follow these instructions:

Desktop:

1) Search for the author's name on Amazon or in the Amazon App.
2) Click on the author's name to arrive on their Amazon page.
3) Click the 'Follow' button.

Mobile and Tablet:

1) Search for the author's name on Amazon or in the Amazon App.
2) Click on one of the author's books.
3) Click on the author's name to arrive on their Amazon page.
4) Click the 'Follow' button.

Kindle eReader and Kindle App:

If you enjoyed this book on a Kindle eReader or in the Kindle App, you will find the author 'Follow' button after the last page.